Joe E. Palmer - Author/Sport:
11997 Foxboro Drive - Brent
Los Angeles, California 9004!
(310) 476-8855

MW01614800

SLIDE, KATIE, SLIDE!

(A Romantic Novel, Turn of the Century,
Those Battlin' Bloomer Girls...
And The Ballet That Is Baseball)

by Joe E. Palmer

SLIDE, KATIE, SLIDE!

by Joe E. Palmer

Property of REMLAP PUBLISHING CO., 11997 Foxboro Drive, Brentwood, Los Angeles, California 90049-4110 - (310) 476-8855.....FAX (310) 820-8760 and (310) 204-1901.

Books are available at quantity discounts for promotional use. For further information, please contact the publisher.

Supervising Editors:
   Professor Lou Riggs, Granada Hills, California; Nancy Palmer Eisenbach, Kailua, Kona, Hawaii; Pam Palmer, Santa Barbara, California
Front Cover Art Director: Joseph D. Thomson, Santa Barbara, California
Marketing Director: Aubrey I. Provost, Owner, Palmer Addressing & Mailing
   Company, Los Angeles, California
Printed by: Griffin Printing, Glendale, California

ISBN: 0-9622549-2-4

Previous books authorized by Joe E. Palmer:

ON THE TRACK OF THE RACE HORSE
(Betting and Winning Around The World)*

OLD BASEBALL SCOUT AND HIS PLAYERS
 (Horsehide and Hollywood)*

LOVE ME, LOVE MY BOOKIE
(A Romantic Novel about Gambling-and-Marriage)*

THE SPORTSWRITER (Sports Stories That Couldn't Be Told)

                                        * Sold Out

Slide, Katie, Slide!

DEDICATION

So many years ago (or were those light-years?), it happened at Phoenix, Arizona's Union Depot: An eastbound Southern Pacific express was held long past its scheduled departure time so that a Great Man with a large chest and the legs of a Greyhound could reign over his court. Those were Baseball fans who had arrived early and waited long for a glimpse of him...perhaps even a chance to chat with him.

From the train's platform, the Great Man looked down at an idolizing, small boy who had been brought to the depot by an Aunt and Uncle. And who, from a spot closest to the train, called upward in a trembling voice, "Hi, Babe!"

The center of so much attention looked down at the boy and boomed forth, "Hi-ya, Kid!"

When the conductor finally called, "ALL ABOARD," and the train's wheels were again ready to roll, the boy's Aunt called upward, "God bless you, Babe. We love you."

In her direction, George Herman (Babe) Ruth offered a deep bow and then accompanied it with a kiss blown off his fingertips. He also returned to her small charge the pencil he had borrowed for giving his autograph in the magical moments just gone by. The boy clutched it to himself as one might protect the mightiest coin of gold. Oh yes indeed I did!

Even today, that mighty mingling with diamond royalty remains with me as one of my proudest moments ever.

And this book must be dedicated WITH LOVE TO THE SULTAN OF SWAT, who to so many of us will always be Baseball itself.

from
the Author

PROLOGUE

Top of the ninth inning, one out for the Marberry Burglars, managed by red-haired Katie Crowley Banton. In this 1909 City Championship Game, the Burglars held a 10-3 lead over the Marberry Lions, managed by Muggsy Banton, Katie's Husband.

Edging off first base was a stocky and smiling Burglar veteran, Pete Brancato. The runner on second was towering and glowering Del White. At bat and then on deck were the Burglars' two weakest hitters. It did appear that the game could quickly end at 10-3.

Whereupon, and wearing Emancipation bloomers of cerulean shade, Katie ran from her dugout, her ponytail flying behind her. She told "Blind Tom," the umpire, "I'm taking over for my runner at first base."

Tom thumbed through his SPALDING'S RULES OF BASEBALL. "Well, now, I don't know..."

"If my Husband can be a player-manager, I can too!"

Tom looked to the Lion dugout and Muggsy, strangely getting no objection at all. So he signaled the change to the official scorekeeper. He further took advantage of the pause in action to lift his megaphone and remind everyone in Lions Park that, by the Blue Laws of The Great State of Pennsylvania, the game must end by six o'clock P.M. sharp.

Indeed, Muggsy Banton had been ready to lodge a strong protest against Katie's entrance into the game. But instead, he had nodded in assent, a strangely quizzical smile tugging at his lips.

At first base, Katie replaced Pete. He gave her a smiling/understanding "Happy landings, Skipper!"

Women's Emancipation leader (and now first base coach for the Burglars) Semanthia Smythe looked over her hooked nose and told her manager, "I understand what you're doing, Katie. It's horribly bad Baseball, but then this is only a game. Whereas you're playing for keeps. Good luck, for the rest of your life."

Over at second base, a storm of anger was raging. Del was throwing his palms upward in a frantic beseeching of the blue skies above. Such as, "WHATTHEHELL WAS THAT CRAZY BANTON BROAD UP TO NOW?" His fury had to remind Katie of the evening when he had attacked her body in the darkness of the team's dressing room.

She ignored Del's frantic gestures. With hysteria taking over the kranks (the players' name for the fans), she suddenly broke for second, sliding in safely.

From Semanthia in the midst of the charge, "Now Slide, Katie, Slide!"

Del had remained frozen at second, unable to believe what he was seeing. Finally, though, and with no choice, he broke for third. But far too late. A snap throw from the Lion pitcher nailed him before he could get within three feet of the bag.

Two out. Hoots of derision rained on Katie from the stands, but not from the section behind the Burglar dugout. In those seats sat the screeching Bloomer Girls; whatever Katie did, they regarded as a "trump move."

Katie was having more problems than just being booed. Sliding into second, she had split the bottom out of her bloomers. Although, as the Lion second baseman would remember: He had been mystified by her sudden tug at the seams of those "underpants" as she came into the bag.

Katie seemed so embarrassed that, with a peek at her watch (five-fifty-nine), she melted into a torrent of tears.

Blind Tom moved to her, "seeking some decent way out of the thoroughly delicate situation" (he was later quoted.)

Still sitting on second base, to hide her nakedness, Katie let her torrent become a flood.

She continued that until six o'clock-and-one-minute-thereafter, when the game was called, as per the Blue Laws.

Then she took a quick look at that corner of the Lion dugout where her Husband was watching the mad scene in thorough quietude and a Burglar coach rushed an oversized warmup jacket out to her.

Quietly then did Katie Crowley Banton leave the playing field.

Chapter One

"Here they come!" yelled the fans lining the parade route.

"Oh you Lions!!" other 'kranks' picked up the chant.

"HOT TIME IN THE OLD TOWN TONIGHT" blared a brass band leading the march down Marberry, Pennsylvania's Main Street.

The line of confetti-sprayed carriages moved down the August-hot thoroughfare of the mid-sized steel mill city. Multi-colored streamers rained on them, and more of those trailed. Jammed along the curbs, the cheering crowd pushed forward for a better look at its husky heroes. Some dared run forward for skin contact...even an autograph!

The men in the horse-drawn conveyances, now down to shirt sleeves, tipped their straw hats. The deafening din grew and grew.

From above, stretched between people-mobbed offices of the buildings on both sides of the street, were banners:

WELCOME HOME LIONS   and

WE STILL SAY 1907 IS OUR YEAR   and

OUR WINNING WAY BEGINS TODAY

From an expensive/tastefully furnished third-floor office along the line of parading, a tiny waisted red-haired girl in her earliest twenties missed not a bit of what was happening below. Katie Crowley wore a quietly blue tailored suit, with ruffled white shirtwaist and blue collar. Her greenish-blue eyes, obviously of Irish nature, were wide awake in spite of the hot and muggy day.

She turned to face an older man at his oak wood desk.

He bore a large, well-trimmed moustache. He was tastefully dressed, but, though obviously given to keeping the six feet of himself in the peak of condition, he was nevertheless showing the first signs of gray in his black hair.

James T. Crowley, President of the First National Bank of Marberry, removed his gold-rimmed glasses, then secured them in a leather case, which he placed on top of the official-looking documents he had been reading. He arose, stretched, and joined his Daughter at the window overlooking the growing commotion below them.

"Sure, glad to watch the parade with you. I don't feel like working, and I'm hurting for some excitement, instead of dreary paperwork.

"Katie, my lass, in yon carriages meet the Lions Baseball Club. They came home today from a long road-trip. They're not winning many games, but the fans stick with 'em. Girl, I'd sure like to see today's game against the Blue Sox!"

Jim Crowley looked at his Daughter, and felt good. Her life had been the best part of his. Sometimes he'd even thought of her as "fey," the word the Irish used by the Irish for those whose charm and wisdom had evidently been touched by the Wee People out there.

"Yeah, scrappy bunch of ballplayers, and especially Muggsy Banton, their catcher. In this town, he's so popular, if he ran for Mayor, he'd likely be elected in a landslide."

"Easy, dear ol' Dad, the heat's getting to you...So which one of those players is your 'Buggsy'?"

"'Muggsy'," came the correction. "He..."

His voice was lost in the thundering commotion on Main Street.

The police were suddenly having a hard time holding back the swarming crowd, especially the women who were a considerable part of it.

"Muggsy Banton has arrived," announced Jim, with hometown pride. "Look at the girls go ga-ga! So many of them at our ball park these days, management had to install more powder rooms."

Katie, her feminine curiousness thus sparked, leaned out into the sunlight, intently looking over the latest carriages to arrive.

"Which one is he?"

"There, in that very last buggy, behind the gray, the stocky fellow with the bow tie."

Watching, Katie saw a sandy-haired man, likely in his late twenties, and wearing a red tie, stand up in the carriage and wholeheartedly wave to the shouting crowd lining the street. His lantern-jaw came forth at an almost belligerent angle, which had to make Miss Crowley wonder if his joyful enthusiasm were authentic. His barrel chest, she noted, was nearly popping the buttons off his white silk shirt.

Three other players, mustached as were their teammates, rode with the object of all that attention, but few in the crowd noticed them. "MUGGSY!" captured the sound waves of Marberry PA.

As he passed the Crowleys' window, the still-standing Muggsy clasped his hands over his head, like a prizefighter crowned the victor. This even heightened the noise.

"Goodness, such hands! It looks as if all his fingers are broken."

"Catching is a rough business; that's why the catcher's equipment is called 'the tools of ignorance'. And it's a doubly rough business if the catcher is as smart and aggressive as Muggsy; I mean, he's so constantly alert, always knowing the game situation...even if, injuries and all, he's not quite the player he once was."

Below them, on the jam-packed street, an eye-filling brunette was monopolizing Muggsy Banton's attention. He motioned the tall and amply endowed girl out of the crowd, and she ran to his phaeton carriage. Muggsy reached down, threw an arm around her waist, lifted her onto his lap. The crowd loved it.

"Likely just another of his many girlfriends," surmised J.T. "And she's not bad looking, either...I mean, not bad at all."

"Easy, Dad, or you'll blow a fuse. Oh sure, she's all right. And he IS rather rugged, but I don't see what gets the ladies as excited as all this. He's...well, he's too..."

"Daughter, you're watching him pretty darned close for a girl so all-fired disinterested. Much more of that and you'll break into a 'twenty-three-skidoo'."

"Dad!"

The pink in her cheeks advanced to a darker shade, until the color separation from her red hair was less noticeable.

He enjoyed his Daughter's petulance at being observed.

"I was just making dumb comments. But your cheeks are flushed."

"So kindly stop commenting, dear teasing Dad. It's just that your office is too warm."

"I'm glad it's just that. I was afraid you were running a fever."

She made a face at him, and returned to the parade. But it had moved on. Most of the gathered folks had moved in the direction of the Lion Baseball Club's home field, soft drink and peanut vendors hawking their "tasties" along that line of march.

"Let's eat," suggested J.T., by way of a truce. "Then I'll come back here and work. You can perform more of the tasks your Mother has doubtless given you, aimed at your going high-society."

As if on cue at "your Mother," the office door opened with vehemence. An older woman, likewise a redhead, bustled in. Same as Katie, so obviously her Daughter, she was short of stature. But she was larger in build. She seemed the type with every single situation under control as soon as encountered.

Katie ran to hug her.

"Hi, Mom!"

Her Husband greeted her more quietly, sensing a coming storm.

Clara Crowley eyed the scene expertly before making her next move.

Her clothing showed little of the quiet taste of her Husband and Daughter. Her bright purple dress was set off by a maroon necklace and a huge hat covered with artificial flowers of many shades. Her high-heeled shoes sought rather hopelessly to dismiss her lack of height.

She granted Katie and J.T. an impatient nod. Then she opened fire:

"What are you doing here, Kathleen, may I be so bold as to ask? At this very minute you're supposed to be having a fitting for your new dress. The country club dance is next week, or have you somehow forgotten?"

"No, I didn't forget, but I cancelled the fitting; I didn't feel like it in this hot weather. I'm sorr..."

"You should be!"

Clara turned her biggest guns on her Husband.

"Jim, you know you should have eaten twenty minutes ago. Our Doctor told you quite clearly to be more regular in your habits."

She checked her expensive watch and precisely corrected herself: "Twenty three minutes ago. You promised me you'd do better, yes you did, don't deny that."

"Yes, Dear, but we got wrapped into the parade. You'd have enjoyed..."

"Parade, tiddleybosh! All those loafers with nothing to do but stand around and watch other loafers. And those hussies should be at home tending to their children. The whole of them, such a sweaty, smelly lot. It made me ill to have to push through them, trying to make my way up here."

"Now, Jim, you go eat immediately. And Kathleen, you immediately make another appointment for this afternoon...I must say, it's a good thing I dropped by. I don't know what would become of this family if I didn't keep things moving."

Muttering something about "inefficiency", Clara did an almost militaristic about-face and marched from the office.

"Easy, Dad, don't you work up a fever," Katie told him soothingly, also somewhat impishly, getting back for darts he'd tossed at her as the heralded "lady-killer" Muggsy Banton had paraded by. "Mom doesn't mean to be that way. She's really trying to do the right thing for us."

"I know, Katie, but, dammit, Clara burns me bad when she plays Napoleon. Why should she tell me when to eat, and what?...I feel like going to the Lions-Sox ball game today, rooting like hell for our home team. Then I'll splash down lots of knockwurst sandwiches (or 'hot dogs', the funny name some call 'em now), with plenty of cold beer. So help me, Katie, I'm going! Will you go with me?"

"Dad!" She was so thrilled at his unexpected revolt..."Really?"

"Really really. Baseball has always been my 'most favorite' game. I used to dream of being a Big League first baseman. I had good moves, or so I was told, but, when I tried to hit curve balls, it was always the old 'Get my room ready, Ma, those pitchers are starting to curve me'.

"Worst of all, now I've gotten so lost in dull old regular business matters, I haven't been to a game in weeks and weeks. Lordy, I've missed the sights and sounds and smells of it."

"Hey, Dad, I can imagine how you feel, even though the last time I saw a ball game was when I was seven years old. Remember? You took me out to the Polo Grounds. I even remember the name of the place they stood on: Coogan's Bluff...It was all so exciting, and mostly (in addition to a 'day out' with my Daddy), I remember a wonderful athlete named Roger Breshnahan, who was catching for Philadelphia against the Giants."

"You really remember all that?"

"Sure do. I cut a picture of Roger out of a New York paper and still have it at home, stored away in my 'special things' drawer."

"Amazing! And, to bring you up to date, even today that same Roger Breshnahan is one of the best catchers in all of Baseball, maybe the best. Only now, he's 'crossed to the other side of the street', as sports writers might say."

"Oh?"

"Oh yes, now he's catching for John McGraw's Giants. Along with Christy Mathewson, 'Iron Joe' McGinnity, and Rube Marquard, he's part of probably the best battery in Baseball history...More, to show his versatility in spite of a few years passing, he sometimes also fills in as an outfielder, as needed.

"In fact, I hear that Roger is about to become even more famous: He's working to introduce 'shin guards' to protect catchers' legs. Oh sure, lot of the so-called tough old timers in the game say that's sissy and that they don't want it to happen. But, deep down in their aching bones, I'll bet those old catchers want the shin guards soon as possible."

From the closet, he reached for a bowler to replace his usual business hat, placed it carefully on his head, and examined himself before the office mirror.

"Now, Katie o' mine, I'll be dressed 'in uniform' with the other Kranks, as the players refer to us. So let's go out and see another scrappy catcher, Muggsy Banton of the Marberry Lions."

"GO."

Chapter Two

FAME FLICKERS? I was in Chicago 's Comiskey Park on that bitterly cold and windy day, April 16, 1940, when teen-aged Cleveland Indians fireballer Bob Feller no-hit the White Sox. It remains the only time in Baseball history that such was accomplished on an Opening Day.

40 years thereafter, at a Los Angeles Dodgers' Old-Timers Luncheon, Bob and I excitedly rehashed the drama of that Chicago happening.

Amazedly listening was Bob's young and recent bride. Finally she broke through: "What in the world are you guys talking about?"

To folks in Marberry, Pennsylvania, that summer afternoon was like almost any stifling day in their home acres. They sighed languidly over the high temperatures that had plagued them through June and July. And they looked forward to autumn, which would bring cooling from across the Marberry River.

All the while, steel-mill soot drifted onto their homes and their gardens and their businesses. Still, in spite of routine complaints, the people had long since ceased to warmly resent their dirty air. The mill meant homes to live in, and groceries, too.

For Muggsy Banton, the Lions' obstreperous catcher, that afternoon meant another joyful opportunity to play Baseball.

He arrived at the ball park shortly after noon, preparatory to the two-o'clock game. Then spent a while chatting with early-arriving fans. He liked the close-in contact; so did they. More, team owner Cliff Hartwick claimed that this pre-game habit of his catcher's, getting to know the fans and thus speeding their arrival at the park, not only increased "Baseball identification" in their beings but also increased his beer sales by aplenty.

Next, Muggsy moved across the street to the small frame building that served dividedly as the Lion dressing room and also as the office of manager Cliff Hartwick. Be it noted that visiting players received no such convenience; before games, their players had to dress in their boarding houses, then hike the distance to the ball park, not usually a short hike. After the game, they hiked back over the same trail, bathing and re-dressing in their boarding houses. But those players little minded such "hardships". Mostly, they came from poor backgrounds, often struggling farms.

Off in the corner, Muggsy saw a Lion filling the mitt of a newly arrived rookie with creamy chocolate, while the youngster was being greeted in the manager's office. The veteran catcher seldom initiated such hazing, fearing they might repel some able kid who could help the club. Still, neither did Muggsy interfere. It had happened to him aplenty on his climb upward from the bush leagues. So now let's test the kids for guts!

Muggsy changed into his baggy flannel red-and-black Lion uniform in leisurely style, kibitzing card games along the way. (No gambling in team quarters, the manual of the United League did read. But Cliff relaxed on that rule as long as scuttlebutt told him the games were still small-change affairs, no player getting hurt.)

The catcher also fielded unprintable replies to the usual obscene questions from his teammates, regarding how he might have scored with feminine companions of the night before, perhaps even in dark corners of the train on the return trip to Marberry. Did he perhaps have available any names and phone numbers in his black book, yeah, such as the sexy brunette he'd lifted into his carriage and then she had finished the parade on his lap...how about it, Muggs...any more like that animal?

When Muggsy finally exited the dugout, onto the playing field, early-arriving fans reached another peak of frenzy. Repeatedly, he doffed his cap in appreciation, as Cliff insisted his players respond.

About that crowd: Most of the men were in factory wear. But there were scattered groups in what were obviously school clothes, such being tight, double breasted suits. Or also turtleneck sweaters the keynote item. Those "schoolies", as the players called them hadn't much appeared until lately.

The girls in the stands mostly wore whatever they figured would best attract the guys on the field.

Sitting in the box reserved for the team owner's guests, those seats directly behind third base and the Lion dugout, Father and Daughter Crowley watched the catcher take his swats in batting practice.

"Six years ago," remembered J.T., "in his first season with the Lions, Muggsy was a real hot prospect for the National League. (The National was the only big league at that time, before the American was born and then there was the first World Series between the two leagues, in 1903.)

"Oh yes, a lot of big league teams were excited over him. But he hurt his knee and suddenly they forgot his telephone number. Since then, he's never been as good a player, just a step too slow for the big time. After that, as Cliff Hartwick, his manager, told me on a hunting trip a while back, Muggsy seemed to decide that having a high old time might as well be his No. 1 ambition. Yeah, Muggsy's gone for the bright lights."

"Oh?" was Katie's comment, as she took her first closeup look at the Lion under such discussion. He was then but a few feet away from herself, headed back to the dugout. From this view, the hugeness of his chest and arms was not only verified but also magnified. Still, what fascinated Katie Crowley most of all was not even that lantern-jaw moving in front of him as he traveled; what truly took her was his clear and direct gaze from those deep brown eyes, seeming to know with each step exactly whereto he was headed.

"Anybody who takes a look at that body of his," Jim Crowley-the-fan raved on, "has to call him man of steel. And he's a ballplayer's ballplayer. If I was still playing he's the one I'd want as a teammate."

"So will he always be a Lion?"

"Likely. Cliff wants to make him a manager. So far, though, he doesn't think Muggsy's ready for such responsibility; he thinks the guy is too locked into fun-at-night. He thinks that what his catcher needs is to get married, stop all this late-night running around. But no girl's been able to lasso Muggsy Banton..."

"Hmmmmm......." She further checked her scorecard, which had cost five cents, including a pencil.

The rules of back-then gave the home team the choice of first-or-last-at bat. On this day, the hometown Lions chose last.

Batters were further allowed to choose the pitch-location. But many deemed that "sissy".

The Sox scored twice in their half of the first inning. But the Lions failed to tally.

..... Still 2-0 when the Sox came to bat in the fourth. Their first hope at the plate took a widespread stance and watched Lion pitcher Jumbo Malone come down with a high hard one.

"Bawlllll one," yelled the huge ump, ungraciously referred to as "Blind Tom".

Raging, Muggsy turned on him, "If you couldn't see that was a strike, then you need a big tin cup and a lotta pencils!"

"Button the lip, Banton, or it costs you ten bucks."

"Kill the umpire," raged the hometown fans.

"Yeah, and then ride him outta town on a rail too."

"You're so blind, you should oughta have a seeing-eye dog, ya bum-ya!"

"Fifteen bucks."

"Kill that umpire."

"Awright, Banton, now you dig in and play ball, or you're outta this game, and the fifteen goes to twenty too."

"Blind sonofa....." But Muggsy'd had his say, so he dug in.

In came the next pitch, and the Sox batter lifted a towering foul that drifted back toward the Lion dugout. Muggsy jerked off his mask and raced back after the ball in what seemed a hopeless effort.

Back-back he went, but the horsehide was going into the stands. Still he chased it, not looking to see that he might crash into the low wooden barrier separating stands and playing field.

"Let it go, Muggsy," yelled manager Cliff. "You can't get it!"

"Watch out," shouted the fans seated down front, fearful for the safety of their idol.

But dauntless Muggsy could still see the ball.

As it fell into the first row of seats behind the Lion dugout, he dove for it.

The elusive ball thudded into his glove but then fell away from him as he went headfirst into the stands.

His massive arms flew forward to break his flight.

They closed around a girl he'd knocked from her chair. Simultaneously, their feet shot into the air. Katie Crowley and the catcher disappeared from the view of the crowd as the shouting become cyclonic.

And then.....?

The catcher lay on the wooden floor of the stands. In his arms, pressed against him, was the shapely redhead. Around them, fans were cheering to the skies. But he knew only those blue-green eyes so close before him. And delightful lips that almost touched his.

Jim Crowley was behind/over them, a frightened Father and fan.

"Are you two all right?"

"Sure, Dad," she told him, struggling to arise, also to straighten her rumpled clothing. "Although I could have been frightfully hurt if Mr. Muggsy hadn't caught me. And see, I have the ball!"

Proudly did she exhibit the scarred horsehide.

"Mr. Muggsy" scrambled to his feet, bringing the redhead with him.

As they came into view, the noise rocketed to a new peak. But those emotions were for the moment lost on the Lion catcher. He was gazing at a small, freckled nose...and oh yes, at a figure bewitching.

Then how those fey eyes did grip him!

"You sure you're all right, Miss? I didn't mean to knock you down."

"I'm all right, and thank you for asking, Mr......uh....."

Embarrassing, but she couldn't remember his last name. Though she surely would have cause to know it later on.

"Banton," he told her, miffed that anyone in Marberry wouldn't know who he was. "Yeah...Muggs...uh....<u>Payne</u> Banton."

"From the way these people cheer you, Payne, I guess I shouldn't have had to ask. But this is the first time I've ever been to a Lion game."

"O.K. O.K. <u>Mister</u> <u>Muggsy</u>," charged Hizzonner The Ump, leaning over the rail and impatiently tapping the catcher on the shoulder. "Howsabout a ball game? Some of us wanna get home by supper time, we do!"

"Me?...Oh yeah." Muggsy was lost in the apparition before himself.

"Here, Payne, don't you want this baseball?"

"Naw...give it to your Husband." He jumped the railing, strutting back to home plate. His supreme thought was, he hoped t'hell she didn't yet have a Husband. He'd too often found those to be bothersome.

She returned to her seat, beside her Dad, whose fascination by the whole scene was only slightly less than his fright at what could have been.

For her part in that hasty encounter, Katie had been struck by something perhaps trivial: Rising above his collared shirt had shown a heavy undershirt.

She asked of her Dad, why would players be "so stuffy dressed" in intense heat? The very idea made her skin itch.

"Granted, that's extreme, but then Baseball is probably the most hidebound of all games. Its people think it's almost sacrilegious to change any of the rules and customs from what they were when an army officer named Abner Doubleday started it in Cooperstown...you know, in upper New York state...about forty years ago."

Katie was absolutely fascinated.

"It's like living far back, in another age."

"And," her Father continued, "The fans treasure resistance to change in their game, while too much else is changing. Well, Daughter o' mine, I must confess that I share their as-is wish...at least mostly as-is....Still, it's almost a sure-thing that, before long, someone will introduce better (lightweight) uniforms and playing gear, even while they are scorned for their impertinence. Sure, like I told you, ol' Roger Breshnahan wants to introduce shin guards."

Katie was up to the discussion: "It takes a brave person to be different."

"You bet it does. And, speaking of change, it's surely coming for you Girls too. I'll bet that, pretty soon, a lot of you will grow brave enough to toss your miserable corsets into trash cans and let your blessed bodies breathe...Then watch the other females follow."

No stopping Jim Crowley at this point: "I've been reading about the 'Emancipation Ladies' of the past half-century. Amelia Bloomer was their leader, and the pantalets she popularized were named for her. She persuaded a lot of put-down ladies to throw away their long, hot skirts, to change to short skirts-plus-outside bloomers. All that was done to emphasize the fight for female rights, and temperance too. Sure, the whole movement was tied in with the National Freedom Fight and sometimes violent strikes male workers had to put on. But you Girls, bless you, avoided the violence."

Midst this fascinating discussion with her adored Dad, Katie kept an eye on the ball game before her. The Lions were at bat, but Muggsy Banton wasn't currently getting a turn at the plate. Which could somewhat dim Katie's interest.

And she wouldn't be outdone in the ongoing recital: "We studied it in school, about Amelia Bloomer. Her followers wore shirtwaists, also bloomers dropped to knee-bottoms, with long stockings below those, much like some girls wear today when bicycling. But then, for a while, bloomers disappeared. Amelia and her followers didn't want the clothing controversy to blot out their supreme struggle, which was for temperance and the constitution-guaranteed rights of all females.

"But Dad, I'm amazed that you too are so 'studied up' on this. Believe it or not, Kind Sir, I admire you even more than I used to."

With such adulation, J.T. Crowley was again on his roll of oratory.

"Now, Katie, I'll tell you something you might not know. Today, the bloomer movement is not dead. There have been bloomer-Baseball teams playing in the western USA.

"They've been organized by a schoolteacher out of Temperance, South Dakota, name of Semanthia Smythe."

"I've heard of her too. She's also urging the bloomer-wearing in everyday life. And, though I haven't been brave enough to join in, I certainly admire those styles, cool and comfortable they are, no more skirts dragging in the mud."

"I'm with you there."

"Ol' Dad," said Katie, almost breathlessly, "I do love the way you <u>like</u> us girls."

"Still, and as you have to be aware, let's not speak of Bloomer Girls to your Mother. INDECENT is what she calls them as she, along with her 'high society friends', go up in flames over the mere mention."

While watching powerful-bodied Muggsy at work behind home plate, Katie was also struck by the huge, almost pillow-like glove on his left hand. It was in large contrast to the almost skin-tight gloves worn by the other Lions in the field.

"How can a catcher grab anything with such a clumsy glove?"

"Not easy. Actually, that glove's main purpose is simply to stop the ball and protect his catching hand. You can see how his bare hand is so busted.

"But then again, someone will doubtless re-design the catcher's glove. There's even talk that he might soon have a mask to protect his face, so he won't end his career grotesque-nosed and toothless, as have so many to this point."

"But <u>don't</u> change the sacred rules of the game," recited Katie. "Or shall I be more accurate... 'the grand old game'?"

"Small Daughter, you're learning quick-like."

In the eighth inning, with the Sox still leading 2-0, one out and a runner on second, Muggsy would come to bat. Though he wouldn't do that in a hurry. First he would indulge in a look-back to where a certain redhead was seated. Then, strutting bantam rooster-like to home plate, he stopped a few feet from there, pulled a file from his pocket, and worked it against his spikes.

"Now what...?" an increasingly amazed Katie wanted to know.

"He's trying to scare the Sox baseman," explained J.T., "letting them know he'll cut 'em up if they get in the way of his running."

Impatiently, Blind Tom took out his watch.

"Banton, if you stall thirty seconds more, you're outta this game."

Muggsy continued to file, then looked up innocently, "Now how much time left?"

"Ten seconds, and I'm not whistling Dixie neither."

Muggsy filed another time, arose leisurely, and took his place at bat. His howling "kranks" were with him, and they told him so.

On the first pitch, he dropped a bunt down the third base line and sprinted for first as quickly as a gimpy knee would take him. He beat the throw, and the run scored. But Blind Tom ruled that the ball had first rolled foul before being picked up by the opposing catcher and thrown to first.

On the second pitch, Muggsy swung from the heels, a drive into left field stands that seemed to have home run and tied-u-game written all over it.

Tom again ruled "Foul ball."

"Do the guys on the other team pay you off before or after the game?" the Lion catcher snarled at the ump.

"Shaddup, Banton, and play ball."

Muggsy drove one to deepest center-field. It appeared good for three bases. But, impossibly, it was flagged down.

So the game ended, 2-0, another defeat for the slumping Lions, their fifth straight.

In the dressing room, Cliff managed a grin.

"Hey, Muggs, better days gotta be coming. But, for tonight, I'm giving a little party for Lion stockholders, and some other folks too. Be happy to have you join us. Fun should start 'bout eight p.m."

Muggsy, beaten down over a seemingly endless string of losses, had just slammed a shoe to the floor.

Still he managed a laugh in spite of low spirits. "Sure looks like the hawks have got this team...But thanks, Cliff, for the invite, and sure, I'll be there."

He next shifted nervously. "Uh...Cliff, who...?"

Cliff played it cool and confident, surely anticipating the next.

"Something sitting heavy on your head? Speak your piece, Muggsy."

"So who was the girl I bumped out of her chair?"

"Are you possibly still thinking of that redhead?"

"Cut the kidding, Cliff."

"But I thought Baseball was your main interest...All right, her name is Katie Crowley. Her Dad is President of the First National Bank of Marberry."

Stripping off his dirty woolen undershirt, the catcher tried to look indifferent.

"Will she...I mean, is she going to be...?..."

"Sure, Muggsy, she'll be at the party."

A shout went up from the other Lions: "She'll be there."

"Shut up, or there'll be some split lips."

"For you, she'll be there," Cliff continued. "Even if I have to go after her myself, which I'd have done long ago if I was some years younger. She's a cutie, now isn't she?"

"Uh...yeah, I guess she's all right. 'Course I mostly like my broads bigger than that, but she's all right."

More shouts: "Muggsy says she's not broad enough, but she's still all right."

A teammate turned to Muggsy, "Hey, don't you never think of nothing but dames?"

"Not much. Do you?"

The other considered it briefly. "Come to think of it, I guess I don't either."

Still he persisted, "Uh...Muggsy..."

The catcher eyed him suspiciously.

"Now what?"

"When you landed on the curvy broad, did you get a quick feel?"

He saw Muggsy advancing on him.

"Awright, awright! No harm intended; us guys just wanted to know...Hey, protect me guys. Muggsy wants to kill me!"

Chapter Three

One of my all-time favorite Baseball quotes: Manager Casey Stegen would tell his players, "When in doubt, take two, then hit to right."

Many times have I benefited from that calming counsel and the spirit in which it was offered...many times, in many places, and in countless situations of stress.

The evening coolness was welcome after the steaming day just passed. The dark clouds over Marberry were hopefully noted as rain-filled, though that blessing was seldom bestowed in August.

Trees received the breezes gratefully and gracefully, their leaves dancing for the first time that day.

Men walking home from the muggy mill stopped on street corners to remove their headpieces and savor the cool.

Riding in J.T.'s carriage, Katie said little.

"What's up, Katie? Cat got your tongue?"

"Guess so."

But she avoided his glance.

"Muggsy's a great fellow," he came back, then waved to someone riding by. "Hi, Ed! How's the new house coming? Got the second coat on yet?"

Katie laughed. "All right, so I never could hide my thoughts from you. Payne is nice."

"Who is?" J.T. thought his hearing had deserted him.

"Payne Banton, he said that's his name, your 'Muggsy' did. He was so polite and caring after we took that tumble together."

"Sounds like you've been hit by a bolt of lightning."

Katie took back from her burst of enthusiasm: "Don't be foolish, Dad. I hardly know him."

"From the way he looked you over, I'll bet you hear from him soon. And do you know something else?"

He paused before carefully easing into his next words.

"Maybe there's something to that 'rugged' approach. Did you see Muggsy stand up to that ol' umpire? Maybe I should be more rugged."

Just then, a large lumber wagon went by them, almost sideswiping their carriage. J.T. had to suddenly swerve to avoid a collision.

"Road hog!" he shouted.

Still, as usual for him, dissatisfaction was brief. He turned back to his previous train of thought, grinning broadly as he flexed his muscles.

"'Rugged Crowley', that's what they'll call me, 'fighter against oppression', 'a beacon for the timid'."

"Careful, Dad; you might take on more than you can handle."

He laughed at himself. "I guess you're right. Besides, I've been reading a lot about that man Mohandas Ghandi and his non-violent fight for his Indian people at home and in South Africa. He's most impressive."

He reached into his coat pocket for a newspaper clipping, and handed it to Katie.

She read: "'I have learned through bitter experience that the one supreme lesson is to conserve my anger. And, as heat conserved is transmuted into energy, even so our anger controlled can be transmuted into a power which can move the world...How I find it possible to control anger would be a useless question, for it is a habit that everyone must cultivate and must succeed in forming by constant practice.'

"I get it. When that lumber wagon almost hit us, you allowed yourself a quick moment of anger, then put it behind you, to keep your supply of energy."

"Right! Same way your rugged friend of today, Muggsy Banton, got rid of his anger in a hurry...he almost seemed to enjoy it, didn't he?.....then went back to doing what he had to do.

"And now here we are again, back at home, sweet home."

Home was a large red brick house looking proudly over the lawns before it.

Those were kept so meticulously, a passerby could be inclined to the thought that they seemed too perfect, more like a painting than anything alive. Even as Father and Daughter Crowley rode up the path in those evening hours, a gardener was still working, bent low to the lawn.

"He's here late. Your Mother must have somehow found one lonely old blade of grass longer than the others.

"You're too hard on Mom."

"Just could be, but lawns don't have to be so all-fired perfect. Hey, what say you and I sneak out here tonight and plant a batch of weeds in the middle of all this glamour, put some balance in the scene?"

"Dad!"

As the carriage stopped alongside the house, a young Negro perhaps ten years old and dressed in neat overalls, ran from the stable. He took the reins from J.T.

Luther Lincoln was the son of Birdie, the family's cook and housekeeper.

"'Evening, Mr. Crowley, Miss Katie," was Luther's joyful greeting.

"Hello there, Luther," Katie responded, accepting her Dad's hand as he helped her down from the carriage. "Do you happen to know if we're late for dinner?"

"You're a mite close to that; your Momma, she's been stompin' back and forth some, like she does when she's anxious."

"'Evening, Luther," from J.T. "Better give old Alfred a good rub-down, if you'll be so kind. He seems to be losing all his pep; today he almost couldn't get us out of the way of a rampaging lumber wagon....How about a new horse?"

"Maybe you need one o' them fancy, combustible gas-mobiles that Mister Henry Ford, off in Detroit, just put out," Luther suggested. "They get you to where you're going in a mighty hurry."

"Then what would you do," Katie wanted to know, "with no Alfred to care for?"

"We could keep this sleepy horse for a pet, and I could keep your bran' new gas-mobile in fine runnin' order," offered the youngster, pulling some pamphlets from an overall pocket.

"See, I've been learning all about gas-mobiles from readin' these and listenin' to the man at the garage on Third Street."

The Crowleys looked at each other, amused. But Luther was too much in earnest for them to make light of his words.

To the boy, J.T. promised, "I'll sure think about it."

To Katie: "Now let's check the squall brewing in yon mansion."

Chapter Four

MEMORABLE WORDS FROM BOWIE KUHN, A FURIOUS FAN AND ALSO THE FORMER <u>COMMISSIONER OF BASEBALL</u> (IN HIS BOOK "HARDBALL....THE EDUCATION OF A BASEBALL COMMISSIONER"):

"Writers are as varied as well, people. While some see themselves as wrapped in the folds of the First Amendment, most do not, being content periodically to put on paper their thoughts on the world, for which they receive a paycheck. Mostly they like sports, some rather fiercely and partisanly."

Then thank you, Bowie, for the fierce and partisan manner in which you fought for the Baseball ideals of Jack and Jane fan.

J.T. knew whereof he spoke. Pacing the hallway as she petulantly awaited their arrival, Clara Crowley was in a foul frame of family figuring.

"Jim!" she pouted, pointing at the hall clock, "It's now thirteen minutes after six. You had no business staying at the office so frightfully late. You know we're going to a musicale tonight at the Campbells' home. They're important people, and we can't afford to offend them by being late."

Her Husband let go a sigh of grief. Nothing bored him so completely as the violin chamber affairs which Clara insisted they attend at least once a week.

But Clara was just getting warmed up.

"And Kathleen, where have you been? Did you have your fitting? That handsome Henry Sample had been calling you. His mother is president of my garden club, and I want you to be nice to him."

J.T. faced her straight-on, a la Muggsy Banton: "We went to the Baseball game, Katie and I did.

"We had a great afternoon."

"You took Kathleen to the what?" Suddenly Clara appeared unsteady, almost ready to faint.

"The Baseball game," he repeated, as he casually checked the mail stacked so precisely on the telephone table. "What's more, we'll probably go again tomorrow."

"No...oh my goodness, you mean with all those crude, smelly people?"

"Yes, and how delightful!"

"But...well...I mean..."

"Yes, Clara?"

Nothing she started to say, or could say, made sense to herself.

The Father turned to the Daughter, who had stood off to one side, struggling to hide her amusement at the interplay between Mom and Dad.

"Dad, shall we go up and wash for dinner? I'll bet Mom has a great dinner ready for us."

Clara fed her an appreciative glance. After being so kindly squelched, any sort of victory was to be treasured.

They started up the thick-carpeted staircase, but then he turned back, "Please give my regrets to the Campbells, and tell them I can't make their affair tonight. If you want to go, Luther can drive you there and wait for you."

"Yes, Jim."

Continuing up the stairs, he winked at Katie.

"Thanks to Muggsy, a new era is upon us. I'll have to catch more of his goings-on. Uh, pardon me, Katie, we'll have to."

She seemed grateful for the correction.

Chapter Five

Long-ago British definition of the game of Baseball: "It's a contest in which the ambitious and brave young man who strikes out for himself will take on himself naught but scorn for that attempt."

As dinner was being served, the phone rang.

"It's for Miss Katie," announced Birdie, "from a Mr. Sample."

"Thanks, Birdie; I'll take it on the hall phone."

"Please be nice to Henry," begged her Mother.

"Oh yes, Henry. Tonight? No, I'm sorry but I can't. Mom wants me to play bridge with some of her friends...Tomorrow? Sorry, I just can't make that either. But thanks for asking, and maybe another time."

Clara was standing behind her and hissing, "But his parents are prominent social..."

"'Bye, Henry."

Katie returned to the table, and J.T. applauded her performance.

"Good for you. Never did care for that fellow. Too <u>nice</u>. Probably can't remember the last time he fought for what he wanted."

"Kathleen, you just know there's no bridge game for tonight.

"And you surely could be nicer to my friends!"

Contritely, Katie crossed herself. "Mea culpa, dear Guardian Angel of mine, wherever you are, for that monstrous fib. It should be worth at least thirty lashes with a wet noodle, or however the nuns in our grade school used to put it....But Mom, you know that I...."

The phone rang again.

"For Miss Katie," Birdie repeated.

"Such a popular girl," commented her Dad. "I wouldn't be surprised if a certain Muggsy Banton had obtained your phone number for his vaunted 'little black book', AND is at this very minute ready to ask you for a date."

"No, it's a Mr. Hartwick," Birdie clarified the situation.

"That's all right; he's highly respected," acknowledged Clara. "But who in the world is this 'Muggsy Banton' you're talking about?"

"Tonight? Why no, Mr. Hartwick, I have nothing planned."

"At your house. And he'll be there too? Why thank you very much. Yes, I'll expect your carriage at eight."

As she hung up, J.T. was one huge grin.

"You never take my advice, you just do what you want," complained Clara. "And who in the world is 'he' that will be there? What's going on behind my back?"

"I'm going to a party at Mr. Hartwick's tonight."

"Well, just in case anyone cares, which I'm beginning to doubt, I have nothing against him. He's most generous about giving money to good causes. It's just that he associates with those awful Baseball players, such a rowdy lot they are!"

"So after dinner you might as well go up and get ready for your party, and I just hope none of those sweaty 'ballplayers' are there too...I think you should wear the blue dress, the one with the balloon sleeves and lacy collar that you and I just picked out at The Gown Shoppe. And wear those long, tight-fitting gloves. They're the latest thing in New York City. That should impress Mr. Hartwick and his guests."

"Oh yes, be sure to impress Cliff Hartwick," her Dad offered in devilish style.

"I declare, Jim, I don't know what's this fiendish mood you're in."

"Mom, you just never mind Dad. Sometimes he's simply full of devilment; like you used to tell me, 'Boys must have their strange joys.'"

"But I do hope you'll please check me out before I leave for the party. I want to be sure I'm 'prim and tucker', like you used to say when I was a little girl."

"Thank you, Kathleen. I'll be pleased to check you out."

Cliff met Katie at the doorway of his bachelor-home.

"I'm so glad you could come, Miss Katie Crowley. And say, what a pretty dress! It really blends with your eyes."

Katie laughed, "Now now, Mr. Hartwick; my Dad said you were something of a flirt."

"A minor league one. But I do hope you'll save a dance for this old guy."

"Thank you, and I'll look forward to that honor."

Then wickedly, in a manner that reminded her of her Dad, he lowered his voice: "Just between us, he's inside, in the living room. He was easily the first guest to arrive."

"Why Mr. Hartwick, whoever are you speaking of."

"Of course, my error, Katie (and please call me Cliff). You came here to be with me, now didn't you?"

"Right, Cliff, and to dance with you."

"Still, kind Miss, you will meet a few of my guests, won't you? They'll be so put out if you don't."

"Well all right, just a few."

"Katie, will you take my arm, let me be your escort, cicerone, whatever."

"Delighted, Cliff."

The living room, with decor as masculine and relaxed as Cliff himself, was crowded. Still, the minute Katie entered, she saw Payne Banton off in a far corner, talking in lively style to a large and curvy female of about her own age. Katie made a self-note to forever hate that girl for "rudely disrupting" her own entrance.

Cliff's arm was still taken by her own, as he guided her to his guests.

"Miss Crowley, this is Joe Benchley, treasurer of the Lions."

Benchley was paunchy and bald, coming on blah to Katie, who smiled with the introduction but sensed that Cliff was teasing her with the delay.

"Paul Spencer, one of our stockholders."

Paul was short and fortyish, his gaze leaving Katie feeling quite undressed.

"Oh yes, my sister, Mary Hartwick."

Mary was round and smiling, as if she lived to smile. Katie liked her at once. But where...?

No longer could she see the ballplayer. But she knew he was still in the room. She couldn't have felt his presence more powerfully if he'd been pressing her hand. She tried to glance around without being conspicuous. Butterflies ("flutterbies" she'd called them as a little girl) were dancing crazily through her entire being.

Finally:

"How about over here, Katie Crowley? Let's see which guest is over here."

(Cliff, you stop teasing me!)

"Oh yes, over in this corner is Muggsy Banton, my cantankerous catcher. But then I think that perhaps you two met this afternoon, if not with a 'proper introduction'. So, Muggsy, may I have the opportunity of properly introducing you to Miss Katie Crowley?"

His tanned face was unashamedly eager.

"Hello, Katie Crowley."

"I'm pleased to meet you, Payne Banton."

(From Cliff to himself with an inner chuckle: Greatest play since Harry Houdini just made an elephant disappear.)

So the formality was behind them. And they were lost in the wonder of each other.

"If you two don't mind terribly, I'll leave you together."

It's doubtful that either of them heard his words, far less noted his going.

In a dark blue suit and a maroon (bow) tie, he looked so different to Katie. But the shy, laid-back something that had so struck her was still there. Again, he seemed every bit as masculine, in command of the moment, as he had been that afternoon.

"That sure is a daisy of a dress. Blue is my favorite color."

(Thanks, Mom, for your choice.)

From the porch came Victrola music, with the voice of Irish tenor John McCormack.

I'll take you home again, Kathleen, across the ocean wild and wide...to where your heart has ever been, since first you were my bonnie bride...

Cliff thanked his luck in finding that one in his attic after a long search.

"Like to dance, Katie? Looks like they're going to do The German."

"Oh yes, Payne, I'd love that."

They danced, and then again, and then for the rest of the evening. The now-distant "other world," certainly including the curvy intruder, was blotted from them. Muggsy made sure that NO ONE would take this luscious redhead from his arms. Even Cliff didn't cut in for his promised dance. ("Never take a hot streak for granted," he'd long preached to his players.) Besides, he was busy with the repeated playing of "their song".....

... I'll take you home again, Kathleen, to where your heart will feel no pain. And when the world is fresh and green, then I'll take you to your home again.

"Hard to believe, Katie Crowley, but tonight you're even prettier than you were this afternoon."

"Why Payne Banton, such delightful blarney! But then who ever heard of pretty freckles? When I was a little girl, I did just everything I could to get rid of them. Once I even sneaked a frog into my room and held him or her against my cheeks at exactly midnight, 'cause I'd heard that would make the hideous spots go away. But, no thanks to Mr. or Mrs. Frog, the next morning the freckles were still there. I heard of some other cures along the way, but that awful 'frog failure' sorta convinced me they were meant to be."

While they waltzed: "Katie, you told me this afternoon that you'd never seen a professional game before today. That's hard for me to understand; since Baseball's been my world for so long, I guess I just thought that everyone followed it."

"I'm anxious to see more games. My Dad and I will be out there again tomorrow. He's anxious to meet you."

She rather astounded herself, the way she opened up so early in their meeting and told him of her Dad's sudden resistance to wifely edicts. But she did that, and felt good for the telling.

"Hey, I want to meet him too."

GOOD NIGHT, LADIES filled the house, and the guests began to leave.

"Is it really so late?" she asked. "Or, as the kids say, must we drag it?"

"Afraid so. Can I take you home, Kathleen?"

They laughed, which came easily on this night.

"Looks like it's meant to be," she told him. "Please excuse me while I primp?"

"Excuse with regret....if you don't brush away any of the freckles."

"And, if you'll please fetch my coat, then you may stuff my sleeves in."

She returned, straightened the wrinkles from her long white "New York gloves" of her Mother's urging. She wore them though, frankly, she didn't like the feel of her hands and arms so confined.

They stepped out into the cool and thoroughly delightful Marberry night-air, its joys fed by zephyrs from the river.

"Now let's see, which of those pretty carriages would belong to Mr. Payne Banton? Surely it would be of the brightest colors, also headed by the mightiest steed."

He sniffed at that assumption.

"Carriage? You must be thinking of someone else. Muggsy Banton rides in style."

She followed his pridefully pointed finger, and she gasped.

"You mean that beautiful red gas-mobile? But..."

"Ballplayers don't make much money, so how can I afford that? Is that what you mean?"

"I guess that's it," she admitted, embarrassed that she might have wounded his ego. "It's just beautiful...but so...so expensive looking."

"Katie, I don't mean to come-on a braggart, but I get that question all the time. And I'll tell you, it not only looks expensive; it also is just that. Buying it like to broke me. But I saw it one day and dreamed about it for a week. So I had to buy it.

You might say I became Marberry's J.P. Morgan for a day."

He added, "Here's a duster, to protect your pretty dress." And he pulled the long coat from in back of the seat. But, when he shook it out for airing, a pair of silk stockings fell to the floor of the car.

He grabbed them, quickly stuffing them into his pocket.

Katie pretended not to notice. Still, if only for an instant, she had a sharp flash of warning, remembering her Dad's words on how Muggsy "liked a good time". She would harken back to that flash before long, but for then she was accepting Muggsy's hand as he helped her into the car.

For his part, Muggsy was glad he stood behind her, hoping she couldn't catch his mortification.

"Riding in this car should be fun. Although I've heard they can catch fire or even blow up."

"As safe as a church picnic, but more fun."

He walked to the front of the car, lit a match, and applied it to the gasoline burner.

The gas-mobile shook furiously, then seemed to explode.

Its two passengers were lost in a cloud of dense, black smoke. Nearby carriage-horses reared in sheer fright, and people ran from their homes to check out whatever disaster there could be.

"Who got shot?"

Across the street, a plump woman dressed in only a nightgown stood on the porch of her house, screaming hysterically, "Call the police, there's been a murder!" Whereupon eyes shifted from the smoking auto to herself, framed in the glare of a bright porch-light. She remembered the robe she'd forgotten to slip into. Scarlet-faced, she ran back inside.

Katie hadn't yet recovered. "What happened?"

Muggsy took her hand caringly. "Nothing at all.

"Oh, maybe too rich a mixture of gasoline, though usually there isn't near so much noise."

The next starting attempt was a comparatively smooth and quiet maneuver.

And away they went.

"Oh, what a perfectly plummy nite!" Katie exhilarated, sinking onto the cushion that Muggsy had selected as a backrest. She was wondrously at ease.

Chapter Six

Fact that belies an age-old rumor: Harold Parrott, Brooklyn Dodger business manager and ticket manager, was the steel-trap mind who brainstormed the club's westward march in 1957, to become the Los Angeles Dodgers.

Harold told me, "Forget all the wild tales about (Dodger president) Walter O'Malley conniving to get the L.A. franchise. Walter didn't have to do any dealing; he simply ate from the table that had been set for him. Well, isn't that how any eager guy will react?"

Muggsy and Katie passed the steel mill, where a new shift was arriving. And watched the blast-furnace chase darkness from the night sky.

A few more miles and the river was in view. A tiny trace of moon was struggling to light the water.

"Here's a scarf for that gorgeous red hair," offered Muggsy, reaching behind the seat. Only now he reached cautiously.

"Thanks, Payne, but letting my hair blow gives me a wonderful sense of freedom. Sometimes I fantasize that's how the pioneer women on the plains felt."

Along the river he pulled off the road. He killed the engine.

The desolate spot where they'd stopped was backed by the blackness of tall trees.

She relaxed against the seat-back, content as she hadn't been in a while.

"Great moon," he commented, "at least what there is of it."

"Does a moon remind you of a baseball?"

"Believe it or don't, I'd forgotten that game."

They looked out onto the water and saw the green running lights of a boat.

"That looks like the Robinson's yacht," she ventured. "They're neighbors of ours, and Mr. Robinson goes out there to be by himself while he writes his novels about love and spies and lots of things. They're so exciting. Now at least I know how he grabs his feelings of eerie loneliness."

His hand moved on the bareness of her upper arm.

She pulled ever so slightly from him.

"Afraid, Katie? Hey, I wouldn't hurt you."

"I know that." And she wished she hadn't moved so quickly. He solved that problem by slipping an arm around her shoulder.

"Payne, this is such a fancy car."

"Fancy...car," he repeated, moving closer until his lips brushed her throat, the tip of an ear, her throat again. All the while he was murmuring something she couldn't make out for sure. Still, the low, soothing voice seemed to blend with her somewhat heated feelings of the moment. Never had she been kissed on a proper first date. Now, as his fingers played on her arm, she watched the brown eyes and awaited a soft movement by his lips.

The ballplayer had other ideas, and they didn't include softness.

Relentlessly, he pushed his damp and demanding mouth onto hers.

Caught completely off guard, she struggled against him. But he was too strong.

One of his hands was behind her, pressing her body against his. From the other, and knotted or not, his fingers had expertly unbuttoned the top of her blue dress. And they were swiftly working their way downward.

"Payne...STOP. Oh please don't do this to me."

Briefly he ignored her pleading. Well why not? Hadn't nearly all of "his girls" protested briefly before giving in to his desires, the momentary resistance, as all the guys on the team seemed to agree, to prove they were really "nice ladies"...well, hadn't they all so briefly resisted?

For Katie, some mild mixture of frustration, body heat, and just plain panic took her, as he sought to push her back onto the seat of that gas-mobile.

So what then?

From Kathleen Crowley the tears did flow.

Jolted, Muggsy pulled back, his face burning in amazement.

"Please, Katie, don't cry."

He handed her a large kerchief. To further reassure, he moved off to the far side of the seat.

"Why did you have to be so rough?" she sobbed angrily, struggling to sit upright and restore her dress to some sort of order.

"I liked you, Payne Banton. I wanted you to kiss me, and I never have stood for that on a first date. Still, Mr. Mighty Athlete, in case no one's ever informed you, I'm not a piece of hamburger for you to tear the wrapper off and gulp down in one quick, careless bite, NO I'M NOT."

He had never felt so confused or mortified.

"I'm sorry, Katie, I really am. I'm just not used to someone as classy as you. But I do apologize; now I'll take you home."

Katie had to treasure the thought that she could indeed light a flame in a man so forceful, yet so inwardly thoughtful and kind.

Suddenly she saw too much of importance slipping slipping away. As Muggsy opened the door on his side of the gas-mobile, headed for again igniting the engine, she put a soft hand on his arm.

"Payne...please...wait a minute. I shouldn't have been such a baby."

Still puzzled, he nevertheless closed the door and again sat down beside her. But did not immediately take the hand she laid conveniently beside himself.

She noted that, and rushed the conversation back to matters-Muggsy.

"Please tell me what it's like, being a professional Baseball player. Mostly I've just seen those on the screen at our nickelodeon house."

He brightened some as again he found Katie's hand to place in his own.

"So you like the moving pictures too? Lots of people think they're a fad that'll die in a hurry. But me, I think they're here to stay. My favorite is still THE GREAT TRAIN ROBBERY. A bunch of us guys on the Lions have seen it over and over, 'specially when we've been on the road. That director...isn't his name 'Porter' ....?"

"Edwin S. Porter."

"Yeah, that's the guy. He sure knows how to keep you on the edge of your seat, with his fast action scenes and the music that races with his chases."

"My girlfriends and I also have seen that movie a lot of times. Now the one we're really waiting for, the 'romantic thriller' that's supposed to come out soon, is THE COUNT OF MONTE CRISTO. It's the first movie ever shot out in California, which they say is the home of so many movie stars. I read somewhere that it's about the greatest love story ever, and, I must confess, Payne, I'm taken by those.

"But about your life in Baseball...that's what I want to hear...."

Muggsy moved closer, but his new-found reticence made it plain, there would be no more assault on this night.

"Baseball is a swell life.

"Oh sure, there were times back in the cheap leagues when I got tired of the dumpy rooming houses, even worse than some of those we stop at now. Then there were the rocky ball fields, stuff like that. But I pegged it out because there was something in me that said I just had to..... Then I was sold to the Lions, and this is getting close to the Big Leagues."

"'Sold'? That sounds terrible, like you're a slave."

"Not actually, but the system sometimes comes close to that. If my contract is sold to another team, either I report to the new team or quit the game....Of course, now that we just got a second Big League (they call it THE AMERICAN LEAGUE) some of the players who are important enough just jump over to where they get paid the most. But a lot of the ordinary guys are scared to do that because they can get a reputation as 'rebels'. I just wish I'd hit the top and got important enough so I'd have to make that decision, jump or not jump. Wow, imagine the chance to jump to the best job for joining with the best team...sure, like the Pirates over in Pittsburgh, where I could play with Honus Wagner, probably the best player ever..."

Muggsy stopped then and ruefully laughed at himself.

"Some dreamer, huh? Well it could have happened if I hadn't wrecked my knee. But now it never will."

Katie's hand added an especially tender touch to his. Well, what else to express? But he treasured the gesture.

Katie was lost in the discussion.

"After you came to the Lions, everything was great for you?"

"At least I survived, even in the early days. Though the old-timers on the club sure didn't like rookies going after their jobs. Right after I got here, I came back to the locker room after exercise drills and found my favorite bat broken, my clothes shredded, and my street shoes sprayed with red paint. I had this feeling, either Cliff had done it or he had allowed it to be done, so he could see what I was made of. I mean, this game isn't anywhere like a tea party, good guys or no good guys. Just no room for crayfishing.

"So what was I supposed to do, be a meek little 'pretty Percy', like the players sometimes called scared rookies? Naw, for some kind of gesture I just hauled off and decked the guy standing next to me, even though he was a lot bigger than me, and even though he probably had nothing to do with ruining my stuff. Well he decked me, and we went at it pretty good for a while.

"But I guess that must've satisfied Cliff.

"A few days later, I found a fifty dollar bill in my pants pocket, which more than covered all my stuff that had been ruined. It had to be from Cliff, and then I knew I was part of the Lion team. By now I'm doing O.K., bum knee and all. I make enough money to rent a house with Jumbo Malone, one of our pitchers. Maybe we'll even buy the house. He's lost the hop off his fast ball, and has about as much chance of hitting 'the Bigs' as I do."

"Payne, sounds like you've found the good life."

"Yeah...good life," he said without the most of certainty. "But some things are missing."

He didn't elaborate on that, and Katie felt that she shouldn't pry.

Already, and more by the moment as he recovered from what had been a severe setback, Muggsy was fancying being close to this lively redhead. What he'd been denied, what he'd sought so boorishly...all that still burned with him and grew hotter by the moment. Still he knew he must be extremely patient for THAT. Of course, he had no clue, how her warmth matched his own.

"Katie, I'll bet your life's been a lot more fascinating than mine."

"Not really. Of late it's consisted of pushing-off from my Mom, who's really a sweetie but is also determined to have me on top of the local social heap. I hate that thought! I truly want to go to the University this fall. But she's against that. She says it will cost me a chance to be a supreme debutante of Marberry.

"I'm counting on my Dad as my ace-in-the-hole to free me."

After which confessions they sat hand-in-hand, silently watching the ripples on the riverbank.

Finally: "It's getting late, Payne. We'd better turn back; you athletes do need your sleep."

"Yeah, darn it. All right, now for sure I'll take you home again, Kathleen."

On her front steps: "Katie, can I see you again tomorrow night, and we can go see a movie? Oh yes, I promise never again to make such a sap out of myself."

Her answer was so instantaneous it even jolted herself:

"7:30, Payne, and I'll be waiting."

The front door of the Crowley home closed between them.

Before long there was a light tap on her door.

"Come in, Dad."

"How'd you know it was me...mindreader or something?"

"Oh, I just took a wild guess."

He was wearing the bright red silk lounging robe which Clara had given him the previous Christmas. Too loud for his taste, but then he wore it rather than hurt his Wife's feelings.

"Have a good time, Katie?"

She hugged him, no mistaking her mood of bliss. And, on the bed where she'd been stretched out, he saw the sports section of THE MARBERRY CLARION.

"Oh my, that good a time?"

"Shame on you, Dad, for being such an incurable Romeo. You stayed up late to hear about Payne and me, so don't you deny it."

He pulled out a white handkerchief and waved it in surrender.

"You win! The more I think about that young fellow, the better I like him."

"Me too, Dad."

Driving home, Muggsy was so joyful, he forgot the soaring speedometer. Roaring through the now-quiet downtown section, his trip was interrupted a shout:

"Hey, you, STOP."

Muggsy pulled over to the curb, watching a bristling policeman approach. Even at night, the shiny badge was disconcertingly obvious.

"You was traveling 'way too fast, young feller," boomed the law's myrmidon. "Bet you was doing maybe 20 miles an hour."

"Who, ME?"

"You, Motorist, I am addressing. See anyone else close by I could be talking to? Night in the pokey would cool off such a smart aleck, is the thought of this Pete Gilhooley, it is."

He flashed his light in Muggsy's face. Suddenly he was all friendliness. "Say, you're Muggsy Banton, you are. I've seen you play lots of times. What're you trying to do, break up the bones of our best catcher ever?"

The ballplayer breathed easier.

"Thanks, Officer Gilhooley." He gunned the idling engine and started to drive hurriedly away while the officer/Baseball fan was still in a forgiving mood.

"Wait there now, Muggsy Banton. A lawbreaker such as yourself certainly can't get away with no toll extracted, as the judges put it."

Muggsy swore, and louder than he meant to.

"Tch, tch, such language! May the saints in heaven not have heard it. And to think that you're the one our youngsters take after, they do. No, you must have a fine, and here it is: I want your autograph for my boy, young Pete. He thinks you are the greatest man alive, that he does."

Muggsy sighed heavily in easement, then reached under the seat to pull out a new baseball and to write on it, "To Pete Gilhooley Jr., from your friend Muggsy Banton. And may you surely realize it's your Dad is the Greatest Man On Earth."

"Oh say now, Muggsy, thank you so much. Your sins are absolved, as Himself Father O'Halloran, my fine parish priest, would put it. But don't let me again catch you endangering life and limb, speeding in this devil's contraption. Now you get on home before I further fine you a ball for myself, which I just might."

For sure, Muggsy also and quickly fulfilled that forfeit, then drove away.

Alone in her room, Katie stood at the large window and watched the small chunk of moon grow dimmer. The wind blew in against her and framed her trim body in the expensive lace nightgown.

In her hand was the baseball the catcher had given her that afternoon, after together they'd tumbled to the floor.

It had to remind her of Muggsy, so rough and scarred, yet also strong and reassuring.

Chapter Seven

From THE TONIGHT SHOW and former catcher Joe Garagiola: "You'll have learned a lot more about our game when you understand why there are no umpires on Baseball cards."

The Marberrians forgot the heat that so recently had taunted their tiredness. Once more, as autumn moved at them, they brought warm clothes down from their attics. While mill-flames had to cut through damping skies on each morning.

As the Lions approached the end of another season, almost every afternoon of their home stand saw Katie Crowley in a front row seat behind their dugout. In her hand would be SPALDING'S BASEBALL GUIDE FOR 1907, that copy to be quickly tattered from overuse.

Thanks to that guide, plus admonitions from her Dad and Muggsy, Katie learned quickly: Nine innings to a game unless it ended in a tie and extra innings had to be played...Three outs for each side in each inning...A ball hit over the fence in fair territory is a "home run".

The local umpire, referred to as "Blind Tom," fascinated her for the tight hold he kept on the game. Also for the definite manner in which he called balls-and-strikes, safe-or-out.

"He's a local guy," Muggsy told her. "Works in the mill all night, then in the afternoon umpires games for us or for the stupid Burglars, the so-called Baseball team across town.

"I never could figure how ol' Tom keeps up this pace. But I guess when you love something like he loves Baseball, you can do anything for it. "The way I heard it, he was a fast-balling minor league pitcher, headed for the big show. But then his arm went dead. I guess his umpiring helps to make up for the chance he lost...His job-idol seems to be "Silk" O'Laughlin, the showboat Big League ump. On the side, Tom once told Cliff, his ambition is to use Silk's famous line: 'Only two people are infallible, the Pope in religion and Yours Truly in Baseball'. But so far he's been reluctant to try it."

"Must be lonely out there," noted Katie..."him against all of you."

"Yeah, tough working alone. Watch Tom, and you'll see he's behind home plate till there's a base runner. Then he has to move out behind the runner, and also call balls-and-strikes from out there. But then it's been the same in the Big Leagues. Now, as we hear it, they're gonna have two umps per game. Hey, maybe it happens here too!

"Still, then it wouldn't be so much fun, 'cause we couldn't pull stuff on Tom. Well, you watch: if he has his eyes on a ball hit to right field, his back has to be turned on third base, and a runner can 'cut the bag' without touching it. Or the third baseman can slow the runner rounding third base by grabbing his belt.

"Getting to like Baseball?" Muggsy asked.

"I'm crazy about it, especially about the Lions, who surely are 'coming into full stride', as a CLARION writer named George-something just said it. And he's surely right; you've won eight of your last eleven games."

Again, late on a Saturday morning, the two of them were in a downtown cafe featuring lunch for 15 cents. On that afternoon, the Lions would play the Cougars.

"Wearing something blue, Katie?" Muggsy asked searchingly.

"Yes, and thank you for asking, Kind Sir, but I don't think a gentleman should know just what is that blue-something. But yes, Miss Crowley is law-abiding."

"Then please recite your lesson, little girl."

She folded her hands and spoke primly: "Baseball players are a terribly superstitious lot. And you, Payne Banton are as bad as any of them, maybe worse than most. When you see a dray carrying nails, you are sure you will have good luck...When your center fielder comes in at the end of an inning, you insist that he steps on first base before heading for the dugout. And, since I was wearing blue when first we met, you insist that I wear something blue each and every time I come to see you play."

"Correct, little girl. You get one hundred percent for this lesson."

"I'll never get over last Tuesday's game when I forgot something-blue. You couldn't get a hit, you made two errors, and your Lions lost, 12-1."

"Rookie, don't ever again pull that boner, or you could get shipped back to the bushes in a hurry, like even with a ticket to Tuskegee."

"Or even with a pass to Paducah?"

"Or even that."

"Horrors! Then I better get my ship in order."

Katie's eyes followed a trayful of pies and pastries that a waitress was carrying by.

"Oh dear, that apple pie looks yum-yummy. But I don't know if my 'figger' can stand the strain."

"You got nothing to worry about," he told her, giving a desirous look up and down herself.

Reassured, she still asked, "Will you eat half the piece of pie?"

Suddenly she wondered if that had been the right thing to say. She and her Mom loved to share food, but J.T. would have nothing to do with such a practice.

(Some questioning from Katie had dredged up the reason for that rock-hard stand: J.T. as-a-child had an Aunt with 15 nieces and nephews. Then his most shocking remembrance reverted to the time when Auntie had invited the 15 to a birthday party at her house, featuring a marvelous collection of small pastries. Young J.T. had firmly set his mind and heart on one of those, featuring luscious apple chunks in a golden crust, all that topped with a fluffy cream.

Auntie had other ideas. She insisted that each and every piece of her pastries, and that included J.T.'s dream dessert, be divided into 15 slices. Oh the trauma for a small boy! Then for Katie's father, the absolute shock from that day had never disappeared. And never again would he even consider food-sharing.)

Muggsy Banton was not loath in the same fashion.

"Sure, Katie, pleased to split a piece of pie with you."

He motioned to the sexy young waitress who'd been serving them. She came to their table in eager fashion, her "bedroom sort" of dark, flashing eyes never leaving the male seated there.

"One piece of apple pie, please, Miss, two forks, and two cups of coffee," he requested, giving the arduous girl but a casual look.

"Yes, Sir," she came back, clearing the luncheon dishes.

"Mr. Payne Banton, you have that young Miss absolutely bewitched. Did you see the way she looked at you? When you get your coffee, better look under the cup for a phone number...But then I'm sure that, being a man, you already noted on the name-tag over her large bosom that her name is Barbara Mooney."

"I caught Blondie's look, but I didn't look back. I only have eyes for you."

"Why how sweet, Payne, to put it that way...Oh good, here's the pie. Shall we cut it in half?"

"Not unless you're particular. Why not each of us go at it from our own side?"

Lost on them was the amused attention of the other diners.

Later: "Thank you for those beautiful roses you sent me. But you shouldn't spend so much money on me."

"All right, no more flowers; anything to please you, Katie."

"Hey, Mister, don't take a girl so seriously, especially not this one!"

"I'll work at that. But how would you like to go to a party tomorrow night? Friend of mine asked me to bring you. He's got what they call a 'ping pong set'."

"Oh sure. I was reading about that new game...Sounds like fun...But...oh oh....now I'm not sure about tomorrow night."

"You mean you have a different date for then?"...His disappointment was so strong that she was excited more than ever. She wanted to leap to the other side of the table and hug Muggsy.

"There's a dance at the country club, and Mom pushed me into accepting an invitation. It's with someone I don't care for, and I've continually turned him down. If I do that another time, both of our Moms will throw conniptions..."

"Trouble with this world of today, not enough conniptions thrown."

"You think, Payne, we should restore the balance?"

"Yeah, that's it. We'll form a club and call it 'Conniptions Unlimited'."

"Swell idea, Payne, and I'll be delighted to attend the party with you...But now, before we head for the ball park, aren't you going to show me your scrapbook, like you promised?"

"Sure will, Redhead; only it's not yet a real scrapbook, just a lot of clippings to put in a book some day when I'm old and retired, nothing else to do."

Back in his gas-mobile, he brought out a cardboard box holding many tales of himself, and photos too, dating from his beginnings.

"Is that you in the sailor suit and knickers?" she asked him.

"I'm afraid so," he answered, quickly moving to another clipping.

"But you were darling!" she told him. "And that was your Mom with you?"

"Sure was," he said warmly.

"She was completely lovely."

"Sure was."

"What's this one?" she asked, indicating a picture of two eager teenagers in decrepit Baseball uniforms.

"Me and a real good friend," he replied with decided wistfulness, "back when we started our Baseball careers together, in the bushes. Now he plays for Washington. He sometimes even gets to catch Walter Johnson, who's known as 'The Big Train' and who some people, including Cliff, say is probably the greatest pitcher in history. But I'll never get a chance like that."

"I'm so sorry." And again one of her petite hands sought one of his, big and beaten.

"Yeah, well..." and he shrugged his shoulders..."like Cliff teaches us, 'just hit the ball where it's pitched'. And then look at it this way, the other guy's up there, so he didn't get to meet you. I'm down here, so I did. Which I figure makes me a winner by miles."

Katie was so overwhelmed by that last, she felt tears coming in a hurry. But, rather than get too emotional before Muggsy, she turned her energy back to the clippings.

"This gambling story, what does it mean, THREE BASEBALLERS CHARGED WITH CRIME?"

"Not nice, is it? But there was something so puzzling about it, I never did throw it away. Gamblers tried to fix some games in a minor league one notch below ours. The players in that photo were supposed to be involved.

"Two of 'em confessed, and were suspended from Baseball for life. (Can you imagine a more terrible punishment?) But the third one, the tall boy in the middle (Yeah, the dude wearing the moustache and beard), Hubert Jorgenson was his name..."

"Nice looking young man, but whyever all that hair on his face?"

"Lots young players do that, trying to look older and tougher and even sexier. Believe it or not, I once did too."

"No!"

"Oh YES...but anyway this Hubert, he disappeared. Since he was the key witness in the case, too hard to convict the masterminds who engineered the whole thing. Somehow, though, I've always had the feeling that Hubert guy was innocent and someone was trying to frame him."

"But if he was innocent, why run away?"

"Probably got scared. Whatever happened, it was too bad he got mixed into it. He was a hot first-base prospect; lotsa big league teams were after him.

"Now here's a good picture, President Teddy Roosevelt throwing out the first ball at a game in Washington, D.C.

"I don't have many 'heroes', but Mr. Teddy's one, so honest and dynamic."

"You sound just like my Dad when he speaks of Mr. Teddy."

Came that afternoon before game-time. Katie reviewed what she'd learned. ..... A "stolen base" is not an offense for which you summon Officer Gilhooley. ..... The distance between the pitcher's mound and home plate used to be fifty feet. But, in the mid 1890's, and because the fans had wanted to see more hitting instead of so many strikeouts, that distance had been increased to sixty feet, six inches. ..... The fact that so few blacks attended the games was attributed to the fact that their own players were not allowed in "organized ball" but had to play in their own leagues. There was opposition to this, including such as Muggsy and Cliff, who avowed, "A ball player is a ballplayer, whatever his color!" But they were currently outvoted.

..... When two are put out on the same hitting sequence, it's called "a double play".

..... The team trainer tended to the physical needs of his players. Although, as Muggsy had explained to Katie, few minor league teams could afford a trainer. On the Lions, Cliff filled in as part-time conditioner, rubbing down severely aching joints with a mixture of vaseline and some "hot stuff" supposed to have come from the cactus of Mexico...When Cliff wasn't available, teammates gave each other make-do rubdowns. If the hurt wasn't worse than a bad bruise, the advice from other players would likely be, "Aw spit some tobacco juice on it, then forget it!"

..... The National League was the oldest Big League. The American League was formed by an educated and religious athlete (later sports editor) named Byron Bancroft (Ban) Johnson. Supposedly he had formed the new league as a protest against the brawling, umpire-baiting of such National Leaguers as New York Giant manager/catcher John McGraw. Muggsy had told Katie, "If I'd had a choice between playing in the two leagues, I'd have taken the National any old day over the 'sissy ball' in the American."

..... Until recently, each team had been permitted only one coach on the field unless multiple bases were occupied. Now, two coaches were permitted at all times.

After his team's pre-game drills, Muggsy joined Katie in the stands. By then she had company in the persons of a rather dumpy mid-thirtyish man of sour attitude ..... and a tall, blonde girl of striking proportions. Eye-catching in a black silk dress-suit, she was vibrant, a strange contrast to her bored escort. In his broad brimmed hat, Prince Albert coat and diamond studs, gambler was etched over him.

Muggsy liked the girl every bit as much as he disliked the man.

"Payne," said Katie, "I'd like you to meet Elsie Peabody, my best friend, and Dr. Phillip Sutton, Elsie's fiance."

"Happy to know you folks. I've heard lots about Payne Banton," the blonde came back. "Lately, all Katie can talk about is Baseball. So I had to come out and see this game that has her spellbound."

From the doctor: "Think you'll win today, Muggsy? I've heard there's good money bet that your sore-armed pitcher can't last more than five innings."

"I'm afraid Philip is not only one of those who not only wagers on Baseball but has done so heavily against the Lions in this game today," explained Elsie.

"I don't know about betting," Muggsy said. Then he decided to set a trap for the gambling doctor. "But if Bugle Nose isn't looking sharp early, he probably <u>will</u> get pulled."

Having said that, Muggsy noted the doctor making a quick gesture to a seedy-looking man seated several rows back. That one arose and hurried toward the back of the ball park, where there would be telephones.

While Philip Sutton leaned forward so confidently on his malacca cane, said to be the good-luck guarantee for all men-of-chance.

Game-time was nigh, and Muggsy said his goodbyes.

"Just a minute, Muggsy, please."

Before them, camera at the ready, was a lanky, thin-faced young man, in his early twenties (and serious at his work, it was evident).

The Lion catcher could then have sworn that some quick and disliking glances passed between the photographer and the doctor.

"Hello, George," Muggsy greeted him warmly. "What can we do for you?"

"If you please, I'd like to get a shot of your party."

"Certainly. Folks, meet George Periwinkle, a fine Baseball reporter and photog for our CLARION. I keep telling George he sure reminds me of someone I've seen before."

From Katie: "Now that you mention it, I get the same idea."

George seemed uneasy at such remembrances.

"Time's short; let's get this picture, so Muggsy can get back to work...now if he'll please move closer to Miss Crowley."

"With great pleasure! I can't get close enough to Katie to suit me."

Elsie laughed joyfully, clapping her hands at the rejoinder.

The dour doctor merely straightened his black tie.

As Muggsy was leaving, Cliff came up from the dugout. He was introduced to the visitors.

Then the manager turned to his catcher: "Unless my sight daily deceives me, Miss Katie Crowley has become quite a Baseball fan.

"Muggsy, why don't you bring her into the dugout for today's game?"

Muggsy wondered if Katie would like that scene, doubtful language, tobacco juice and all.

"I'd love it," she soothed his doubts however unspoken they were. "Though I did promise to sit with Elsie and Philip."

"Forget us," urged Elsie. "We're in love, and we'll probably forget you by the second round."

"<u>Inning</u>, dearest," the doctor corrected her.

"Whatever. Katie, scat! Off with Payne you go to the dugaway."

"Dugout. Dearest."

"Whatever. Scat scat!"

As Katie passed by Elsie, the blonde squeezed her hand and murmured, "Payne's awfully nice."

The redhead's answering smile said plainly, "I think so too."

Then she bent forward and whispered, "Elsie, please cross your fingers for me. I just hope I don't act stupid before all those men."

Chapter Eight

WATCHING "THE BALLET THAT IS BASEBALL" OVER A LOT OF YEARS, I'VE SEEN AMAZING PLAYS. Still, the near miracle to top them came in the very first major league game I ever attended. It was in 1935, as I'd reckon the years. Though for me dates have been a weakness.

The Yankees were playing Cleveland at Yankee Stadium, "the house that Babe Ruth built". And a Cleveland Indian hit a low line drive that was clearing the field-level barrier in left. It seemed a home run for sure. But the Yankee youngster out there wouldn't give up on the ball flying past him. He left his feet, swooping into the stands. He made a backhanded catch while in-flight. The fans out there likewise caught Tommy Henrich as he somehow hung onto the baseball.

Oh so many years later I reminded Tommy of that catch.

"It <u>was</u> my best ever," he reminisced. "But I'm amazed that anyone remembers even reading about it, let alone you were actually there."

This I have frequently found: The mightiest are 'most always the humblest.

The other Lions, relaxing in the dugout before the game, seemed embarrassed when they saw Katie heading their way. She clearly noted that and started to tell Muggsy that she should return to her seat. But already he was making a speech:

"Listen, you guys, there's a lady gonna sit with us today. So watch your language, and spit your juice at the other end of this dugout, see!"

The players removed their caps of pillbox design.

Whereupon Katie stood up and told them, "Oh, please keep your caps on. I'm so happy to be with you, but I don't want to be a bother. I'll just sit over here with Payne."

That was the healer. The players grinned at her understanding, relaxing as before.

Except that one Lion hissed at another, in what had doubtless started out to be a whisper, "Whoinhell's this 'Payne' she's talking about. Guy with her sure looks just like ol' Muggsy used to catch for us even yesterday."

That was the complete problem-solver. Muggsy and Katie joined in the uproarious laughter that followed.

"Katie, you've already got 'em loving you," exulted the catcher. "But hey, you relax now while I confab with Cliff and Bugle Nose Stankorsky, our starting pitcher for today."

What followed was as easy for Katie to hear, seated next to the three of them, as it was certainly an education in the world of Baseball.

Muggsy had raged at the gambling-proposition words of Dr. Philip Sutton, that Bugle Nose would not last six innings. Back went his thoughts to another day with another team when he'd heard that a certain "knowing" big gambler had supposedly received information which urged him to wager considerably that the ballpark on that day would have a capacity crowd, which was 2000 fans.

The solution back then was simple for the home team, determined as it was to discourage the attendance of the wagering set at its contests. The boss, adept at counting crowds from a perch he took far out in the left-field stands, signaled his assistants at his count of 1900, and no more fans were admitted. That maneuvering cost the home team some dollars, but it cost the conniving gambler a lot more of them. Which seemed a small enough donation to the glorious game.

So on this occasion in the Lion park: Muggsy told Cliff and the somewhat gimpy-armed Bugle Nose (who'd wounded his throwing arm by falling on it i the shower room the previous day) about Dr. Sutton's bet.

First and foremost the Manager was furious that word of the injury had escaped the team room, drifting out to the gambling crowd. Cliff vowed to find the culprit on his team and then get rid of him.

Next that "brain trust", also calling in the coaches for advice, went to figuring how it might be assured that Stankorsky would go six, so the doctor would be sure to lose his money.

"I've heard about that bozo Sutton," Cliff told the others. "Think it would help Bugle's arm to keep going if we used some hot stuff on it after, say, the fourth inning?"

One of the coaches volunteered as how that would be a great idea.

Muggsy suggested that, to best conserve the wounded wing and cause it the least amount of wear and tear, he'd call for a lot of slow stuff from Bugle Nose, down and away, to get the batters to hit ground balls. And have the infielders play back some for those, to be in superb position for them. For today, forget about strikeouts, which was Stankorsky's usual bill of fare.

Another of the coaches suggested that, when the groundskeepers came out to rake down the infield, they wear boots brimming over with water. So the water would spill onto the dirt and make it softer, slower, slowing the ground balls even more. He remembered that once in a bush league he'd seen it pulled off.

At that last advice, Cliff covered his eyes. "Oh my sainted Aunt! To think I should hear the suggestion of such sculduggery on my own ball club."

To the coach who'd made the suggestion, he gave a handshake of appreciation: "Of course we can't do it, but I do admire your team-spirit."

Bugle Nose said his injury hadn't been big-big in the first place, but now, after hearing of the dirty gambling situation, his wing felt a lot better.

"I'll last at least six, never fear," he told the Lion conclave.

"Time to play ball," Muggsy finally announced to Katie. "Cliff can answer your questions."

"With pleasure," volunteered the manager. "I thought I'd never be alone with this lovely girl."

Just then the batboy stuck his head in the dugout.

"Mr. Hartwick, Blind Tom wants to see you at home plate."

"Damn!" muttered Cliff. "I never could get lucky for long."

He excused himself and left the dugout. Katie picked up a catcher's glove from close by. She tried it on her small hand and felt lost in its comparative expanse.

Just then the Lion right fielder, playing catch with the second baseman, cut loose with a hard and wild throw that zoomed toward the dugout and the redhead.

"Lookout, Katie!" yelled Muggsy, who saw too late what had happened. "Duck!!"

As though she'd done it forever, Katie reached up with her gloved hand and expertly caught the ball just in front of her face.

Relieved applause from the Lions nearby: "Sign her up."

"Yeah, probably do a lot better than the shot-to-hell catcher we got now."

"You all right?" asked Muggsy, running toward her, pale and frightened.

"Sure. Hey, that was fun. I wish I were a man, so I could play ball."

"I'm so glad," he breathed to her, "that you're not a man."

Chapter Nine

About knowledge: "This book of universal information will tell you all you need to know about life-and-living," insisted the salesman at the front door.

"Don't need it," growled the Husband. "My wife tells me all that, and a lot more besides."

Before that day, Katie had eagerly picked up a smattering of what-is-Baseball. Now she would advance on the scene:

"Can of corn" was the players' term for a high fly ball.

Third base was known as "the hot corner".

It was considered good strategy to use a "southpaw" (left-handed) pitcher against a team with many left-handed hitters.

Butterflies nearby were considered an ultimate in good-luck. Likewise a barrel-full of nails.

Just as players referred to fans as "kranks," so did fans refer to the athletes as "krankies," which was perhaps understandable when one noted their pint-sized salaries. No doubt, to stick with the game they had to love the game.

"So much to learn," observed Kathleen Crowley as she sat in the dugout with her Payne Banton while the Lions were at bat.

"Yeah, so much. Just for instance, watch the Cardinals' rookie pitcher out there on the mound. He's easy to hit; he tells us what he'll throw."

"He <u>tells</u> you?"

"Sure does. Watch close: Before he throws smoke (a fast ball), he rubs his pitching hand on his shirt. Before a curve that will break in on the hitter, he digs his right foot into the dirt.....Keep your eye on him. Now he's rubbing his hand on his shirt."

Katie, striving to miss nothing he said and nothing that happened on the field, took another look at Muggsy's eager eyes. At work he simply radiated joy.

Sure enough, the next pitch was a fast ball. The waiting Lion batter slapped a base hit between first and second, into right field.

"But how can he keep on playing 'up here' for any amount of time?"

His chest swelling past even its usual protrusion in appreciation of "up here," Muggsy told her, "He won't stay in a sharp league for long, unless someone wises him. Now, if I was his manager, I'd also see that he learned quick-like to throw a spitter. It's made great pitchers out of some guys who otherwise might have stayed just ordinary...yeah, like 'Happy Jack' Chesbro, on the New York team in the new American League.

"But for now this kid will probably have to be sent down a notch, where he can learn the basics of pitching, for sure learn 'em better than he has so far."

"Poor boy. I'll bet his Wife..."

"He's not married."

"Well then, his girlfriend and his family will feel so bad when they hear he's failed this chance. Oh look, he's digging his right foot into the dirt. That means a curve ball."

So it did. Another Lion hit, and a run crossed the plate.

More of the same did follow, so out came the anguished youngster. He was replaced by a tobacco-chewing old timer with no giveaways for Lion hitters.

Muggsy came to bat and immediately took a pitch in tight (close to the body). Lion players charged the mound, quickly joined by enemy players, and a fight seemed the next order of business.

But Blind Tom somehow kept all of them apart. Doing that, he also took a wild punch to the side of his head, whether or not that was accidental or merely some player's finally realizing a longed-for cheap shot at an umpire. Overall, though, Tom seemed to enjoy the tremulous peacemaking job (requiring much muscle as it did), as fully as the players seeking a scrap.

Through it all, Muggsy sat beside Katie on the bench.

"Surprised I'm not out there in that so-called fight, joining in with a lot of guys who mostly don't know how to fight, but mostly just push some and yell at each other...surprised I'm not joining that?"

"Yes, sort of."

"I'll give you three good reasons for why-not: First, I enjoy it a helluva lot more sitting here with you. Second, my bum knee doesn't need that brawling or whatever half-way imitation of a fight it might be."

"So I'm doubly glad to have you here."

"But the third reason, that old pitcher out there for the Cardinals is a friend of mine. Matter of fact, he was my best buddy back in my home town of Schantzville.

Did a lot to get me started in this game. Yeah, and besides, we're some kind of shirttail relatives. Now why would I fight him?"

"So why would a 'best buddy' throw at you?"

"No way he wanted to hit me, and, even if he did, he doesn't have enough speed left to hurt. Naw, he just drove me back from the plate so I couldn't take my best swing. It's all part of the game. His team wants to win every bit as much as ours does."

"Oh?" Though Katie still held some doubts. "Maybe his pitch is soft, but the baseballs I've held seemed mighty hard to me. Hitting in the right spot, I'll bet they could still hurt a body."

Muggsy chuckled, "Hey, good thought, and especially in the early innings when the one ball we're allowed per game hasn't become too out of shape and soft.

"Anyway, ol' Hal, that pitcher is a real fine guy, plenty of class. Matter of fact, I talked to him before the game and he wants to meet you, after the way I raved about you."

"Thank you, kind sir."

"You're welcome, lovely lady."

"Love to meet this anomaly who is such a gentleman but still throws hard baseballs at a buddy."

Thus did Katie learn infinitely more of the game called Baseball.

The game played on: Muggsy cracked a two-base hit to center field, then scored on a single by Butch Holcomb. The home hopes held a 3-0 lead, and were rampaging.

During the Marberry club's next-at-bat, the redhead asked Muggsy, "Did you ever get hit in the head by a pitched ball?"

"Just once that was really bad. In a cheaper league, I'd been hitting like crazy. So their catcher cut the ball on the razor-sharp part of his belt buckle. He did that so the ball would bob and weave and do tricks even crazier than when it's spit on or paraffin is rubbed on it or it's scuffed by sandpaper. And then I couldn't track it so well when it came toward me."

He showed Katie the blade-like corner of his own buckle.

"That's terrible!"

"Yeah, isn't it? Anyway, after he gashed the ball, on the next pitch it was absolutely out of control. It came up to the plate waist-high, in a perfect spot for me to slug it a mile. But then, all of a sudden, it zoomed at my head and caught me square on the temple. They told me later, I still hadn't come-to when the ambulance reached the hospital. They thought for sure I was dead. In fact, some nut had already thrown a sheet over my head. But I came up yelling, like what was going on? And, in a few days I was playing again.

"I had to come back in a hurry or get laid off the team without pay."

"How frightening, Payne, that I came so terribly close to never knowing you!"

"Yeah, I'm glad too, we didn't lose each other...But here's the payoff on that beaning: A couple of months later, I was at this party, and who should throw his arms around me but the catcher who'd cut that beanball. He wanted to make sure I was all right. He apologized like crazy. Said he'd come to the hospital to see me, but I was in such bad shape for the first 24 hours that they wouldn't allow visitors.

"It had scared the daylights outta him when he thought he'd killed me. He promised he'd never again cut the ball so deep, and, believe me, I learned the same lesson for the rest of my career...Hey, Katie, it's all right. I'm here with you. Aw, baby, please don't cry!"

"But Payne, it's just that... Oh, I know I'm not supposed to be so forward, but I have to tell you, Payne Banton, I love you, truly I do."

"Oh, and I love you, Katie Crowley. I just never want to be without you."

So it was, in the stifling heat of that home-team dugout, in Lions Park, Marberry, Pennsylvania, on a late-summer afternoon in 1907, the ballplayer and his lady pledged their devotion.

Chapter Ten

"One who bets into a cold deck is a gambler pure and simple, especially simple."
- Wise Man from out of the East

Final notations on "that day" and "that game":

For the first four innings, Bugle Nose Stankorsky sailed securely with a 3-0 lead over the Cardinals.

But, in the fourth, Muggsy noted that his pitcher was beginning to labor, no doubt from the injury to his arm the day before.

Muggsy looked into the stands and saw Dr. Philip Sutton grinning, as he would later describe to Katie, "like a Cheshire cat with a bowl of herring". The doctor was gaining confidence, Bugle Nose would not last out the sixth inning, and so he (the doctor) would win his big bet. Confidently, Sutton patted his studs for more good fortune.

Somehow, though, no scoring by the Cardinals in that fourth.

Likewise in the fifth, Bugle Nose's discomfort and wildness were becoming more obvious.

Going out for the sixth, Bugle Nose told his anxious manager, "Don't worry; I'll get 'em out this time around."

"You sure, big guy? If it's going to hurt your arm, we'd better pull you right now, let that idiot win his lousy bet.

"Never!" vowed Bugle Nose.

The first two Cardinal batters went down on long line drives. But there followed a single and two bases on balls. Bases loaded.

Bugle Nose was wild and high on the next three pitches.

Muggsy signalled to Cliff, make sure someone was ready in the bullpen.

Following which he went out to talk to his pitcher.

"Whatcha think?" he asked Stankorsky. "If you walk this guy, you see a pinch-hitter who's owned you for years."

"I'll get this one!"

His next pitch was fouled a mile high, drifting away from Muggsy with help from a sudden late-afternoon breeze, surely no chance for the catcher to grab it. But Muggsy, fiercely wrapped into the situation at hand, wouldn't give up. He finally made a backhanded stab of the ball, out past third base, to end the inning, still 3-0. Impossibly, Bugle Nose had lasted through six innings, beaten the bet.

The crowd was on its feet, yelling appreciation for the impossible play just made, though little realizing what was behind it.

As Muggsy headed for the dugout, he passed the box where Dr. Sutton was seated. He paused ever so briefly to stare straight into the angry eyes of that one. He also noted the confusion of Elsie Peabody, what in the world was going on?

Without breaking expression, Muggsy continued his walk to the dugout.

When the final out was registered in the ninth inning, Muggsy gave Katie's hand a final squeeze and ran for the dressing room.

But equally hurrying, surging out of the stands, was the large and hyped crown of hometown kranks. They fought their way over the diamond, past the policemen who tried to stop them. Soon, Muggsy was in the middle of the frantic mob; everyone there fought to get near him, to touch him, to slap his back, to grab his cap and run away with it if the opportunity showed.

As they pushed forward, a girl in their midst called out, "Way to go, Lover Boy!"...She was the brunette who'd joined him in his carriage on the day when Katie had first seen the Lions parading down the main street of Marberry.

She moved up to Muggsy, who planted a big kiss on her cheek, then was gone.

Such an afternoon it had been!

But were more shock-waves in store?

Chapter Eleven

It's not easy for any boss to consistently say "the right thing." Walter Alston, a noted manager of the Los Angeles Dodgers for many seasons, practiced the art, largely by remaining silent when there was no real need to speak. Still, even for Walter came the time of reckoning: In the final inning of the deciding game of the 1962 National League pennant chase, the Dodgers held a narrow lead over the San Francisco Giants. L.A. needed help from its bullpen. Alston had that available in his flame-throwing Don Drysdale .... But then, UN-believably, he had said, "No, I'm saving Drysdale for tomorrow (for the first game of the World Series.)" He brought in scatter-armed Stan Williams, and shortly after that the Giants had won the game, also the pennant.

So too could Cliff Hartwick, manager of the Lions, speak improbably.

Once Muggsy and the other players were out of sight, most of the fans had hurried away to home and dinner.

Except for the small cleanup crew working through the stands, only Cliff and Katie remained in the dugout. No change needed for Cliff, since he did his managing in a business suit, which made him a Baseball exception. Still, as he had noted, the manager of the Philadelphia Athletics, of the newly-formed American League, likewise guided his team in street clothes. That one was Connie Mack, whose full name was Cornelius McGillicutty, though the Baseball writers had reportedly been responsible for its shortening, to suit the convenience of their type-space requirements.

Cliff had been impressed by the style of Connie Mack. He felt that the more formal dress added to his authority. Although, if Muggsy would ever take over managing the Lions (as Cliff fervently hoped he would), Cliff understood that his ebullient catcher was far too much one-of-the-boys to ever wear coat-and-tie in the dugout.

For this moment, Cliff was lighting a cigarette, relaxing against the back of the dugout.

"Tough game that one was. I feel more tired than if I'd been playing. But today was like winning a doubleheader; we not only beat the Cards, but best of all we put down that creep Sutton.

"Don't misunderstand me, Katie. I'm not against all gambling as such. When there've been horses running nearby, I've been known to spread a few bob over the premises, searching for longshots.

"But when it comes to vermin like Sutton hanging around ballparks, that's something else. He has too bad a reputation, trying to use money to get people to do his dirty deeds...I hope we've now seen the last of him for a while."

Katie had to feel badly that Elsie, her best friend, was tied up with such a shady individual. But how can you tell anything to a person in love?

"Anyway, Cliff, you're now just five games behind the first-place Bears."

They looked out over the diamond, so carefully kept that it appeared almost manicured (nearly reminding her of her Mother's front lawn.)

Out there at the moment, some small boys were demonstrating to each other how they'd have played, had they been in the game just concluded. They played minus bats and balls, but their imaginary antics lacked no enthusiasm as they shouted and ran.

"They 'most always come in after the game's over," Cliff told her. "They love to run around the field, 'playing big guys'. I know just how they feel; I did the same when I was a little kid."

Just then the youngster on the pitcher's mound threw an imaginary ball to the plate. The "batter" swung a "bat," and all of them turned to watch the "ball" disappear over the center field fence for a monstrous "home run".

Cliff and Katie responded with vigorous applause. The "players" took deep bows in the direction of their audience.

Cliff further reached into a rack above his head and pulled down a tattered batting-practice ball. He tossed it to the boys on the field, so "the game" could proceed with increased fury.

All fine and good, the scene had been. But then Cliff Hartwick would open his mouth too widely, and the wrong words would come out.

He inhaled, pulling a newspaper clipping from his coat pocket.

"See this in THE CLARION today, Katie? That reporter George Periwinkle has been giving Muggsy a heavy buildup. (Good Baseball writer too, like he knows his stuff. Yeah, like he's been close to the game somewhere or other. But I never heard of him as a player.)"

"I missed today's paper. Dad left the house early and took THE CLARION with him, 'bad ol' Dad'".

She took the clipping and read:

"For years, Muggsy Banton has been a devil-may-care figure on the Marberry Baseball scene. He has craved his Baseball life with the Lions, but has seemed to think far more of the fast life after-hours. Now, quite suddenly, the ballplayer has taken over from the good-time guy in him; he's giving his team the fighting field-leadership it's sorely needed.

"Who knows what might happen before the United League race is settled. The Marberry Lions are zooming up-up!

The mystery: What has changed Muggsy Banton? Could it be the charms of a certain redhead?

"Interesting," spoke Katie, but now her voice was somewhat guarded and cool. "Except that the credit for Payne's playing improvement should go to himself."

"Wonder who's that redhead. If she's all that Periwinkle says, we ought to put her on our payroll. Katie..."

His tone went from light to serious. "Katie, it's hard to believe the change in Muggsy you've brought about in such a short time."

"Oh?"

Cliff felt her tensing, and knew he should back off. But some stubborn streak pushed him forward. She reciprocated by moving slightly from him.

"Really, Katie. You've made him the serious-minded guy he should have been years ago. When are you going to marry him and finish the job? He certainly needs you. I need a good manager. With you to take care of him, Muggsy will be just the man to lead my Lions."

Katie threw up her hands in angry Irish protest.

"Cease fire, Mr. Manager Hartwick! You're too terribly self-caring in your plans, pushing them at other people. I mean, you're too damn pushy!!"

Katie took back some, but not much: "My Dad taught me, there are extreme times when such words are allowed in conversation, yes, even by a lady. And, come hell or high water, right now I'm damned angry with you. You'd better know, I'm not about to open a nursery to take care of you or Payne, or your team or anyone else...Also, and however incidentally, Payne hasn't even asked me to marry him. Oh yes, I like him, and he likes me. More, Cliff, to feed your over-romantic soul, yes,

I love Payne, and I'm sure he loves me. But times have changed, and all that 'love' doesn't mean we must rush to get married.

"In fact, at this moment, I'm not even sure I'd say 'yes' even if Payne did ask me to marry him. Maybe I'm just not convinced he's left his wild life behind him.

"I'm not even sure that his 'love' goes past his desire for my body...Or maybe I'm not even ready to give up my dreams of graduating from college. ...But, sure as shootin', I won't rope Payne into marriage just to help your blessed ball club. So please back off, Mister Hartwick, then let's try being friends again."

Cliff offered an apologetic half-grin. "You're a real Irish firecracker, Katie Crowley, oh yes you are. All right, so I was dead wrong for meddling."

"Apology accepted, Cliff, AS LONG AS YOU NEVER DO IT AGAIN."

They sat there together for a while, silently, looking into the distance.

After that interlude, "Cliff, I hope you'll forgive my unseemly language just used."

"Oh don't apologize! I thought you were rather magnificent."

They continued to sit there, saying little, till long after 'the players' had gone home, and the shadows that had reached third base and home plate at the end of the game now covered the dugouts.

Then a spruced-up Muggsy, red bow tie in place, would appear to take his lady-love out to dinner.

Over that repast, his being was still dilated with the charge from the events of that afternoon.

Katie, likewise thrilled with and for the man opposite her at-table, worried even more when she was close to him. For his swollen hands and the obvious pain from them, however he tried to hide him.

He noted her caring.

"Don't worry, Katie. This pain's a great friend of mine, because it tells me I'm still an active player. Hey, if I take care of me, maybe I can be like that Jim O'Rourke, who used to catch for Mr. McGraw's Giants. I read the other day that, at 48 years old, he's still doing a helluva job playing and managing in some league out West. What a lucky guy, to have logged so much time out on the ball fields!...."

Katie churned inwardly, but said nothing. For, in her comparatively few years on this planet, she'd already learned well: True love means giving freedom to that other "special person". Never had she learned that better than in refusing to try to dissuade a boy named Johnny from enlisting for gloried combat service....Now, facing another potential crippler of a man she'd grown to love, the sometimes unreasonably brutal pastime of stopping pitched balls all day long, she had no path to follow but the gritting of her teeth and then, as the players put it, pegging it through the next game.

Chapter Twelve

As befits my somewhat-aging, nearly all of my "heroes" are in the legendary past. But even today, as I work with the Los Angeles Dodgers in varied venues, "I get that old feeling" (as a song put it) when I encounter Don Drysdale, a member of the team's broadcasting crew.

"Big D" remains topmost among pitchers I have watched. Others, and certainly including Sandy Koufax, were dazzling for a few years. But Drysdale was the "big stopper" for 14 unyielding seasons. Or perhaps Willie Mays said it supremely, "To dig in against Don was just like making an appointment with the dentist."

On a night soon to follow, Muggsy Banton was a dinner guest at the Crowley home. He was received with warmth by J.T., with more warmth by Katie, but with disquiet on the part of Clara. Would the sweaty lout advancing on her home track dirt over her fine rugs or shred them with his hobnail boots? Would he (horrors!) even take up his peas on a knife?

Only on Muggsy's arrival did her fears begin to vanish. The ballplayer who came to her home was as bright and ruggedly polite a young man as she had met in a while. Not even hobnail booted! Still she allowed herself continuing doubts.

Luther Lincoln never shared his mistress' hesitations. He greeted Muggsy with a recounting of that one's base-hits and assorted victories over the past week. He promised the gas-mobile would be thoroughly washed and polished on that evening.

"Three-out-of-four-secured, which means I'm hitting .750," he told himself as the dining room doors were thrown open.

The meal struck all present as a masterpiece, for Clara, in spite of trepitudes, had gone all out in preparation. Giving in to Katie's pleading, she had moved back into her own kitchen to prepare the goulash which was her culinary specialty. She'd fixed that same sinfully-delicious dish for J.T. not very long after they'd met; she'd strongly surmised that the goulash had begun her young man's processed thinking of marriage and herself simultaneously.

"I'll prepare dinner for your Payne," she'd protestingly told Katie. "But it does seem a waste of time. These crude 'ballplayers' probably don't care a mite how a meal tastes, 'long as it fills their big bellies."

"Now, Mom, you taught me a long time ago that prejudging people isn't fair. I just know you'll like Payne a lot."

The parental reply had been "Hmph!". But the goulash had emerged in full glory alongside fresh garden peas (Clara needed that doubt-and-fear answered!) and heaping golden soleratus (baking soda) biscuits. Dessert: piping-hot spiced-plum koliches.

The first break in Clara's meticulously built train of objections to her guest came when he repeatedly praised her cooking: "Greatest meal since I left home!"

After which J.T. told his family, "I'll bet you girls didn't know that the Mayor of Marberry once presented Muggsy with the key to our city."

Clara looked up, vastly impressed, also silently admitting that Henry Sample had never received such a tribute.

"Aw, it was nothing," protested Muggsy. "Mrs. Crowley, this strawberry jam is sure tasty, and...." But his diversion went nowhere.

"It was too something," Katie went on. "Cliff told me all about it: In your fifth year with the Lions, the Mayor appeared at a testimonial banquet with a full house of dignitaries and fans. You were voted most popular _and_ most inspirational player on the team. And...."

"Easy, Katie," warned her Father, "or you'll run out of breath."

There was no stopping her: "The Mayor gave you the key to the city. What's more, he said that, considering that you overcame what could have been a Baseball career-ending injury and went forward to continually play-to-win, you were a wonderful example for all the young people of Marberry. Soooo, there."

Applause from J.T. "I was there to hear that speech, and, believe me, Katie, his speech couldn't touch the one you just made."

"The Mayor is high in the social set," thought Clara. Thus she was further wound into the dinnertime conversation:

"Tell me, Mr. Banton, what do you think of these newfangled 'flying machines'? Isn't it frightening, the things that are being invented to disrupt our lives, like the gas-mobile too? It just seems to me that the world is going crazy."

"I'm afraid I can't agree with you, Mrs. Crowley. Sure, there are big changes here, more on the way, in our style of living. Now I believe that we must respect their newness, and go slow in using them for our enjoyment. But we _must_ use them. Or how can they be developed to the fullest?"

"No!...I mean, really?"

"Yes, I think so. Those Wright Brothers in Kitty Hawk have already taught us a lot about flying. And I think that very soon our military people, even up to President Teddy Roosevelt himself, will be convinced, the skies are as important a place for fighting a war as is the ground."

For the very first time, Clara looked at the resolute and barrel-chested visitor in some admiration. And oh yes, he had taken up the fresh garden peas with his fork.

The prestigious meal ended, but J.T. found so much to discuss with Muggsy, it looked as if the young people would never be alone.

Still, thanks to Clara, they finally escaped.

"For goodness sakes, Jim, stop being such a gabby-body! Don't you know Mr. Banton and Kathleen want some time to themselves, away from us 'old folks'?"

Which, coming from Clara, was a "whole lot of relenting," as Katie observed to Muggsy when they strolled from the house, arm-in-arm.

"I'm glad, because your Mom and Dad are such real fine folks...Now, shall we go for a drive, or just walk off that great meal?"

"Let's walk. This night air is too glorious to pass on."

She didn't add her further thought, that she wasn't again quite ready to be parked on some lonely road with him. She wasn't even sure if she feared him or herself the most, her being was that filled with the warmth of the man walking beside her.

"Walking's plenty all right with me......But say, that was some dinner, best I can remember. Where'd your Mom learn to turn out scrumptious biscuits like those?"

She stopped and faced him. "Payne, now you're just teasing me!"

His puzzlement was genuine.

"You know that I made those biscuits," she said slowly, giving each word its full effect.

"You did?"

"Yes, I did, all by my itty-bitty lonesome."

"Gee, now I like 'em even more. But how was I to know you made 'em?"

"Well....somehow I just thought you'd know."

Muggsy, lost for another comeback, pulled down on his shako cap. "Anchors away!

"Oh yes. Damn the torpedoes and full speed ahead."

On the fringe of Marberry's business district, they turned a corner. And something up ahead stole Muggsy's composure. He jumped toward the entranceway of a nearby store, pulling the surprised redhead with himself.

"Stay here for a minute," he pleaded. "Pretend you're looking at the stuff in this window."

"Why?"

"Oh...nice furniture, isn't it?"

Katie continued more curious than cooperative. She left the window and looked up the street.

"Now I see," and she laughed delightedly. "It's that girl who rode with you in the parade, the day I first saw you. She chased you too, after the game on the day I sat in the dugout with you, and then you hugged and kissed her. Or did you think I missed you two acting like a couple of lovebirds and her calling you 'Lover Boy'? Honest, I'm not really blind or deaf, no I'm not, LOVER BOY."

"Aw..."

"Payne, please introduce me to her."

"I would but..."

"All right then; if you won't, I'll introduce myself."

Trapped, he saw no way out. "Oh, all right."

The approaching tall and amply-provided brunette was dressed in most colors of the rainbow, those blatant against Katie's quiet style.

"Well hello, Muggsy," she said in a husky voice. "Where've you been keeping your adorable ol' self? All the girls in the show have been asking for you; they're lonesome for your cuddly company. We've heard rumors, but nobody knew nothin' for certain."

"Uh...I've been busy," stuttered Muggsy, trying hopelessly to think of some excuse for hurrying on.

"Aren't you going to introduce me to your cute girlfriend?" asked the newcomer, giving Katie a complete lookover.

"Bell, this is Katie Crowley. Katie, meet Belle LaFrance."

"So glad to meet you, Belle."

"Likewise, Dearie. Then you, being so Irish, should get it straight from the hip that my name too is from the sod, Mary Murphy I was.

"So you're the dolly who's taken our Muggsy from us? Well, if we gotta lose him, I'm glad it's to someone like you. There's too many sharks swimming free.

"Us girls in the show sure wouldn't want one of them to grab our boy."

Belle's oversized bosom heaved as she spoke, and Katie drew a better picture of her stage attraction.

Muggsy, against whatever comparisons, was busy regaining his composure.

"Uh...yeah, Belle, so how's the show going?"

"SRO," she told him, "as a lot of your Lions will back me up....Say, I wish you two would drop by some night real soon. We've got some great new routines knocking 'em for a loop. We even got a great piano guy playing straight outta Scott Joplin, oh great ragtime! He uses a time pattern from some guy named Europe. Really makes the house (and us girls!) jump."

"I'd love to drop by, see your show," Katie told her. But Muggsy looked itchy with the invitation.

Belle turned to Muggsy for a final time: "It hasn't been near as much laughs since you stopped coming around. We miss your homely face and dumb jokes."

"Well, I won't keep you two no longer. Just take the best care of this lug, Katie, or you'll have to answer to a gang of us girls."

With those last words, her voice almost broke in high emotion.

"I'll do my best, Belle. And I'm so happy to have met you."

"Me likewise." Then Belle was gone.

"She's nice, Payne. And so far gone over you."

"Aw, Belle's all right," he admitted, ignoring the last observation. "We were good pals."

"Whatta pal with whatta figure!"

"Yeah, I guess so."

They continued their walk, passing a soda shoppe complete with marble fountain.

In the window was a blaring sign: Exciting new treat: SUNDAES.

"Oh, those are fun!" Katie told him excitedly. "They're a confection someone in New York, or was it London, dreamed up: ice cream, syrup, nuts, whipped cream, and a cherry on top. Mom and I split a monster one, with strawberry topping. Sometime when we're not so full, you and I should try the special, the hot fudge sundae."

"I'll try anything once," Muggsy ventured in daredevil fashion. "But can we eat a sundae on a Wednesday?"

"So much for you, Joe Miller and your Joke Book."

"But say," he went on, "talking about crazy ideas, did you see the pictures of those 'Emancipators' in yesterday's paper? Ever see anything as foolish, not to mention downright indecent, as those broads actually walking our streets wearing 'outside bloomers'? The story said they were screaming like banshees about 'freedom for all women'. Freedom from WHAT, I'd like to know? Them crazies oughta be locked up where they can't hurt no one."

Her expressing of rising petulance made it clear, Katie was miffed at his positive male assurance...even perhaps over-positive?

"I think that women will bring about many changes before long. Men had best be ready."

"Katie, I'll tell you this for damn sure, those changes better not come till us guys are ready for 'em. But hey, did I tell you about when I played ball in bloomers?"

Whereupon Katie was glad for a chance to end the present confrontation.

"You wore bloomers? Oh my....."

"Oh yes. A bunch of years back, not long after I first joined the pros, I was out West during the off-season, picking up some bucks playing in exhibition games...just another wild kid roaming the USA for the first time.   "One of those Bloomer Girl teams (from Arkansas, I think, or was it Kansas?) played a game with the team I played for. Their manager was a cranky, hook-nosed ol' broad named Semanda Smith, or something like that. But we had to admit, she knew a whole lot about Baseball and how it should be played. She had whipped her girls into being reasonably good players."

"But you wore bloomers too?" Katie was impatient for that part of the story.

"Betcherboots I did, and I could get away with it because I didn't yet have whiskers on my young-boy face. Then see what happened was, when we played 'em, their catcher had to take the day off because it was....well, you know...the start of her special time of the month. Our team had two catchers, so our manager asked me if, for an extra twenty bucks, I'd mind wearing a wig and bloomers and go out to catch for the Baseball broads' team.

"I told him, for twenty I'd swim through crocodiles, but that, if he or anyone else gave away the secret, I'd bust their heads. Yeah, I caught for the girls that day, sort of high-pitching my voice to make it sound right. I got three hits, and dated 'my team's' pitcher that night. Boy, was she ever fast, once she dropped her bloomers...I mean, when she got back into a dress.

"But that was a long time ago, Katie. Now I prefer more sensible girls like you."

Miss Crowley wasn't too enthused over that last. Still, she subdued such feelings, also those on Emancipation, growing stronger as they were.

"I wonder," mused Muggsy, "whatever happened to Semanda Smith. Probably still out on the prairies, trying to stir up trouble with her...haw!...silly emancipation ideas that she preached to anyone who would listen. I'll tell you this for sure, Katie, no matter how much Baseball she knew, she wouldn't dare butt into our games up here in the better leagues."

There could come times of remembering that bold proclamation.

Chapter Thirteen

Still another "hero" who today is handshaking-close: Bill Russell, coach (and heir-apparent to the managership?) of the Dodgers, was one of the mightiest athletes I ever watched, which means he dredged the most from his abilities. As a center fielder in '67, he was a gazelle to do no wrong. But then Maury Wills gave out; the Dodgers needed a shortstop in a hurry, and called on their ATHLETE for the quick change...Bob Scheffling, longtime big league catcher, manager, and scout, said this, "Russell is so great, the fans will never appreciate how easily he does it all. But oh, what EVERY single big league team would give to grab him! In any deal, Russell's the player they want most."

Bill has forever carried that young-as-a-choir-boy-look. I tried long and mightily to stick the tab TERRIFIKID on him, but an unappreciative scene wouldn't latch on.

After a while, Katie and Muggsy headed back to her home.

The touchy subject of Emancipation having passed for the moment, they held hands again. And passed a store window displaying women's shoes.

"Like those green slippers in the back row?"

"Oh sure," he murmured, trying badly to act interested.

"I declare, you're just like my Dad. He simply hates to window-shop, though Mom tried for years to get him into it. But about the only time he'll stop to look is when they pass a variety store. Mom never objects to that."

"Oh?"

"But yes. When Dad was single, and such an eligible young bank executive, oodles of debutantes set their caps for him. But he didn't crave the society life they wanted to push on him; all he wanted in his free time was to hunt and fish. Then one day he was needing some fishing line; he walked into a variety store where he met this pretty young clerk."

"Redheaded, of course."

"But of course. She told him she simply loved to hunt and fish, even if that was sort of a fib and she didn't know much about either of those."

With no effort, Muggsy finished the story: "So he married her. Before long she forgot hunting and fishing and went big for high society."

"How'd you know, Mister Smarty Pants?"

"Male intuition," he said haughtily, and she made a face at him.

"Men think they're so smart."

"Well we are."

"But just wait till all us girls wear 'outside bloomers' because then we'll be emancipation with a capital E."

Muggsy took a mock swing at her, and she ducked. While an elderly woman passing by gave a look that disdainfully said, "We---lllll."

The young lovers moved away at a rapid pace.

"Payne, we must be more proper."

"Don't wanna be proper. Wanna follow my animal feelings, which you arouse."

Katie could well have offered "Touche" from her French classes.

"Anyway, you guessed right about Mom and Dad. Worse, she just never let up on her society-push. She's run over Dad for a long time, but, as of these last few days, that's ended. Suddenly he's decided that next weekend he's going fishing with some buddies, for the first time in years. Now I just wonder who E-mancipated his thoughts."

They turned the corner that brought the Crowley home into view. And they stopped in amazement.

The bright red gas-mobile in the driveway gleamed even brighter than before.

"Just great!" Muggsy exulted. And he handed Katie a dollar bill.

"Please give this to Luther from me."

"He'll be so excited. He's had his eye on a baseball in Schroeder's window; he's been counting his pennies till he can buy it."

"No sense his wasting the dollar," Muggsy came back. He reached under the seat, carefully now as the found-stockings had taught him. He pulled out a shiny new baseball.

Following which, in his shirt pocket, he found two passes to Lion Park.

"Please give Luther all this. He deserves it, and more."

"Those big eyes of his will simply pop out of your head. Payne, did anyone ever tell you you're a most generous man?"

"Aw....no. It's just that I went through rough times, and I think it's important for young people to have fun, enjoy some of those 'good things' <u>now</u>."

He stood close to her, and Katie's lips were read; he hadn't come to them since the crude happening on their first night together.

To Katie, the spot where they stood seemed perfect for the occasion: under a massive elm which gave a darkened and soft aura to the ground below. And his hand gave hers the needed assurance of his warmth for herself. Still, she needed much more than assurance; she wanted desperately to be kissed long and firmly, tenderly but with passion to match her own.

He read her desire, but decided the time was not yet.

Gently he kissed her cheek.

"You'd better go in now, Katie Crowley. It's late, time to train it."

Trying to mask her letdown, she gave him a matter-of-fact, "Yes, Payne Banton, it is late, now isn't it?"

At her front door, she handed him her key. Muggsy unlocked the door.

"Thank you, Payne, for a wonderful time."

"I didn't get to see enough of you. We've been together only since ten o'clock this morning. Not enough!"

"Why thank you, Payne. What a sweet thing to say!"

"Tell you what, our next day together we'll start at five A.M. Only tomorrow, maybe you'd better not get up so early. 'A girl does need enough rest, to keep the roses in her cheeks', or so my Mom used to say."

"I'll match that with what my Dad told me, 'A ballplayer has to be in the best of shape to keep the sting in his swing.'

"Helluva smart guy, your Dad. But, thanks to the Pennsylvania Blue Laws, we don't play on Sunday. Maybe I'll sleep till noon or later."

Something he'd said dug into her. She moved away from him, if slightly.

"Hey, Katie, what in hell is wrong?"

"How can you sleep till noon? You told me you promised your Mother you'd go to Mass on Sunday."

"Oh and I do, most of the time ..... at least some of the time."

Katie started to say something else, but let it go. Giving him an offhanded "Good Night," she moved quickly into the house, locking the door between them.

A puzzled Muggsy was "hung out to dry" on the front steps. Finally, he shrugged his shoulders and drove home. But didn't sing on his way.

Came the next morning, and he phoned Katie: "How about you and me for eleven o'clock Mass?"

After the bad night she had spent, wondering if her questioning his religious habits had been a resented intrusion on his personal life, his voice had come on as heavenly music.

"Oh yes."

"I'll pick you up at ten-thirty."

"I'll be ready."

"And I'll stop being such a bossy biddy," she told herself, "but oh I do love that man, and I want our life together to be as-close-to-perfect-as- can-be."

"I'll handle Katie Crowley carefully," Muggsy told himself. "She's the keg o' dynamite I've looked for all my life, and I'm gonna be careful that the blast goes off at a time as-close-to-perfect-as-can-be."

Chapter Fourteen

"May you live all the days of your life." - A Leprechaun from the fields of Killarney who refused to be identified.

Ever since Kathleen Mary (name added at Baptism) Margaret (name added at Confirmation) could remember, her Mother had sought to dominate her...even to own her. Seeking to meticulously groom Katie for "society life," Clara had picked the clothes Katie must wear, the schools she must attend, and, of course, the men she was to be seen with.

Katie loved her Mom, if sometimes in a resentful sort of way. She told herself, she realized that Clara was thinking of her "happiness". Nevertheless she could feel squashed by that over-love from above.

For Katie there had nevertheless been a special time, days and nights so romantically memorable: At eighteen, attending a private Catholic school for potential debutantes, she had met Johnny Johnston.

Johnny was tall and trim, with sparking brown eyes forever in search of a laugh. His rumpled blonde hair seldom seemed to fall into the same configuration two times in a row.

He had been a high-ranked Engineering student at the nearby university.

Then he and Katie had met at a dance arranged by a "social counselor" at her school and likewise at his. Between the two young people sparks did fly. Romance on-the-wing was instant. They would be together whenever possible and even sometimes when it seemed impossible. They loved to walk through the woods near her school, attend the theater in a nearby town, also to take joyful turns reading favorite books to each other. Henry Thoreau's Walden Pond was their idyllic spot.

On the days when Katie wasn't supposed to leave her campus, they met in a darkened grove not far from the campus.

Katie was alive then as she never had been. How she looked to each moment with Johnny!

Her idea that an abundance of chatter was the key to a good time was quickly left behind. Katie learned the quiet contentment of being with someone she wanted most to be with. She loved it that Johnny was a paradox who could at times come on so serious and at others so carefree. She was joyful to be changing, to have shed "dull old Kathleen".

But WAR had come. The Rough Riders of Teddy Roosevelt had ridden in Cuba. Johnny enlisted, martial tunes rushing him onward to the battlefield "to save freedom". Heard everywhere was REMEMBER THE MAINE, TO HELL WITH SPAIN.

One weekend had remained before their parting. Katie and Johnny met by the tree they knew as "theirs," Johnny deliriously dashing in his Private's uniform. As they clutched at moments about to explode away from themselves, his lips had moved through her red curls.

"Katie Crowley, I'm crazy about you."

"Johnny, dearest..."

"Katie, before I sail, can't we get away from here just once and find alone-moments to remember?

"Please meet me here tomorrow evening, same time. I know this daisy of a place up the coast where we can listen to the ocean breaking on the rocks. Watch a million stars. I promise to get you back on time on Sunday night."

At that moment, whether Katie Crowley got back on time or didn't was of the least interest to her.

"Oh Johnny, it sounds perfect. I'll tell the school I'm visiting relatives."

When she had gone to meet him the next evening, there was a note on their tree. His outfit had shipped out for Cuba that day.

"I love you, Katie, love you so terribly much. Please wait for me."

Letters from Cuba had respoken his devotion.

The end of the war, and Katie had never been so full of the joy of living. Paradise seemed within reach.

Still, as she would brusquely learn from the casualty list only two days after the shooting had stopped, Private Johnny Johnston had died in Cuba. The jungle's "Yellow Jack" had been his killer. So his patronym would never be hers.

After that, little had mattered to Katie Crowley. Two more years of meaningless schoolwork, parties, teas, and a stream of men who approached her...all were promptly forgotten.

Her most-respite from feeling useless came in the hours she spent as a volunteer nurse's aide, serving wounded veterans in a military hospital.

Still she longed for life with a new flavor, and, some day again, perhaps even some of the sheer joy of living she had learned from Johnny.

Perhaps the University was the place to start. Johnny had thoroughly loved it. But then Katie Crowley had watched a parade with her Dad.

Nor had Payne (Muggsy) Banton's life coursed smoothly as the proverbial sheltered lake on a warm summer's day.

Chapter Fifteen

Did you, a Baseball Fan, ever have the desire to meet a Manager of true greatness? Then see BANG THE DRUM SLOWLY. Therein, actor Vincent Gardenia is Walter Alston and Joe McCarthy and Sparky Anderson and Connie Mack and Roger Craig, all bound into one UN-forgettable portrayal. I mean, if you like Baseball, you can fairly flip over this soul movie of the horsehide existence.

Payne Banton, Baseball player-to-be, had been born in and raised on the tough side of Schantzburg, Ohio. His widowed Mother, a scrubwoman, dwelt voraciously on the written works of Thomas Paine, concerning politics and religion. So what else but to name her son after her literary idol?...Oh yes, because you've doubtless noted the inconsistency, she did get the last-name spelling mixed with the name of John Howard Payne, who wrote HOME SWEET HOME, her favorite song. By the time the error was discovered, she decided she liked the mistaken version and let it stand.

"It's an unusual name to put on a kid," he would later admit, "and it got me into lots of fights in school. A kid named Percy and I easy got to be the toughest kids there. But we were good friends, so we never did square off to see who won the title, as they say in the sports pages."

Payne had been only ten when his Father had died from a bottle-blow to the head in a bar-fight. After that, no other way to go except jobs to help his Mother, also using his ever-ready fists to get him out of difficulties along the way.

He also met "the American game" known as Baseball. He soon had thoughts of little else.

Early-on, Napoleon Lajoie, matchless second baseman for Philadelphia and then Cleveland, became his horsehide god. Payne Banton was set and determined that he himself would some day soon become at least the second greatest second sacker in history, alongside "Nappy", whose tattered photo he forever carried in his back pocket...

Toward attaining that dream, he had wanted to quit school after the eighth grade. But Mom, forever his guidepost, had stopped that premature move.

"Stay where you are Son, right there in school. You're a smart boy. If you're educated, you'll go places, maybe even be a famous writer like Mister Tom Paine. It won't be easy, because, as Mister Paine told us, 'There are times that try mens' souls'. But you can be as great as you want to be."

Payne listened respectfully to Mom, but his dreams still centered on making the double play like Nappy.

He entered high school, also worked night in a livery stable for any small wages that could help out at home. By then, though, his thoughts would travel in one direction, one only: a straight line leading to the local ballfield.

Mom saw what was coming, and steadied herself; no writer in her family.

Early-on, Payne wasn't distinguished in the Baseball trade, certainly no legendary "born athlete." Worse, because he was small of build, he was pushed away too often, denied any chance to play ball.

But came the time when he'd again pleaded to join in and someone pushed him too hard. A catcher with stunted brainpower knocked him to the ground and sneered, "Beat it, Shorty!"

The boy picked himself out of the dirt, and, for a short moment, stood where he was.

The other players had turned away.

"No guts," was their judgment on the little guy.

Calmly then, Payne had advanced on the bully and knocked him down.

Surprised, the others turned back for another look.

"All right, Shrimp, you asked for it," sneered the catcher, who returned to pulverize the cocky kid. But that one cocked his right hand and again threw it. Again the big boy went down, this time tasting blood.

"Dirty fighting," he muttered, coming woozily to his feet and heading for a distant spot before the small dynamo could get more of him. Getting cat-calls even there from onlookers of the brief brawl, he quickly sneaked away.

While admiringly the others had swarmed around young Banton.

"Kid, you sure can fight!"

"Yeah, see him throw that dynamite right?"

"Like a slingshot. But now who'll catch? Whatshisname has run off and hid."

Few it seemed were anxious to handle a job as rough as the one behind the plate. Less-risky positions were more to their taste, since they held little desire for broken fingers so common to catchers, to say nothing of broken noses in those days before the coming of face-masks.

"I can catch," bluffed Payne, his dreams of being another Napoleon Lajoie giving way to necessity.

So it was, on that day, an "unimportant" game in Schantzville saw a different face behind the plate. For his trouble, that one gained two badly swollen fingers where foul tips smacked him, also a black eye from a collision when he successfully blocked a runner trying to score.

When he went home that night, Mom saw the carnage and wanted to weep. But she knew her Son wouldn't like that. So she settled for listening to his excited account of that Baseball day.....how, after the final out, the fellows had swarmed around him, pounding his back and beseeching him to return. Oh, but life was beautiful. Mom would do naught but put beefsteak on his black eye, also give him a pan of warm water for soaking his bruised fingers.

On the next afternoon, at the park, the home team's manager told him, "You're my catcher from now on, if you'll just let me teach you a few things so you'll do a better job and keep your body all in one piece."

The boy, however hopeful he had been, just stood there, too stunned to speak.

"Well, you want the job or not?"

"Yes, Sir!"

"Then go to it, Muggsy," the manager proclaimed, forever tagging him with the nickname of John McGraw, the scrappy field boss of the New York Giants.

Muggsy Banton, as fans would forever-after know him, resolved to live up to his brand new tag, even if it sometimes meant starting a fight to pep up his team.

After a while, he wondered how he could have considered any other job but catcher. Back there he was really in the middle of the action, with so much to learn and a manager eager to teach, to correct, to give approval when that was earned, also near-bite his head off when he repeated a boner. The latter, be it noted for Muggsy's eagerness, was increasingly seldom.

Someone told his Mother, "You've got a promising player in your Son."

"Whatever he is," she answered proudly, "he'll be a great one."

So it was that the back-pocket photo of Napoleon Lajoie gave way to one of an oncoming catcher of star ability, one Roger Breshnahan. That one was moving from the Baltimore Orioles to the New York Giants, where he would pioneer the face-mask that would make life for catchers such as Muggsy Banton far more comfortable in pursuit.

But, even with his newfound devotion to Roger B., it's doubtful that Muggsy stopped often to consider that, up in Marberry, Pennsylvania, a lovely red-haired girl named Katie Crowley likewise kept a picture of Roger in a special place.

Now the game of Baseball had truly become Muggsy's life.

Late each night he was still reading books with advice from the mightiest players of the day. Mom too caught the fever, and, with added earnings from working extra hours for "the family cause," she presented her Son with a book detailing special advice for anyone who would be a catcher. Naturally those notes were penned by a certain Roger Breshnahan, who told how he handled the slants of the Giants' "indomitable duo," Christy Mathewson and Rube Marquard. Urged onward then by such love from above, in giving him that treasure of a book, Muggsy would read even later at night, play even harder in the afternoons, and seek to put in still more working hours to help support their home. Busy life!

With his fierce desire to learn, Muggsy had also followed the writings of a Baseball Writer out in "far-west" Chicago:

"The day when a batter can select just where he wants the ball thrown is fast coming to a close. Further, the catcher may soon be given even more bodily protection than he is "spoiled with" today. He may work his position with leather guards on his shins! Is it possible that Baseball, so long the game for rough and rugged males, will soon turn into a 'sissy sport?' This is what old-time players want to know, following disquieting reports that, farther West from here, there are Baseball leagues for (get this!) Bloomer Girls. At least for those, since they don't throw as hard as males or hit it as hard, their 'ultimate in protection' seems to consist of sliding pads and brassieres.

"Some extremists among old-time ballplayers are fearing that, in times not far off, players will actually go to gloves with padding, believe that or don't."

Muggsy read and was impressed. For sure, he wouldn't be one of those advocating "sissy ball".

Although, as he lay in bed at night and could admit it to himself, he sometimes had to admit to his "tough and rugged" self, he wished his body...well...didn't ache quite as much.

For him, little time for parties, girls, or any other such distraction to cut his playing (and reading) time.

He sought tactical advice from any veteran players, especially catchers, who would spare him a few minutes.

Soon the improvement in his game was plain to be seen. His throws gained in accuracy. His handling of pitchers was more worthy of respect. And he wasn't satisfied until he became the fastest runner on his team.

Even Mom caught diamond fever, coming to the games whenever possible, cheering for "her boy" and his team. She also worked extra hours on scrubdown duty so she could put on a chicken dinner at home for the team. (No chicken like hers, was their attesting.)

Muggsy's barreling-out chest projected even farther. He had the swellest Mom in the world!

Just after he'd finished his third year of high school, a minor league scout saw him play. The scout would then visit the Banton home.

"Mrs. Banton, I want to offer your Son a professional contract. We can't pay him a lot at first. But I feel sure he'll move up fast and then earn a lot more. In ability, and certainly in desire, Muggsy's got what it takes."

"Please, Mom, let me go with them," pleaded her 17-year-old.

She swallowed hard as the very last of her otherwise-dreams took flight.

"All right, Payne. We can't have a great Baseball player wasting away in school."

So what if his new teammates, in a town 80 miles from home, turned out to be either worn-out old-timers or dreamy kids, too many of those with doubtful ability? Every one of them was someone to learn from, or he wouldn't be playing for pay.

Mom came to see Muggsy in his first professional game. He got two base hits and threw out three runners attempting to steal, to test the arm of the raw rookie catcher.

Still, the enemy players of that day wondered further what the new arrival was made of.

"Throw at his head," their manager told his veteran pitcher, noted for his control, if no longer for a fast ball. "We'll see what he's got gut-wise."

When Muggsy came to bat in the third inning, the pitcher obeyed orders, zinging one at his chin. Muggsy hit the dirt just in time.

He jumped out and approached the sneering pitcher.

"Don't do that again. My Mother's in the stands."

In came the next pitch, far too close for comfort. But this time the rookie was ready; he moved back a step and dropped a bunt down the first base line. The pitcher lumbered over to field the ball, seeming to have time aplenty to make the play at first base unassisted.

But Muggsy, thundering down the baseline, timed his spring perfectly to meet the pitcher just in front of first base, slamming him into the dirt as he attempted the tag. While the ball fell from the old fellow's hand and rolled toward the dugout, Muggsy made it to second in easy style.

The pitcher was helped to the dugout, his bruises forcing him from the game.

On the next pitch, Muggsy stole third. A long fly ball to left, and he trotted home, sealing a 1-0 win.

"I'm so proud of you, Payne," his Mom said at the depot that night.

A lump jammed his throat as her train pulled out, but no time to be homesick. Too much Baseball to be played.

The next years were rough for the kid catcher. He learned of tank towns, cheap rooming houses, greasy spoons, too.... He played on fields barely advanced from the rock-pile stage. His team traveled in the most bedraggled of chair cars. There were fights on the field, more with enemy kranks.

All of that slowed Muggsy not a whit; he was finally traveling the road he cherished most. And it was hard to believe he was actually getting paid to play.

He sent most of his paycheck to his Mom, scrounging by on what was left.

Finally he moved up to the Colts, Allied League, just two jumps from the dreamed-of "Bigs".

There was a day, in the Colt ballyard, when Muggsy came to bat in the ninth, a teammate on first and no outs, the ball game knotted at 1-1. His manager told him to wait until the second pitch, then bunt the runner to second.

Still, and on the first pitch, Muggsy cracked a two-base hit against the left field fence. The Colt runner scored with the winning run.

As the appreciative crowd rose and shouted, "Mugggseee," the cocky catcher strutted back to the Colt bench.

His manager, snarling, met him head-on.

"You fresh punk! I ordered you to bunt."

Unbelieving, Muggsy finally managed to blurt out, "But I drove in the winning run!"

"I don't care if you drove in 50 runs. I gave you orders, punk, and you ignored 'em. You next paycheck shrinks by twenty clams, so laugh off that one, MUGGGGSEEE..."

Muggsy was ready with a sharp answer, but an older player standing nearby motioned him to button the lip.

Then someone handed him a telegram.

The manager saw him reading, hands shaking.

"Bad news?"

He showed the manager: Mom had a stroke. Not long to live. Was asking for him.

"Gotta go home right away," Muggsy told him, trying to force back a sob.

"No more trains tonight. I'll drive you there."

In the manager's carriage, they rode all night. Vaguely did Muggsy remember, somewhere in the middle of the ride, the skipper cancelled the fine.

They arrived with daybreak. A nurse met them at the hospital door.

"Please hurry, Mr. Banton...please."

"I'm so proud of you, Payne, and what you're doing," Mom told him.

Then peacefully did she die in the arms of her Son.

Muggsy, the tough kid, broke down.

"It's my fault, all my fault. If I'd stayed here and worked, she wouldn't have had to work so hard. I'll quit Baseball."

"Son, it surely wasn't your fault," the doctor told him. "Nothing you could have done would have made a difference. She told me over and over, what made her happiest was your doing so well at what you wanted to do."

"Anything I can do for you, Muggsy, let me know," his manager told him before returning to the team.

"Nothing more than the lot you've already done, and thanks a whole lot."

"Come back to the team when you're ready."

"No. I'll never play ball again."

Muggsy meant that.

Or certainly thought he meant that.

Chapter Sixteen

For me, the absolutely UN-forgettable Baseball moment came in the late innings of the final game of the 1963 World Series, at Dodger Stadium. Dodgers had won the first three games, and led 2-1 in this finale. With two outs, the Yanks loaded the bases. Mickey Mantle faced Sandy Koufax. Speak of Armageddon! The noise was so intense, it seemed the stadium could topple from the tremor. Then Sandy struck out Mickey. And "the Blue" had won it all.

For a week after the funeral, Muggsy had wandered aimlessly through the streets of Schantzville.

He told himself he was looking for some kind of job there, anything but Baseball. Every time the game was mentioned, he walked away.

Then he reported back to his Manager, in that one's tiny office.

"I'm ready to play ball," he announced resignedly, nodding politely to a well-dressed, smiling man who stood close by. Muggsy was sure he'd sometime or other seen photos of that one in a big league uniform. Even now, the trim body and erect stance had Baseball-born written all over it.

"Great to have you back, Muggsy," from the manager, "but you're not playing for us any more. We've sold you to the Marberry Lions. Meet Cliff Hartwick, their owner and manager."

In his joy, Muggsy came off the floor. The Lions were in the United League, top minor circuit, the last stop before "the big show."

Still the youngster shoved his elation deep into some corner of himself. Time to celebrate later; now he had to deal his hardest.

He stepped forward and shook hands with Hartwick. "Glad to meet you, Sir. How much money do I get?"

The visitor stared at him in utter amazement.

"Boy, now I've heard everything. Listen, busher, you're getting the chance of your life, moving up to the Lions. You can deflate your fat head and turn the financial worries over to us."

The youthful catcher wasn't completely sure of himself after that brusque comeback. Still he decided to bluff it through.

"Nothing doing, Sir. I know your catcher. My arm is better than his, and I can outrun him. Besides, he never plays more than 110 games a season; I've averaged 130. And your second catcher is out with a broken wrist."

Cliff stood fast: "We'll name your salary."

"Tell you what, Mister Hartwick, I'll make it easy on you. I'll settle for 25 bucks a month under what your first catcher's getting, but that's for the first season only. After that, you'll know I'm a lot more valuable than he is."

"I've seen some wise guys, but you're the...."

"Do I get it?"

"No!"

"Then I'll stay here for a while," Muggsy proclaimed, all the while trembling inside, fearing he'd gone too far. "I like this town and this team, and I've got a manager who's teaching me plenty."

"Looks like he means it," the Colt manager noted to Hartwick. He was enjoying the unheard-of cockiness, finding himself pulling for Muggsy. More, though he couldn't/wouldn't stand in the kid's way, he hated to immediately lose the capably confident catcher.

But Cliff had thrown up his hands in despair. "Oh hell, I...oh, all right. But listen, Junior, if a word of this gets out, you're fired on the spot. I'd never live it down, a busher making a sucker out of me."

"Mister Hartwick, your secret is safe."

Still the Lions had heard stories of the fresh youngster headed their way. And had prepared a worthy reception.

After Muggsy's first day in the Lion park, he went back to the dressing room to find his street clothes shredded and his catching gear doused in red paint. He stood there, rather dazedly looking at the ruination, feeling the eyes of the other players on himself. Same old story: could he take it?

Working to mask his shock, he faced them.

"Who ruined my stuff?"

Buck Jackson, the rangy and mean-looking center-fielder, stepped forward.

"You could say, rookie, that I thought up the party."

Viciously, he gave Muggsy the back of his huge hand. The new arrival crashed into a locker on the way down. For a minute or more, he lay on the wooden floor, wiping blood from a cut nose.

The other Lions laughed knowingly.

"Just another loudmouth!"

"Yeah, no guts. This rook'll be gone in a hurry."

Reeling badly, Muggsy came to his feet and waded in. Jackson pounded his jaw with a one-two volley. The kid again hit the floor.

Manager Hartwick, till then a spectator, walked over to Muggsy and offered a hand rather than let the beating continue.

"Muggsy, you all right?"

The caring words brought shame to Muggsy. What the hell was he doing on the floor, bleeding and getting laughed at? NOBODY had ever beaten him down. He brushed aside the helping hand and went after Buck. A left dug into the big guy's belly, and the ever-faithful right exploded on Buck's jaw. Buck hit the wall, taking a bench with him as he went down.

"Busher's got guts!" yelled a Lion.

Buck charged back, but Cliff moved between them. He had allowed the hazing because he too wanted to know more about his newest player...and had let it go farther as some kind of payback for what he considered a putdown by Muggsy on their first meeting. But he didn't want to see his catcher badly hurt, and he knew that, even with Muggsy's guts, Buck was too big and too strong.

"Enough, Buck. Muggsy can take it; that's all we wanted to know. Now you two guys shake hands."

Each of the players hesitated, not wanting to quit.

"I said SHAKE HANDS, and I mean it," Cliff ordered forcefully.

They shook hands, and Buck added, "Hey, welcome to the Lions, Muggsy Banton. Lemme tell you, you throw a helluva right hand."

"And you're sure no patsy."

Before long, Muggsy had broken into the Lions lineup, with a first-game accumulation of four hits, six runs driven across the plate, and two runners thrown out trying to steal second.

After that, he was seldom replaced. The fresh kid set the league on fire with his give-all brand of Baseball and his constant search for a scrap.

The Lions, who had lethargically faded to third in the standings, caught fire with their rookie catcher. A month before the end of the season, they took over first place. They won the pennant going away.

Everywhere the Lions had played, Big League Scouts gathered to watch the fireball catcher.

"He's got what it takes," said one of them. "How does he live?"

"No night life," answered manager Hartwick. "Strictly a ball player. He lives just for that."

"I'll make him an offer he can't refuse," said a Scout.

From another: "I'll top whatever you offer."

With the pennant stowed away, the Lions had but to play out their schedule. Most of the players eased off in those last meaningless games, but not rookie Banton.

So it was, in the ninth inning of the last game of the season, with the Lions leading the Bears, 11-0, Muggsy still slid wildly into third base, arriving late and sending the third baseman flying.

Muggsy also tore the cartilage in his knee, plus fragmenting the kneecap. He went off the field on a stretcher, straight to surgery.

"He'll be back next year," Cliff told the Scouts, "good as ever."

But the injury-wise ivory hunters had shredded their juicy contracts for Muggsy and had gone looking for hot prospects elsewhere.

Oh, a few of them persisted, coming back the next spring for a desperate look-see. They quickly observed that Muggsy's prime speed was gone. No more that essential QUICK that makes a Big Leaguer.

The realization of dreams-taken-flight at first shattered young Banton. Still, after a while and with careful counsel from Manager Hartwick, he could philosophize/rationalize: "A few make it to the top, but most don't...But one thing's for sure: I'll have a lot more fun from now on. 'Bright Lights Banton' they'll call me."

Thus would he then live.

Muggsy Banton, the "almost guy" still thrilled the fans with his scrappy style. In the nine years he had been a Lion, he had six times led them to first division finishes. But, after his first season in town, the team had never made first place. Forever lacking, along with the speed, was that final inspiration that could have taken them to a pennant. Muggsy was having too good a time.

Finally had come the day and night when he met Katie Crowley.

Chapter Seventeen

**"From some Baseball 'Wise Man' who would be heard:
'If he's quick, even a little guy is a big guy' "**

Baseball "experts" can insist that just one man can't make a team GO. But, when a destined leader firmly grasps the rudder, then who can deny the sudden momentum gained? Such as when Muggsy did the grasping, the Lions won as never before.

Manager Cliff had formerly taken a let's-see-what-happens approach to sometimes letting his pitcher shake off Muggsy's signs. But he soon realized that almost-never would his "new" catcher stand for that. And the pitchers likewise came to that truth. Muggsy had cast off his admittedly eager but still fun-bent attitude. Now his play-to-win spirit would inflame all the Lions. Again witness: If an enemy runner charging home plate had to be blocked, he would be, no mind that aching knee.

Nearing the road trip that would end their season and just conceivably see them win a pennant, the Lions had won 15 of their last 17.

Still some writers doubted. They praised the spurt, but still told readers that catching the first-place Bears in this season was just too much to ask. Now if the resurging Lions could just carry the present pace into next year!

No matter pessimism. Reporter George Periwinkle hung tough: "This is the year for the Lions."

Some hours after still another Lion win, Clara and J.T. were at a formal dance at their country club. As they waltzed to "AFTER THE BALL," Clara complained, "It's a crying shame that Katie didn't come to this lovely affair. All of our best people are here, but did our own Daughter show up? Oh no. She's out with that 'Muggsy' again. Jim, you really should talk some sense into her; seems you're the only one she listens to these days."

J.T. figured silence to be the best reply, as they continued to maneuver the crowded room, with whatever difficulty: "Clara, let's go home. Ouch! Whyinhell can't people dance on their own feet?"

As Marberry's mayor and his Wife approached, the orchestra was continuing its medley with "THE BLUE DANUBE."

"See the Lion game today?" the mayor asked J.T.

"No, but I hear we won again, thanks to Muggsy Banton's home run in the bottom of the ninth. Sure wish I'd been there to cheer our guys on."

"We were there," the mayor's Wife was anxious to assure them. "Harry and I see as many games as we can. And isn't that Muggsy simply fabulous?"

"Say," added the mayor, "isn't that your Katie we've seen him with lately?"

Clara was almost put to rout by that one, but she quickly recovered.

"Oh yes, he and Kathleen have been together a lot. He's such a fine young man. Jim and I are quite fond of him."

"Seems to be a helluva guy," the mayor uttered fervently. "Wish our Lucy would find someone like him."

"Fine young man," repeated Clara. "Baseball players live such clean, healthy lives, you know."

J.T. coughed too loudly, and Clara kicked at his foot.

Mercifully, a loud version of "HOT TIME IN THE OLD TOWN TONIGHT" ended the conversation.

At that moment, Katie and Muggsy were parked by the river.

"Same old moon," noted Muggsy, "only now it's full-size. I sure missed you when I saw it last night."

"Oh?" Her tone was decidedly edgy.

"Yeah, I was out with some of the guys."

"Also with some of the girls, including Belle."

He was caught dumbfounded. "How'd you know?"

"Word gets around. By ten o'clock this morning, I heard it from three different busybodies."

She hadn't intended to say anything. Still, once it was out in the evening air, no use stopping. Katie was hurt, and made no secret of that.

"Tell me, Payne, are your other friends too good for me? Or are you just afraid I wouldn't fit in with them?"

Muggsy came up bristling, "Wait a darn minute! Whatinhell's wrong with my going out with other people once in a while?"

"Not a single thing wrong with it. Go out with Belle every single night, if she's who you want. Now please take me home."

She turned her back to him. But the quivering of her shoulders was more than he could take.

"Katie, what's wrong with us? We've never quarreled before."

She stayed where she was, her back to him.

He moved to her, one hand barely brushing a cheek. She continued to retreat. So he leaned over and whispered in her ear, "I'm so sorry, Baby. But honest, I was there last night just so I could be sure. And now I am. The old life means nothing to me anymore; all I want is to be with you."

Quickly did she come to his arms.

"I'm sorry too, Payne. I was hasty and hateful, a real Irish bitch. But I missed you so much last night, so jealous at the thought of maybe another girl in your arms. Payne, can't you have other friends and me too? I do like Belle, and, if the others are your friends, I'll bet I'd get along splendidly with them."

"Katie, that's how it'll be. Only I want to be alone with you as much as possible."

"Oh yes, I want it to be that way too."

He took her arms and held her a short distance from himself, looking into those blue eyes no longer clouded.

"Katie Crowley, I love you so awfully much. Will you marry me? I may not be much of a Husband, but no one else could ever care for you the way I do."

She pressed back to him. "Oh yes, Payne, I will marry you...tonight or tomorrow, whenever-wherever you say. I'm so terribly in love with you. I may not be the ideal Wife, with my awful temper that flares too easily. But I do want to spend the rest of my life with you, no one else."

For precious moments, their embrace left no need for words. Then Muggsy broke the spell: "On that first night, Katie, I made such a mess of things. I was afraid I'd ruined it all. So I made up my mind I wouldn't try to really kiss you again until it would mean a lot."

Now it did, and the blast furnaces in the distance must have been envious at the heat generated.

So their engagement was a reality. But so was their coming separation, as the surging Lions made ready for their final road trip of the season.

Two days later, back at their table in the coffee shoppe, the ballplayer and his lady examined the gloomy prospect of weeks of "apartness."

"It'll sure be lonesome, Katie. I used to enjoy these trips. But not this one coming up....without you."

"Payne, it isn't right for us to be separated.

"Let's get married right now, and make this trip our honeymoon. Unless, of course, I'd be in your way on the road."

He took her hands in his. "Katie, you just know you wouldn't. But I thought, well, maybe when the season's over and we have the money I'll get if we win the pennant..."

"No whens or ifs, Payne Banton. Let's get married NOW."

"Katie, on the road, it's such a rough life. We ride in beaten old chair cars. We stop at cheap boarding houses because they won't let 'vulgar Baseball players' in decent hotels."

"NOW, Payne."

"We eat wherever we happen to be at meal time, which means some horrible hash houses. Honest, it's no life for a high-class girl such as you. We have to take it and like it, because it's our life."

"Sounds like the most wonderful life, with you," she cooed, as she finished her sandwich.

Muggsy's resistance was ebbing. Still, convinced he had to do the right thing for his Bride-to-be, he continued his negative barrage: "Your Mother probably would want you to wait until time for a big wedding."

"I doubt that, Payne. You just don't know how Mom's changed. She is now one of your most ardent fans. The other night, at the Charity Ball, she and Dad talked to our mayor and his Wife, who are also red-hot Baseball fans. Which finally convinced Mom that ballplayers are worthy of unlimited respect."

"Well I'll be..."

"In fact, last night when I went to my room, I couldn't find my Spalding Baseball Guide. Mom had snitched it and was reading all about the great game. She didn't quit until after midnight. She kept Dad awake all that time, asking him about home runs and stolen bases and errors, and all that."

"Never would have believed it...But getting married in a hurry is..."

"We'd be together through every wonderful day and every simply fabulous romantic night."

No struggling with that last, which had become his foremost dream.

"Yes, Katie...NOW..."

The same sexy young waitress who'd had eyes only for Muggsy was slithering to their table, showing her every curve.

"Mr. Banton, I'd better chain you to the table."

"Stop teasing. Can I help it if I'm irresistible to that there Barbara Mooney?"

But no note-with-phone number was slipped to the ballplayer.

Instead, the waitress brought two cups of coffee and one large slice of apple pie a la mode, with two forks.

"But we didn't ask for dessert," protested Muggsy.

"Compliments of Madame du Bois," the young girl told him, looking oh so soulfully into his brown eyes and managing to brush him as she served his pie.

Madame du Bois, fulsome and gracious owner of the coffee shoppe, was beaming as she followed her employee to their table.

"I do hope you lovely people aren't offended by my anticipating your wishes. I have seen affaire d'amour in the joyful eyes of both of you from the first time you visited my little cafe together. Now I hear of what-you-call 'engagement' and this dessert is my tiny way of wishing you a lifetime of marital joyeux."

She picked up the check previously left, tore it in two, and put the pieces in the pocket of her apron.

"In Ma Belle France, we have the saying, 'comme il faut'."

Katie volunteered, "That means 'as it should be'."

Madame du Bois was more than pleased with such understanding.

"Oh, but the Mademoiselle speaks my tongue! Yes, it means just that, and I am sure that your amour for each other is as it should be. May you forever love tenderly."

"Oui," offered Muggsy, which was his entire French vocabulary. For which the Madame bent down and kissed his cheek.

Katie told her, "Madame du Bois, you must please come to our wedding."

"Oh, but yes. And when?"

"Day after tomorrow, 10 A.M., St. Mary's Church."

"I will surely be there. Oh, I can look at this magnifique man and even now know he will be the grande amour for his exquisite woman."

After Madame du Bois had left their table, Katie commented, "Mister Cliff Hartwick is a lucky man."

Muggsy came up short from a bite of pie a la mode, and looked quizzically at his Katie.

"Sorry, I missed that. Cliff is <u>what</u>?"

"Payne, you are so naive, when you are supposed to be such a man-about-town...You mean you didn't know about the sizzling romance in progress between your manager and Madame du Bois?"

"Well I'll be! Us guys figured something was going on, the way Cliff's dressed so sharp lately and been even more upbeat than before. But we never suspected...Why that sneaky old sonofagun, and I thought I knew him so well."

Katie was enjoying her role as "informer."

"Try hard, Payne, and you might remember...who introduced Cliff and Madame to each other?"

"How in the world should I know?"

"If you'll look back to the time when you and I brought Cliff to lunch here, you performed that grand formality. Oh, I remember thinking on that day, it was like tossing a match into a dry forest. Boom! Off it went."

"Now ain't I a helluva great guy."

"I'm not usually much at gilding the lily. Still I must admit, I do think you are."

Chapter Eighteen

My favorite wedding toast? No contest on this one: "Here's to those moments of sheer delight. Then fanny-to-fanny, the rest of the night."

St. Mary's Church had seldom known such an enormous gathering as filled every inch of its space when Katie and Payne were wed.

So many friends and fans wanted to attend that police were summoned to preserve order, if they would be needed.

The officers could have gone on their way, as Father Dennis Matthews, the Pastor, explained it: "It's an orderly crowd, and will remain that way. Besides and begorrah, all these fans of Muggsy Banton know that, if it's commotion they want, their man will surely display it for them on the diamond, he will."

The church altar was enveloped in flowers. When those kept coming, the sacristy was turned into a floral storehouse. Finally the excess was dispatched to a nearby hospital.

The wedding, though hastily planned, was everything Katie had dreamed of.

She and J.T. waited in the vestibule, at the rear of the church, and heard George Periwinkle sing AVE MARIA.

Father and Daughter hugged each other one last time before the ceremony.

"Now, Dad, you get rid of that big tear in your eye."

"Soon as you lose the same in yours. But I'm glad I'm giving you to a good guy."

Finally, they were strolling up the aisle, the bride in a pale blue gown of taffeta and lace, with a light veil shadowing her red hair. It was the creation that had long topped her romantic fantasies.

Clara, fidgeting in a front pew, had many times heard the recitation of those dreams, and, when she had sensed that wedding-time was nigh, had quietly asked her dressmaker to begin preparations as desired.

But, even with that headstart, it had come to crunch time in the last few days.

Clara now breathed deep thankfulness to the dressmaker who had worked without letup, days and nights, to somehow have the desired gown ready on time.

Up the aisle, in front of Katie, walked Elsie Peabody, the maid of honor. Near the front of the church, she was startled, and hurt too, noting that Dr. Philip Sutton, her fiancee, was not in his seat. But Elsie was not one to blare forth her inner sadness. Smiling, she moved forward.

"Nervous, Muggsy?" asked best-man Cliff, just before they left the sacristy.

"Yeah, some, but I'm glad we didn't wait."

"I'm glad for you. When that lucky bluebird sits on a guy's shoulder and digs in, the guy has to realize it's his time to GO."

Near the front of the church, the other Lions watched.

"Gee," whispered Jumbo Malone, "I guess we didn't know all about Muggsy after all. He seems so...so different."

From Skeeter Newman: "I think she's what he's needed."

"Quiet, you mugs!" hissed the huge Buck Jackson, who had once given Muggsy his brutal introduction to the Lions. "Ain't yez never learned 'bout being quiet and re-spectful?"

From a back row, Miss Barbara Mooney gazed longingly at the groom.

Kneeling in mid-church, Madame Blanche du Bois fingered her beads, while her eyes seldom strayed from Cliff Hartwick, now at the altar with the groom.

At a signal from Father Matthews, Muggsy accepted his Bride from J.T.

The couple moved forward to the altar steps, where they knelt.

Offering encouragement to the slightly quavering bridal couple, the flames of the tall altar candles refused to die, however they were made to dance merrily by the new autumn breezes advancing through the main church doors.

"Do you, Payne Banton, take this woman...?

"And do you, Kathleen Mary Crowley....?"

Soulfully they found each other's eyes, waiting longingly for the words of binding.

"Jim, she does look so happy."

"Yes, Clara, and beautiful. You were the only bride that ever matched her for loveliness."

"I now pronounce you Man and Wife."

Chapter Nineteen

From manager Casey Stengel: "Do I think my players should be married? Hey, now, you lissen and lemme say, for every woman who makes a fool outta a guy, there is two ladies who make men outta fools."

"Muggsy, you don't have to play today," Cliff told his catcher in the dressing room before the game, "being that you might be knocked out from all the wedding commotion of this morning."

From the back of the room: "Skipper, you're mixed up. It's tomorrow morning when he'll really be knocked out."

Muggsy glared down the intruder, then told Cliff, "Katie insists on my playing today. The wedding gift she wants most is for us to win today...win big."

Butch Holcomb stuck his head in the door, "Everything's ready at home plate."

As the astonished Muggsy walked onto the field, still another wagonload of gifts was being unloaded. While a massive delegation of presenting fans stood 'round the brightly wrapped boxes.

In the stands, people were on their feet, cheering wildly, "Bring on the bride, she's a lot prettier than the groom," and similar sentiments.

So Muggsy walked over to where she sat.

"I'll go if you promise to stay with me," she told him, clinging timidly.

"Bride, I just got through promising I'd stay by your side for a lifetime. But I'll gladly repeat that vow over and over."

He lifted her over the railing, onto the playing field. Which brought an even greater crowd-reaction.

At home plate, the mayor of Marberry was making a speech:

"The citizens of Marberry are indeed proud and happy to honor a number one citizen and his most charming bride. We want them to accept these small gifts to show our esteem and civic appreciation, and ....."

"Ah siddown, Yer Honor, and shaddup!" roared a foghorn voice from behind third base. "Let's get on with the Bride and Groom."

A booming chorus of kranks supported that, so the mayor, after a deep bow, sat down.

The newlyweds opened as many of the packages as was possible before game-time: Jewelry, perfume, hankies, and kitchenware only began the collection for Katie...oh yes, and harpsichord for her living room.

For Muggsy: an order for a new suit, shirts, a promise of a year's supply of fuel for his gas-mobile. For both of them: linen, and a silver service from Cliff. From the other Lions, there was a bat wrapped in dollar bills.

The climax was a case of beer from Blind Tom, with a card: "To my pal Muggsy."

"So play ball!" boomed the ump. "Now gimme any lip, Banton, and you're outta this game before it starts."

In the third inning, with the game scoreless and the Lions' Herky Jackson on second, Muggsy came to bat. Passing the seats down front, a shower of rice covered him.

"Hey, 'benedict', hit it out."

On the first pitch, Muggsy lined a hit over the Sox second baseman, into right-center field. Herky scored, the first installment on Katie's requested wedding gift.

From first base, Muggsy yelled to the enemy second sacker: "Hey, Dum-Dum, I'm coming down on the next pitch."

Which he did, easily beating the throw from the catcher.

From second, he shouted to the third baseman, "Get ready, Egghead; gonna visit you right away."

On the next pitch he stole third without a throw from the catcher, so rattled were the Blue Sox.

By now the visiting team was raging, and their catcher snarled at Muggsy, "Try to steal home, if you got the guts; let your Bride see how ya look with no teeth, 'cause in-the-chops is where I'm gonna tag ya."

The pitcher went into his abbreviated motion, guarding against another base theft. But Muggsy hadn't even waited for that. He crossed home plate standing while the discombooberated moundsman still held the horsehide.

The hometown fans gloried in Muggsy's daring, telling him so as he jawed with the fuming catcher.

"Hate to say 'I told you so'," he taunted that one, "but..."

"You cocky bastard! Next time you come my way, I'm gonna bust your head open."

"Trouble with you is that you don't trust people; hellfire, I told you I was coming down. Where you come from, doesn't anyone tell the truth?"

Muggsy headed for the Lion dugout, the whole team up to meet him and pound his back in their joy.

By demand, Muggsy came out for more applause from the hysterical crowd.

He called to Katie, "There's a starter on your wedding gift."

"I love it, but let's have more, a whole lot more, beat 'em 20-0."

In the sixth, with two runners on base and the score still 2-0, Muggsy again advanced to the plate.

"O.K., wise guy," threatened the Bison receiver, "you steal more bases, make us look bad again, I told you what's gonna happen, bust your head open."

"You mean you'll lose your paycheck? Awwwww, poor 'ol Bisons."

"No, matter of fact, the skipper promised, you don't steal no more then the fine is canceled."

"O.K., joy boy, I'll be nice to you and won't steal this time around."

In came the pitch. Muggsy Banton swung from the heels. The horsehide was but a faint blur as it took off for distant pastures, up-up, long gone from the ballpark.

Continued delirium in the stands as Muggsy circled the bases.

The catcher flung down his mask in disgust.

"Hey, why ya mad? I kept my promise to you and now you get your paycheck."

"Hurray for my Husband," shouted Katie.

"That's my Son-in-Law!" Clara told anyone and everyone who would listen.

On top of a house across the street that ran along the left field fence, an old man was fuming, "Drat it. That's the tenth ball been hit through my windows in the last two weeks. Once Muggsy and the Lions started this hot streak, I told dummy-me, 'Sam Streck, it's sure time to put up the storm windows.' Then like an idiot I didn't do it. Oh well, hurray for Muggsy and his Lions!"

For that day, all resistance had faded. The Lions delivered Katie's wedding gift, 20-0.

Chapter Twenty

"Traveling on trains back in the early 1900's, those cars pulled by steam engines," reminisced an old ballplayer, "we had two great choices. We could close all the windows and near-die of heat and suffocation. Or we could open the windows and get absolutely blanketed with soot...But do you know what, we loved every bit of it because it gave us a chance to be professional players."

On that night, the Lions-plus-one left town in a cloudburst. But the downpour couldn't keep their fans from the depot; they stood shivering under umbrellas, their continuing cheers shaking down the thunder from the skies...until finally the train was out of sight.

In their chair car, Katie and Muggsy watched the rain pounding at their window. In unison they sighed happily.

"You're the first girl ever to ride with us on Esmeralda," Muggsy informed his Bride.

"On what?"

"On Esmeralda. That's what we call any train we travel on."

"It's a simply beautiful railroad train," protested Katie, resting her head on his shoulder. "And its gaslight lanterns are utterly romantic."

"Happy wedding night, Mrs. Banton."

"Oh the same to you, dearest Husband."

He suddenly sat up straight, and, despite her protests, held her at a distance. Then in mock sternness, he demanded, "How come you didn't wear anything blue today at the game? You took a chance on jinxing us."

"Payne, how can you be so sure of yourself?"

"Welllll, I didn't see any blue, and I thought..."

She pulled him closer, whispering, "When we're finally alone together, I'll prove to you, dearest lover, I would never jinx you."

Early the next morning, as the train chugged along through the heavy mist, Muggsy shook her gently.

"Wake up, Sleepyhead. Time for a brand new day, our first entire day-ever of wedded bliss."

She stretched out luxuriantly as the stiff seat allowed, trying to peek through the fogged windows.

"At least it's stopped raining," she announced delightedly. "Now look, the sun's trying to peek through. Oh, what a simply glorious day!"

"I sure wondered, Bride, what you'd look like first thing out of bed in the morning. My, you are still so beautiful!"

"You tell such sweet fibs, I'll try to make you at least kinda close-to-honest by tiptoeing off to the little girls' room.

"Don't hurry back."

She turned back in her departure to again face him, appearing miffed.

"I don't think I like that. Why not hurry back? Are you tired of me already?"

"Oh gosh not, but the guys have to change into their uniforms."

"IN-teresting. So what if I refuse to leave?"

"Don't know. Hey, shall we find out? I sure don't fear comparisons."

"Given that mighty assurance, I'll depart. Just knock three times when you're all...oh, sorta reasonably decent...sorta kinda. I mean, a girl doesn't get many such chances.

"I'll miss you. Still, for being such a smarty-pants, we might not win today's game by more than 15 or 16."

After a while, Esmeralda wheezed to a halt.

"We're here," Muggsy announced. "Mrs. Banton, I'm pleased to escort you."

Cliff was cautious as he led his players off the train.

"Don't be surprised at anything that crops up from now on," Muggsy warned his Bride.

His words were barely out when SPLATT, a foul-smelling egg flashed through the air, breaking on his clean, grey uniform-front.

From all around the depot, the egg-shower continued, sometimes implemented by rotten fruit.

Finally the spattered Lions reached the safety of the waiting-room.

"You all right?" Muggsy asked Katie.

"They hardly got me.....But I don't understand all this."

Combing shells from his hair, Cliff explained, "Kranks do it out of loyalty to their home team. Ours in Marberry are certainly no different."

"Yeah," added Muggsy, "this is mild compared to what we get in some towns. Katie, maybe I'd better put you on the next train home."

"Never! Anything you can take, I can take better."

With a sideways glance at the nearest window, Muggsy caught a movement that alerted him.

"Keep talking, all of you," he hissed. He dropped to his knees and moved toward a bucket of water, the depot's fire-fighter.

Cliff grinned knowingly, "See one?"

"A lot of 'em. They're sneaking up to the windows to fire another round while they figure we're trapped in here. Keep talking."

"Now as I was saying, KATIE," Cliff spoke loudly, "these people sure get worked up. Why, did you know..."

"When I say 'ready', you open this window, quick," Muggsy told Jumbo Malone.

"You don't really mean it, Cliff?" Katie moved the coverup conversation. "Why, I never would have thought..."

Up went the window, and Muggsy shot the bucketful of water through the open space. The drenched hometown fans dropped their rotten eggs and were lost in the morning mist.

"Now let's eat," came from Herky Jackson. "That diner across looks about as inviting as we're going to get."

"But mightn't they poison our food?" Katie wanted to know.

"They might. Still, in enemy towns, it's a chance we gotta take, or starve."

The famished Lions took over the eater, most of them at the long counter.

"Hey, bridal couple, there's one empty table in here," observed Cliff. "You can sit there and we won't think you're snobbish."

From Katie, "Thanks, Skipper, but the counter suits us just real fine and dandy."

Muggsy's glance at her was loaded with equal parts of love and pride.

As bacon and eggs were served, Katie looked over the dingy, badly-lit room. "This is the wedding breakfast I've dreamed of."

"Madame, will you have champagne with your eggs and bacon?" Cliff wanted to know.

"No, I prefer black coffee."

"Good choice," said Muggsy. "Their bubbly bottles would likely be set to explode in our faces."

That afternoon, the Lions won, 1-0, with a Muggsy Banton steal of home in the ninth inning.

"How lucky can a girl be?" Mrs. Banton wanted to know. "The wedding gifts just keep coming. I'd be all-a-twitter about tomorrow's game, except that mostly I'm looking to tonight with my man."

In their drafty rooming house cubicle at last, so smugly and snugly did the bridal couple face each other to exchange kisses that grew from quick and frantic to lengthy and soulful.

During which, to remember a bit of passionate prose from sometime/somewhere:

> **Tenderly he undressed she.**
> **And boldly she undressed he.**
> **Before both lovers addressed each other.**

But suddenly an apologetic Muggsy backed away.

"I should have turned off the lights."

"Oh...why?"

"I've heard that girls want it that way, 'darkly romantic'."

"Not this girl. As we climb between these faded but ever-loving sheets, I want to see HIM and have HIM see ME. What I'm stumbling to say, Mighty Mate: Let's us leave just nothing undone."

Lights finally out, Muggsy lifted Katie Crowley Banton onto the rickety old bed.

Then resolutely followed her there.

Chapter Twenty One

Remembered from Jimmy Dykes, when he managed the Chicago White Sox: "Getting your team known as the toughest in your league, as my team certainly is, can be worth six or eight wins in a season. Let's face it: The prospect of facing spikes coming in high can make some family-men grow faint and filled with...now what's that fancy word?...yeah, filled with <u>IN-souciance</u>."

The weeks that followed were merry ones on the road, as the Marberry Lions pursued the pennant in an unyielding, anything-goes style of Baseball.

They spent five days in each town, with Katie at every game. She felt the few setbacks perhaps even more than the Lions themselves, because their experience with losing was more deep-seated.

After each series, off to a new town in Esmeralda, while uniforms hung out the train's windows to dry. At each stop then would come the hostile depot-salute of rotten eggs and fruit, with sometimes a spattering of mud mixed in...or even a shower, full-stream from a fire hose.

Oh yes, every day (and every night!) brought unequalled chills and thrills to the Bride of Muggsy Banton.

"Expert" admonitions that the Lions should-oughta-wait-till-next-year before getting their hopes up lost credibility with each passing day as the Marberry Club closed in on the league-leading Bears. Led by the living flame that was the NOW Muggsy, manager Cliff's club was more than the opposition could handle.....Finally the Lions found themselves in first place, just a game away from winning the pennant, with three battles remaining, all at the Bears' park. The Lions would win the championship streamer, "the gonfalon" unless the home team could sweep the series.

"We're gonna win," Muggsy predicted in utter confidence.

"Oh yes we're gonna!" Katie echoed his words of triumph

But the first game went to the Bears 10-3. They pounded Jumbo Malone from the box in the second inning and scored as they pleased.

The Bears repeated in the second contest, 3-2, despite a steady pitching performance by Bugle-Nose Stankorsky.

Muggsy had a supreme chance to put away the pennant in the ninth inning of that one, the score 2-2, bases loaded, two out, count three-and-two. But his powerful swing contacted nothing except ozone. Worse, his long-injured knee gave way. He fell to the ground, unable to arise. The downhearted Lions swarmed around their leader, watching him roll helpless in the dirt.

Katie ran from the stands to her Husband's side. A doctor was called from the crowd.

"It's in bad shape," the medic told Cliff. "Must've re-torn some of those ligaments."

"Does it hurt a lot, Payne?"

"Naw!" he lied to his Wife, as the doctor probed the damaged area. "I'll be back in there tomorrow."

"Please don't, Muggsy," begged Cliff. "You've got other seasons ahead of you."

"Gotta play. That game is our last chance, and we've come too far to blow it now...Ouch, dammit, Doc, not so hard!....Look, Katie, this happens lots. If it didn't, I'd be in the Big Leagues."

He softened then, squeezing Katie's hand, telling her and the other Lions so reassuringly, "I'll be behind the plate tomorrow, and WE WILL WIN."

It was a tense team of defeated Lions that walked back to their rooming house, while Bear fans followed them from what seemed a safe distance.

"G'wan home, ya bums!" yelled those kranks.

"Yeah, 'n where's your mighty Jumbo? That phony couldn't break glass from three feet away with his so-called 'fast ball'."

That last should have been left unsaid.

Jumbo Malone rushed from the straggling Lions and grabbed two of the home-towners by their collars. With no effort he jerked them off the ground.

"Think I'll knock your stupid heads together till your teeth fall out."

The captured duo pleaded, "Honest, we was just kiddin'" as the huge pitcher dangled them like dolls high and away from himself.

Cliff tapped Jumbo on the shoulder.

"Relax, Big Guy. They just wanted to rattle you. Don't give 'em the satisfaction, filing a battery charge against you in their home town, with the judge likely a Bear krank too."

Jumbo melted to an awkward grin. "Oh awright, Boss. But can't I please throw 'em in that horse-guzzling trough across the street?"

"Be my guest."

While the captive hecklers still wailed for mercy and their comrades sought safety in watching from a distance, Jumbo dropped the two of them into the cold and slimy water.

The other Lions cheered his performance.

After which Jumbo yelled at the distant remaining Bear hecklers, "Tell yer stinkin' team I'll be back on the mound tomorrow and beat the socks off 'em."

As the Lions continued on their way, Jumbo had this anxious thought:

"Hey, skipper, I am pitching tomorrow, ain't I?"

"You bet you are, Jumbo. You'll do just what you told 'em, beat the socks offa them stinkin' Bears."

A carriage passed the again-high-spirited Lions. Katie and Muggsy (his knee heavily wrapped) sat in the rear.

Shouting as they went by, the catcher pointed to a barrel in the open section behind the seat occupied by himself and his Wife.

"Nails!!" he yelled, pulling out a handful and dropping them deliberately back into the barrel.

To Baseball players, that was the surest sign of impending victory, the sight of nails.

"Honest, I didn't plan this," Muggsy continued to shout. "This carriage just happened by and it was our only chance for a ride. Then the nails just happened to be in that barrel in the back. HONEST."

As the carriage passed on by, Katie was somehow looking the other way.

"They have some of the cutest houses in this town."

(She was hoping/praying that her Husband wouldn't learn the truth: While his knee had been tended by the doctor at the ball park, it had taken her most frantic efforts to find a carriage in alien territory, also to set up the nail scenario.)

"Good luck," Katie would read from quotes of an onsurging Baseball firebrand named Branch Rickey, "is but the product of fervent design."

"I'm so proud of my Husband," spoke Katie as she undressed before his constant gaze. "He was the life of the party this evening, even though he'd refused to take any heavy pain pills because he was afraid they'd slow him down in the game tomorrow. Oh yes indeedy, he's the most wonderful man on this whole earth."

"You're the wonderful one; you haven't complained once through the whole trip."

He was seated before her, a heat pad on his bad knee. He watched her unbutton her dress, and, with a catlike motion, slide out of it, down to her underclothes, including (finally!) her lace underpants.

"Complained?" she protested, wrapping the word in warmth. "No bride ever had such a glorious honeymoon...But say, wasn't that a happy surprise, Cliff throwing a party tonight? I'm still drooling over those big steaks."

"And the cold beer too! Then getting tickets for the burlesque for the whole team, except of course for this bridegroom, who can have just one naked girl in his thoughts.

"He'd better have just one."

Outside their window, a clatter of tin pans and brass horns had begun.

"Just Bear kranks determined the Lions won't sleep tonight," he explained. "But we'll sleep anyway, and tomorrow we'll wallop 'em."

In bed, she secured the pad on his aching knee, then cuddled close behind him, making Muggsy relaxed and comfy in almost every possible way.

"'Night, Muggsy."

"Why Katie, it's the first time you've called me that."

"I know. I just wanted to see how it sounded, coming from me. But I like Payne better, at least for a little while. 'Night, Payne darling."

Some minutes later: "Katie, I can't sleep. Your undressing got to me."

"I thought you'd never say that. I was beginning to worry about my bumps and grinds. I mean, I don't expect to be another Belle La France, but..."

"Belle's don't go one-to-a-hundred with yours."

More minutes later:

"Katie, I can't believe you'd do that for me, so you wouldn't hurt my knee."

"Payne, dearest, I've dreamed of when I'd do that for you."

"I can hardly wait," he told her, "for the next time I hurt my knee."

The next day saw Muggsy back in the lineup with bad knee and terrible hurting, all such ignored in his desire to WIN.

End of seventh inning, no score.

Katie, watching her Husband force each moment of action, ignoring the pain, wanted to cry. Still, each time he looked back at her, she was smiling and waving excitedly to him.

"Win, Payne, WIN."

In the ninth, game still scoreless, two out, bases empty, Muggsy managed to get hit on the hip by a pitched ball. He hobbled to first, from where, of course, he was no threat to steal. So the Bears concentrated on the batter, who was Butch Holcomb.

On the first pitch, Muggsy completely crossed up the Bears, stealing second, diving in on his belly. His teammates carried him off the field as Cliff held back a sobbing Katie.

"Leave him alone, Katie. Muggsy doesn't want sympathy."

"All right, Cliff. I just didn't know anyone could be so selfless."

Bobo Gentry went in to run for Muggsy. Butch Holcomb punched a single into center. From second base, where Muggsy had so agonizingly put it, the tie-breaking run did score.

The final Lion out came on a line drive to the third baseman.

"Win it for Muggsy!" yelled the Lions as they took the field for the bottom of the ninth.

Jumbo struck out the first two Bears. But the third batter sent a long, looping triple that reached the fence in deepest center field.

It looked bad for the Lions, with the Bears' heaviest hitter coming to the plate. But Jumbo seemed unruffled. He calmly stepped off to one side of the mound and retied his shoes. He also motioned for Gentry, now the Lion catcher, to come out and join him.

In the stands, a young girl looked adoringly into the eyes of her boyfriend, then asked, "You know so much about Baseball; what are they talking about?"

The boy returned her gaze and wisely assured her that the pitcher and the catcher were discussing what to throw the next hitter...indeed, heavy strategy going on at the mound.

Out on the hill: "Some game," commented Bobo. "Didja catch the brunette babe about six rows behind third base? Lordy, whatta pair o' knockers!"

"She's all right," Jumbo agreed. "But hey, I know some real snaky dolls want to entertain us here tonight, seeing as how our train doesn't leave till tomorrow and return us to our same-same old ladies. You want in on the fun?"

"Oh yeah."

The Bear danced off third, ready to swiftly score the tying run.

The batter set himself for his best swing.

From around the field, the Lions yelled encouragement to their pitcher. He smiled back at them, plainly reassuring them, "Nothing to worry about."

Jumbo then bore down and struck out the Bear batter on three steaming pitches, each more of a blur than the one before.

THE MARBERRY LIONS HAD WON THE PENNANT.

At the Marberry depot, fans were waiting in huge numbers. Following which, the parade down Main Street, where Katie once had her first glimpse of Muggsy.

Close by her side on the high rear seat of the carriage, Muggsy responded to the cheers of the mob by repeatedly doffing his cap.

"Sounds like they love their Lions," Muggsy volunteered.

"Obviously, but then you're not the only celebrity in this-here family. Just look up at Dad's office."

He did that, and saw a mammoth banner which Clara and J.T. thrust forward into the breezes:

WELCOME HOME, KATIE CROWLEY BANTON...

Chapter Twenty Two

I used to know a talented outfielder named Gerald Walker. Gerry performed repeated wonders of fielding and hitting for Mickey Cochrane's power-packed (American League champs in 1934, won World Series in '35) Detroit Tigers. Still the Tiger said frankly, "I do love to play Baseball. But honestly, by the end of another <u>long</u> season, I wouldn't walk across the street to see some other team play in a World Series. But oh how I loved the celebrating after we won!"

On the night of the champion Lions' return to Marberry, the Bantons sat on the front porch of their home (the one Muggsy had formerly shared with a teammate.)

They watched the torchlight victory parade march by.

Some of the marchers carried large signs: MUGGSY FOR MAYOR.

Blaring bands added to the uproar.

"I'm so glad, Payne, that you didn't let that foul ball drop into the stands, like Cliff told you to. If you'd just let it fall, where would we have met?"

"Some time-some place," he said confidently. "It just had to be."

Katie's voice took on a softer but more sinister tone: "You're so right, Mister. But I had it all planned, you'd fall with me, then fall for me. That's why I wore my enticing dress that day. And, if you can keep a dark secret, I just might reveal that to you."

"Cross my heart. Tell me the terrible truth."

"See, Mister, you didn't really fall into the stands."

"I didn't? Did an earthquake knock me in?"

"No, but when you got close enough to the front row of box seats, a female tornado named Katie Crowley reached out, grabbed you by your shaggy locks, and pulled you in. She'd seen the rugged cuss that's you, and she knew she had to have you to warm her bed every night forevermore."

"Am I glad that designing dame happened along!"

They snuggled between the sheets, bodies aglow for lovemaking.

"Payne....?"

"Yeah.....?"

"More news for you if you can stand so much excitement in just one day."

"Do tell me."

"The next Lion catcher will be here in June."

"Katie...oh, Katie baby."

He had been drawing her closer to himself, but he stopped anxiously.

"Can I...is it still all right?"

"Oh yes, Payne, and please with no time lost. I've never loved you quite as much as I do tonight."

Carefully she moved above him, to protect the injured knee.

Chapter Twenty Three

My matchless Mother, who seemed to have a special saying for every occasion, would add this one: "A happy marriage is like the story of the two bears, Bear and Forbear."

Later that night, in nightgowns and robes, they sat by the open window and listened to the dying sounds of the pennant-winning revelment.

"I wonder where Cliff is tonight," mused Muggsy. "After the blowout at city hall, when he was given the key to the city, I didn't see him anymore."

"Dearest Payne, you are so naive. When we got off the train today, didn't you see Blanche there waiting for him? Then, as soon as the ceremony at city hall had ended, and she was there waiting for him, the two of them jumped in his carriage and were out of there like greased lightning."

"Well twenty-three-skidoo!"

"I learned more about her," his Wife told him: "For some years now, after a severe stroke, her Husband has been paralyzed and comatose in an Army hospital about a hundred miles from here. She visits him every Sunday, though he probably doesn't recognize her.

"In between those Sundays, she told me, God will understand if she and Cliff live their lives to the fullest. So make your own guess whether or not she and your skipper are alone-together somewhere tonight."

"I'm glad as hell for Cliff. He's a neat guy. Keeps on an even keel after seeing some rough times."

"Oh? Do tell."

"His family, real well off they were, wanted him to go to college. But he wanted to be a professional ballplayer. When he told his family about it, his Mother swung to his side. But his Dad disowned him. Said ballplayers were a bunch of tramps, no decent man would join up with them, all like that."

"He came to Baseball anyway, but his Dad, whom he loved so much, would have nothing to do with him from then on."

"Poor Cliff."

"But that wasn't his only terrible bruise. See, there was this girl. Emma her name was. From what he told me, Emma was special. They started dating and it got serious in a hurry. But her Dad, a wealthy guy and supposedly one of Cliff's teams' biggest boosters, stepped in...Cliff had asked Emma to marry him. She'd said YES, and brought him to her home so he could ask for her hand in proper style.

"She had first thought that, for sure, her Dad would be crazy about her marrying Cliff, since she'd often heard her Dad rave about him as a player. But her Dad met them on the front steps with a buggy whip, drunk and yelling something about 'scummy ballplayers', how he'd teach one of them not to touch a decent woman. He swung the whip at Cliff. Emma grabbed for it, lost her balance and fell down the steps. Fractured her skull. Died the next day."

"Oh no!" breathed Katie, burrowing her face against her Husband.

"Yeah, and Cliff never really got over it. He left that town, shattered, but never stopped playing ball. Was in the Big Leagues for 12 years, a helluva third baseman, from all I've heard. But, at least until now, he never fell in love again, just settled for Baseball life, that was all he cared about."

"He must really love the game to have taken so much heartache for it and still stick with the scene."

"Yeah, and some day, when ballplayers are accepted everywhere, we'll know it was guys like Cliff who kept the scene alive in rough times."

"...Guys like him...and like you too."

Thoughtfully, Muggsy drew her closer to himself.

"No, I'll never deserve credit anywhere near what he does.

"Because of the game, he once lost what he wanted most. It must have been damn hard for him not to tell Baseball to go to blazes. Me now, it's easy to love it even more than I used to, because it gave me YOU."

Below them, street lamps were turned off.

A breeze from across the river touched the thinning trees. Those waved a loving GOODNIGHT to the newlyweds.

Katie was almost asleep when Muggsy touched her one more time.

"Girl, now I have news for you."

Hazily she tried to return...

"Oh?"

"Yeah. I forgot to tell you, I'm the new manager of the Lions."

"So what's new?" she yawned.

"Well I'll be damned; you women are amazing. You already knew it by some intuition or whatever you call it?"

"Oh no. Just that Cliff told me on the day we were married. I was supposed to keep you 'on tenderhooks' (he said) till the end of the season."

"Well I'll be damned," he repeated, and returned to his pillow.

"Payne," she whispered, shaking him.

Now he had trouble returning.

"Yeah?"

"Pardon me if I seemed flip. I think it's just perfect, you being manager of the Lions."

They cuddled closely, both of them drifting away.

"G'night, Katie Crowley Banton."

"'Night, Manager Muggsy."

Chapter Twenty Four

Quote sometimes laid to New York Yankee manager Miller Huggins: "Schoolboys who wonder why they must study decimal fractions finally get their answer when figuring Baseball averages."

Among Cliff Hartwick's multiple memories of Baseball, "the tale of the telegrapher's town" reigned as one of his best-loved.

There had been early springs in the 1870's-and-onward when Cliff, a fiery young infielder with the Fort Wayne, Indiana Kekiongas, of the ruling National Association of Professional Baseball Teams, would form an "All-Star" team from professional ballplayers living in and near-to Marberry. It was a fine way for those players to "get the feeling going" before training camps opened. They would thus gain an edge in toning bodies perhaps grown soft over winter months. They would further grab a chance to take in the glorious aroma of freshly-grown green grass at the earliest possible opportunity.

Little doubt, the mightiest of the athletes to perform for Cliff was a veteran lightning-like second baseman from the Troy, New York Haymakers, Sam Streck.

"Moved like greased lightning, Sam did," remembered Cliff. "A ball park could go just plain hysterical when he was ready to steal another base. In the field, he was death on double-play balls."

In the middle of one such "All-Star spring," manager Hartwick was buried under multiple telegrams from Hillsville, a town some 80 miles distant from Marberry.

On such wires those were! They could run to three or four pages in length, as the sender begged Cliff to bring his guys to Hillsville for games with their town team.

Cliff would recall with a chuckle that the wire-sender's name was Bill Bailey, just like in the 'won't you please come home' song.

"I figured those wires were costing ol' Bill a fortune," Cliff looked back, "so he had to be some well-heeled krank who could afford to pay us decently for showing up. Still, another piece of the puzzle: There weren't a whole lot of people in the Hillsville area. Now where in the world would he get the big crowd he seemed sure of?

"Still, all that pleading had continued over the wires until Cliff, so fascinated that he had to know all the answers, agreed to the Hillsville visit for his team. He scheduled two other games along the path of buggy-travel, to make the four-day jaunt financially feasible.

"Our guys had a ton o' fun on that trip," he would later tell Muggsy. "We saw new sights, made new friends, while breaking even in the four. Still, as I had suspected, not too many kranks showed up for our games. But those in the parks passed the hat most generously, to help pay expenses.

"Bill Bailey, who had sent all those long telegrams? He was a helluva friendly guy and a krank of no small proportions, on fire to see a game. I mean, he just couldn't wait for the regular season to start....Above all, hearing that Sam Streck played for us had just sent him to the skies. He'd seen Sam play 'in the Bigs' and was wild for a chance to watch him up-close in his own (Hillsville) ball park, also to meet our peerless second-sacker in person. He even got Sam to autograph a photo of himself.

"Besides, Bill owned most of Hillsville, maybe all of it for what we could prove, and that certainly included the local telegraph office. So it had cost him almost nothing to send so m any long and persuasive wires."

Cliff thoroughly enjoyed the telling of that tale.

"After the doubleheader at his park, he took all of us out to a great country dinner at his farm. We ate our fill of beef and chicken and corn and biscuits, following those with strawberry shortcake and apple brandy. You bet too, we 'talked ball' with Bill long into the night.

"Icing on the cake, that was, in realizing what a grand life is the Baseball life."

Chapter Twenty Five

Now wasn't it Lynwood "Schoolboy" Rowe, ace Detroit Tiger pitcher in the 1930's, who offered this sage observation on nuptials ahead of Anne Landers or Dear Abby: "Marriage is a course in the three R's, which are romance, rice, and rocks."

In 1908, William Howard Taft (out of Cincinnati-Ohio, not far from Buckeye State home of one Payne Banton) would become the 27th President of the United States. And President Taft would also be emblazoned on History as the only U.S. President who would later be Chief Justice of the Supreme Court.

Robert Peery, on the good ship Roosevelt, would discover the North Pole.

New York City was in a tizzy over its first subways.

Such drama intrigued the newly-captured heaven of the Payne Bantons, but still was washed over by their fervor as they first "set up house."

Following the Lions' championship season of 1907, winter, as per usual, arrived in Pennsylvania's Marberry. The frigid invader conquered all but the giant blast furnaces. Those still spat defiantly at the frozen world around themselves.

While the Banton band played on:

Katie had her first (even if rented) home to tend, and for her that was the beginning of fulfillment. She relaxed from the over-exacting (or so she thought) restrictions of her Mother's prim home-style...as, HORRORS if a spot of dust might somehow be found on the piano or mantlepiece.

COMFORT keyed the lifestyle of her Husband and herself.

The other Lion Wives, most of them nomadic movers over the Baseball landscape for long years past, found no problem in accepting new "club-member" Katie Banton's unquivering ways.

Most importantly, Katie had her Payne.

For his part, the new Lion manager had likewise and finally learned the meaning of contentment: Katie was his to come home to.

When spring would return, there would be more Baseball to make life even better.

All the while, Muggsy's rugged body was conditioned by the furnaced insides of the steel mill.

In the midst of which came an early-December Sunday of plentiful food, long walks, loafing, and loving.

That evening found Muggsy stretched out on the divan.

Katie entered the living room, modeling her newest (latest fashion) negligee, a gift from her Husband/Lover.

"I love this gown.

"Black silk makes me feel absolutely wicked."

His eyes stayed glued to her, and he began his move from the sofa.

"Payne, we've been married since last September, almost four months. Don't you think we should start being more reserved?"

His forthright answer to that was to pull her to himself and kiss her 'till she could scarcely breathe.

"Don't like being reserved, especially with my Katie."

"Well, frankly, neither do I. But I thought I should at least be a proper lady and make the suggestion."

Wanting to stretch out the delicious scene, as even a proper lady might, she got out her sewing.

Unexpectedly, at least in her scripting, he disappeared from view.

She heard him opening drawers, then loudly closing each one.

"Payne, what on earth are you doing?"

"Looking t'hell for a clean handkerchief. Whereinhell didja put 'em?"

In the bedroom, she opened a drawer and pointed, "Right t'hell there, where they always are."

He was standing behind her, his hands gentle but heated on her hips.

"I do believe this maiden has wandered into a trap."

"Katie, I adore you."

"Oooooooohhhh, Payne!" Suddenly she was (again) quite "en negligee".

Still, even in such blissful hours, a foreteller of tempest would approach their doorstep:

Several afternoons later, while Muggsy was laboring at the mill and Katie was busy with her housework, Elsie Peabody made an unexpected visit. The big blonde, whose wedding to Dr. Phillip Sutton had recently and unexpectedly been postponed until late January, showed a face fairly dragging on the floor.

"Come in, Elsie, if you can wade through all this junk. I've been cleaning out closets. Honestly, I don't know how Payne ever collected so much absolute junk.

"But hey, girl, what's wrong?

"You look absolutely awful!"

"Katie, I came to say goodbye."

Katie couldn't believe the words she'd hear from her best friend.

"WHAT?"

"Philip has left me."

Elsie's sniffles advanced to sobs poured onto an already wet hankie. "For the last two days, he didn't phone. Today I got this letter from New York, no return address."

Katie read:

Dear Elsie, I'm sorry, but I can't go through with the wedding. It's hard to explain, but I fear I can't stand the confinement of married life. I hope you will understand and will some day forgive me. Goodbye. (signed) Your friend, Phillip.

Katie put her tender arms around her absolutely disconsolate best friend.

"Elsie, this is terrible."

"I should have suspected something when he postponed the wedding. But no, stupid me, I loved him so much, anything he did was all right."

Katie led her to the sofa and sat down beside her.

"I'm going to visit my Aunt in Chicago," Elsie said mournfully.

"Right now I'm in too much of a muddle to think straight.

"Maybe new horizons will some day bring me back," was her grandly romantic (prophetic?) furtherance.

"Elsie, I'll miss you so much. But gee...well, if you just have to go, maybe it's best that you do for just a little while. You'll surely meet someone much better for you than Phillip is or ever would have been. Payne said he had a very shady reputation."

"No, I'll NEVER love again," was Elsie's dramatic reply, replete with gestures..."NEVER."

"Oh, Elsie, I'll miss you."

"Same as I will you, Katie. For always and always, you've been my best friend."

Sadly the two did embrace; then they parted company.

"I feel so bad over what happened to Elsie," Katie told her Husband that evening as she set the dinner table.

Muggsy, hammer-in-hand, worked to loose the lid of a case of beer and started loading the bottles into the ice box.

"Yeah," he said casually, snapping the top off a bottle and taking his first large swig of the evening, also letting out a loud and contented BURP. "Too damn bad that happened to a good ol' gal like Elsie. But she'll live through it. Funny though, and just like George said, I too keep thinking I saw her doctor before, somewhere...someplace. For sure, I only know I didn't like him. Elsie's well rid of him.

"People all get their share of unhappy times. Hey, look at me; I took some bad bumps, but I wound up getting you."

"Thank you for 'getting me', I think, whatever that means."

She kissed the side of his nose.

Muggsy grunted, and rubbed where her lips had landed.

"I'm offended! You didn't use to rub away my kisses."

"I don't like nose-kisses. Never did like them."

She moved her lips to his neck. "So how's that?"

"Very nice. Say, Lady, I sure hope your ol' Husband don't come till real late tonight. You're a sexy number. Love to be alone with you, know what I mean, take off your shirt. Then we could fool around, know what I mean?

"Thank you, Mister lecherous old iceman. I'd adore to fool around with you too. Did I ever tell you, one of the things that first attracted me to you was your nose? I've always paid particular heed to people's noses, like as a viewing glass into their characters, know what I mean?"

"Dope!"

He swatted her backside.

"So romantic the iceman.

"But oh my, what's that awful odor?"

"Comes to me like burnt beans."

"Oh my goodness, it is the beans. I left them on too long."

Wildly he kissed her.

"Whoinhell cares about lousy beans?"

"OOOOhhhh, Payne! Now I really feel sorry for Elsie."

George Periwinkle stopped by the next day, and heard about Elsie.

"Awful thing that is, hurting such a sweet girl."

"Yeah. Have a beer?"

"Thanks, don't mind if I do. Really, though, that Sutton oughta get his teeth kicked in. Wish I had a shot at him right now."

"You liked Elsie a lot, didn't you?" asked Katie.

"So much that it hurt like crazy to see her with another guy, above all with that nose-in-the-air Sutton. But she never knew I was alive. Oh well, time to write off that lovely dream."

Which last deduction could later prove that reporter Periwinkle was indeed not omniscient.

Life dared to go on in Marberry, even against Elsie's sorrow.

Muggsy's wintertime labors in the steel mill were hard spent, but now he could better put up with the rugged toil. He had Katie to return to each evening. And then the thoughts of spring, fast approaching, when Baseball would again take over his working hours.

When the millwork occasionally slacked off, there were hunting trips into the mountains with J.T. and Cliff. He had first asked Katie to accompany them. But "like Mother-like Daughter," she soon decided such forages weren't for her; she wasn't one to pursue discomfort or enjoy the killing of animals, even for food. Besides, the child within her was more-more a definite presence felt.

"I'll be your snow bunny, Payne, holed up in our warm and comfy hutch, waiting for big daddy rabbit to come home."

"For sure then, I'll make it back home sooner than I usta, sweet mama bunny."

Before the Bantons could realize it, March had again swirled upon them. Time to go south for spring training! True, it wasn't far south, a slightly sheltered spot out of the wind-and-snow belt, less than a hundred miles from Marberry. But the sparse miles took little excitement from the training trip.

Hard to believe, considering the glories preceding them, but such journeys were the best part of the Bantons' life together.

Manager Muggsy had his work cut out as he made the change-over from just-player.

From the patient teacher that was Cliff, he learned about directing the conditioning of his men, a task previously owned by Cliff.

Muggsy would also decide which players made the squad, and, toughest of all, would have to tell others they were traded or else cut adrift. He sometimes found himself wishing he hadn't been so thoroughly "one of the boys" in all his playing days.

At least most of the older players appreciated their manager's situation. One of them, an outfielder who'd been especially close to the Lion catcher, got the word early, via the grapevine, that his timeworn legs wouldn't be acceptable for another season. Before he quietly left the camp, not waiting to be pink-slipped, he penned a note for his manager:

> **Muggs: I won't put either of us through the torture of you having to cut me. It's been great, playing with you all these years, also playing the nights away. Now I'll quietly get lost. But hey, if you're ever looking for a good ol' Lion coach to help you whip the kids into shape, you know where I live, and I'll be here quick-like.**

Before long, Muggsy did find in that faithful friend the ideal coach-confidante for himself and his Lions.

Along those cutting-loose lines, manager Banton stuck like glue to a policy learned from Cliff: When checking out the swarm of bright-eyed rookies who showed up for the Lion camp, he concentrated on NEVER learning their first names and thus making the dismissal of any of them a thing of pain for himself. He would merely post a roster on the bulletin board twice a week; the absence of any of them on golden list was a tidy dismissal. Of course, if Muggsy could place any of them on other teams, he'd surely do that.

All the while the new player/manager had to sharpen his own abilities before the start of another season. And daily heat-treat his ouchy knee.

Oh yes, he usually found time to be with Katie for a while in early afternoon. When he thought he was too busy for that, Cliff chided him, "Act like a Bridegroom before any ho-hum days set in for you and her! Go home and grab a nooner. It'll be a lot of dreary hours before glorious tonight is here."

Long gone were the training camps when after-dark would for Muggsy mean carousing with the other Lions, seeking the delightful company of "Baseball Annies," as the femme followers of the scene were tagged. Then any old night on the town for the roaring Lion gang could end in a fun-filled barroom brawl. In emergencies, "good ol' Cliff" bailed them out of the pokey.

All of which Muggsy could now remember with quiet fondness.

In the twilights, he and Katie sometimes rented a carriage. (They'd come to camp on the train with the rest of the Lion squad and assorted Wives...some of those admittedly on hand to make sure their mates stayed out of trouble at eventide.)

On those carriage outings, sometimes the Bantons would enjoy a swim at a nearby beach, that in their newest-style bathing suits. Muggsy's was a sleeveless one-piece suit. Katie, he thought, was dangerously dazzling in a shirtwaist, pantaloons, her hitherto unbared knees, calves, and neck open to the breezes.

Or the Bantons might visit a nickelodeon, the first of which had recently opened in Pennsylvania's McKeesport. The evening's performance offered a 20-minute screen performance, with piano accompaniment, for five cents; Oh yes, amazing it was and well attended by those who could afford the fare.

Still, as it seemingly must happen to all, disquieting waves did roll onto the Banton shoreline.

On a spring-training evening when they were buggying through a pastoral scene, they stopped by the side of the road. And grew lost in watching a fetching sunset.

Another couple rode by on a tandem.

"Did you notice that girl wearing bloomers?" asked Katie.

Muggsy muttered something that might possibly have indicated YES, as he dozed in the buggy seat, and rhapsodizing in the concert of the creek and crickets.

"Hey, wake up, Husband! Doncha like my company anymore?"

"Yeah...uh...what? ...Sorry, Bride. What were you saying?"

"I spoke of bloomers. I said, in some places women are wearing bloomers."

"I should hope! I once listened from the top of the stairs at our house in Schantzburg. Mom was giving 'lady advice' to a niece of hers. Mom told her that 'decent ladies' must wear bloomers, clean ones too. Otherwise it could be embarrassing in a train wreck."

"Oh, Payne, I mean modern bloomers that can be seen, not old-style underpants bloomers. In lots of places, girls wear stylish bloomers called pantalets, or pantaloons."

"Indecent!"

"Not at all. They cover all private parts. But tell me, Mister Smarty Pants, from where came the word 'bloomers'?"

"You got me, Missus Know-It-All."

"In the last century, there was this lady, Amelia Jenks Bloomer, who died thirteen years ago. She came from Homer, New York, where she was married to a newspaper Editor. She also put out a paper named THE LILY, which pushed TEMPERANCE, also THE LIBERATION OF WOMEN.

"To emphasize her preaching, Amelia wore something called 'Turkish pantaloons', which were worn under a skirt reaching to the knees and the pantaloons down to shoe-level. Now Mrs. Bloomer wasn't the first to wear those pantaloons, but she made them famous because she wore them wherever and whenever she lectured, which was a lot of times. (Then, after a while, those pantaloons got to be known as 'bloomers'.) Well, she felt she had to find some way to come on outstanding, to emphasize her teachings."

"Indecent nonsense!"

But Katie wasn't about to climb off her soapbox, which perversely she enjoyed even more because of the obstinate male who was her audience.

"For a while, the Bloomer movement died down, though there were small groups continuing to push it. When I was a little girl in Marberry, I remember how some awful men used to chase those ladies, even throwing mud at them and yelling things like (Let me see if I can remember...) 'Heigh ho, the carrion crow, Bloomer Girls are all the go. Twenty tailors take the stitches, but it takes these girls to wear the britches!'"

"Wish I'd been there to throw mud with the other guys."

"There were even some mean little boys following the men, chanting the same awful thing, and throwing rotten eggs. Oh, it made me so mad, I wanted to join the lady marchers, but Mom wouldn't let me go. Anyway, the Bloomer Girls just kept on marching, and I loved 'em for that."

"Indecent," snorted the broken record that was her Husband.

"Now other ladies are picking up where Amelia Bloomer left off...like the 'Gibson Girl' that just went by on the bike, wearing 'athletic bloomers'. And I've been hearing more about Semanthia Smythe, a schoolteacher out of Corncrib, Iowa. She and her Emancipation followers dress in bloomers for any and all occasions."

For Muggsy a light suddenly turned on: "Yeah, Semanthia Smythe, that was her name, the hook-nosed broad that used to manage the Bloomer Girls Baseball team I once played for. Granted, she knew a lot of Baseball, but she and the other broads looked so ridiculous, running around in their underwear.

"Emancipation of indecent women, haw! The idea has to die. Broads oughta stay home, barefoot and pregnant, that's what they oughta."

After that, and almost instantly, there came between Mr. and Mrs. Banton a wind of icy texture. Katie found herself distanced from her Husband, the first time it had happened...but not necessarily the last.

After a while, they would again be washed over by the lovely scene, and would finally return to holding hands.

Katie, somewhat scared by what had happened, decided the bloomers-and-emancipation subject should be a taboo subject for themselves, at least for the immediate THEN. She had lost no faith in her beliefs. Still, in the fact of Muggsy's blatant chauvinism, she wasn't sure she could properly control her responses if the touchy topic was quickly resurrected.

The utter joy of that pastoral evening had not been broken. But it definitely had been bent.

Chapter Twenty Six

Oh yes, in today's Baseball, there are/have been players of high authority, those easily matching the "most" of old-timers in that respect. When a noted St. Louis pitcher was asked how he'd react if his catcher gave him pitching advice, he responded, "It won't ever happen...because I simply won't stand for it."

Corroboration from his catcher: "Y'know something? He tells it the way it is."

After another day of rigorously prepping his Lions for the coming season, Muggsy sat with Katie in a tree-filled park that was gracefully accepting the shadows of evening.

Her back was against a massive oak tree which, in the best of springtime fashion, was showing the first signs of new life.

Muggsy's head was in Katie's lap, a treasured posture from which he departed only to sip from the beer bottle in his hand. Mostly, though, the Lion manager settled for admiring glances at his well-favored Wife, pondering the prospect of the nighttime ahead when she would be his to lengthily love. Occasionally he would glance past her to the darkening sky.

"Hurry up, you old nighttime, for me and my gal!"

But for now....

"Did I tell you, Katie, that in a few days the Big League clubs will start moving in here to play us?"

She bent down to kiss his forehead in the most of empathy.

"They'll be heading through here from their southern spring bases on the way to starting their seasons."

"Does it make you feel badly again, wishing you were in their Big League shoes?"

"Sure, sometimes. Mostly, though, I'm adjusted to big frog-in small pond."

Tears came to her, as she buried her lips on his forehead.

"Strictly between You and me, Dearest God," she breathed silently, "thank you everlastingly for Payne's bad knee."

Came April and the end of spring training. Time to head for home, Lion Park, and the brand new season of 1908.

Again the kranks were waiting in overflow numbers at the railroad station.

Again the mayor escorted the Bantons into a waiting phaeton, which would lead the parade down Central Avenue.

"I'm so self-satisfied," confessed Katie, "that I feel almost ashamed. Imagine little ol' insignificant me with the most popular fellow in town!"

"Yes, my Princess. And where shall I tell the royal coachman to drive this carrier on its golden wheels?"

"Same direction it's been headed, which is straight to heaven."

And further again, from J.T.'s office floated a mammoth banner, held at each end by Clara and J.T.:

WELCOME HOME, ALL THREE BANTONS.

Before the first pitch of the new season, Muggsy gave the capacity crowd his own version of a ceremony that had long been seen-to by Cliff:

"We asked Mr. Teddy Roosevelt to be here today, to throw out the first ball. He deeply wanted to join us, but has notified us that he's too busy training more Rough Riders...just in case. So Blind Tom will do the honors."

The crowd went wild over that show, mentioning the idolized President.

Thus it was that the 1908 season of the United League of Baseball Clubs did open to wildly appreciative attendance-sellout games.

In each city it was plain as the nose on any face that hope for a pennant sprang eternal.

But soon it was just as evident, the hard-playing Marberry Lions were simply too much for their opposition.

When the Lions ran, it was as if the Devil himself were chasing them. When they slid into bases, few were the basemen brave enough (foolish enough?) to face their steel.

Manager Muggsy Banton cared not whether his men scrapped with umpires or with enemy players. But heaven help the Lion who didn't rhubarb with SOMEONE. Almost every game saw another of them ejected for arguing too long, with too much fervor.

With each game, the Lion faithful came to idolize their field boss the more. It seemed nothing Muggsy did could be wrong.

This was never shown more convincingly than in a home game VS the Panthers.

Muggsy, at bat, had just watched a third call strike sail by him.

"Yer out!" blared Blind Tom.

Muggsy turned and said something to Tom.

From the stands, the crowd let out an unmuffled roar of protest.

"Kill the umpire!"

"Naw, killin's too good for the bum. Let's tar 'n feather him, ride him outta town on a rail."

The Tom-tirade continued without letup until game's end. As the last out was made, sealing a Lion loss, the fans poured onto the field, bent on punishing Blind Tom before the park police could move in to protect him.

One oversized bully made it, shoving the ump to the ground and jumping on him. Then another, moved onward by that first successful attack, threw dirt in Tom's face.

Finally the police managed to scatter the mob, but even then some of the fans were reluctant to leave. As the officers escorted the frightened ump out of the park and into a paddy wagon for a safe journey home, still more angry spectators stood by, muttering threats.

In the Lions' dressing room, Cliff told Muggsy all that had happened after the players had sped for their quarters following the final out.

"Muggsy, you got super-loyal people out there. If you asked them, they'd likely burn down city hall."

"Not that bad, I hope."

"That bad it definitely is...you just don't know your own power in this town. So, starting tomorrow, I'll have to hire more auxiliary cops, to ring the field immediately after the last out."

"I hope they didn't hurt Tom. The poor guy was just doing his job, trying to make a living."

"He got a few bruises, and a mouthful of dirt, that's about all."

"Hey, I'm glad, and please tell him I said so."

Reporter George Periwinkle moved to Muggsy and asked, "Just what was it that you said to the ump after that called third strike? Your kranks figured you were mad as hell at Blind Tom because he blew the call."

Muggsy was shocked.

"Oh no! All I told Tom, when that third strike sailed by me, right over the heart of the plate...honest, all I told him was, 'I'd give ten bucks to have that last pitch over again'."

Still the time had come when the ballplayer was just one side of Muggsy, as fervently attested to by the other Lions:

"He's not the same guy he used to be," said Skeeter Newman. "Remember, he used to hang around this dressing room for an hour or more after every game, playing poker and swapping yarns about Baseball and broads.....remember?"

"Yeah," Jumbo Malone joined in, "then we'd go out together and raise fifty kinds o' hell, 'way into the morning. Now, soon as a game's over, he's the first one dressed and outta here. Said she'll have a tub of hot water ready for his aching feet, then hand him cold beers while he sits there soaking."

"Maybe I should get hitched," added Skeeter, "'soon as I find a rich and gorgeous girl who's too proud to let me work."

Came June, then the day when Katie went to the hospital.

"I'll be so lonely there, Payne, without you."

"I know, Katie baby, and I'll miss you the same, even more. But you and the new Lion manager have got to have the absolute best of everything, all the care that a hospital can give you."

"Payne....?"

"Yes, Katie...forget something?"

"It's just that....well, you won't be too disappointed, will you, if it's a girl?"

"Why of course not! I'll love her every bit as much, even twice as much if she looks just like her Mama...Besides..."

"Yes, Payne?"

"Besides, maybe it's about time for lady managers. Might be more exciting that way."

How prophetic could he be?

On the field during warmups before that day's game, Muggsy collared George. "Need a special favor."

"Whatever, you got it. Gotta keep you cool and composed on this big day."

"Thanks. Katie's close to delivering. Just in case there's news from her, the hospital will call here. I'll sure appreciate your camping near the phone."

"You got it."

For eight innings, a scoreless ball game.

No news from the hospital.

The top of the ninth saw the Bears go down in order.

With one out, the Lions loaded the bases. Muggsy at bat. He took two called strikes. Then figured the next pitch would be a "teaser," on the outside of the plate.

Muggsy's guess was a near-disaster.

As the pitch zoomed inside, there was a shout from George, "IT'S A BOY!"

Muggsy never saw the pitch. He was turning to the catcher and yelling, "IT'S A BOY!"

Plunk. The horsehide caught the Lion catcher on the back of the head.

The field came up to meet him.

All the Lions ran to home plate as the winning run was forced across the plate.

For what onlookers at the plate took as a long time, Muggsy lay motionless. Finally, though, he blinked his eyes, seeing all the anxious faces above him.

"Wild pitch, ol' Dad, and you got beaned," the enemy catcher told him. "Sure glad I had a hunch; some voice from above must've told me to call for half-speed."

Muggsy saw George above him. And he remembered.

"IT'S A BOY," he yelled another time, trying to stagger to his feet.

Frightened as they hadn't been in a while, Cliff and George tried to restrain him.

"Can't wait. Gotta get to Katie. Come on!"

With his two friends supporting him from each side, Muggsy hobbled to first base to make the play, and the victory, official. Then they helped him to George's carriage. Off to the hospital. Flying up those steps, George worked to keep Muggsy moving in a straight path. At best, the results were tottery.

Muggsy's spikes made a loud clatter on the hospital floor. The solemn-faced nurse at the front desk protested in stern fashion:

"Sir, will you please be QUIET?"

Both the new Father and George tossed apologies over their shoulders as they continued an awkward attempt to tiptoe to Katie's room.

He slipped in there, while George waited in the hall.

"Katie, Katie baby! Are you all right?"

"Well of course. Did we win the game?"

The baby boy was brought in to Katie and Muggsy.

Soon afterwards, the proud Grandparents arrived.

"What a darling!" cooed Clara. "Such an adorable chin."

"That is far more than just a chin," Katie informed her Mother. "It is the BEginning of a genuine lantern-jaw."

"Doesn't look a bit like your chin, Ma," mused her Father. "I wonder where on earth he could have gotten it."

"I go for those blue eyes," raved the new Dad. "They remind me of a pretty little girl I once met on the floor at the ball park. Name was O'Brien, or something like that. I heard later she'd been kidnapped by a second-rate ballplayer."

"What a terrible fate," added J.T. "I heard she could have sampled some other guy, name of Henry."

"Don't let 'em tease you, Mom," put in Katie. "Henry Sample was a lovely boy. Trouble was, when he found out he couldn't hit a curve that broke on the outside part of the plate, he had to send a wire to his Mom, 'Get my room ready, these professional pitchers are too much'."

"Anyone can make a mistake," Clara was pleased to admit.

Muggsy put a big arm around her.

"I have a peachy keen Mother-in-Law."

"Why, Payne, what a nice thing to say." And Clara wiped away some tears.

"Time for all visitors to leave," announced the nurse.

Katie's parents left, joining George in the hall. But, at an insistent call from Katie, George entered the room long enough for a look at the new arrival and a kiss on Katie's cheek.

Then the Banton parents were alone.

"Thank you, Katie, for our son, and for the chance to know you and love you."

"You're welcome, Big Daddy. I wouldn't have missed any of it, nor what's to come. Oh I do love you!"

Chapter Twenty Seven

I REMEMBER A QUOTE attributed to Philadelphia Athletic immortal Frank (Home Run) Baker who in 1913 hit the unheard-of total of 13 round trippers: "Playing ball is fun. But winning is the most fun of all! ... No, let's correct that: Winning big is closest to heaven."

The remainder of that '08 season passed quickly, with the Marberry Lions finishing a full 12 games ahead of the second place Bears.

Wrote reporter Periwinkle:

"The Lions can thank Muggsy Banton for their success. He's as smart a manager, as inspiring a leader as we've seen in many moons. This scribe places his abilities right up there with those of a famous name-alike, John "Muggsy" McGraw (AKA "Little Napoleon"), the indomitable manager of the New York Giants."

"I've got a damn good press agent," Muggsy told Katie on a relaxing Sunday morning, as she nursed baby Jimmy, named for his Grandfather.

"George didn't say half enough. You're not just a smart Manager; you're the best by far. I wish I were writing for the CLARION: I'd really tell the readers in superlatives, in spite of some obvious tactical errors I've seen you make lately."

"Izzat so?"

"Yeahzat's so. Although, I grant, it's hard to be perfect."

"Thank you, 'finicky mom' for your generosity. But you'd better stick to arranging flowers and let George handle the reporting. Probably he can better understand that, when your best bunter shows up with a hangover and can't play, then maybe the situation best calls for hitting away."

"How'd you know what I was referring to?"

"'Cause I don't like giving orders I don't want to give, even if sometimes I have to give 'em and they can lose ball games."

Katie struggled to unravel that Baseball-ese, then said, "Uh...O.K. Still, with all the speed on your ball club, I'd do a lot more hitting and running."

"Bullshit! You talk like home runs are nothing."

"Payne, I asked you, please, don't talk like that in our home."

"Double big fat bullshit! Anyone who knows can tell you, guys who hit home runs eat big steaks. Singles hitters make enough for hamburgers....Katie, you sound more and more like Semanda Smith, or whatever was the name of that bossy bloomer broad."

She caved in, "Oh Payne, I am sorry. This was supposed to be fun-talk, but then it got out of hand, and I don't see why you had to use your nasty words too. ... Well of course it would be impossible for me to manage; I don't know nearly enough about the game, even after all you've taught me. And maybe Miss Semanthia Smythe doesn't either, certainly compared to you. Oh Payne, please don't be mad at me; it makes me feel so terribly bad."

Just then, Cliff arrived on the scene. He caught the chill somehow pervading the Banton household.

"You two used to get along rather nicely, as I remember it."

"I was telling him what a great manager he is. But the conceited pup is arguing with me, so I'll praise him more. I'm onto your tactics, Payne."

She emphasized that last by mussing her Husband's hair.

"Quit that!"

She mussed some more. He jumped from his chair, flung an arm around her waist and pulled her to the couch.

"You asked for this, Katie Banton."

"Oh no, Payne, NO. Please don't tickle me! Beat me if you must, but please...you know I just can't stand that."

Screaming in protest, she rolled off the couch, onto the floor. Muggsy, now thoroughly fired, followed her, grabbing her again before she could go free. And resumed the furious tickling of her.

From the easy chair where he reclined, Cliff drawled, "In the midst of your obscene rasslin' match, if anyone is interested, I heard a great story today; seems there was a traveling salesman who..."

"Give up, Katie? Promise not to muss my hair again?"

After which he tickled her some more, his gnarled fingers working amazingly quickly under her arms, then up and down the sides of her. There was nothing Katie could do against all of this, because Muggsy was sitting on her stomach, holding her prisoner.

"I'll promise ANYTHING, yes I will, if you'll...please...let me go...let me up, oh please!"

One last, and extended, administration of his hands over her body.

"But this is nothing compared to what you get next time, if you force a next time."

"Whatever will Cliff think?" she asked, coming off the floor, embarrassed as she re-secured her blouse that had been opened from neckline to waist.

With the warmth created in herself by the wrestling with her lover, she also sincerely wished that Cliff was elsewhere by a long distance.

Muggsy's thoughts were doubtless similar, because he added, "Who the hell cares what Cliff thinks?"

"About my story," the Lions' owner went on...."this salesman was going down the street, and delightfully he bumped into a farmer's Daughter. Then they, oh, whatthehell happened then? You cave-folks have me all discombooberated; well, maybe it was a lousy story anyway. So let's talk about our hunting trip. You got those maps, Muggsy?"

Thus for the Muggsy Bantons, time did march merrily. But the return of a big blonde could shatter the easy going.

Chapter Twenty Eight

Of all the Baseball tales oft' told, few get more telling-mileage than this: Hall-of-Fame Cardinal pitcher/baserunner Dizzy Dean slid hard into second base, to break up a double-play, and was beaned by a thrown ball...Blared the next day's headline: <u>X-RAYS OF DIZZY'S HEAD REVEAL NOTHING.</u>

Soon then did come an eventful afternoon in late April, during Muggsy's second season of leading the Lions.

On that afternoon, he was at the Lions' ballyard, guiding his team to still another win.

Katie was at home with Jimmy, contentedly so. She was also putting her Husband's numerous clippings into a scrapbook.

When a knock sounded on the door.

On the front porch stood Elsie Peabody, Katie's best friend, returned from her jilting-exile. In bright red bloomers, she was more stunning than ever. At least so thought Katie.

Then joyously the two best friends hugged each other.

"Katie, you look just wonderful. And can this be Jimmy? He's so husky; he'll be a real followup of his Daddy."

"Oh my, if Payne heard you say that, he'd just burst with pride.

"Elsie, it's just grand to see you again. Why haven't you written lately? And let's look at those bloomers! Elsie, on you they look positively splendiferous."

"Certainly," agreed self-assured Elsie, "because now I am <u>living</u>. And, as some poet said, we look the way we feel. Katie, I have been where women have at last learned the true meaning of life....LIBERATION.... FREEDOM."

She accompanied the last words with dramatic hands-in-the-air gestures.

Before such a storm, Katie simply had to give ground.

"Please sit down, Elsie, and tell me just everything about you."

"I'm now a Bloomer Girl."

"So I see."

"Our leader is Semanthia Smythe."

"Yes, I've heard about her."

"Our life-goal is the emancipation of all women."

"Oh my!" Contented Katie had to suppress a giggle.

"I've never been so serious," Elsie told her, ruffled by Katie's reaction. "Katie, it's a tremendous movement, by far the greatest thing that's ever happened. And guess what: I might soon be made a District Chairwoman."

Katie acknowledged the evident importance of that.

"We are out to undo the wrong perpetrated on centuries of suffering womanhood, just like you, housewife Katie Banton."

"Me? Suffering? But I've never been so happy in my whole life."

"That's your delusion of now. By the way, what do you think of my bloomers? I'm not sure red is my best color."

"I..."

"That's the way I feel too...how can you know till you try?

"Now, Katie, just you relax and let little Elsie get you straightened out."

"Sure, Elsie...sure."

Katie was too rocked on her heels by "little Elsie's" overwhelming self-assurance to utter more. She merely collapsed on the couch and waited for the tempest to wear out.

"I just arrived in town with Semanthia. She's our absolutely SUPREME LEADER for this part of the country. She's striving to bring back the best of all worlds. As you know, the movement slowed down some after Amelia Jenks Bloomer died in 1894."

"I read about that."

"Glorious Semanthia and her followers, certainly including myself, are fighting to revive our cause, in spite of all the ignorance and narrowmindedness we constantly encounter from stupid...ugh!...men.

"I told Semanthia that Marberry would be a plummy central base from which to carry on our vital recruiting processes."

"You do look great in bloomers," Katie had to again admit.

"You, Katie, and all my other friends will look just as great in them.

"As you leave the old, worn-out degraded life behind you."

That last, accompanied by rather violent gestures, so amazed Katie that once more she could gather no counter-argument. So she and her best friend retired to the bedroom, where Katie tried on the red bloomers.

"See, I told you you'd look just fantastic in them."

"No, Elsie, there are types, and then there are types, and I'm not this type."

"Nonsense! It's just that these are 'way too big for you, Katie. You'll come on simply super in your own size and style. I have some in my hotel room that will be just perfect for you. I'll bring them by here tomorrow."

Katie was horrified by the thought of Payne somehow being at home when Elsie arrived with her style show.

"I just don't think..."

"Nonsense! You'll see that Elsie knows of what she speaks."

After which the two girls chatted about other matters.

Elsie tried on some of Katie's hats. But paid little heed to her new gowns.

"They're pretty if you like them," she agreed in a put-down manner, "but they'll soon be completely displaced from modern thought. Oh I know, Katie, you think I'm going overboard. But soon you'll see, Semanthia and I are completely right. As she says, we are one hundred percent right, and the only reason we can't be more right is that there is no more than 100 percent."

Katie remembered when a high school teacher had used that line in a class attended by Elsie and herself, also how impressed Elsie had been by it. But she figured that clarifying the point would be inappropriate for this moment.

"A little while back," Elsie was continuing, "we had a bonfire dress-burning in the middle of downtown Rochester. You can bet, just all of my gowns went into those happy flames, there in New York.

"FREEDOM. This world was made for women too, maybe even mostly for women, considering the important of the lives we live, against the degraded existence of...ugh!...mere men."

That night, when Katie told Muggsy what had happened (of course excluding certain pertinent passages in her narration), her Husband thought she was joking.

"She wants to do what to women? Guess I'm slow tonight; those extra-inning games, even when we win 'em like we did today, take a lot out of a guy on a hot day like this one was. Anyway, Katie, beg pardon but I don't get the point of your funny story."

"Please pass the butter. No, Payne, I'm not joking. Elsie insists on 'liberating women like your wife from shame and misery'. Can you imagine me being 'liberated' from you and Jimmy and our wonderful home?

"For damn sure, now I've heard everything. Someone ought to have a helpful but forceful chat with Elsie, explain the facts of life."

Katie had long since learned this about Muggsy: He blunted no words for nicety-sake.

Her coffee cup raised to her lips, she put it down suddenly.

"I've got this simply stunning idea: Elsie needs a man."

"She sure does, a real man to take her to bed every night and show her what makes life worth living."

"Payne, please stop being so utterly crude. I mean the companionship of an intelligent and understanding man who'll rid her of the most outlandish ideas she got from Semanthia Smythe...not that I think all those notions are so bad."

Muggsy, determined to enjoy his dinner, ignored the last part of Katie's heated discourse. Instead he asked her, "Mrs. Cupid, which man are you thinking of chasing to that big, busty blonde? ME? Gosh, I'd hate to be stuck with that awful job, but then you know I'd make almost any sacrifice for my darling Wife."

"Certainly not YOU. You're my man, and I'll scratch the eyes out of any female that even winks at you, including Elsie, maybe even especially Elsie.

"But what about George Periwinkle? He's awfully nice, and he told us, right here at this table, that he likes Elsie a lot."

"I don't want to get mixed up in matchmaking. If those two are meant for each other, they'll get together without any help from us."

"Payne, you can get so awfully unromantic. Why don't we ask George and Elsie to dinner here tomorrow evening?"

"You mean Elsie in her bloomers in this house? Naw, I don't think...."

"Oh please, Payne. Pretty please?"

He'd forever found it difficult to refuse anything to his Katie.

"Well...."

"Oh thank you, Payne, thank you so much. And I promise, I won't do any matchmaking, once they've met again."

"So O.K., Mrs. Cupid. So now what's for dessert?"

The next night's dining at the Banton home seemed to be fully enjoyed by both couples, no matter the Emancipation currents swirling around them.

Katie chose the pale blue dress that Payne said "did the most for her."

Elsie wore white bloomers sprinkled with large green polka dots. Long black stockings anchored those.

She was annoyed that "ignoramuses" had taunted her as she walked up the Bantons' residential street on that evening. But she had paid no visible heed to such boorishness.

Muggsy and George refrained from opinions on her costume, neither feeling qualified to handle the subject without acidity.

Dinner-talk was strictly small chatter: From Muggsy, "Did you see the great story in today's paper about Teddy Roosevelt's latest speech, what it means to be American?"

From Elsie: "I was fascinated by the article about the motion picture producer David Griffith, who said he'll soon make movies to surpass his others. Oh my!"

Then trade-talk: Hubert noted that Boston Pilgrim pitcher Cy Young had amazingly won 20 games every year he's pitched for the Pilgrims, and some years had won 30-or-more. "His arm must be made of India rubber."

"I read," offered Elsie, "that they call him 'Cy' instead of his real name (Denton True) because his fast ball streaks through the air like a cyclone."

Wow! Muggsy and George were considerably admiring of this knowledge, and Elsie glowed at that. "Oh," she then said casually, "I read a lot about Baseball, because our Emancipation leader, Semanthia Smythe, is wild about it. But most of our women know little or nothing about the game, so Semanthia gets lonely for conversation."

Grudgingly from Muggsy: "When it comes to our game, she knows a lot."

From George, to lighten any disturbing waves then in the air, "Katie, this is easily the best meat pie I ever ate. Muggsy, with such great cooking, I don't see how you keep your weight down."

From Muggsy: "Yeah, I got this weight problem...I can't wait for the next meal."

"Here we go again, Joe Miller Joke Book of 1741," was his Wife's rejoinder.

Katie was further determined not to get the Baseball conversation of that evening pass without her own contribution:

"When it comes to rubber-armed pitcher, how about the New York Highlanders' Jack Chesbro? He's started, and won, two games pitched in two days. And he told his manager, Clark Griffith, that, if necessary, he'd pitch every day in a week."

Muggsy's glance at his Wife was indeed filled with pride for such an expose of knowledge on his game.

After dinner, Elsie volunteered to help Katie with the dishes.

"I accept your offer. We'll do 'girl talk' while the men are relaxing."

George and Muggsy went to the porch for a round of cigars.

"Nice girl that Elsie," commented Muggsy, "even if she's gone goofy on that Liberation hokum."

"Yeah, great girl, and what a body, even if she does wear those silly bloomers. I could go for her, but I don't suppose I have a chance."

"Don't be too sure, George. You might have a lot better chance than you think; it's hard to know a woman's deep-down feelings, especially some of the crazy, mixed-up broads of today. They don't have their feet on the ground like our Mothers did.

"Yeah, George, down deep that Elsie just might have a passionate yearning for you. I could've sworn, couple times during that meal I found her giving you the eagle eye when you were looking the other way."

In the kitchen:

"George is nice, isn't he?" asked Katie, as she brought down the soap from the cupboard.

"He's all right," was the grudging admission from Elsie, as she carefully secured an apron over her bloomers, "as far as men go. But they don't interest me any more. Semanthia has liberated me from all that nonsense...Oh, Katie, I do like your dishes, such pretty patterns."

"Thank you. I had something of a battle with Mom over them; she wanted me to get more 'straight' patterns, like hers. But I won that battle for my own house. And know what? More and more, as I establish independence from her, in a loving way, we're getting to be good friends like we never really were before."

"I think that's wonderful. And, speaking of friends, I admit I would like to have some man for a good friend, as long as he respected my independence as a woman, free of all those bonds that used to be. Maybe I could even accept your George on that basis, but I doubt that he or any other man I've met is ready for such advanced and intelligent thoughts."

"Payne said that George is strictly a high-class guy," noted Katie, forgetting her no-matchmaking promise in the tempest of the moment. "Also one of the very best Baseball reporters he's known. He says that, in the 'human' sort of way George covers the game, he shows an understanding that almost no reporters come to. Although we've never learned the WHY of that ability."

Elsie, seeing that Katie's campaign was picking up tempo, then retreated.

"So phooey on men! All they're good for is to break a poor girl's heart, once they think they've got her locked up as 'only a bird in a gilded cage', like the song puts it. Then they walk out, leaving her flat...Of course, Katie, in deference to you, I think we can make Payne the exception to prove the rule."

"Oh?" Katie wondered if she should be grateful for such crumbs.

"But now I have some special news for you," announced the blonde guest, as she wiped dry the dishes that Katie handed to her. "Or maybe it's too soon for telling."

Any slightly-miffed feeling of Katie's was then washed away by curiosity.

"Oh please, Elsie, at least one little hint."

"Well, all right, but only because we're best friends."

"Semanthia and I have this superlative idea. There's another Baseball team in Marberry, as I understand it."

"That's right...the Burglars, of the Federated League, which is a lower classification than the Lions' United League. But Payne says the Burglars are 'rotten-lousy', and almost always wind up in the cellar."

"The cellar?"

"That means in last place."

"Well," announced Elsie in grand style, "then why shouldn't the Emancipators buy the Burglars and install a woman as a manager? We have lots of money behind us. Katie, you'd be amazed at the names of some of our biggest backers, Wives of rich and famous men, even if they're still scared stiff to let it get out that they're our 'angels'. One of their Husbands is terribly high in government."

"Oh? Please, Elsie, just one hint."

"No, Katie, I can't...I promised Semanthia I wouldn't to anyone....But I can tell you that the Husband of one of our biggest donors managed a team in the World Series just a few years back. If I tell you, promise not to tell Payne?"

Promise confirmed, and information passed along.

"Oh my!" exclaimed Katie. "Payne said that couple was so happily married!"

"'Happily married' is as 'happily married' does," said Elsie the sage. "But I promise, Katie, when I can give the other names to anybody, you'll be the first to know."

At which strategic point in the conversation, Elsie Peabody put down the dish towel. She further gathered herself to her full (and considerable) height, preparing for the announcement she would then cut loose:

"Katie, we want you to manage OUR Burglars Baseball team..... that is, ours as soon as Semanthia completes the deal to buy them, which should be any day now."

Muggsy's Wife quickly withdrew her hands from the dishwater. Hands on her narrow hips, she stared at huge Elsie in disbelief.

"Sorry, Elsie...I guess I didn't hear right."

Elsie repeated her pronouncement. Katie broke up in laughter.

"Me? Manage the Burglars? Why, that's about the funniest joke I've ever heard."

Elsie was taken aback by the rebuff, but still marched forward.

"It's no joke. Semanthia and I are dead serious in wanting you to manage the Burglars. Not only for your knowledge of Baseball, either, but also because hiring the Wife of the famous Muggsy Banton would be a prestigious coup in this part of the state."

Elsie quickly threw in her ace: "Believe me, you'd be extremely well paid for your work."

"But....but....Elsie, the Burglars are Payne's pet hate. He calls them 'the sloppiest bums in the history of the game'. It's gotten so we don't even mention them in this house, unless we want to turn any good day into a sour one.

"Besides, I know almost nothing about Baseball."

"Oh? Just a little while ago, at dinner, your Payne said you know more....what was it he called it....?"

"Inside Baseball."

"That's it. He said you know more inside Baseball than most of his players."

"He was just being kind. Besides," she protested, handing the last of the cleaned dishes to Elsie, "women just don't manage ball clubs."

"Granted, the old-fashioned, downtrodden women wouldn't dare. But the new, progressive, LIBERATED women will jump at such a chance. We'll even make you General Manager and Manager of our team."

"No, no, I won't, I never will! I won't even think about it. Payne wouldn't allow it."

Disdainfully, Elsie sniffed, "Too bad about His Majesty. Are you his slave? Don't you have any freedom? No, of course not. But Emancipated women will grasp at any such opportunities to march forward in our brave new world.

"Katie, I'm ashamed of you."

That put-down did hurt, but Katie strove to ride over it with no animosity. Best Friends, she had long ago decided, are hard to find, and well worth struggling to keep.

Smiling through it, she placed a gentle hand on one of Elsie's.

"Sorry to disagree, Elsie, and you know I don't want bad feelings to ever come between you and me. But face the situation as it exists: After all my years of supreme no-purpose, I'm now the 'contented kitten', Wife, and Mother. I love things as they are, and wouldn't do anything to disturb them...Come on, girl, let's rejoin the men."

"Oh all right, but won't you at least come to our rally tomorrow night at the town hall? It'll be BIG , and I promise you'll love it. Besides, it'll be the first time I've presided over something so enormous. I'll be real nervous, and it'll mean a lot to have you in the house, giving me support."

That plea was hard for Katie to reject.

"Really think I should?"

"Sure, why not? At least sip the delicious waters of the brave new world for all women."

Katie clapped her hands at the oratory, smiling devilishly.

"Well...oh, I don't think that will hurt anyone or anything. Payne and the Lions start their next road trip tomorrow evening, so he surely won't know.

"Understand, Elsie, I'm not really against your movement. I know there's much good in it. Women who support themselves and can do as good or better at the same work a man's performing certainly should get pay equal to his.

"Today, sadly, she's lucky to get paid half of what is his paycheck."

"My, Katie, what a great speaker you'd be for our movement!"

"Still," Katie demurred, "the way you're going about it seems just too radical, so unnecessarily hurting to so many families. Couldn't you perhaps tone down the blaring and get the same results?"

"Confidentially," admitted Elsie, "I almost sorta-kinda feel the same. I told Semanthia that, too. But she wants it her way, and she is, after all, OUR LEADER.

"And sometimes it does take radical actions to wake people from their apathy!"

When the evening at the Bantons' wound down, George helped Elsie into the black cape she'd brought with her. Its darkness against her blonde tresses did, he thought, make her even more stunning.

"Elsie, may I walk you to your hotel?"

She fished for a negative answer. But what came out was, "All right, George. Thank you."

They walked mostly in silence through the cool night.

George was satisfied just to be by Elsie's side. He hoped the feeling went both ways, but her reticence kept the matter in doubt.

For Elsie, that night indeed held warm thoughts of the lanky reporter. But she put them aside..."Why bother? Men are just too much trouble."

Back at the Bantons', Katie said nothing to Muggsy about Elsie's ideas regarding the purchase of the Burglars or of her own managerial possibilities. Again, no use getting him worked up by mentioning the next night's rally, especially on their last night together for some weeks.

Still, Muggsy had heard rumors: "Know what someone told me today (but then you can't believe this anyway), he said those stupid bloomer dames, the Emancipators, isn't that what they call themselves, are out to buy the Burglars and make some dame (which I guess would have to be Semanda Smith) the new manager. Can you possibly imagine that bad comedy happening, and right here in our own home town?

"Well, like I told you, and surprisingly enough, old lady Smith does know a lot of Baseball. But no team of men would ever knuckle down to a dame. Besides, old dumbo-what's-his-name that owns the Burglars would never sell them. They're a bunch of sloppy bums, but they make pin money for him because the kranks still need their Baseball when the Lions have to be out of town, even stinkin' Baseball."

Katie sat at her dressing table and combed her long, red hair before braiding it for the night.

"Payne, I don't see why you're still mad at the Burglars. So their Manager called you a few names in the paper. So what? Why not just forget it?"

"Never! He called me a one-legged tramp. Nobody talks like that about Muggsy Banton without someone paying for it."

"But why don't the Lions ever play the Burglars, at least once a season? It should be a real crowd-pleasing gate attraction."

"Cliff once suggested it, but the Chief of Police nixed it. He said both players and kranks would wind up tossing a riot.

"And now the stupid Emancipators, in their stupid bloomers want to buy the stinkin' Burglars," snorted Muggsy. He had to grab his sides 'midst an almost ungovernable spell of guffawed laughter.

"If those Emancipators bought the Burglars, I don't know who'd be worse off, the stinkin' Burglars or the dumbo dames walking around the ball park in their underwear."

Katie thought it best to bite her lip and turn away.

"Just kills me, it does, when I think of most dames at ball games. What a sick joke! Did I tell you what happened to Bugle Nose Stankorsky on Ladies Day?"

Almost curtly, Katie answered in the negative. She didn't dare turn and face her Husband.

"See, 'the Nose' was supposed to pitch last Saturday, against the Chiefs. They're the team he's pretty much owned for a long time, like just toss his glove onto the mound and they're whipped. But this time, just before the game, he asked me to please use another pitcher.

"Remember," said Muggsy, fighting to hold back his bursts of laughter, even as he told Katie the story, "that was the day Cliff was trying out the new idea of all women admitted free, a rose given to each of them, crud like that."

Katie recalled it clearly. She had thought the sight of so many ladies in the park, some with men but more of them within their own female groups, was such a pleasant relief from the usual loud-talking, all-male crowd.

"But," Muggsy went on, with assorted haw-haws thrown into the telling, "Bugle Nose told me he couldn't stand the screeching of the stupid dames in the stands. Said it wasn't just the noise they made, but mostly the crazy things they'd yell at. To them, a great catch was nothing to get excited about, but a high pop fly was sen-sational. Then they'd start screeching, and nothing had even happened in the game, but it would turn out that some dame in a funny hat had just walked through the stands."

Katie was unbuttoning her dressing gown and stepping out of it. She knew her Husband's piercing eyes were on her, and he was ready to move on her. She knew that although her back was to him.

"So they can yell at strange times," she told Muggsy, "but what's the difference as long as they have fun? You 'superior' males have got to admit, it's probably true that hardly any of them have had Baseball explained to them like I have to me."

Muggsy ignored her calm reasoning, and continued with his non-stop orgy of male-type recollections: "Now you know me, Katie baby. I'm THE BOSS os the Lions; if I say one of my men pitches, then dammit he pitches or he gets fined twenty bucks, out of his next paycheck. But last Saturday ol' Bugle Nose begged so hard to be let off. Said that, if I'd agree, he'd work an extra game whenever I asked him. Well, understanding manager me...."

Katie, then stepping out of her pantalets, was grinding her teeth so hard that she bit her tongue, and had to struggle against crying out against the pain.

"Well, understanding me, I knew what he meant; them stupid dames drive a catcher crazy, but he's got no place to run and hide, so he might as well settle in and face the music.

"But what my ol' buddy Bugle Nose was begging for seemed reasonable, since pitching is such a high pressure job, especially for a guy like Bugle Nose who can get so worked up out there on the hill."

Katie turned to face Muggsy as she sat on the bed and began to slowly remove her stockings from her trim and well-shaped legs. For the way he was coming unstrung at the sight, Muggsy was having trouble proceeding with his narration, but still he talked on, though he was locked onto the thought of the night of love to come.

"So I told ol' Nose, 'Okay, sit it out', and he was so grateful that for a minute I thought he was gonna lick my hand.

"I used Three-fingered Brutz on the mound that day, as I'm sure you remember. He's so deaf, the dames' stupid hollering couldn't get to him. He beat the Chiefs, remember, gave up just two hits.

"Yessir, those dumbo dames that don't know no Baseball are sure nutty nuisances at the ol' ball game."

One more round of haw-haws, and Muggsy had talked himself out. He retreated quickly to his copy of the CLARION. Katie, doubly glad she hadn't mentioned Elsie's idea to him, quickly slipped into her nightgown and slid into bed. Soon Muggsy was there beside his apparently sleeping Wife. He reached to untie the top ribbon of her gown.

She acted as if he'd awakened her, and moved away, every so slightly, but the gesture was definite.

"Aw...c'mon Katie, it's our last night together for a long time. Aw, Baby..."

Again he approached her, and still another time she moved from him.

"I'm sorry, Payne, but please, not tonight, all right? I'd better be ready to go to Jimmy; he seems to be catching quinsy, and he's so restless. Besides, you'll need your strength for tomorrow's game, and then the long train ride too."

Muggsy, his built-up passions having to suddenly evaporate, same as for put-off Husbands over the ages, had no true defense versus wifely negatives.

So settle in, Muggsy Banton, to your lonesome. As the SHOWBOAT's famed Cap-n Andy used to shout, "It's only the BE-ginning."

. . . .

• • • • • • •

Baseball advice that might endure through the ages: Brooklyn Dodger manager Charlie Dressen (1951-53) would tell his guys how to emerge from a game's crucial spot, "You just keep on playin'...I'll think of something."

For Katie, the following day went wrong.

It came on sultry, too sticky for any comfort at all. Nor did Jimmy's wails of misery help the situation. True to his Mother's diagnosis...although she had mostly invented his illness on the spur of unharmonious moments of the night before...Jimmy was sick. He told the world about it, as lustily as only a one-year-old boy can proclaim.

The CLARION of that morning didn't make the day any more joyous for Katie. Most of its front page had been given over to deriding the Emancipators and their impending rally of that evening. A blaring cartoon showed them parading under the caption: **PROTESTING MISSES AND THEIR MADAMS, EACH OF WHOM HAD YET TO LOSE HER BLOOMERS**.

Katie heard Muggsy chuckle at breakfast, reading the caustic cartoon and accompanying stories, then adding corresponding opinions of his own.

She wished she hadn't agreed to attend the rally. If word of that somehow got back to Muggsy, the lovely tranquility of their home would likely be blasted to smithereens, even past the discord of last night.

By afternoon, Katie had decided to skip the rally. After all, "General Elsie" would be so busy, she wouldn't even notice Katie's absence.

But what upset Muggsy's Wife even more: She had eagerly wanted to see the last game of this Lion home stand, be close to her Payne a bit longer.

Still: "I'm sorry, Payne. I just can't leave Jimmy while he's sick; anybody I got to sit with him just wouldn't care as much as I do!"

"Sure, Baby," he told her with a hub. "I understand." And truly he tried to.

"Payne, I guarantee you're not feeling worse about our separation (this afternoon or the weeks ahead) than I do. But surely in a few days Jimmy will feel better. Then I'll see if I can leave him with Mom, and I'll catch up with you on the road. Now hurry, or you'll be late getting to the park. I'll have your bag packed by dinner time. Mom will watch Jimmy while I go with you to meet Esmeralda."

"You're the absolute greatest."

"As long as you think so, Payne dearest, I want no more."

Even at that late moment, he considered a "nooner", but sadly the idea seemed self-defeating. The guys had told him that such delights were limited to honeymoon times. And of late he had suspected that they were right. There was something out of sync about fondling Katie while she was insisting that he hold Jimmy.

In spite of any cheerful talk, Katie's own frustration didn't lessen. The day grew hotter, and Jimmy protested his misery in more volume.

In the heat, the ice-box door seemed to expand. Whatever, it wouldn't close. Before the repair man arrived, most of their food was spoiled.

Katie, pushing furiously onward, started to pack Muggsy's suitcase. But his shirts hadn't been returned from the laundry. She reached her peak of woe when she burned her hand on the stove. Too much! In the bedroom she flung herself onto the coverlet and cried huge tears.

After a while, she arose, looking at her streaked face in the mirror. Then she was able to laugh at herself.

"What a sight, Katie Crowley Banton, art thou!!"

Came a knock at the back door. It was the delivery boy from the meat market: "Here's your order, Mrs. Banton. Mr. Campbell says to tell you he's real sorry. He said he knows Muggsy hates liver, but it's all he had left by the time you phoned him. A lotta ice-boxes must've gone sour today; we had a big run on other meats."

"Please thank him for the liver. Put it in the ice box and I'll pay him tomorrow."

When he came out of the house she again called to him. "Have you heard how the Lions are doing?"

"Yes'm, a while ago. Game was tied, 9-9, end of fourth. Looks like they'll be playing till dark, if the heat don't get 'em first."

"Anyway," she told herself, "I'll have time to freshen up and fix dinner."

"Can't hear you good, Mrs. Banton," he shouted up her way.

"Never mind; just talked to myself. Thank you again for the meat."

"Yes'm."

By the time Muggsy finally arrived home, Katie was in cool, white linen, and dinner was ready. But her Husband was in an absolutely foul mood.

"We lost, 13-11, in twelve, and I got tossed out of the game. Well, why shouldn't I tell off Blind Tom? Their guy was out at home by a country mile; that's what beat us. That stupid ump oughta be put away where he can't hurt no one!

"And those glass-armed chuckers o' mine can't pitch decent enough for an old ladies' home."

She brought him a chilled mug of beer.

"But you're still leading the league by three games. You're just tired tonight. Drink your beer, Payne, you'll feel lots better."

"Leading the league, ha! Couple more games like today's, and we'll be lucky still be in the lousy league."

Jimmy started to cry again, and Muggsy grimaced.

"It's the heat," Katie explained. "He's almost well; the doctor said so."

She brought in dinner.

"Liver?!? You know how I hate liver. I'd rather eat dirt."

"Liver was all Mr. Campbell had left, except for some sawdust. I guess I could have baked you the sawdust in tomato sauce."

He didn't think that was funny.

"A lousy meal to come home to."

Katie tried, and desperately, to push back her anger. "I'm sorry, Payne. I did just everything I could to make our last meal together for a while a nice one. I even fixed some of the rolls you like so much. But, even if you don't like my meal, you could be polite. It's been just a terrible day."

Fighting back more tears, she turned away from her untouched plate and fairly flew up the stairs. Too tired to care anymore, she again dropped onto the bed, letting the sobs come.

For every minutes, Muggsy sat at the table, gazing in terrible loneliness at the empty chair opposite himself. From the nearby back room, naught but silence from the sleeping Jimmy, finally "worn to sleep" from his unending screaming of the afternoon.

Finally the Husband too headed upstairs. In the bedroom he leaned down to kiss Katie's forehead.

"Sorry, Katie, for being such a lousy heel."

That helped a lot.

"It's all right, Payne. This heat beats up on everyone. Oh, did you find your shirts on the hall table? They came so late, I haven't yet gotten around to packing them."

"Yeah, they're all socked away in my bag. Thank you more than I can say, and now I guess it's time to go."

"I'm afraid so. Oh, that must be Mom downstairs, come to sit with Jimmy."

Just before they left the house, Muggsy approached his Son's bed for a last look and a gentle squeeze of the baby hands.

"Sure getting to be a bruiser."

"Sure is," agreed Katie, proudly linking her arm in her Husband's.

"Yells like a trooper, too. And hey, will you look at that jaw stick out!" bragged Dad. "Give him a few more years and he'll be telling off Blind Tom as good as his old man does it."

"Really, Payne, he's just a year old."

"O.K., so he's not quite ready yet," admitted the Father, pushing back a wisp of reddish blonde hair that had fallen over Jimmy's forehead. "After all, I didn't have my first scrap till I was four."

"Same here; I had one when I was four."

"Three," corrected Clara from the doorway. "The little boy next door said something highly uncomplimentary about your favorite dolly. You then gave him a good beating. He cried for a long time. All the little girls in the neighborhood referred to you as 'Naughty Kathleen'. But, as I remember, no one else said things not-nice about your dolly after that brawl..."

"Oh the memory of a Mom!" gloried Katie, hugging Clara.

"Get going now," Clara bade them, "and good luck to our Lions. Also, please tell Bugle Nose to stop telegraphing his curve. He's flicking his left ear just every time before he comes in with that pitch."

"Hey, Mom, helluva sharp Baseball tactician you're getting to be. Howsabout signing on as a coach with my ball club?

"But, speaking of Bugle Nose, he won't be with us for a few days. He got knocked out of today's game in the third inning. Said his arm didn't feel right. Said he felt something give last night when he was helping a ladyfriend move furniture up at her place. So I told him to take a rest from pitching and moving furniture. But, Mom, when he joins us again on this trip, I'll sure lay it on him, that curve-giveaway you spotted."

A few minutes later, after delaying Muggsy's parting from home and family as long as possible, he and Katie finally had to leave for the depot, to face their first being-apart since they'd been wed.

It was almost dark as they walked through town in the coolness.

"Lots of people on the streets," noted Katie. They must be out to watch the Bloomer Girls parade."

Oh, how she immediately wished she hadn't made such a knowing observation! Still, the fact was before them: Coming down Main Street were hundreds and hundreds of women. The marchers seemed to number at least a thousand, for their seemingly endless surge forward.

There were tall women and short ones, pretty and plain and ugly ones too. But they were alike in that each was bloomered, to bring inescapable attention to their fervently expressed issues.

At the head of the suffragettes were Elsie and a tall, hook-nosed woman who seemed even more furiously intent than did her femme compatriots.

"Well, I'll be damned!" muttered Muggsy. "That's ol' Semanda Smith. Been a coon's age since I put on a wig 'n bloomers so I could catch for her ball club. But hey, I'd never forget that gawky ol' dame."

"E-MANCIPATION," shouted the horde of oncoming females.

"Someone should oughta turn a fire-hose on 'em," snorted Muggsy. "If I had time, I'd do it myself."

Katie bit her lip so hard that it would be sore for days, a solid reminder of when she'd nearly screamed at her man right out there on Main Street.

The wave of women continued to pass by them, torches lighting up the evening and making their banners easier to read:

WOMEN MUST BE EMANCIPATED.
Give us the vote!
and
LET'S BLOOM IN OUR BLOOMERS
also
We demand the vote!

"I didn't know there were so many stupid dames in Marberry. Guess a lot of 'em flew in from outta town on their broom handles."

Impossibly, Katie pushed back more anger, while she sought to continue the farewell hours on an even note, leave good thoughts about good-bye.

"The CLARION said there'd be more than three thousand of them at the rally tonight."

"A lotta dizzy dames with nothing to do. They oughta be home barefooted and pregnant."

Instead of flinging his chauvinism back in his face, she brought up something she'd kept on the back burner:

"Payne, I..."

He knew that hesitant look. Concern was heavy on her head, but she wanted to spare his feelings while still making a strong point. He'd long since learned, a desirous Katie Crowley Banton was just about as easy to deny as a runaway truck headed downhill.

"Shoot, Katie. I've got a tough hide."

"Payne, will we ever be able to buy our house instead of just renting it? Now, when we need repairs, it takes so long for our landlord to get around to them, and it costs so much for us to rent. Worse, everything we pay for the rent is gone forever...my Dad taught me that.

"It would be wonderful if we owned the house...if we could just make payments on it and dream together of the day when it would be all ours...I know Mom and Dad would lend us money, to help out for just a little while."

She felt his tensing at that last, and wished she hadn't said it.

"You know I won't accept money from them."

"But just a small loan for a little while...?"

"You KNOW I won't accept money from them," he repeated heatedly.

He would take a short minute to regain his calm, then came on quietly, "So we won't be buying for a while. Cliff would give me a raise if he could, I but the improvements on Lions Park cost him a lot."

Those had been turbulent moments; now Katie knew when to quit.

By the time the depot and Esmeralda were in sight, they were again holding hands, dreading the moment of separation.

"Payne, I'm going to miss you terribly."

"Oh me too, Baby. Join me, please, soon as you can. And don't worry about money; after the season ends, I'll put in some extra hours in the mill and help our situation, to take the best possible care of you and Jimmy."

One more hug. Then Muggsy was gone for a long time.

Watching Esmeralda fade into the distance, Katie then turned toward home, lonesome as she couldn't remember when.

Chapter Twenty Nine

There was the manager who ranted to Baseball beat-writers gathered before him, "To you bleep-bleep so-called 'intellectuals', <u>liberty</u> means the right to mind every bleepin one else's business, especially mine!"

Walking then through downtown Marberry, Katie stopped to watch the parading Bloomer Girls pour into Town Hall. She felt the awful need for something besides her self-pity of the moment, some other thought-medicine for the sudden gap in her life. And oh how she wished she hadn't rejected Muggsy last night, for whatever silly reason.

Around the stream of women, the male onlookers had increased. They jeered at the bloomered females, who jeered back by ignoring them.

Heard by Katie: "Poor miserable broads, they don't know what they want next. Worst thing could happen to 'em would be for wishes t'happen."

"Yeah, fouled up as they are, if they got their stinkin' "equality", then they'd be twice as confused as they are now. Real soon then, they'd run home to the guys who provide them and their kids three square meals a day, with a roof over their head."

"Yeah, then they'd drop their underpants when they're told to, no silly speeches given in the meantime."

The last drew a generous round of guffaws. Katie moved quickly away to the fringe of the women-watchers.

As the last of the paraders entered Town Hall, someone touched her shoulder. "Well hello there, Katie Banton."

She turned to face a bountiful brunette, of loose and limber "cowgirl design".

"Betty Holcomb, what on earth are you doing here?"

"Oh, just a curious kitty watching all these other tabbies, same as you...also observing the stupid ol' dirty-talkin' hounds."

With this last, she jerked a thumb in the direction of a knot of jeering men nearby."

The Wife of Lion third baseman Butch Holcomb looked cautiously around herself to make sure no one was listening.

"C'mon Katie, let's you and me go in to watch the hullabaloo. After all, who'd be hurt by our just taking a sneaky peek at what goes in the old corral. I mean, for sure, this mess couldn't happen in my ol' safe-and-sure Oklahoma."

"Does sound like fun. But I'd die if anyone recognized us!"

"We can go in the side door and sit near there. We can leave as soon as it's over with."

"Weelllll, all right. Like I read in a book somewhere, 'If I dood it, I get a whipping. But I dood it anyway'. Heck, what harm can it do? And it should be fun, seeing my friend Elsie Peabody in action.

"But I can stay just a little while...got to get home and relieve Mom from baby-sitting."

Thoughtfully, Katie paused for a minute, then added, "Honest, Betty, Muggsy and all those other 'superior' males sneering at the parade made me so mad, I liked to throw up."

"Amen, Sister Katie, Amen."

Spurred on by empathy, Katie continued to unload:

"I'm still tasting blood from where I bit my lip, not telling that Husband of mine what's what and how dumb he can be when he sets a mind to it."

"Amen again. Maybe we'll at least get _that_ much out of this Emancipation thing, that we can all just say what we think!"

When the Marberry Town Hall was filled, the earth had cause to quake.

Elsie, in purple blouse and bloomers (the latter covered with white polka dots) and long legs encased in white stockings, took the podium.

"You ladies should be proud of Marberry, whether it's your home town for always or just for tonight. It has been chosen as the site of this historic meeting for this mightiest of movements. Certainly, the female citizens of the world will be re-energized by our gathering here tonight, speaking out as we must."

The tremor increased, and wavering hearts took courage.

As Elsie gestured wildly, the ladies came to their feet. In unison they shouted with her, "EMANCIPATION WILL BE OURS."

Like the others, Katie felt an inner surge of fire, especially when the females jamming every cranny of the hall gave out with a resounding BATTLE HYMN OF THE REPUBLIC to the organ's thunderpeal.

Outside the hall, complacent males were unaffected by the commotion.

"Hiya, Pete," a smallish and withered old man greeted the cop on duty: "What the hell's going on in there, some religious revival?"

"Tell you, Sam Streck, those goofy dames sound like they're having a fit, then falling in it. But the chief says they gotta be protected from any and all harm."

From Sam, the mighty baseballer of another time, "Man, it's gettin' wilder by the minute. I'm glad my Bessie's safe at the library."

"They sound insane, like a tent-revival that's out of control, like I once saw in Oshkosh. Hey, like you, Sam, I'm glad my old lady is visiting her sister. She's gettin' old, and sometimes fuzzy-thinking, but at least she has more sense than to take up with jazz like this."

Back inside the hall, their Wives yelled as loudly as the others, also chanting the movement's own battle cry:

> "Down, down with men, we'll never be slaves again.
> Whatever the cost and how long the fight,
> We'll win this battle in DE-fense of right."

Semanthia Smythe, dressed in all-black, then spoke: "Ladies of Liberation, let us never forget June, 1948, a time etched in the life-blood of our movement. It was then that our brave forebears, Elizabeth Cady Stanton, Lucretia Mott, Martha C. Wright, and Mary Ann McClintock, issued the call for convention for the rights of all women. They met in Wesleyan Chapel of Seneca Falls, New York and adopted our sacred Declaration of Principles, did those 68 women and the 32 brave men who stood beside them. Now, if you'll all please stand, together we'll re-read those principles and re-affirm them...Please read from page 3 of your programs, joining me:

> 'We hold these truths to be self-evident, that all men and women are created equal. But the history of mankind is a history of repeated injuries and usurpation on the part of men toward women, having in direct objective the establishment of an absolute tyranny over her...We hereby assembled demand for women the right of equal education, the right to teach and preach and earn a livelihood. It is also the sacred duty of women of this country to secure for themselves the sacred right to the elective franchise.'

"Now please be seated, and Sister Peabody will continue the meeting."

More wild cheering followed, and Elsie gave it several minutes to build before she raised her hand and urged its subsiding.

As Elsie would re-take the podium, somehow, from out of the hall's throng of females, she spotted Katie Banton. She quickly called Semanthia to her side and feverishly whispered something. The pinch-faced leader nodded with newborn brightness framing her face. Katie saw Trouble crossing the road in front of her. But it was far too late to escape.

Elsie stepped forward to the front of the stage.

"Glorious Sister Emancipators, we have with us the forceful and talented lady who will soon be one of our most accomplished workers. She's the new manager of the Marberry Burglars Baseball team, living proof that all women can succeed at anything. Let's give Sister Katie Banton a big, big, big hand and get her up here on this stage."

She pointed out the redhead, and all eyes followed her direction.

"No!" gasped Katie.

From Betty Holcomb: "Girl, you've been had. Me, I'm makin' tracks, fast tracks out of here before my Butch finds out and hangs me from the old oak."

Quickly, Betty vanished out the side door, into the night's darkness.

Deafening shrieks demanded that Katie move up to the stage. She tried, above the din, to signal NO to Elsie and the women near her.

"Get her up here!" demanded "General Elsie".

Determined hands pushed Katie aisleward, and others would move her stageward. Finally, with seemingly no choice, unless she wanted to physically struggle, she gave in and completed the journey up to where stood Elsie.

"You shouldn't have done this. Payne will be just furious."

"So who cares about stodgy old Payne? Of course he won't like it. Men never want to see their women do anything worthwhile; they just want us at home doing the dishes and minding the kids.

"Sister Katie Banton," she told the wildly excited assemblage, "will now address you enlightened Emancipators. Katie, tell our ladies how you'll manage the Marberry Burglars Baseball team."

Finding herself choiceless, Katie faced the lusty ladies.

"Speech!" yelled the frantic femmes.

"That's our girl!" yelled Bessie Streck, quite evidently not at the town library.

"E-mancipation," screamed Sarah Gilhooley, definitely not visiting at her sister's house.

"Girls, Sisters, Eman...I really haven't decided...."

She turned to Elsie with a hopeless palms-up gesture. "I really don't know what to say. Of course I won't manage the Burglars."

"Thank them for their confidence in you; tell them you'll give your all for Our Glorious Cause."

No place to run or hide, and Katie, on the edge of tears, hated making a scene in public.

"I'll tell them what you said, Elsie, but I'll back out tomorrow."

"Thank them."

"Thank you, ladies."

They liked that, as clearly noted by their screaming applause.

"Great, just great," said Elsie. Obviously she adored being "seneschal"-top dog.

"Payne will be furious, even though I only pretended to accept...just to get out of here alive."

"Phooey, double phooey on your old Payne."

Elsie again turned to the audience: "Sister Katie Banton will prove again that women can do anything men can."

"Only we can do it better!" called out a fat woman in the hall's back row of seats.

"DOWN WITH ALL MEN," chanted the assemblage. And they continued to chant it as they left the hall.

When Elsie reached her hotel room after the rally, Katie was waiting.

"I bribed the clerk to let me in. Elsie, I'm backing out right now."

Elsie's expression showed hurt.

"But you promised to do it."

To emphasize her feelings, she flung her hat onto the bed.

"Elsie Peabody, you tricked me into it," Katie told her angrily. "I just accepted rather than embarrass you. Now, when I back out, as I must and will, they'll blame only me."

"The CLARION already has the story, and there's no way to reach their press room this late at night," fibbed Elsie.

"That moon-eyed George Periwinkle interviewed me after the rally," the blonde continued. "He said he wanted to talk to you too, but you'd beat it out of there in such a hurry. And do you know, he even had the gall to ask me to go out with him tomorrow night 'to further explore the story'? As if I'd lower myself to go out with any mere man."

"Then will you please give me his phone number?" asked Katie, all the while having the feeling "she was kicking a dead dog," as Muggsy would have phrased it.

"Look, Elsie, I know you have it, because you told me so. I'll phone him and kill the story. He won't like it, knowing he's been deceived."

"I lost his phone number," Elsie fibbed again. "I lost it on purpose, you could say, because I wanted no connection with that...that moon-eyed man."

"Elsie, I don't think you're being honest with me. And we used to be best friends."

Elsie was stung by that. "I'm sorry, Katie. I'm just doing what's best for all of us."

"Payne won't like this," repeated Katie.

"And why not, I'd like to know," Elsie returned to the attack. "He should be proud of you, especially when he realizes that your success as a Manager is due to his teaching."

"Who'll take care of Jimmy while I'm working? I can hardly ask Mom. She'll be every bit as furious with me for 'accepting' as I am with you for tricking me."

"We'll handle all expenses for the best of day-care for Jimmy. I told you that, with our organization, money is really no object."

Elsie led Katie to the sofa, and sat down beside her.

"Look, Katie, I'm sorry for not being above-board on all this."

Katie was finally turning loose the tears that all evening had wanted to flow. The big blonde put an affectionate arm around her chum of many years.

"Look, Katie, it hurts bad that you don't want us to be best friends anymore. I hope and pray that some day soon we get that back. I'll never forget that when Phillip, that...that beast...ran out on me, it was you that stood beside me, to hold me together when I just didn't want to live anymore. Now I need you again, and I know there's some pain for you...well, at first...but I'll bring you through it like you did for me.

"Katie Banton, stop working up reasons why you won't take this job of managing the Burglars. Why, we'll pay you two hundred a month plus a most generous expense account. Are there any other Marberry girls you know of who make that kind of money?"

Katie's mouth flew open in amazement.

"But that's forty more a month than Payne makes! You couldn't possibly be serious, paying so much for an inexperienced manager like me against what a professional like Payne can make."

"But I am serious. Our motto says, anything men can do, we can do better. So we should get paid more for 'better'...Tell you what, Katie, if you'll stop this mindless arguing right now, I'm sure I can get that paycheck up to two-fifty a month plus the expense account. Oh yes, that many 'spondulicks', or big bucks, or call them what you will."

In Katie a tremor was growing.

"Why, with all that money, we'll soon buy our house, instead of throwing the money away on rent, like we do now. Payne would have to be proud of that."

But then Katie remembered something her Dad had taught her: "Don't ever undersell yourself. When you have received what seems the best offer you'll get, strike for just a little bit more."

"All right, Elsie, I'll take the job at a starting salary of (gulp) two-seventy-five."

"You've got it, Burglar manager. I knew you'd come to your sense. I may even borrow a few dollars from you; you're now making considerable more than I am."

"Any old time...But one last condition: You'll have to pay me two months salary to start with. So, when Payne comes home after this road trip, we'll be able to make a down payment on our house."

"It's a deal. Come to the Burglar park tomorrow morning at ten. We'll sign the papers and give you the two-month check."

"But are you sure the Burglar owner will sell?"

"We offered him so much money, he couldn't possibly turn us down."

"My, this does sound like a high-powered operation."

"Strictly. As I told you, big-name, big-money ladies are behind the movement...So how about coffee and crumb cake to seal the deal?"

"That cake sounds especially good. It's been a long night and I'm famished."

Of course, no way to predict the concussions to follow.

Chapter Thirty

This quote was reported to have come from New York Yankee owner/beer baron Jacob Ruppert: "Money is junk. Anyone who hustles for it can make all the money he wants. Now what is truly difficult is to get along with people. Like I got to try getting along with my player Babe Root." (Colonel Ruppert seemed to have trouble remembering "Ruth".)

"I hate to sell," said the Burglar owner the next morning in his woebegone office at his dingy ball park.

"But I can use the money, especially the large loot that Miss Smythe is throwing at me. Yeah, I'll sell, though I'll catch blue blazes for selling out to women, especially to these 'Emancipators'.

"Frankly, Mrs. Banton, if the new manager was a Johnny (or Jane)-come-lately, I still might back off. But in your hands...well, the team has to get better. The sorry manager of ours was leading a bad team. And, if your Husband has given you any decent part of his Baseball savvy, as I'll wager he has, then go to it!"

He signed the document of sale to the ladies of liberation.

Just as promptly, Elsie handed Katie a check for five hundred and fifty dollars. A proud Katie put it carefully into her purse.

"Now I want to talk to my team," announced the new manager.

"They're on the field, waiting for you," said the ex-owner. "No game today, so naturally they're expecting the day off."

"We'll see about that. I never heard of a last-place ball club getting a day off in mid-season. What they'll need is plenty of work."

"Suit yourself. They can be mean guys, at best not what you'd call 'nice people'. Although, to maybe give them a break, maybe that's because they've sunk so low into losing. I think the flighty term is 'the insouciance of defeat'."

"But please do watch out for Del White. Nasty bozo he is. In fact, he's so thoroughly nasty, I figure he had to be born that way."

"My Husband told me about Del. Outstanding long ball hitter. Cliff Hartwick said Del wanted to play for the Lions, but the Lions don't want drinkers."

"Uh....one more thing, Mrs. Banton, and I hope you'll accept this in the cautious spirit in which it is offered..."

Katie didn't like the ominous tone.

"I hope you'll please avoid any personal contact with the players, especially going into their dressing room."

An uptight Elsie moved forward. "Oh, why is that? Why can't our manager go anywhere in our park?"

The former owner shifted his feet uncomfortably, evidently wishing he hadn't introduced the subject.

"Tell you what, Miss Peabody, we had an ugly scene a week ago. I've repeatedly warned my manager that no girls were allowed in the dressing room, but, whatthehell, he'd got so he didn't give a sh...sorry, ladies...didn't care anymore. Then one morning last week, couple of hours before game-time, the kid who sorta fills in as our clubhouse boy, came running up to this office after me, real scared he was. He said our players had a girl down there and they were going too far, roughing her up, you know what I mean. I put out an S.O.S. to the cop working this beat, guy named Gilhooley, to get down there in a damn hurry. We hit the dressing room just in time to get the girl off the floor, you'll pardon my blunt language.

"After she got her clothes back on, I had to pay her off real solid, to keep her quiet. But at least we kept it out of the papers.

"Mrs. Banton, I hope I haven't shocked a fine lady like yourself. I just wanted you to know what you can be up against."

Elsie, angry as Katie had ever known her, stepped forward.

"May I ask, Sir, why you waited until the deal was signed before you told Katie this insulting story?"

He fidgeted for a moment, then admitted, "Guess it was because I didn't want to blow the money for the sale."

"Which means," Elsie continued her stormy state, "that you are just as dishonest, just as 'cruddy' I think the expression is, as other men."

"I reckon that's so. Still, a deal's a deal."

She turned to Katie, "If you want, we'll stop payment on the check and invalidate the sale."

Semanthia stepped forward, likewise in a tizzy, but this one was differently directed.

"Now wait a minute, Elsie; I wrote that check. What right have you to interfere in this manner?"

"Because Katie is my Best Friend, and I think she's been legally wronged in signing before she was given full information. Please stay out of this, Semanthia....... Well, Katie, stay or go?"

Another hard gulp from Katie before she spoke boldly.

"I need the money. I'll still manage the Burglars....But thanks Elsie, for the support."

Katie and Elsie and Semanthia headed for the field.

"Elsie, I wish you and Miss Smythe would please not come with me when I talk to the team."

"And why not, I want to know?" asked a still highly ruffled Semanthia. "We want to see men taking orders from a liberated woman. And it is our team."

"I know what I'm talking about, Miss Smythe. I understand ball players, or at least I think I do. These unhappy Burglars might put up with one woman, but three would be too many, especially here in their home park."

The used-to-be owner had followed the women from a distance, but now he stepped forward.

"Never mind what you ladies might think of me; I still suggest you listen to Mrs. Banton. She makes sense."

"Oh all right," muttered Semanthia. But she needn't be uppity. I know players too."

She turned to Katie, "You win this time. So all right. But I happen to think that I too understand Baseball players. And I find your high-handedness to be offensive.

"Just be sure in the future, whenever or wherever your represent Our Movement, you're properly attired (in bloomers.) That's firm in your contract."

"But..."

"She's right, Katie," Elsie told her friend. "It's in the fine print. But you'll look great in our new styles. Swell chance to show off your great legs."

With which she turned and followed Semanthia's unhappy exit from the field.

From her first look at "the crummy park across town," as her Payne had often described it, Katie had been disappointed almost to the point of being sick. She was that used to the well-kept Lion home field, with clean stands and a manicured field.

At the Burglar's home, the dirt was rocky, the grass was in the final stages of expiration, and unpainted fences showed gaping holes. The stands were likewise untended, badly in need of paint and a thorough sweep-up.

At home plate, in street clothes that generally showed more neglect, Burglar players waited sullenly. Few of them were shaven, as Muggsy, same as Cliff before him, had insisted the Lions be at all times.

Summing the dismal situation, Katie decided that what she had to work with was even less (far less) than she had expected.

"All team members over here," she nevertheless called out in what she hoped sounded like authority. Or had it been but a squeaky-voiced effort?

The players slouched forward, ready for rebuke.

"They act half-dead," observed Katie. "No wonder they're in the cellar. They move like zombies."

"They've been breaking training at a fast clip," the deposed owner told her. "Whether that followed losing, or vice versa, who knows?"

The Burglars faced the pair before them.

"All right, guys, meet Mrs. Katie Banton, your new manager." After which he hastily left Katie to her solitary troubles.

The players had, "Let's get this fool meeting over with," all over them.

Katie tried not to show the fear she felt. She had to bluff her way through or lose all chance of success in this crucial first meeting with her team.

"You Burglars better know, you're about to become a winning ball club."

Derisive laughter from those facing her.

She stepped forward to confront a stocky man with an expanded midsection. From the start, he had seemed less hostile than the other Burglars. She felt safer confronting him as a managerial starter.

"You there with the big mouth and the even bigger gut, what's your name and what's so funny?"

He removed his cap.

"Put your cap back on. Tell me, what were you laughing at?"

"Name's Brancato, Ma'am. Pete Brancato. I've been the second sacker for this so-called ball club."

"So tell me, Pete Brancato, what's the big ha-ha?"

"What you said, skipper. Just like that, we're supposed to start winning. I've been in Baseball fifteen years and I sorta doubt it can be done...anyway, not with this stinking outfit. We've been buried in the cellar for so long, we just feel comfortable there."

His teammates nodded in sullen chorus.

Katie began to realize what trouble she was in with this thoroughly beaten club. Briefly she considered the course that was easiest and maybe wisest, which was to simply turn on her heels and run away. But the house-saving check was in her purse, with lots more to come.

"Pete, you're one of the players I'm thinking of most when I plan the work-load for this team. Now the book on you says you can play ball. If you want to stay, you'll help us a lot. But you'll have to first lose that ton of lard you're dragging around. After that, you can work like blazes for your job."

"Lawsy now," spoke one of the other Burglars, "the round man has sure been told by the pretty lady, ain't he?"

Laughter or none, Katie still felt she had won the opening round.

Quickly she moved in with another volley, "Any of you that don't want to play on this ball club, speak up right now. If possible, I'll sell you or trade you as fast as I can, providing I can find a team willing to deal for you, after the shoddy playing most of you have shown of late. If I can, I'll ship you to the team of your choice."

Another Burglar spoke up, "I wanna leave. Don't take orders from no skirt, that's for dang sure. First, if I have to, I'll find the guy that invented poverty."

Katie smiled at him in confidential fashion. "Fair's fair. Each of us must decide whether or not we want to eat...But about the 'skirt': I can solve that one for you. The owners of this ball club just informed me, it's in my contract, I must wear bloomers when I'm managing, to, as they say 'emphasize the purpose of their movement'. Hey, between you guys and me, I hate the thought of wearing bloomers on a ball field. But that's my fault for not reading the contract's fine print."

Another player chipped in, seeming to offer his bond of harmony.

"I got a brother-in-law what's a lawyer...well, no, he's really more shylock and ambulance-chaser than he is a real lawyer. But, if you want to talk to him, Miz Banton, I'll call him."

"I appreciate that," said his new manager. "But I'm afraid the dye's cast. Now for sure it's bloomers that I'll be wearing."

The first malcontent spoke up again, "Now for sure I gotta go. My Wife would for sure kill me if I played ball for a lady walking around the field in her underpants."

Shades of Muggsy Banton! But even Katie, beginning to feel at home in her new circle, joined the uproarious laughter at that one.

"Well, she sure would kill me!"

With which declaration, he turned and left the park.

Katie asked the others, "Any more of you want out?"

No more forward movement for purposes of resignation.

"Then we're ready for a workout. Please change into your uniforms."

Deep and dark sullenness replaced the brief laughter from the Burglars. Hadn't they been promised the day off?

"We'll have morning practice today and every day until you are a winning ball club."

A huge, seedy man stepped forward. He wore dirty jeans and a ragged undershirt. He spat on the ground in front of manager Katie, then coldly stared at all of her, his eyes working to undress her.

"I'm not practicing today, and you can like it or not."

Katie surged back, returning the bloodshot glare of the towering Burglar who obviously hadn't shaved over a lot of days. This was her first major crisis. Katie Banton, lady manager, had to meet it head-on or know that her new role was finished. She had to regardless of the trembling that rocked her inner being.

He spat again, this time even closer to her shoes.

"So you're Del White, I do believe."

"Yeah, pretty lady. Now how'd you ever guess that?"

"Your reputation goes before you. You're the troublemaker that Cliff Hartwick wouldn't have on his ball club, little matter how desperate he was for a long-ball hitter. Still, it looks like you're on my team, at least for today. And that refusal to cooperate takes twenty from your next paycheck. Any more bad-mouth and it's thirty. Plus, if I catch you drinking in this ball park, it's forty....and you'll immediately be suspended indefinitely without pay."

Amazement, even whistles of surprise swept through the players.

Del attempted a comeback at Katie, but, as soon as he opened his mouth, evidently decided he'd best close it. This dame just wasn't to be wrestled with, at least not at this very moment... He allowed himself another leer at her, thinking of some day to come.

For the moment, though, he pedaled backwards until he was hidden by a knot of Burglars.

"Anybody else refuse to work?"

Nobody dared.

"So one last note for each and every one of you before you get into your work-suits: Starting right now, get the whiskers off your faces. You'll dress (and act!) like gentlemen at all times. On the road we'll travel first class, and we'll see if we can't get into some decent hotels."

Their pleased expressions said that no more cheap trains or third-rate boarding houses or smelly hash joints would suit them just fine. Manager Katie had figured right-on when she'd demanded this concession from Semanthia, counting on it as a solid argument for her reception by the players... So often she had tried to persuade Muggsy, get the Lions better traveling accommodations. He and Cliff had acquiesced to some degree but had never carried it up to her wishes.

With her Burglars, the boast of "better living" would not...simply could not...fall into failure, little matter how much of the plentiful Emancipator dollars she and Elsie might pry loose from Semanthia Smythe. Semanthia might well be a reasonable person, but her ideas on how ball players were entitled to live were every bit as stodgy as Muggsy's.

Half an hour later, the Burglars returned to the field, shaven as instructed. But what ragged and filthy uniforms they did wear!

"Those are easily the dowdiest monkey suits I've ever seen," she told Pete Brancato.

He grinned ruefully while still trying to tape up a tear in a hopelessly shabby pant-leg that seemed determined to drag in the dirt.

"Yes'm, sure are raunchy, aren't they? Our last owner and our last skipper, the owner's brother-in-law, in case you didn't know it...."

"Yes, I knew that...which was the reason the manager couldn't get fired."

"Hey, Lady, you really do know your way around Baseball, now don't you? Yeah, they didn't give a sh...I mean, beg pardon, didn't care a bit how we looked or how we played, long as the two of them could get loaded on pigs-knuckles and bock beer just every night of the week."

"No wonder you're buried in the cellar...or, I'd better say, we're buried," she told Pete, also watching the last of the leaden Burglars straggle back onto the playing field in their sad suits.

"Over here!" she called with all the authority she could summon, same time wondering if it were truly her voice throwing out orders like a drill sergeants's, or maybe like a second-class imitation of Muggsy McGraw...or even Muggsy Banton.

They shuffled slowly over to her. She again looked over them, realizing further what the ex-owner had meant, indeed there were troublemakers out there.

Del White looked especially menacing, though Katie had to note that he too had shaved. And there was actually a clean undershirt peering up from his ragged unie shirt. He was doubtless trying suddenly to make a good impression on her, so she'd remove the crippling fine. No doubt, Del would take diligent watching, decided his lady manager.

But this was definitely a further time to establish authority. GO, Katie.

"You doubtless object to fundamentals in mid-season, but you're going to get them. So start yelling now. We begin with conditioning."

She nodded to Bob Little, one of her coaches.

"Give 'em calisthenics," she ordered. If he resented her tone, no sign of that.

After twenty minutes of painful stretching, the Burglars were groaning in the agony of it all.

"Keep it up, Bob, but faster!"

Ten minutes later: "Enough for a few minutes."

Exhausted, the men fell to the ground, as Katie motioned her two coaches to her side. She knew both were of high reputation in Baseball after Big League careers, and she was anxious that they not only remain but also cooperate with her.

"I've got good reports on your two. I do hope you'll stay."

"Count on me, Mrs. Banton," said Slewfoot Keller, with high enthusiasm. "Hard work is what these loafers gotta have."

"You two may call me Katie."

Slewfoot liked that informality. "Yes'm, Mrs. Ban...uh...Katie."

"Me too, Katie," coach Little assured her. "And I do like your style. As you probably know, there are some good players on this team, once they get their sloppy shoulders back to the wheel."

Katie grinned, already gaining in confidence.

"I'm glad I can count on your two. Now, Bob, you take half the men and hold bunting drills."

"Sure, Katie. Only, if you don't mind the suggestion, Slew knows lots more on bunting than I ever will."

"A manager must never be reluctant to take advice properly given," Muggsy had often told her.

So: "Good thought, Bob. Slewfoot handles the bunting drill. Bob, you take the rest of the men and work on a sliding drill. I remember that you once stole 48 in a season for the Orioles."

Coach Keller glowed that someone still remembered.

"Bob, you keep the sliding drill going till you're seeing results, then keep it going some more. Tomorrow, after batting and fielding practice, we'll do more of same. And this afternoon, since there's no game, we'll devote to running the lard off these guys, also more batting practice."

"Good show!" Bob came back. "There'll be raw hides around here, but these fuc...pardon me, Katie...THESE BUMS WILL SURE RE-LEARN HOW TO HIT

THE DIRT, also along the way remember what it's like to eat some dirt."

An hour-and-a-half later, she told her coaches, "Enough for now. Send them around the field twice, and we'll stop for lunch."

"The most fun I've had in years!" bubbled Slewfoot.

"Enough of that," he then yelled at the players.

Premature sighs of relief as the players turned for the dressing room.

"...after two laps around the field, and I mean all the way 'round."

Groans, but no backtalk. Evidently the fine assessed against Del White was keeping them in line.

When they started to run, Bob added, "Last bum around the field does an extra lap and misses the fried chicken spread the skipper's laid out in the clubhouse...with biscuits and all kinda good stuff..."

The Burglars, who had been loping, picked up the pace.

Last one in was Pete Brancato, he of the excess lard. He tried to slip into the dugout before manager Katie would notice. He almost made it.

"Brancato," she yelled, "another time around!"

Standing on the dugout steps, he looked at her pleadingly against that penalization.

"Aw, by the time I get in line behind the chow-cheaters, all the good grub'll be gone."

For the moment, Katie didn't relieve his seeming death-struggle by telling him that his share of lunch had been stashed aside..... That much did Banton already value the services of Brancato.

She merely told him, "Serves you right, Pete, for collecting that brew-belly."

Pete managed a laugh against his agony. Something told him he still had a job, and this one with a ball club that would settle for absolutely nothing less than winning.

"O.K., Mrs. Banton...Skipper...'The boss always knows best', that's what Mister Connie Mack used to tell us."

Now it was Katie's turn to glow for being included, even obliquely, in the company of one of Baseball's grandest gentlemen.

Back again that afternoon for more fundamentals, followed by an intense batting drill.

"It's for pitchers, too," ordered the manager in vehement tone. "They hit as often as anyone else."

The Burglars' respect for her continued to increase with her in-talk that proved she was no stranger to their game.

"Katie Banton," announced Slewfoot, "I do like the way you get things done. Easy to see your Husband's influence. I've admired him for so long; he's a sure-fire ballplayer's ballplayer."

Katie had been desperately lonesome for her Payne, but somehow never as much as at that moment, listening to her coach rhapsodize on him. It helped to salve her solitary anguish, the thought of how pleased Payne would be, her added paycheck allowing them to buy their home!

At least she thought he would be pleased.

Chapter Thirty One

A reporter once asked the general manager of a Baseball team if he considered that his new manager had made some progress. The GM had to chuckle at that one; from his college days, he remembered that there was an Italian word which sounded almost identical to progress. The Italian dictionary indicated that the word meant "no navigation."

Katie would push onward in her managerial (navigational?) quest.

Before afternoon drills on that initial day as Burglar field manager, she was on the phone:

"Hello Imperial Laundry: This is Mrs. Katie Banton, manager of the Burglars Baseball team...Yes, you heard that last name correctly: Banton, manager of the Burglars."

(She had wondered what that last would sound like when finally uttered. Truth to tell, she now liked the way it rippled off her tongue.)

"I want to speak to the head person at your company, please."

The laundry boss came, listened, and "boggled" in language as strong as he thought he could get away with, speaking to a lady. Pick up all the Burglar uniforms promptly at 4 P.M. of that very same day, have them cleaned and patched by the next morning, also deliver them to the ball park by 10 A.M.? (Holy moses, did this dame also want him to talk on water?)

More from Katie: "Whatever the added (reasonable) cost for the hurry-up, we'll pay it. Just don't rob us or give us the sloppy work you gave the last owner of this team."

The Imperial Laundry staff was pledged into high gear.

"Good! But your driver'd better have a strong nose; these suits smell something terrible."

Later that afternoon, as Katie was leaving the ball park, Del approached her.

His blustery anger seemed to have vanished. Still, careful Katie played the scene (in the vernacular of ball players) "like walking on eggs".

"Mrs. Banton, I'm sure sorry for shootin' off my mouth."

Just what Katie had expected. So handle him as her Payne would, with any maverick member of his squad. Which was, give leniency but certainly not take him all the way off the hook.

"All right, Del. Just don't let it happen again."

She turned to walk away, but he was following her. Clearly the scene was far from finished.

"Mrs. Banton, won't you please take off the fine?"

(Damn, how it killed him, this having to plead with a smartassed broad, especially with one who aroused such other reactions in him, those gripping his body and raising its temperature. All he really wanted most was to belt the redhead (just once!) for humiliating him, then ride that luscious body all the way to heaven!)

He tried the little-boy expression. Some girls had told him he was super at it, dropping his eyes a bit while he pleaded for what he wanted.

"Mrs. Banton, right now I'm damn near broke. My landlady's giving me fits for being behind on my rent. I just gotta have all of this coming paycheck."

She searched his dark eyes for sincerity. She felt for certain that the other Burglars would be awaiting the results of this clemency plea, this finding out who/what was the real Katie Banton, their manager. Her future was on the line.

To lighten the situation, she looked straight into Del's searching eyes. From that lofty I'm-the-boss perch, she then gave him her best carny-operator pitch.

"Hey, mister, being broke's no fun, is it? So tell ya what I'm a-goin' to do."

"Yeah?"

Hope leaped onto his craggy face, while still he ogled her breastline. His staring shook Katie, but she stuck with her pitch.

"Yeah! Instead of paying the whole fine this month, you can pay half of it out of your next paycheck...we'll deduct that...then the rest won't be taken out till next month."

His thick lips, dampened by the travail tearing at him, compressed tightly on each other.

So this bitchy broad had won this round but he'd get a return engagement, make sure that one was on his terms.

For the moment, he backed off completely.

"Yes, Ma'am."

She remembered her Payne telling her, "When a player's gotta be set down, still leave him with some face-saving."

"Show me a ton o' ballplaying, Del, and next season we'll talk about giving those bucks back to you."

As soon as she had released that one, she realized she'd carried her good-guy act too far. But that high-hanging curve ball she'd floated up over the plate was long since long-gone, swatted over a distant fence. Probably, as Katie dolefully reflected to herself, she wasn't meant to be a dramatic actress or a comic or whatever.

Again his lips tightened noticeably, and this time he made no control effort. He repeated "Yes, Ma'am," turned, and walked away.

Came the next morning and the CLARION blared this full-page ad:
COME OUT TODAY AND SEE YOUR NEW BURGLARS PLAY THE WOLVES. IF YOU ARE NOT PLEASED WITH OUR IMPROVEMENTS TO DATE, WE WILL CHEERFULLY REFUND YOUR PRICE OF ADMISSION.
(signed) Kathleen Crowley Banton, General Manager and Manager of the Burglars Baseball Club.

"Will the Wolves agree to giving refunds?" asked Elsie, as the two of them, brightly bloomered, rode to the ball park that afternoon in Elsie's carriage.

"Yes, they have agreed to the refunds as long as their share of the gate receipts is at least a hundred dollars per game. For sure, they're not sitting in a cloverfield of money like we are. In fact, George told me yesterday, there may not even be a Big League team (or at least very many) can match our cushion."

"So what does that grubstreet reporter know about anything?" Elsie scoffed.

"You're too hard on George; he's really a fine young man and reporter."

After which Katie grew pensive.

"Believe me, I'm not looking forward to facing the public in these bloomers. I'll bet a lot of people will give me a bad time."

"You're helping to lead one of history's mightiest causes."

"Maybe so, Elsie, but, for the moment, a ton of flutterbies have taken over where my placid tummy used to be....Mom told me to give back this job, forget the money. She thinks I'll make Payne insanely angry, though I don't really know why.

"My Dad hasn't said much at all. Lordy, if I don't get his support, I may still back out."

"Stay in there, girl. 'You done right'. ...Stay in there."

At Lions Park, leaving the carriage and heading inside, before many stares and raucous catcalls, Katie's embarrassment grew, as if she truly were out there in public in her underpants.

But then, as she looked at the early arrivals behind the home dugout, some kind of miracle happened, it did: There was her Dad, standing and waving a king-sized banner: HURRAY FOR MANAGER KATIE. Go Burglars!

Just as suddenly her feelings fell into focus.

In the dressing room, the lady manager faced the gang of men who were her team.

With mushrooming confidence, she and Elsie had decided the ex-owner's "panic" story of what had happened to the girl down there had been grossly overstated. And didn't any manager belong in her/his dressing room, to spur the players onward?

Before her, Pete Brancato, clearly one of those who had to produce or be released, was tying his shoe laces as nervously as would a rookie ..... While Del White and his buddy, outfielder Slugger Ennis, a huge pair weighing maybe 500 pounds between them, leaned against a back wall, pulling on cigarette butts. No, correct that: they had been so pulling when Katie entered the room. But quickly she had brought their attention to a newly-painted sign above their heads:

THE BURGLARS WILL WIN WITH STRONG AND HEALTHY BODIES. No Smoking or Drinking (other than the consumption of beer distributed daily to players by management) will be permitted in this room.

Immediately, the cigarettes had been doused, while players exulted over the fact that they no longer had to put out for their post-game beer.

Katie had hoped for such a reaction. In fact, when Muggsy had begun his infant season of managing the Lions, it had been J.T. Crowley himself who had suggested to the new Lion field-boss that such a policy would be highly profitable, health-wise and not only for the alcohol-control established...but even more for the good feelings brought forth from the players. Or so J.T. had learned it in his too-brief years of professional Baseball. So Muggsy had adopted the idea and been grateful.

She hoped that, when he found out she had acted likewise, Muggsy would approve. Funny now...the more she was around her own ball park, "her Payne" had become "her Muggsy". She had an idea, when he knew that, he'd like that too.

Del seemed wholly unimpassioned on this occasion, a burned-out matchstick hanging loosely from those large lips. Except that, when Katie dropped her lineup card, and, in bending to pick it up turned her blue-bloomered behind in the direction of the players, a murmur swept the men in the room. Looks of knowing amusement passed between Slugger and Del. Those two leaned close to each other to exchange what Katie had to suppose were leering remarks. But Katie let the moment pass.

In that morning's drills, she had noted that some of the Burglars' lazy attitude had already seemed to evaporate. Without a single exception, the players also came on far more impressive in their cleaned-and-patched suits.

.....And grateful was manager Katie for such small steps forward.

"Our first game together," the lady told her men.

"Let's be a wide-awake ball club!"

The Burglars took the field for infield drills, a quickened pace noted by fans already in the stands.

"Lots better," Katie caught from a front-row customer. "They look almost alive, and when last did we see that in this crumby ball park?"

"Yeah, but can you believe the way this place was cleaned up in such a hurry?"

"And how about the well-dressed look, or at least as much as could be done in a hurry with those wormy suits that had to come from Methuselah's father?"

Katie heard that and was pleased. So another full-page ad in the next morning's CLARION would tell that all-new uniforms were on the way, of a revolutionary lightweight texture, BUILT FOR SPEED, which was what the Burglars would feature.

Another something different for the notorious day: The night before, Katie, Elsie, and Semanthia had huddled, seeking something to highlight the premier contest of the new Burglars.

From Elsie: "Katie, I've got this simply stupendous idea.

"Since we were little girls, you told me you wanted to be a great actress, emote before the multitudes like Bernhardt."

Leaning back in her chair, Semanthia had drifted into lovely memory: "I once saw Sarah Bernhardt on the stage in New York. It was one of my most exciting times ever, along with watching Rube Waddell pitch and Wahoa Sam Crawford play the outfield, imagine those two miracle-men as teammates! Talk about perfection in motion!! First I saw Bernhardt on Broadway in CAMILLE, then I went west to see Crawford and Waddell. First I saw them with Grand Rapids, in the Western League, then next they would play against each other, which seemed a waste of, might you say, concentrated perfection? ....By then, Sam was with the Tigers and Rube was burning 'em in for Connie Mack's Philly team.

"Even in my enemy roles, those two were still magnificent to behold. And that Ty Cobb, even from his Baseball beginnings, had been pure poetry in motion, even if sometimes a notably nasty man."

"Please, Semanthia," Elsie reproved her friend, "we're trying to set up something special for tomorrow's game, something exciting to start people coming out to our ball park."

"Sorry, Elsie," the older woman returned apologetically from her daydreaming. "Sometimes, like any old fool, I get lost in my recollections. So how are we going to get the fans on our side, other than by winning?"

"It's this way," offered Elsie: "Katie has told me how Muggsy has made a speech to open the new seasons...so, tomorrow, before the game..."

Thus it was, on Katie's first day as manager of the Burglars...the very first occasion when a woman would manage a team in a high minor league...Elsie had to fairly push a reluctant lady manager to home plate.

But, once up there, Katie grabbed the moment for her mightiest effort.

As she moved the megaphone to her lips, a silence came over the crowd, broken only be a hoarse cry from down the right field line, "I love my Wife, but oh you bloomer kid!"

Matching that was a blast from high above home plate: "I love my stenographer but twenty-three-skidoo to you too, Kiddo."

Katie smiled while waiting patiently for laughter from the larger-than-usual crowd to die down. Then she told the kranks, "Thank you, so many of you, for coming out to help us celebrate what we in the Burglar family consider the start of a new and exciting and winning era.

"We are deeply grateful for your patronage, and, to honor that spirit, I asked Mrs. Edith Kermit Carow Roosevelt, Wife of Teddy Roosevelt, our glorious President of the United States...."

As forever, thunderous applause at the mention of the idolized First Family.

..."To throw out the first ball here today, to celebrate the cause of Women's Liberation, the importance of which Mrs. Roosevelt is so keenly aware."

Scattered hoots and mocking calls from the stands at that point. But also cheers, especially from the crossover Lion fans catching the relation to Cliff's and Muggsy's speeches at their opening days.

Loudest shrieking applause of all from the wildly vocal section of bloomered

Emancipators behind third base.

"Unfortunately, she's too busy searching for Mister Teddy's dinner in Oyster Bay. So, regretfully, she had to decline our invitation. Surely next season!"

More heavy applause.

"Because of which circumstances, we're pleased to have Blind Tom filling in for 'Mrs. Teddy'. So let's play 'Burglar ball'. That name will be appropriate, you'll discover, because we intend to steal every base in sight!"

Whereupon, Blind Tom, taking over at home plate, added, "Pullllayyy Bawlll."

Several hours later, much of Katie's melodrama had been doused by the rugged realities of Baseball: The Burglars had lost, 11-8, four ghastly errors killing their chances. Still, the home team had never quit. And they <u>had</u> initiated their run-run campaign with three stolen bases, one of those a completely UN-expected stolen base by overweight second baseman Pete Brancato.

Less than 10% of the paying kranks had asked for (then promptly been given) promised refunds for nonsatisfaction.

"But hey, we didn't look anywhere near as dead as before," observed Slewfoot, sitting with Katie and Bob Little in the dugout as the crowd departed.

He added, "Probably we were trying too hard to turn it around in a hurry. But Del looked almost like his old self, with those two shots over the fence in deep left."

From Bob: "Most of the guys are for you, Katie. But I say let's get rid of Hasking, Brumbaugh, and Wilson. They're definitely past the age and stage where they'll put out in the runnin' game you're after."

"I agree," Slewfoot came on. "When you're shot, you're shot."

"Consider it done," decided Katie. "But what about Slugger Ennis? Can he still cover enough outfield to help us?"

"Not nearly what he usta, up in the big show," offered Bob. "Still, he's got plenty of smarts to make up for added age. He's also important for a quieting effect on Del. Plus, if he can get within shoutin' distance of hitting like he used to, he'll definitely be a plus for us."

"About my idea too," offered their skipper. "So we keep him. But what about Brancato? .....Was that steal a fluke? He booted an easy grounder, and looked sorta shaky."

"Ol' Pete is still one of the best double-play guys in this league," said Bob. Once he gets back in shape, as I'm bettin' he does in a hurry, and finds the rhythm with the new shortstop we'll bring in, he'll help a lot. He's an artist at keeping a team loosey-goosey, which we need so damn badly."

"I'll go with that," Slewfoot tossed in. "Pete'd have to be a tomfool to blow this chance."

The manager and her coaches sat there for a while longer, checking out the remainder of the Burglar roster. Decision: Two outfielders, a shortstop, a right-handed pitcher and a reserve catcher were to be released as soon as able replacements could be brought in. Above all, they sought Harvey Houdini, flashy third sacker from Albany.

"We sure can use the Houdini touch." And her coaches roared in agreement.

"When my Husband sees how we've improved our situation all 'round, I want him to be proud of me!"

"He'd better be!" was Slewfoot's vehement reply.

For the moment, though, Katie told them, "It's late. We'd better be traipsin' along, get you fellows home to your families."

"You're right, by hokey," Bob confirmed that. "Gee, ain't it funny, when you're lost in your job, how time slips away?"

"I'm for that," Slewfoot noted. "So let's 'leg it trippingly' as I once read in a fancy book."

The conference broke up in laughter. Indeed, better times for those Marberry Burglars seemed to be on the way, though facing rugged roadblocks.

Chapter Thirty Two

Not all terrible typos happen in newspapers, some sheets can be pleased to know. When I once prepared a release for Harold Parrott, Ticket Manager of the Los Angeles Dodgers, this was supposed to blare from the top of the page: "REVISED NIGHT-GAME STARTING TIME AT LOS ANGELES COLISEUM - NOW 15 MINUTES LATER"...But lo and behold, after the release had been proofread (??), printed, and delivered to Harold's offices in the peristyle end of the Coliseum, he asked me, "Pray tell, howinhell can games 'start 15 minutes after starting time'?"

After Katie's first managerial effort, the wire services reported that here indeed was a new situation in Baseball: Elsie Peabody, Marberry, Pennsylvania chapter-head of the Women's Emancipation Movement, which had purchased the Marberry Burglars, was now also the manager of the Burglars.

Finding such in the out-of-town sheets, Katie was glad to find no picture of herself accompanying the mis-statement....no picture such as the MARBERRY CLARION ran across page one, showing herself and Blind Tom at home plate before the game.

She was further glad for the stalling time that such errors and omissions bestowed on her. When Muggsy would finally learn what she was doing with her team, and then finally saw her Burglars in action, she wanted a ton of improvement.

More about the CLARION story of that game: Reporter George Periwinkle's account of Katie's first game as manager did not reek of joyful satisfaction. Still, George injected hope for the future: "Manager Banton shows much Baseball savvy. Give her time to effect her changes."

More too about the photo run on the CLARION'S front page: Background for the shot was a legion of Emancipators (bloomered, same as Katie) in the stands.

The ladies shown were of all ages and sizes, and shapes, in the process of wildly cheering from their seats behind the Burglars' third base dugout.

Underneath the photo was a caption: WHAT CHANGES TIME HAS WROUGHT, CAN ANYONE STILL REPAIR?

Katie took that caption as bawdy male whimsy. Whereas Elsie and Semanthia were outraged by it.

"We'll soon put the bonehead louts in their places!" ranted the blonde.

"Bet we will!!" echoed Miss Smythe. "Before long, we'll have managers in the Big Leagues too."

Not yet ready to reveal her "secret" to her Husband, Katie avoided writing to him while he and the Lions were on the road. She also managed to be unavailable when she was most certain that he would phone her.

On that three-week road-trip, Muggsy was baffled by the lack of communication with back-home. Still, he allowed, there was no figuring the female mind. Maybe, in his absence, Katie was relieving her loneliness by a return to Marberry's social mill.

Oh yes, he did think the newspaper story about Elsie managing the Burglars was a real ol' knee-slapper.

"Haw! Imagine that stupid blonde broad trying to run a ball club. With all she doesn't know about this game, she'll make the stinkin' Burglars even worse than they used to be."

"But Skipper," interjected Butch Holcomb, "do you honestly think that 'Elsie Nobody' is no-class enough to actually go onto the field...I mean in full view of the kranks...out there on the field in her dainties?"

"No doubt! She's so indecent, it wouldn't surprise me a bit if she undressed right there with the stinkin' Burglars."

Butch wondered, "Whatever happened to old-fashioned girls, like our Moms were, and like your Wife and mine still are? I know for sure, neither of them would go near those revoltin' Emancipation rallies I've been readin' about."

After being battered in Manager Katie Banton's debut, the Burglars shed more of their woefulness with each game to follow.

They again met the Pirates, and this time had a 3-3 tie after eight innings.... Still, (it's not so easy for the leopard to immediately change his stripes) in the ninth, their infield fell apart, racking up three atrocious errors.

Katie's team still wouldn't quit. In the bottom of the ninth, they loaded the bases. Pete Brancato brought the home crowd up and cheering with a steal of home. Still the Pirates won, 7-4, as the frustrated fans jeered the home team in bottled-up disappointment pitted against faint hopes.

A day later, and thanks to a three-run homer by Del White, the Burglars had a 5-1 lead after seven. Katie was daring to dream.

In the eighth, the visiting Alligators blasted the Marberry pitcher from the mound, deadlocking the game at 5-5. They would have taken the lead but for a crushing double play started by Slugger Ennis; running at full speed, though the play looked hopeless, he picked a line drive high off the right field fence, then fairly rifled it back to first ahead of the runner who had been rounding the bases on what had seemed a certain extra-base hit.

The game would then go 13 innings, finally being called by Blind Tom because of darkness.

Katie still didn't have a "W" in her column, but she was feeling more optimistic about her team.

She called Del White to her office and told him that, for his all-out play, she was rescinding the fine.

He liked that, and thanked her. She felt she had handled the situation as a good Manager should. But then some demon told her to add, "Just don't do it again!"

She saw the bitter expression return, and he stomped from the room.

Again she remembered, too late, what Cliff had told her: "An important part of managing is in knowing when to button your lip, or else sink the ship."

So manager Katie Banton would continue struggling, and learning. Too obvious it was, hostility feeds on hostility; and there had been too much of unfriendly fire in herself ever since Del had sought to humiliate her before the Burglar squad. She'd barely scratched the surface of bitter learning in the world of Baseball.

After the joyful jolt of seeing the Burglars almost win a game, attendance began to rise. Somehow/something had happened to the awful-awful team, though the paying customers couldn't fully realize what it was.

They no longer asked for refunds. All right, Katie had meant that give-back policy for one game only. Still, as successes had come so slowly, and with Elsie's O.K., she had left the refund sign posted on ticket booths for a while longer. That last was done with over-strong objections from Semanthia, who did not like "the movement's" money handled loosely. But soon Miss Smythe abated her protest.

Along with which, as the crowd-count steadily rose, it was evident that more help must now be taken on at Burglar Park. This problem Katie handled without any consultation with her female associates. She anticipated their abhorrence to the hiring of more (ugh!) men for the Emancipator-owned ballyard. Still, the present crew of workers out there advised her that it was against "sensible thought" to hire females to serve the sometimes unruly males that made up most of the game's attenders. Katie hired more males, and this time both Elsie and Semanthia blasted her policies. They stormed at her.

After that discord with her compatriots, Katie's solitude increased. So often would she wish that Cliff was close by for counsel. But he and the former Blanche du Bois were honeymooning midst the gentle glories of Old Cape Cod. Explanation: A short while back, Blanche's long-invalided husband had passed away. Then she and Cliff had quietly declared their union. Katie wished them the most and the best. She knew that Muggsy felt likewise.

In matters of Baseball, if not the heart, Katie would find herself relying more on Semanthia. She soon realized how knowing Muggsy had been when he said the older woman had a sharp understanding of the game.

Katie never did learn for sure whence knowledge of diamond stratagems had come to Miss Smythe. Oh yes, there had first been hazy sorts of stories/rumors/suppositions from Cliff; he seemed to remember that Semanthia's Father had been a long-gone Baseball player of high athletic ability but limited personal judgment, finally kicked out of the game for betting against his own team. Later, Cliff had told Katie, he had checked with diamond associates, learning that the transgressing Smythe had then run out on his Wife and a flock of children, leaving them with little to subsist on. Years later, "out West" somewhere, he had died penniless in a small-town jail.

He'd bet a good buck, Cliff did indicate, Semanthia had been a Daddy's Girl who'd learned Baseball at his knees, then found utter disillusionment when Daddy had desecrated both his family and the game he'd taught her to adore.

Elsie verified, Semanthia's Father had run out on his family. Well, didn't that add up to a logical start for universal man-hating, same as with Phillip and herself?

Indeed, sometimes Katie grew so "piffed" at Elsie and Semanthia, she felt she'd have to bite off her tongue to listen to any more of their anti-male bitterness.

Again, though, and relating to the language of Muggsy, "Hey, nobody's all bad!"

Amazing, Katie found it, how often the strategies passed on to her by Semanthia were so in line with the thoughts of her coaches, Bob and Slewfoot.

Something else that manager Banton learned about Semanthia: That one was every bit the advocate of go-go Baseball that Muggsy was. Which meant that Semanthia too was almost fiendishly devoted to bunting, hit-and-run, run-and-hit, steal bases at every opportunity, outthink the opposition to its grave. So often, listening to the older woman's admonitions, Katie could almost feel that Muggsy had never left her side.

But Miss Smythe would never send down advice during a game. Though time would prove that she almost never missed a Burglar home contest. After a game, she was pleased to meet with the Burglar manager and point out both her good and bad moves of that day. Her favorite expression was "Reap and garner, leaving nothing for the gleaner." Translated, as Katie took the Baseball advice of both her Husband and Semanthia, then melted all together, "You win by not giving the other team an even break!"

Therein too was something notable about Semanthia, or so thought Katie: In their discussions of strategy, Miss Smythe discussed the players strictly as just that, not letting her embittered opinions of men-as-such foul the conversation. Which, thought Mrs. Muggsy Banton, even her obdurate Husband would have found every bit as admirable as she did...However improbably, she wished that Muggsy and Semanthia would sometime meet, get to know each other on chatting terms as they came together on their best-loved subject, which was, of course, the ballet that is Baseball.

Katie longed for the chance to then linger unbodied in the background, listening to such a knowing skull-session on the game's intricacies.

Semanthia's favorite Burglar, no doubt of it, was Pete Brancato, the quick-thinking second sacker now slavishly thinking to extend his playing career via extra hours of workout each and every day....also by, according to the prime scuttlebutt pervading the Burglars, restricting himself to one relaxing beer each evening with the guys in the confines of the dressing room. It was further stated by those with whom he would later take dinner, that he near-religiously pushed himself away from the table much sooner than before his "rehab" had begun.

"Face it," he told Slewfoot, "how many guys on-the-slide have you known who get a final extra chance such as our pretty skipper has given this guy? No way this dum-dum will blow an added chance to stay in the game, even if as a player for a little while only, then finish it out as a coach. Bet your bottom buck, Slew, I'm gonna peg it every inch of the way.

"Maybe even," Pete would continue, his face coming to a glow, "I could, miracles granting, someday be a manager...aw, even if it was in the low minors. But I'd still be in this game somewhere, Slew, which I just gotta be. Without Baseball before me, why should I go on living?"

"You got a solid thought there, Petey," Slewfoot agreed.

"Yeah, and you can quote me, for Mrs. Muggsy I'll go through fire-or-flood any old time she asks me. All by herself she rescued my Baseball, yes she did."

While about the same time Semanthia was telling Katie, "As my Mama used to tell her kids, 'you did good' when you saved that little round man for our team. My but he's a goer! I mean, he's Connie Mack's kind of player. Now we'd better hope Mr. Mack doesn't come looking for him again, at least as a coach. Just don't bet that won't happen! The way news in Baseball travels like a rocket, I wouldn't count a whit on Pete as a Burglar after this season. Come to think of it, I've seen Mr. Mack's scouts in our stands at least a few times lately."

Soon would come the day when the Marberry Burglars appeared on the field in brand-spanking-new uniforms of bright blue pongee (same material and hue as Katie's on-the-field bloomers.) Those also sported a cream-colored stripe down the side of the pants, that stripe the same shade as the blouse which Katie daily wore at work. Monkey suits made for speed, they were indeed.

Harkening back to what Katie had observed from her very first trip to Lion Park with her Dad...the suits of heavy wool, and heavy undershirts too, all of which seemed to overwhelm the players on the hot and sultry days of Marberry summers...harkening back to such a dreary sight, Katie would settle for no less than pongee. Again, the new and lightweight undershirts, lighter and free of itching, were optional for such of the Burglars as felt comfortable with change-over in a hurry.

The fans loved the svelte appearance of the new suits. Most importantly, as Katie got it, the Burglars themselves were high on them.

Slewfoot told Katie he'd heard Slugger Ennis almost ecstatic over the slim/trim/speedy effect of the new suits: "Hey, I'd better finish out my career right here in these sexy things. Bet you I can go from first to second a couple of clips of a stopwatch faster than I used to."

And "Oh my," Brancato reportedly had added, "that I have to see. Slow as I still am, I'll bet I can put on one of the old suits and still outrun you going in the new silks."

"Then I'm gettin' outta here!" Del had reportedly finished it off, in a rare burst of good humor. "When either of you old geezers tries any runnin', for sure the sky'll fall down."

Which report manager Katie did embrace. It was the first time she'd heard of happy talk among her formerly sullen performers. She hoped the turn-around was not of a "fugacious" (fleeting) nature.

Came the Burglars' first game-appearance "all dressed up with some place to go," as a popular song put it. This time they took no chances on losing to a late-inning uprising by the opposition. Led by still another of Del's moon-shot homers, they gave Katie her very first managerial triumph by 9-1 over the league-leading Alligators. On succeeding afternoons, they followed with 10-1 and 14-0 clobberings of the same team.

The long-suffering, too-long-hushed Burglar fans began to loosen their chords:

"Hey, we got a ball club at last! I sure never thought that dame could cut it as a manager. Howinhell did she bring 'em back from the grave?"

"Yeah, by jingo, I thought they were headed for the scrap-heap, for sure. Why, I've seen a ton of Baseball teams in my time, and not much more'n a couple o' weeks back, I wouldn't-a been surprised to see 'em lose every dang game for the rest of this season. This broad must really reach 'em like twenty-three-skidoo!"

Still, some weren't impressed:

"So we won three lousy games. That bloomer babe just sweet-talked the players into hustling for a couple of days. They're just cozying along with her as long as they have to, to keep their shaky jobs, not have to work 9-5 like the rest of us slobs."

"Yeah. Before long, she'll drop her silly bloomers, crawl home to her kid and her kitchen. Which for sure is where all dames everywhere oughta be, in their proper place, barefooted and pregnant."

But the last noted were among the mild scoffers of Burglar-dom, even in its present exalted state. Easily the most vocal put-downers of Katie's club were the pure Lion fans, who still bragged they wouldn't be caught dead near Burglar Park. They sniffed or else outright loudly laughed at the improvement reported for the other team in town:

"Haw! Just one ball club in Marberry. Them sissy Burglars in their monkey suits of 'Chinese silk' you only oughta see in a babe's boudoir will just never approach the class of our Lions, no chance they'll do that."

"Yeah, probably the next thing that bossy bitch'll do is talk them hot-pants mugs into wearing lacy underpanties. She just don't understand, ballplayers was meant to play smart, hairy, sweaty, and <u>dirty</u>."

Still, when the Burglars swept the next three games against the tough Crocodiles, more diamond doubters would cross over to new-sprouted hope.

Just no one, it seemed, was more of a Katie-booster than the CLARION'S George Periwinkle. Daily he wrote hurrahs for the job she was doing, with equal praise to her players for the manner in which they'd responded to new and fresh leadership.

When Katie left the park after a series-opening 9-2 demolishing of the Gorillas, George was waiting by his carriage.

"I wanted to tell you, Katie, I do indeed like the way your team's playing."

"Oh thank you, George. I can't tell you how much that means from someone who knows and understands the game of Baseball like you do. Now, if we can just get more speed into the lineup, we might really go somewhere, like farther up in the standings than the 9 games out of first place where we are now....Oh yes, the new suits help a lot in giving our guys the _feeling_ of lighter and faster. But it'll really take a ton of hard work to turn that feeling into reality, with hard work and plenty of personnel changes too. We still have guys, however hard they are trying, who are too far over the hill to adjust to our run-run game.

"But you can write it, George: WE WILL FIND THE PEOPLE WE NEED."

"Myohmy, Katie Banton, it does sound like you cotton to your job."

"Cotton to it? I absolutely adore it. And I can't wait for Muggsy..."

"When did you stop calling him 'Payne'?"

"Since I really got into this game, George, got a real feeling for it, I knew then why he's called 'Muggsy'. I think he'll forever be that to me.

"Still, as I was saying, I just can't wait for Muggsy to see how the Burglars have turned around. And especially for him to know that now we'll be able to buy our house, with the added money I'm earning."

"Sounds like a golden future for the Bantons."

"Oh I hope so, George, I truly hope so. Mom seems to think I've gone up some....almost some primrose path and will destroy our family....but I hope....she's wrong."

"Can I drive you home?"

"Yes, please, and thank you. I was going to walk, but these days I get so tired a lot more easily. See, I am again, and definitely, with-child."

"Another big surprise for Muggsy."

"Oh yes. And it'll sure help this poor ol' child-bearing lady if you'll also drive me by the Daylight Nursery, on Eighth Street, to pick up Jimmy. I sure do miss him during the days, and then a lot of nights I don't see him as much as I want. When I'm meeting with Semanthia, Mom will usually come over to sit with him."

"The nursery it is," and he helped her onto the seat. When he ran to the other side and fairly vaulted into driving position, she was taken by his grace of movement. So, she imagined, was his mare, who seemed to try to match her master's show of enthusiasm, leaving the ball park.

"George, you have good moves. Are you sure you weren't an athlete?"

He was obviously embarrassed by the question.

"Oh, I just try to keep in shape....you know, some running, watch my diet, all that..."

To push away from the discomfort her question seemed to have caused him, she changed the topic with an obvious sort of question: "You covered the game today?"

"Sure did. My editor used to mostly take me off Baseball unless the Lions were in town. Now he wants me to cover as many Burglar games as our schedule will allow. Oh my, Katie, but your team has this town gabbing.

"But I also cover a bit of everything else too...even society doings and the police blotter. Just this morning I interviewed Elsie on new plans for the Emancipators. Miss Smythe sat in too, but she didn't say much. Kept looking at me funny, like was I someone for real?"

"How did the interview with Elsie go?"

"Great as I look back from here. But then I'm one-sided; any chance to be near that girl makes it a great day. I asked her again for a date. But, after a slight hesitation when it seemed she might finally break down and say YES, she got her back up again and fed me the same old NO."

"Keep trying, George. You know how badly Dr. Sutton treated her. That left her sour on men. But, (and pardon me if I'm an interfering ninny), I honestly think she'll come around. From little things she's let-slip to me, she really likes you."

"Sutton's a skunk, all right. Some day, Katie, I'll tell you how much...some day..."

Katie didn't push that, though her girlish curiosity was tough to hold back.

"I'll wait for you while you run in and get Jimmy. Then I'll take the two of you home again, Kathleen."

Which bestowed on her another spasm of loneliness for Muggsy.

"And congratulations on the new-one to be. What'll suit your wishes, a sister or a brother for Jimmy?"

"Whichever will be great, but, just between us, I sorta hope it's a girl. In the years ahead, there will be so many new opportunities for women, and I want to see her get the most and best of it."

"Right now, you must be mighty tired, Mama Banton."

"Oh yes I am, and there's still the Emancipation rally tonight at Town Hall."

"Yeah, I'll cover that one too. No end to the working day for drudges like you and me...."

Reaching home, lonely Katie wanted so much to invite George in for dinner, but she knew how the neighbors would gossip. She settled for dreaming how grand it would be when Muggsy was home again.

Immediately she had to ruefully laugh at that awful miscalculation. Wait a minute! As soon as the Lions returned from their long road trip, Muggsy's jutting jaw leading the march, she'd be taking her Burglars on an equally long road jaunt. Maybe at best, one saving night in between the two. Better settle for dreaming of (finally) the off-season in their own home, hard to actually believe that such a dream was on the edge of coming true.....But there was so much she hadn't stopped to consider when she'd signed on with the Burglars.

All right, Daddy J.T., let your little girl say it again: "In the dark and gloomy tunnel, no light at all till you push out of the other end." ....How often Daddy Jim had given her that advice at bedtime when she'd brought up a childhood problem at bedtime. Then one of their favorite scenarios: She would crawl under the darkness of her covers until she could finally peer out from the other end of the bed. Oh how joyously they'd then laughed together as he re-tucked her in, giving her the treasured Daddy-hug, doubtless a best part of little Katie Banton's entire day and night.

These days, she worried some because she didn't see much of J.T. She feared maybe he was staying somewhat scarce lest he betray his anxiety, same as his Wife's, how her changed career might disturb the tranquility of her marriage. He'd often told her, he considered money to be "gross" if it chased away the true joys of life. But, she wondered, how could dollars grossly needed be "grossly spent"?

Finally, Katie was laughing at herself. Of course all would be right with herself and Muggsy. Hadn't their marriage been made in heaven? She'd better stop herself from becoming another Gloomy Gussie!

Chapter Thirty Three

I knew this Baseball manager who delighted in spouting bits of (so-called, anyway) wisdom.

As when one of his young players was about to be married, the field-boss would tell him, "Son, you've got the situation plumb struck out if you know why we call our language 'the Mother-tongue'. Which is because the Father seldom gets to speak it."

Two hours later, Clara was caring for Jimmy, after (again) urging her Daughter to please walk away quickly from the Emancipators and Burglars before her precious marriage exploded.

"Kathleen, pardon my shopworn statement, but I <u>have</u> been around longer than you, no matter how narrow you regard my view to be. I've had time to learn about men, and I'm telling you, money or no money, your Husband will simply not stand for what you're doing. I can see him embarrassed...and angry...oh my, I'm near panic when I even consider the extent of it."

Facing her Mother, Katie felt her back stiffening.

"And what does Dad say of the terrible climax you've conjured?"

"Kathleen, that's perhaps what frightens me most. When I try to discuss it with him, Jim gets very quiet and moves away from me. I grant you, I often talk too much, but at least Jim usually answers me with some grunts if he doesn't like the trend of the conversation. Now he turns completely silent. I swear to mercy, he's as frightened as I am.

"Or maybe I should better say, at least he's tried to close it."

Squarely was Katie facing her Mom. You might almost say that was in the manner of Muggsy squaring off against Blind Tom.

"Mom, I do love you for caring. Still I must say, this comes to me as one of those almost never-never times when Mother doesn't have to know best. Payne and I understand each other. We'll be fine, and we're going to be living in a home that's all our own. What could be better?"

It was a defeated Clara who moved off to care for Jimmy.

Shortly after, Katie was back in Marberry's Town Hall, staring into the eye of the Emancipation storm. Which is to say, the hall was SRO for howling women.

More complexities for Muggsy's Wife: After Semanthia's stern admonition that she read the fine print in the Burglar managerial contract, Katie had discovered still another fine-print covenant. Which was that she must attend the conducting of all Emancipation meetings within twenty miles of her home or even those meetings "conveniently close" to her place of residence in other cities where the Burglars were playing. All such attendance in bloomered attire.

Katie thought that unreasonable, but she saw no way out.

Now another rally "VS male tyranny" would begin.

Katie sat on the stage between Semanthia and Elsie, waiting for Elsie to gavel the meeting to order, while she read her latest letter from Muggsy.

'Dear Katie, I miss you more than I thought I would. My lonesomeness is stretched something awful, about like stretching a single into a three-base hit. Katie, why haven't you joined us on the road? Why don't you phone or even write? You're never there when I call. I phoned your Dad's office, asking him to get you to phone me. But he was hesitant as hell, not like him at all, said he hadn't seen you much. How can that be? We'll be playing the Bears next week, you know where we stay, please phone me, this is driving me nuts. I heard about Elsie managing the stinking Burglars, running on the field in underpants. That's the funniest story, also the vulgarest. What happened to decency? We've won some games, but bad things happen to us, sometimes it beats on me and all I wanna do is get jagged at the nearest saloon, but I have not and I better not. So I tell the guys, take two and hit to right, better days comin'. Like Jumbo was hit in the leg by a line drive, now Bugle Nose has a sore arm... I sent 'em home for treatment. We're so short on pitching, maybe I'll take the mound, haw. Katie Baby, here's something else, paper said Elsie's the prettiest redhead in the history of Baseball. Did that stupid broad really dye her hair red? What a stupid setup, redhead Elsie in her stupid underpants with a stupid team. Katie please answer this soon. Your loving Husband Payne.'

Katie had a hard time holding back the tears.

Elsie sensed her friend's emotions. "You all right?"

"Yes, thanks. Sometimes Muggsy, the big bum, breaks me up."

"Men are so insensitive."

Whereupon Katie could but send this thought to Muggsy over the miles, "Papa Banton, you'll be so proud of me, I just know you will."

She put the letter in her purse. And again watched the utterly hysterical house before her. Which caused her to remember something Muggsy had told her, the hoary bit of Baseball lore that every year, when the season is about to open, many "Grandmothers" die a convenient death so their progeny can take in the opening game. Likewise, on the night of that Bloomer Girl rally in Marberry, thousands of wild-eyed women jammed Town Hall. They did that after deserting home for the tempestuous evening with reasons every bit as dog-eared as the Grandma-yarn.

To illustrate:

Outside the building, a man walked up to a faithful henchman of the law, and stated, "They're going crazy, Pete."

"Sure are. But thank the Lord mine ain't trying to make a silly spectacle of herself with this buncha screaming meemies; she's at the hospital, busy wrappin' bandages. Ozzie, you and I are damn lucky to have sensible Wives who ignore all this (Haw!) Liberation nonsense, Liberation from WHAT I'd sure like to know. We give 'em a place to live and clothes on their backs and three squares a day, what more?"

"Yeah, and I'm glad my Wife's bummin' around with her friends at the library tonight....Now can you believe this, I saw Mrs. Butch Holcomb, you know, she's the Wife of the guy who third bases it for the Lions, hanging around and chatting with these screaming meemies. Wait'll Butch hears about it, and especially that this ain't the first time she's been seen with these banshees. The way Butch rules his house, he'll just blow the roof off!"

"I even heard Sam Streck's Wife joined this dizzy gang, did you ever hear the likes of that? Seems like Sam, who you know was one of the greatest ballplayers ever, deserves better in his later years. But no. And the way I heard it, Sam even got so mad from hearing all the junk about 'feminine freedom' that he really told off his old lady. He up and belted her too when she sassed him back, though I doubt the old guy is any more strong enough to hurt a fly. But now his silly Wife's seeing a lawyer about a divorce. Imagine? They been hitched nigh onto fifty years."

"Yeah, I guess nothing's sacred anymore. Decent world's shot to hell."

While inside the auditorium their Wives "at-the-library" and "at-the-hospital-wrapping-bandages" yelled as lustily as did bloomered Betty Holcomb. By now, eminently fired with the Emancipation ideals, Betty had to be wondering why she had run from the scene on the night of the first rally. Like Katie, she sometimes wondered quaveringly what her spouse's reaction would sometime be. But the fact that her Butch had gone on the Lion road-trip without leaving grocery and rent money for herself and their two youngsters would again urge her revolt onward.

Up there on the stage, Elsie was ranting onward in like thought: "All that men do is make life miserable for us. But we've had a bellyful of that nonsense. NEVER again."

Her followers screeched approbation at every word.

Gesturing furiously, Elsie continued: "Girded with the uniform of truth, we shall give our city, our state...yes, our whole nation and the entire world the benefit of our enlightenment. We shall go forward, ever forward to break the hideous chains which have for so long held glorious womanhood in miserable, trembling bondage. We'll gain the right to vote, along with everything else so dearly due us."

When the din finally subsided, at least somewhat, Semanthia took over the podium:

"Glorious news, emancipated Sisters! Samples of our latest-style bloomers have arrived from the fashion centers of New York City."

Onto the stage did her helpers bring large cardboard boxes.

"We have bloomers in all colors," shouted high-pitched Semanthia. "You girls will never be at a loss for a quick change, whether your mood be serious or lighthearted.

"We have pink bloomers and brown ones, as well as red, black, and green. Then, oh yes, there are the combinations: pink-and-black polka dots, blue-and-yellow stripes, also orange-and-white checks. Oh yes, we also have plaids in red, green, yellow and purple, also complete mixtures of those shades."

"So let's see 'em," came a holler from down-front via a husky young girl who had fresh-off-the-farm all over herself. Katie had to wonder what excuse that tow-headed one had used to escape her family for an evening.

Semanthia turned to Elsie. "Sure, let's model the new stuff."

Elsie didn't want to hurt her friend's feelings, though she shuddered to consider elderly and long and lanky Miss Smythe as a "model". The best she could then do was to settle for an indefinite, "Uh...you really think so?"

Katie, listening to that verbal back-and-forth, shared Elsie's thought but definitely: Elsie and some of the younger ladies present were far better suited for the modeling role. But how to keep from wounding a friend?

Semanthia latched onto the indecision, motioning Elsie and Katie to follow her offstage. Shortly they would return in the new-style bloomers.

Squeals of joy came from the gathered freedom-fighters, who pressed forward toward the stage without the least hesitation. They placed orders with the blonde and the redhead, also viewed the showings of other young Emancipators who tore open cartons and held the different-style bloomers before themselves.

Semanthia, lost in her pathetic prancing as a "model" was doing sparse business.

"Oh please," Elsie requested in a low voice to some of the throng shoving forward, "won't some of you ladies order from Miss Smythe?"

There was a distinct hesitation, but finally some of them assented.

"Honestly, Elsie," beamed Semanthia, after the order-taking was completed, "I just never dreamed I'd be such a success at showing off new styles. Though I will confess to you and you alone, I used to secretly hope I'd some day do that. I hoped that from clear back when I was a grade-school Miss out in Corncrib, Iowa."

"Oh yes, you did a grand job."

Elsie was just turning back to the audience for further announcements, when, from the balcony of Town Hall, six "girls" in granny gowns and wigs stood up and proceeded to yell in voices definitely un-feminine. At their feet were bulging paper bags.

"G'wan home, ya witches!" shouted one of the obviously-male intruders.

"Yeah, ya indecent naked dames, g'wan home and cover up your underdrawers."

"In this decent town, we shut down dirty shows."

Amazed, those on-stage brought their attention upward to the balcony, which perfectly targeted themselves for the hecklers. Those reached into their paper bags. Back went their arms, and the reigning Emancipators were caught in a torrent of rotten, foul-smelling tomatoes.

"Stop it!" screamed Semanthia, dodging but not well enough as a bullet of red struck squarely on her face and another spattered her plaid bloomers.

"Grab those...those animals," ordered General Elsie. "Grab 'em and toss 'em oooouuuuuu.....ouch!"

That last exclamation was occasioned when an apple, somehow mixed in with the tomatoes, somehow struck her mid-section. Even then, Elsie might better have remained silent instead of drawing attention to her substantial self. A pulpy barrage would blast her from head to toe.

Katie, remembering a "Better than a hero be, retreat and return another day" line from some bygone military tale, had quickly taken her barely spattered self to a wing of the stage, from there to peek through a curtain-tear at the hectic happenings now furiously increasing in intensity.

For her part, Elsie seemed to know naught of retreat.

"I'll show you...you...beasts!"

She fired back every bit of red fruit still fit to be tossed.

Her first few shots went wild, but soon she found the range.

"Help...I can't see," protested a deep voice whose owner was notable for an oversized proboscis. His eyes filled with tomato pulp, he clawed wildly for help in seeking somehow to regain his bearings.

Not so bravely, his companions suddenly shared his panic.

And certainly the assembled females took courage in their overwhelming numbers as they swarmed over the intruders.

Off came the wigs, and six embarrassed males, now in utter bondage, tried hopelessly to fathom their way out of the pickle into which they'd worked themselves.

Rip! Off came the granny gowns covering their street clothes. The men were then bound in the tatters of those.

"Throw the bums out!" shouted Elsie, again in command.

"Wait a minute," suggested Katie. "I want a look at those two biggest guys."

The femmes holding that duo in check faced them toward the stage and Mrs. Banton.

"I thought so. They're Bugle Nose Stankorsky and Jumbo Malone; they pitch for my Husband's ball club, the Lions. Their arms are supposed to be hurting...aaawwwww, the poor babies..."

Seated near the balcony action, Betty Holcomb affirmed the identification: "That's who they are."

Emphasizing the thought, she picked up two tomatoes from the bags brought in by the male invaders. And smeared them into the faces of the now-helpless Jumbo and Bugle Nose.

"Take that, ya tramps," she crowed at them in utter joy. "I just wish my Butch was with you. I'd sure give him one too, right smack in the kisser, for his lousy leavin' me 'n three kids without any money to live on while he's on the road."

"Betty, you just wait till he hears about you," Jumbo fairly hissed at her, "how you're out in public in your dainties. He'll beat the tar outta you!"

"I'll be waiting for that," she retorted. "Tell him too, by the time he gets back home, I'll have filed for divorce for non-support, and our house'll have new locks on it, so he can sleep in the park for all I care."

Spurred on by the bravado already shown, other "liberated females" now grew brave enough to come forward and identify the intruders.

"That bald one's my Husband, much as I hate to admit it. Wait'll I get the bozo home again!"

"The skinny geek is mine, and he's gonna sleep in the garage for a long time to come. But first gimme two o' them tomatoes. Oh, I've waited a long time for the chance to plaster <u>him</u>, after all the times he's slapped me around."

Soon all the would-be "grannies" had been identified.

Pushed onward by an inspired thought, Katie called her friends into conference. They were seen to talk in tones of high excitation.

"You mean...?" asked Elsie delightedly.

"Just that."

"Ideal idea," bubbled Semanthia. "Katie, my admiration for you has grown a thousandfold."

The assembled Emancipators, with their confused captives too swarmed over and trussed to make movement possible, watched the huddle on the stage and waited. Finally, Elsie stepped forward.

"First, some of you girls drag those lowlifers up here. Better come by way of the back stairs; some of those slobs are too fat to hand down over the front rail. Then just to be sure, a bunch of you down-front sit on 'em till we're ready to do what we're gonna do."

"While you're at it," Semanthia added in her screeching voice, "take off their pants. In case one of 'em breaks loose, he won't be near as likely to run out into the street in his underdrawers."

"I've known it that way too," yelled the tow-headed "farm girl".

More squeals of delight from the ladies, more wails of protest from the helpless males.

Elsie continued her orders: "Another twenty or so of you go out and get all the rottenest fruit and eggs you can find. There's a market open about two blocks down the street."

The delirium of pure joy reigned in Marberry's Town Hall.

After some twenty minutes, the ammunition was on hand.

"Now for the fun!" yelled Elsie.

"But we didn't mean no hard feelings," pleaded Jumbo. "Can't you broads just take a joke?"

"You girls can't do this to me," wailed another of the would-be raiders. "You're gonna ruin my best go-to-meetin' shirt!"

"Hold 'em tight, girls," called Elsie, "I mean real tight. Too much fun coming to miss a single bit of it."

"Don't worry, Miss Elsie," called the tow-head, now planted firmly on the massive chest of Bugle Nose. "And ain't this fun...most excitement I've seen since baby brother fell through the hole in the outhouse. But we got these guys caught tight as chickens ready for pluckin'. And hey, this banana-nose is kinda cute. 'Long as he's wrapped and ready to go, I just might take him home for a pet."

She reached down and rumpled the Stankorsky locks.

He looked up at her delightfully developed body and grinned pleasurably in spite of his present predicament of doom.

"And my Pa can sure get a lot o' farm-work outta him," she added.

For that prospect, Bugle Nose stopped smiling.

That bucolic interlude ended, Elsie resumed her orders.

"Bring 'em up to the stage."

The men were passed forward by way of eager feminine hands.

Finally, they were deposited in a pile at the front of the stage.

"Now stand them against the back wall."

Done as commanded by eager feminine soldiers.

"Pass out the stinking fruit and eggs.

"Everyone gets a shot. But naturally, the Wives of these skunks get the first tosses."

Orders carried out, and then the execution squad was ready.

"Now...aim...FIRE."

Chapter Thirty Four

Oh yes, the Ballet that is Baseball can also hold times of appalling sadness. And this is a remembrance of the wanton wastage once viewed therein.

Playing center field for the 1978 Los Angeles Dodgers was mercury-swift and power hitting Glenn Burke, recently out of the University of Nevada-Reno baseball and basketball programs.

In the Dodger dressing room, I observed that lighthearted Glenn and the rock from his ghettoblaster formed a delightful core of Dodger team unity. A veteran Dodger pitcher told me, "These are the happiest, loosey-gooseyest times we've known down here. It's made us a TEAM."

Hall-of-Fame Dodger coach Jim Gilliam further stated, "Once we cool down a bit of Glenn's feistiness (something somehow characteristic of kids from the troubled Oakland area), we figure Glenn to become another Willie Mays."

Then did a "terrible" secret leak to the press (as I heard the inside story), in premeditated style by a team official whose code of personal ethics would allow for no differentiation. Because, as revealed, Glenn Burke was a homosexual. Ten years later, the news didn't figure to raise a ripple. Still, in those alarmist times, few protested as Glenn and his God-donated talents were dismissed from the Dodgers. Soon, he was no longer a member of the ballet.

Any fan could weep some for man's inhumanity to man, and to Baseball.

On the evening after such riotous happenings, and following another Lion road-win, Muggsy returned to the boarding house...sometimes referred to by the players as the "spite-house". Their reasoning: The awful food served there was an attempt to get even with any players from out of town.

Muggsy found this wire awaiting himself:

**Have learned that your Wife is a leader of lousy
Emancipators, and Butch's is loudmouthed member.
Both walk around in their underdrawers. And your
Wife is managing stinking Burglars. Thought you
and Butch would want to know.**
(signed) Jim Stankorsky

"Hey, it's gotta be a gag," protested Buck Jackson with furious rage, when he'd seen the wire. "Bugle Nose'll do anything for a laugh."

"Yeah, funny as hell," retorted Butch. "Skipper, when do you and I hustle back home? <u>Right now</u>? Just wait'll I get my mitts on that dumb broad o' mine!"

"Buck's probably right, it's just a gag," said Muggsy, trying to stay cool though it was the last thing he felt like. His hand shaking, he stuffed the message into his pants pocket and hurried down to the telephone, Butch at his heels.

"Buck, it's no gag, at least about Muggsy's Wife, it's the <u>truth</u>," Herky Jackson told him when Muggsy was out of sight. "Some of us saw the correction from that first 'blonde lady manager' story. It was buried way back in the paper three or four days ago, the correction was. We figured Muggsy saw it too, but we thought he just didn't want it talked about, such a touchy thing about his Wife."

"Gosh, Herk, this could mean bad-bad trouble ahead."

"<u>Could,</u> my eye. It already does. And have you seen Butch? He's stomping around like a crazy man. I sure wouldn't wanna be in his old lady's bloomers. I mean, once in a bar I saw him jump his skull and clobber a broad over nothing at all."

On the phone, with Butch leaning over his shoulder in panting rage, Muggsy called a sportswriting friend at the local paper. Something was pounding at the manager, a haunting phrase which hadn't made sense, or maybe he'd shuffled it from his thoughts because he couldn't afford to have it make sense. But now it was becoming part of a terrible picture: "the prettiest redheaded manager Baseball has ever known" ... redheaded ... redheaded **manager** ... his Wife, **KATIE**. Still, he waited, even prayed, for a last-minute stay of execution...

"Hello, Jerry, this is Muggsy Banton. Fine, how're you, Kid? Yeah, helluva game today, sure was. Jerry, who's managing the Marberry Burglars. I heard it was that stupid Elsie Peabody broad...isn't it?....Jerry....well, isn't it?"

There was a long pause while Muggsy listened.

"Well of course I don't know, and I wanna know, or whyinhell would I call you?"

Again Muggsy listened, taking it between the eyes, turning pale for the awful knowing. Still, he fought for composure.

"She is, huh, she really is? Thanks, Jerry."

He turned to the raging Butch, "Yeah, it's that way. We'd better head on home."

As Muggsy turned to the front door, headed for a telegraph office, he didn't even turn to see Butch sitting on the couch by the phone, sobbing in his sudden loss of equilibrium; he could think of nothing else to do but pull off one of his heavy shoes and fling it at the oversized mirror on the wall. The explosion from that must have resounded all the way to Marberry. At least, by the time he gathered himself sufficiently to phone his home and hear the stern voice of his Mother-in-law, he was told that Betty had taken the children and "gone away somewhere". Butch would, he was further told, next hear from an attorney regarding "divorce for non-support". Butch's productive career ended at that moment; he had lost the people who meant most to him.

In his haste to then make his rounds, Muggsy bumped several people, and they muttered angrily.

In the telegraph office, he grabbed a blank. His mind and eyes equally fogged, he still managed to wire:

George, please meet me 3:50 train tomorrow afternoon.

When Muggsy stepped off the train in Marberry, reporter George Periwinkle was waiting for him. The manager's shattered look was even worse than George had feared. He had re-read the wire from Muggsy, wondering desperately if there were anything he could do to help.

But it didn't happen that way. Several times he had almost phoned Katie to warn her of Muggsy's scheduled arrival. George had this dread of being a busybody, perhaps even hurting more than helping.

So he'd never called Katie. Now, seeing his demolished friend coming off the train, he sincerely wished he'd warned her. He remembered lines from an old song sometimes heard in burlesque houses:

Oh, I wish I'da done what I almost done when I had the chance t' done it. But sad me, the doin' never got done.

He grabbed Muggsy's hand. "Hi, good to see..."

"When did it happen?"

"Right after you left town. But Muggsy, she got tricked into it."

"Why didn't you tell me?"

"I guess I thought..."

"Where is she?"

"Burglar ball park. But Muggsy, you look awful. Didn't you sleep at all last night?"

"Let's go!" Muggsy hurried for the carriage-stop, and even the agile George could hardly keep up with his frantic haste.

In the carriage: "Katie didn't want the job," George repeated. "She got tricked into it... Hey, Muggsy, can what she's doing really be so bad? She told me she wanted to make some extra money so you two could buy your house. I mean, is that so awful?"

"Katie shouldn't have done it," came out robot-like, for he'd repeated the words to himself innumerable times. "What hurts most, it's my own Wife sneaking behind my back and stabbing me."

Soon, the revivified Burglar park was in sight. Before George's prancing mare had been urged to a halt, Muggsy was out and running through the brightly re-colored gate leading to the grandstand, that too newly painted and spanking clean. Even the distracted Lion manager had to notice that the scene was far from the dirty, disintegrated wreck of other days. Though for the moment he would hardly stop to consider the changes in the ball park. Other sights caught his practiced eye.

The impressive new scoreboards told him the game was 6-6, bottom of the tenth inning.

In a glance, Muggsy took in the big crowd, and, shockingly to him, the new blue-white, skin-tight suits of the Burglars. But what truly bombed his senses: At the first base coaching box was his own petite red-haired Wife in blue BLOOMERS...HIS KATIE.

Muggsy swore, then started for her, but stopped. The Burglars had runners on first and third, one out as indicated by the scoreboards.

The Cougar pitcher went into his stretch, not daring a windup at that point.

Still absolutely UN-believing, Muggsy watched in frozen fascination as Katie ground the heel of her right foot into the dirt.

"My signal....she's using it for a bunt!"

The stocky Burglar batter, whom Muggsy remembered as a former big leaguer of note, name of Brancato, took the sign and set himself. The baserunners likewise got the message. The Burglar on first moved two steps toward second, then another cautious step. The runner on third likewise wandered cautiously from the bag. In came the pitchout; it was high and wide, but still Pete got wood on it, dropping a lively bunt down the first base line.

Muggsy had to be amazed how the slimmed-down Brancato did motor down the line toward the bag.

The Cougar catcher finally trapped the ball. Too late to nail Pete at first. But a perfect toss to second nailed Slugger Ennis, the runner going in with spikes high.

That throw to second was what Katie had counted on, the mistake her plan was built on. Off third, and usually ignored as a base-stealing possibility, Del White had acted nonchalant, even disinterested through the first part of that action.

In the instant when the Cougar catcher fired the ball to second, Del threw all his bulk into a mad dash for the plate.

The massive tangle then caused by Slugger's charge into second (landing all over the Cougar shortstop as that one tried hopelessly to throw to home plate even though Slugger was called out), meant that Del could finally ease up and almost walk the final yards to the plate with the winning run.

The play had worked as perfectly as Muggsy had repeatedly diagrammed it for his attentive Wife. Though he'd seldom noted that she was quite so attentive or heard her ask many questions afterward.

Again, Muggsy's words of amazement were unprintable.

The home crowd whooped it up. A fan darting for the exit behind Muggsy stopped long enough to slap the lantern-jawed stranger hard across his back.

"Bee-yoo-ti-ful double steal, eh brother? And howja like that bunt of Brancato's? Shows what a great manager can do for a gang o' has-beens, turning 'em back into shines. Well, it's gettin' late, and my Missus will have victuals on the table. So I better be on the hike, but I'll see you out here tomorrow. Sure don't want to miss any of these Burglar games, the way our guys are playing like a new crop of young men."

The enraptured fan was then lost in the crowd storming the exits. But Muggsy stood still, staring at the diamond.

He saw his Katie leaving the field, trying to escape the portion of the fandom that surrounded herself. Soon, their congratulatory hands could wax careless.

Muggsy went after her. But that swarm of fans on the field, each of them seeking to personally reach and touch and congratulate a Burglar, blocked his path. Still he fought his way toward her.

"Hey, where you headed, rough guy?" asked a man of huge proportions who was almost knocked down by Muggsy's charge toward Katie. "Aincha got no politeness? Oh hey, I know you! You're Muggsy Banton, aincha? Gotta tell ya,

Muggsy, that little Missus of yours is one smart manager, yeah, gotta tell the world she is. She's really wakin' up these other teams that have just been bummin' their way through their jobs. You just gotta be goshdarned proud of your little woman."

Likewise heading onto the field from their down-front seats along the third base line, a swarm of bloomered Emancipators was screaming wildly:

"Hurray for our Katie Banton. Anything a man can do, a woman can do better."

"You tell 'em, girl. Katie's provin' this world was made for Emancipated women to take over."

Katie finally ducked into the dugout and was headed through the door that led away from the field, toward her team's dressing room.

Muggsy called to her, but no way could she hear him against the din.

After which Muggsy completely ignored the people in his way, 'midst his frantic rush to get to his Wife. People in front of him noted his charge. Most of them escaped his furious path. Still, one tall and older lady with a hook nose was sent sprawling, for which she made lament as she lay on the ground and watched him continue to barrel forward.

"So, Muggsy Banton, we finally meet again," Semanthia spoke disdainfully. "A beast like you, no wonder Katie deserted you for a new and better life!"

Through the dugout door Muggsy then hurtled himself. In the fading sunlight, he stood in front of a small wooden building newly marked "BURGLAR DRESSING ROOM. All Others Stay Out."

But no Katie in view outside that door.

As his worst fears drew him to the room, he heard her voice. Katie was <u>inside</u> the dressing room with her undressing players.

Muggsy bolted for the doorway.

Inside, the Burglar players sat on benches, most of them already stripped to the waists, fumbling with shoes and socks and belt buckles, sweat pouring from their overheated bodies.

Katie stood just inside the door, facing them.

"Great game, guys. That finally lifts us out of the cellar. Tomorrow we..."

"KATIE..."

Amazed, she wheeled to face him.

"Muggsy...MUGGSY...I thought you were in..."

At that moment, she couldn't remember where she'd thought he was. But it didn't matter. She ran to him for a hug of greeting. He backed off in terrible anger.

He grabbed her roughly by an arm and fairly shouted, "Katie, you come home with me right now. You oughta be ashamed of yourself, in here with these guys undressing, and you naked in just those...those..."

Katie had never been humiliated like that. She pulled loose from his rough hold, and faced him eye-to-eye, as she or he would an umpire in a fierce confrontation.

"Muggsy, I don't need talk like that," she told him in a voice that was supposed to come on controlled.

Several Burglars stepped forward to face the Lion manager, defend their own.

"Cool off, Mister, you're gonna blow a gasket," Brancato told him. "Wanna back off for just a minute, then start again?"

"Drop dead, Brancato!"

Slugger Ennis made a move forward, but Katie took over.

"Please let me handle this," she begged her audience. She turned back to her Husband, trying to restore equilibrium in the room, to save something from the shattered moment.

"Muggsy, aren't you proud of me? I'm making money at what you taught me about Baseball, so now we can buy our house."

Same old scenario: "Oh, if I had that last pitch back." But as soon as she'd turned it loose in front of her players, there was no recalling it: By insinuation/innuendo/whatever, Muggsy had to be shamed by what she'd said before his sworn enemies.

The feeling of shame those words touched off carried Muggsy to absolutely uncontrollable rage. Again he grabbed his Wife's arm in an iron hold, trying to pull her to the door. But now her Irish blood was up for sure; she fought for freedom from his gnarled hands as she'd never dreamed she would again after their first night in his gas-mobile, by the river.

"Muggsy, let me go!"

"Katie Banton, you come home with me right now. You joined these tramps when you knew how I hate their guts. That's dirty pool."

Again he told her, "You oughta be ashamed of yourself." And tears of frustration and rage began to fill her Irish eyes. She'd never imagined she could be quite so angry at anyone.

Del stepped in, grabbing Muggsy's arm and jerking it loose from Katie.

"Why you stinkin' little jerk! Call us tramps, will ya? I'll slam ya through that wall and then stomp ya."

"You and what other ten tramps, Boozehound?"

As other Burglars moved forward to back Del, the dressing room scene was moving out of control.

Fearing for her Husband's safety against such numbers, and seeking to mute her churned feelings, Katie moved between him and her onmoving players.

"Enough. Let's not get foolish."

To her storming mate: "How can you act like this? I thought it was the old Burglar owner and manager you hated so much, not these guys. I thought for sure, after I started managing here, you'd feel differently about this team."

In what was meant to be a softening touch, she forced a smile and told Muggsy, "Sometimes I don't understand my Husband at all."

It was a futile attempt to lighten the cyclonic scene; Muggsy was in no mood for a cooloff.

"Katie," he yelled at her, "you actually had the guts to join the stupid Bloomer Girls. Now I find you near-naked in this dressing room. You're not only indecent, you're disgusting."

As tears gathered on her face, conciliation deserted Katie. She stamped a foot down hard and glared at her Husband.

"Mister, you've said too much. And so I'll tell you what I've learned about life while you were gone and I was silly enough to think I was missing you: I've begun to realize there's something mighty worthwhile about the Emancipation movement. Now, after facing your bullying today, I just found out what it is. Yes, Mister I'm PROUD to be one of the Emancipation ladies, in dress and also in determination, to uplift womanhood from the dregs into which such unfeeling clods as you have dropped us and kept us. Muggsy, get out of this room in ten seconds, or I'll stand back and let these guys throw you out!"

He laughed a laugh without joy.

"Sure, I'll get out, then I'll wait for you to come crawling home. But I'm damn well telling you, Woman, when you do, it'd damn well better be without this stupid job...and you showing a dress, not just your underpants."

One last laugh of derision at the Burglars ready and fighting-eager to close in on him.

He turned and left the room.

"What happened?" asked George, when Muggsy returned to the carriage.

"Bad scene; it was one bad scene. I caught Katie actually with those stinkin' apes, while they undressed. No telling how many of 'em would have been butt-naked a minute later, if I hadn't come in when I did...and she didn't seem a single bit disturbed by any of it! I told her off. When she comes home, I'll tell her a lot more."

George moved the horse into action.

"Better come to my place, Muggsy, and cool off over a beer or two."

"You're probably right, George, but Katie sure'd better quit that fool job.

"Or maybe I just won't take her back."

Leaving the park in Elsie's carriage, Katie told her, "Muggsy actually called me indecent and disgusting, right there in front of my players."

The tears were fighting to finally break loose. Elsie handed her a hankie, and told Katie, "Let 'em flow, Girl, like the rest of us have done over the insults of mere men."

After a while:

"Gee, Elsie, maybe I'm even getting rusty in the head and don't think so straight anymore..."

"Don't talk like that! How can you blame yourself for what men are?"

"Anyway, I sure wish he hadn't talked like that. If he wanted so badly for me to quit, all he had to do was ask me. But he talked just terrible to me, and, Elsie, you know I've never been an indecent person."

"Well of course not, but men, dirty minded as they are, always talk like that."

"Right now, I wish I were dead, I truly do."

"Katie, right now you're way down, and you need help from friends. I'm supposed to meet Semanthia at a tea shoppe where they serve heavenly kolaches with spiced peaches. Between that, and the straightening out we'll give you, you'll know just what to do to handle the slob you've called your Husband."

Chapter Thirty Five

"We do not comprehend ruin until we ourselves are in ruin."
- Heinrich Heine

It was after ten o'clock that night when Muggsy walked onto the darkened front porch of his equally darkened home. Through the shutters, he could barely spot a light showing through from the back bedroom, which for himself and Katie had been the scene of so much glorious lovemaking.

Almost completely blacked out was that scene, matching the doom of Muggsy's mood. Still, reposing on the screen door, attached to the wire mesh by a hairpin, was a note in Katie's handwriting, the expensive white bond on which it was penned cutting through the night in almost fluorescent style.

Lighting a match, the emotionally scarred Husband saw that, yes, the message was for himself. He worked it free, then took it out to the street to read by lamplight:

To My Husband: I do not wish to see you, here or elsewhere, ever again, until you sincerely apologize to me in front of my players for your terribly hurtful accusations of this afternoon.

In the meantime, when my Burglars and I go on the road, you may temporarily move back into this house. When the Lions are on the road, Jimmy and I will live here.

Should you require anything vital from this house while I"m living here with Jimmy, please notify me through Mom, and we will briefly vacate the house for your convenience.

To repeat what I told you this afternoon, the Women's Emancipation Movement, of which you have now made me such an eager member, teaches well this undeniable fact:

Enlightened womanhood of the present, also of the glorious future-to-be, will never again have to kowtow to the boorish and sadistic domination of mere men such as you.

(signed) Kathleen Crowley Banton

The words written thereon were certainly not Katie's. Muggsy knew that as surely as had his Wife when she had sat in Semanthia's hotel room earlier that evening. And when, in her shattered state, she had allowed Elsie and Semanthia to dictate "her message to Muggsy".

Even the hairpin attaching the message to the screen door had seemed unfamiliar to Muggsy, just not the same as the ones he'd removed from his Katie's red hair so it would flow long and luxuriant for lovemaking times. He now guessed that the pin belonged to Elsie, and in that assumption he could not have been more correct. After she and Elsie had reached the Banton home later in the evening, Katie had late-opted for one more chance to settle with Muggsy minus any written note. But Elsie had quickly closed off that choice with a definite, "Tonight, Katie, you don't know your own mind. Go to bed and get some rest. Leave yourself in the hands of your best friend, who certainly knows what's best for you."

That mission confidently accomplished, and with "Katie's note" to her Husband securely in-hand, Elsie had then attached it to the screen door with one of her own hairpins and left the scene.

Still, even when Muggsy had finally returned home to read the note and then try the door with futility because it was bolted shut from within...even at that moment, Katie had been sitting in the dark of their living room, only short steps removed from him as he read "her note." She waited for his knock.

But Muggsy did not knock, though he had started to.

So his Wife did not next run to him, though she had been ready at his earnest entreaty.

As she heard his retreating footsteps, toward the front gate, she ran to her-and-his bed, falling on it and sobbing terrible tears.

Katie Crowley's dream castle, so many years in the building, had seemed unshakable. But now it was a hopeless rubble of hostile mis-communication.

Still, retreating footsteps or none, Muggsy hadn't left his home in a hurry on that night of disaster. He had sat on his front steps for a time that confusedly reached him as maybe a few minutes or maybe long hours. Hey, whoinhell knew or cared? Finally and hopelessly, he arose and departed. At Marberry's depot, he caught the next train back to his ball club.

In a darkened corner of a railroad car churning through the night, he sought to retreat from the shock which possessed him.

Not to be, that relief. From the next car he heard a barbershop quartet dallying away the long hours of travel:

I'll take you home again, Kathleen,
Across the oceans wild and wide-----

That treasured rendition further shattered something within himself.

Muggsy Banton, through his lifetime the unconquerable scrapper, now begged of some far-off Providence that his severed existence and its tearing pain would somehow and quickly cease to be. He pleaded that the train on which he was a passenger would somehow crash to destruction, and of course lost on him was the realization that other human beings would likewise by lost. Oh yes, he had, as the players on any constantly losing team would put it, "hit the pit."

But Whoever/Whatever writes such scenarios would not allow Payne Banton such a quick and easy way out of his torment. Forced to return to him were the words from his cherished Mom: "Son, what we buy, we pay for."

The next morning found Muggsy rejoining his team. But it was a while before he could again take that scene in full perspective, such as the news that equally torn-up Butch Holcomb, the team's veteran and always dependable third sacker, had deserted them. He had told a teammate that he was heading for Oklahoma, where he suspected that his Betty was hiding out with their children at her parents' home.

Those same hours found Katie foregoing her's and Jimmy's usual morning visit to Clara for a loving chat. Somehow she wasn't yet ready to tell her Mother what had happened. She feared that "I told you so," however muted or even unspoken, would still fill the air around themselves.

Instead, after leaving Jimmy at the day nursery, she stopped by Elsie's apartment.

While the two girls sipped tea and chatted, the phone rang.

Oh but Katie was excited: "It's Muggsy! He tried to reach me at home, to apologize. Now he's calling me here, I just **know** he is."

"No," insisted the blonde with an affected yawn, "it'll be George...again."

She advanced on the phone with a confident (cruel, thought Katie) smirk.

"Yes, George, of course I know you love me. Frankly, it touches me not a bit.....How did I know it was you? Well, who else pesters me quite so constantly, day and night? .....Now go away.....GET LOST."

Down hard with a decisive BANG went the phone's receiver. Katie silently reflected, 'twas a wonder the instrument didn't shatter as it hit its cradle, so much of Elsie's emotions were then spent on it.

"That, Katie Crowley, is how to handle a persistent pest."

"Elsie, you could be nicer to George. I mean, he is such a thoughtful, considerate person."

"Not me. Little Elsie has learned the real truth of the opposite sex, with their horribly bloated self-importance: At heart, they're nothing but cowards, seldom with any aim stronger than the taking of our precious bodies. But I for one will never again be dominated by their cheap efforts and their forever-duplicity, double-dealing, or whatever we may best call it."

Katie reflected, her friend had almost always been talkative. But now every chance for her to speak seemed an excuse for an oration on her newfound beliefs.

Devilishly, the Burglar manager pondered what strident bit of elocution would issue from Elsie should she merely be asked for a glass of water. Katie reflected, she'd like to share that with Muggsy. But then suddenly and soulfully, it struck her again that she had no idea if, when, or indeed ever she would ever again see her Husband. Indeed, the idea struck her with such a jolting inner sorrow, she had to suddenly retreat to the bathroom, to absorb it in her aloneness. As Muggsy would have put it, "whoinhell else understood or cared a bit?")

Whether or not Katie realized it or didn't, she was already beginning her own drop before she hit the pit.

Chapter Thirty Six

Rogers (The Rajah) Hornsby is remembered by fans of a bygone era as Baseball's mightiest right-handed hitter and one of its stormiest players. He would far rather practice his batting stroke or argue with umpires than spend his time in philosophizing. The latter he put forth about as often as he would smilingly leave home plate after striking out.

Still, a friend of The Rajah once related to me that, when in comfortable companionship away from ballpark surroundings, Hornsby would sometimes offer this quote from Samuel Butler:

> **"Marriage at best is a vow,**
> **Which all men and women either break or bow."**

For once-lovers, Butch and Betty Holcomb, now terribly torn from each other by activists concepts, the hours went forward sadly, swiftly, but briefly.

Having tracked his Wife to her parents' home just outside of Enid, Oklahoma, befuddled Butch performed his mightiest contrition in seeking to glue their marriage back into the lovely affair it once had been.

Not that Butch had any love for the prairie-filled Sooner state which had taken its formal name from words meaning "red people." All he seemed to see out there were piles of red clay with coyotes and rattlesnakes running rampant...plus endless Indians, their land stolen from them by the U.S. government. Those clung to a sole surviving dream: soon becoming oil millionaires, as had so many in their tribes.

For Betty's part, having quickly become known as a highly vocal (and fashionably bloomered) Emancipator in Oklahoma, life on the run from her Husband was her current way of going.

Yet, Betty was no longer so sure of her stand. After rejecting Butch still another time, she said this to her Mother, while the three young Holcombs listened through a door slightly ajar: "Ma, I gotta admit, I do miss Butch a lot, 'specially through the long nights, and then when the kids ask so often, 'When's Daddy coming home?' Today, in fact, he got to me so much, I almost gave in. But the running-around louse has some paying-up to do for the way he's treated me. Lately, he's hardly ever left enough spondulicks for bread and beans.

"So I've decided, next time Butch comes askin', I'll give him another chance."

Whereupon, Mom let her have it with both barrels, as the folks of Oklahoma put it. Brusquely, she interrupted another blanket-thwacking session on the back stoop:

"Betty, you're playing with time, assuming our loving Lord will grant that. You've especially embarrassed your Dad with all your filly-frollying in your home town in those silly bloomers. Just last night again, he wanted to throw you clean out of this house. But, considering the kids, I hindered him one more time.

"As for your Butch, I don't know how he's been so patient...Grab yourself together NOW, Elizabeth." (Mom used that full name only in the most drastic of situations.)

Betty broke into sobs that had of late fought to break loose. In the warm arms of her Mother, she promised an immediate reconciliation. Yet, before that could happen, her Dad would receive a phone call from the local hotel: Would he please notify his Daughter that her Husband had just hung himself in his room?

Like her Butch, Betty did not then dally in doldrums. Within hours of Butch's funeral on the prairie, she suffered a massive stroke. Quickly she died from its effects, being buried, as she requested in last breaths, "alongside my Butch".

For her internment, her Oklahoma-in-place parents added two stipulations:

The first was in answer to a wire from Semanthia Smythe, inquiring as to the time of burial services for her dear friend and working associate Betty, so she and a Mrs. Katie Banton could attend. The parents quickly wired back, neither she nor any other Emancipation cohorts would be welcome at the funeral.

Following which the parents had the casket opened head-to-foot for public viewing of their Daughter's remains. Which was to grant another of Betty's final requests, that she be buried in a flowery and lengthy dress which Butch had adored on herself...certainly not in the bloomers even she herself had finally come to despise. Betty, from her roots basically a homespun sort of lady, had felt that Butch would then rest more gently alongside herself.

Far away, Katie pressed sleeplessly into her lonely bed. She added a flood of tears for the Holcombs to those for her own crumbled existence.

For herself and her spouse, an almost equally severe separation would continue.

The Marberry Lions Baseball team was still on its length road-trip.

No communication was there between Husband and Wife.

By then, their shocked neighbors had stopped commenting, "Oh mercy me, what a sad situation!" The Banton breakup was simply another bitter but accepted fact of everyday living, as folks turned back to treating their own painful problems.

Along with all else, Baseball continued its lusty ways.

In the world of the Big Leagues, the wrenching rift caused when the new-born and quickly mushrooming American League had been born to challenge the time-tested National was well into being healed. The ongoing World Series between the two leagues was now an accepted annual event.

The Boston Red Sox had made a $400 purchase from Houston, of the Texas League. That amount brought them Tristram Speaker, "The Grey Eagle," an outfielder, who would hit for a lifetime average of .344. And whom many would claim "could shove Ty Cobb into the outhouse when it came to playing the outfield."

As for the eagerly achieving minor leagues, Katie Banton's Marberry Burglars were the chief conversation subject, no doubt about that.

BURGLARS CLIMB INTO FOURTH PLACE, blared the MARBERRY CLARION'S sports page, as Katie's team neared the end of its long home stand.

"Sensing a comet," the Sports Editor was quick to grab a tail and ride, as per an age-old newspaper theorem:

Katie Banton, Manager of the Burglars, is a smart Baseball pilot. It has been a long time since Burglar fans have seen so much fire on the field, so much heads-up, play-to-win Baseball.

But reporter George Periwinkle, for so long loyal to Muggsy in his writings, refused to go overboard on "the other team in town":

Katie Banton is doing a good job. The team is improved in its spirit and overall play.

Which was undeniably true, especially as shown in a game against the Greyhounds, where the Burglars led, 5-4, in the ninth inning.

Again, proof that no game still alive can be dismissed as won or lost, a Greyhound slammed a pitch into deepest center field. He slid safely into third.

The hometown kranks hung tough.

"We'll get out of this mess."

"Yeah, Katie'll find a way to win."

The manager trotted to her pitcher, the Burglar Blue of her saucy bloomers somehow coming on more striking in the late-afternoon haze.

The Greyhound runner kicked at the dirt around third base while he checked with his coach there.

The meeting at the mound broke up after Katie had sneaked the baseball from her pitcher and moved it into the glove of her third sacker.

Her infielders resumed their positions, shouting encouragement to their pitcher.

The Greyhound runner took a step toward home, then another, watching the pitcher's motion. The pitcher seemed to be ignoring him, so the runner lengthened his lead, paying no attention to the third baseman....until that Burglar tagged him with the ball. He tagged extra hard for the undiluted joy of triumph.

"Yer out!" roared Blind Tom. "Game's over."

The Burglars ran for the dugout, WINNERS.

"Whaaa the hell?" came from the dumbfounded runner who'd been picked off, now still standing at third base as the Burglars trotted by him, joyfully headed for their locker room.

Triumphant Marberry fans, led by the screeching Emancipators, shook the stands with their derisive joy.

"Bonehead!" they yelled.

The Greyhound manager ran at his used-to-be runner.

"You...you IDIOT."

The object of his put-down faced him right back.

"So tell me, smart-assed skipper, if you were so damned wide-awake, why in hell didn't you tell me who had the ball?"

"I...you...aw shaddup. I never seen such a brainless scatterpate."

An hour later, after locking her office while she still glowed in her personal triumph of stealing that victory, Katie returned to the player's dressing room.

Only a dim light from the showering section broke the oncoming lightlessness of advancing nightfall.

"Slugger, are you still in there?"

"You lookin' fer my buddy?" answered Del's suddenly ominous growl from the most-distant corner of the room. "Ol' Slug's long gone, yeah, like a home run shot, outta the ball park. Likely he's downtown already, chasin' 'stuff'.

His words were slurred almost unintelligibly. Katie had no doubt as to the cause. She hesitated...when to confront that severe breaking of team rules?

"But he promised to meet me here. We were going to review his contract."

Then a wavering shaft of light hit the whiskey bottle in Del's huge hand, that glass container near-empty.

Just as evident was the hairy massiveness of his naked chest. The rest of Del was covered by only a white supporter, barely sufficiently sizeable for the task.

Angrily, Katie moved toward him, which she definitely shouldn't have. The closer she drew, the more confronting the smell of booze.

"Del, you know drinking isn't allowed in here. This time it costs you, like I told you, those forty bucks."

"Oh sure, pretty boss."

He spoke casually as he worked his bottle-like arms in a warming-up motion. He moved from the bench in her direction, his eyes thoroughly undressing her.

"But I wasn't hurtin' no one, just sorta soothin' my ache for companionship with a shot o' shine."

She suspected he'd already had many shots.

"Hey there, sexy skipper, how about a li'l drinky-poo with your best home runner? In fact, so I'm (hic!) told, after the two I put outta here today, I'm now the whole damn league's very best and (a belch followed at that point)...beg pardon...foremost dispenser of four-basers, as I once saw one o' them stupid reporters put it. Yeah, how's about a drinky-poo to celebrate that?"

"I should say not!"

"Well, shiver my timbers, but ain't we gettin' uppity?"

He moved toward Katie, however unsteadily, with a savage leer that revealed his desires. Clearly noting which, Muggsy's jeopardized Wife retreated toward the door, or at least attempted to. Del was quicker than she, blocking her lane of exit.

"Aw, what's the hellfire hurry, sexy skipper? Let's me and that daisy body of yours spend a skin-night that'll go into the record books forever."

Savagely she slapped at him. "NO ONE talks that dirty talk to me."

"Well, I do declare to goodness," he told her, trying badly to effect a high-pitched voice. "But, to continue our highly intelligent conversation, what's a cute broad like you...naked in your underpants, wasn't that what your old man called you right here in this room?...doing in such a helluva hurry? Hey, your Muggsy's way too far gone from his hot mama for any lovin' tonight, likely out on some town looking for another doll to cuddle close. While I got you!"

Del's discourse on Muggsy, offered with a knowing leer, dug savagely at the fears she'd carried. As she tried again, disdainfully, to get by Del and reach the open door, she tried another slap. But failed miserably in those ventures.

He grabbed her arm and fiercely. Katie clawed at him.

"Aw now, Katie doll, you shouldn't oughta scratched me," he objurgated, as if deeply wounded.

"Tell you what, les' get this party under way with a kissy-poo from your hot lips. Ferdangsure, your Muggsy don't want you no more, but Del'll try to be proper about accepting damaged merchandise...Lordy, you must have a solid case of the warms, living by yourself."

"Could be, slob, but not for garbage like you."

"Awright, uppity pig, if this is the way you want it, I'll sure oblige."

His clutching hand locked on her arm and twisted it brutally behind her. His mouth punished hers with the stink of cheap booze. She wanted to vomit him away, but had no chance to free herself...

Savagely he yanked at her upper clothing, then all of it hung at her waist in a tattered tangle. Her entire being went into terror far past any she'd ever known.

Her free hand reached hopelessly for some shred of the cloth that would cover herself.

"Lordy Lord, will ya look at them knobs! Just as perfect as I've often dreamed they'd be."

"You'll go to jail for this!"

He took another damp swipe at her lips.

"C'mon, Bitch, let's be sensible, done with all that 'jail' palaver. Whaddya think (hic!) some old judge, who's likely a great fan of mine, will say when he hears you came to this team-room in the dark, knowing I or other guys might be here as naked as jaybirds? 'Just another tease', he's bound 'n determined to decide, then fer sure throw it outta court. You'll be the laughin' stock of this town, a scarlet woman forever. Hey, little Sis, you wanna live with that?

"Woulda been like that for the Teasin' Tessie us guys caught down here a while back. She wouldn't have had a chance, with so many of us guys testifying against her. But the stupid sonofabitchin' owner back then paid her off anyway.

"So now, pretty skipper, what say we get you outta them silly bloomers?"

Using his arm that held her prisoner from behind her back, he flung Katie to the floor. She was dazed and utterly helpless as he bent over her, touching her.

When another decisive grip would pin Del from behind himself.

What Katie dazedly saw next was her attacker slamming into a corner across the room.

"You all right?" asked Slugger Ennis, bending over Katie.

Gallantly he restrained a whistle for the sight before himself. As he would hand her a sweaty Burglar shirt from a nearby hook.

Tears flooded from her to briefly replace her anger, as gratefully she accepted the smelly cover.

"Yes, I gue---guess so."

"Ol' Del got carried away by the booze. It can easy happen."

That returned her venom: "Oh sure. Otherwise, the sweet guy wouldn't have even considered trying to rape me."

Satisfied that Katie was recovering, Slugger left her for his crumpled buddy.

"Father, dear Father, come home with me now. The clock in the steeple strikes one," Del quoted from the popular DRUNKARD melodrama.

"Sorry for clubbin' ya, Delski. Honest to Pete, I didn't know I still had that knockout punch. You sleep it off for a while, then I'll get you outta here.

From across the dressing room, his caring for Del increased Katie's anger.

"Oh no! He tried to steal my body, and now he's going nowhere but to jail.

"He'll never again play for this team or any other professional team; his only games will be with the penitentiary bunch."

"Yes'm, skipper, he sure tried to do you wrong, no doubt o' that," Slugger sought to soothe her. "But, 'twas I you, I'd calm some before raising the roof.

"If my sleepin' buddy is kicked off this team, I'm leavin' right with him. So will plenty other guys, I feel free to predict, even including your precious Pete Brancato. Down deep, Pete's pure ballplayer through and through, you'll learn quick-like. I mean, he don't like his teammates being misused."

"Blackmail!"

"Mebbe so. Mebbe even probably-so. Still again, while you high-flyin' society dames always seem to do what you're bound 'n determined to do, ol' Slugger is passin' you some advice, gold-plated but still friendly-like: This was a large part of what I wanted to see you about this evening, at the request of a lotta guys on this here team, yes including Brancato. Same as you likely don't want us to invade your own dressing room, we don't like you coming down here to ours."

"Your room? I'm the manager of this ball club, or did you forget that?"

"No ma'am. But our room's the only privacy we got at this ball park. We don't go for dames in here while we re-lax and maybe move around naked in our 'easy moments', as you might say.

"'Matter of fact, since we've dished it out this far...and I trust you don't mind 'tough talk'"...

Katie ground her teeth in unrelenting anger, while still trying to cover herself.

"The stage is yours, Mister. Tell me the rest of why I'm such a bad guy."

"Oh no, not that at all. But some matters gotta get squared away. See, Pete and I feared we caught some of the same 'tensions' in here, as you might say it, that were bouncin' around before the regrettable incident with the babe in this room before you joined us. Now Pete, being so admiring of you but a guy at heart, 'specially pushed me to speak to you, so I said, what-the-hell, Brancato, I'll try. I'm just glad to hell 'n back I didn't dally an instant longer in finally getting down here...And no, Mrs. Banton, in case you might wonder, Pete 'n me didn't participate in that other girly-bash down here. We hadn't shown up yet, weren't even on hand when the owner and the cop broke it up.

"Now ol' Del, he's sure not a 'cooth' guy, as you fancy people put it. But ferdangsure he's basically a good guy; I know that from a front row seat 'cause I've palled with him here and on other teams. Besides, he's the best-by-gosh long-ball hitter in this league."

Such words of opprobrium for her attacker re-lit the fire in the Burglar manager.

"You're both kicked off this team!" she fairly screamed at Slugger. Following which, however unsteadily, she ran from the room to somehow reach her carriage and hurry home. During her flight in the darkness, she was grateful that no one, including her neighbors, seemed to notice the Baseball shirt she clutched to herself.

Off in the corner of the team room, Del tried to sit up.

And rubbed his aching jaw.

"Dames is hell," he noted dazedly.

"That they be, Delski."

"What say we head for a load of cooling brew?" suggested Slugger in empathy.

"Hits the spot with me, buddy. Maybe even find special stuff in the brewpatch."

"Although," Del added in regret, "it likely won't come one-to-five hundred against what we delightfully viewed here on this evening. Lordy Lord, for a minute there I sure thought, 'Ol' man White, you're catchin' the last train to heaven'."

Chapter Thirty Seven

"For this relief much thanks," was uttered in HAMLET. Doubtless too by many Baseball managers, watching their bullpen heat up in the closing innings of a tight game. Then certainly by Marberry's Kathleen Banton as she would reflect on her narrow escape from the clutches of Del White.

Arriving at the ball park the next morning, Del and Slugger were notified by coach Slewfoot they should appear pronto in their skipper's office.

"Gonna miss playing here, Slugger. Nice town."

"Yeah, but what the hell, there are plenty of other teams in spots as lively as this burg. Why, I do hear of great Baseball in Mexico, with plenty o' them hotsy Senoritas in the stands."

In her office, Katie was waiting for them, trying not to show nervousness.

"I spoke hastily," she told them. "Shall we forget the whole scene?"

No way they'd turn down that offer. Both nodded in relieved assent.

"And I'm sorry," added Slugger, "for shooting off my mouth."

"I'm glad you did shoot it," Katie told him.

"And I sure apologize fer drinkin' in the team room," added Del, "then gettin' carried away...aw, you know what I mean."

"So let's forget it, both of you, as long as not one other person ever hears about it, and they sure won't from me."

Del was trying to say something else, but suddenly he'd developed a severe case of lockjaw. He fumbled with a large ribboned package he'd brought to the scene.

"Oh?"

Clumsily he handed it to Katie. Carefully she opened it.

Inside were a white and lacy blouse, also beribboned underthings, to replace what he'd savagely destroyed.

"The saleslady said all this should be your size, or you can exchange it," he told her embarrassedly, noting the label that showed the store of purchase.

On each of them, Katie kissed a burning cheek.

"Thank you both so much.

"Now, you apes get out of my office, back to running laps. I've got work to do!"

For once, Del and Slugger were relieved to run.

And manager Katie Banton would never again appear in a men's locker room.

Such was Katie's healing-over of sorts.

Still, in days to come, she would ask herself what had made her approach the Burglar dressing room as darkness came on, instead of sensibly arranging to have Slugger visit her office? Possibly, had the boldness of Emancipation burrowed in herself more deeply than she'd dare realize?

What could shock, even shame Katie most and worst: recalling her body-heat, even in the midst of revulsion, when Del had reached out to touch her.

Still, she had struggled against him...well, hadn't she?

Or was Katie Banton less-good than she'd estimated?

Her Muggsy had been gone for so long. The thought of perhaps never again knowing his powerful love had left her with achingly wakeful nights.

After which Katie Crowley Banton's nights would only worsen.

When she took her Burglars on a road trip, how to handle the situation, one all-alone lady among so many male animals?

Face it, on the road the players had each other for company, in addition to easily finding "Baseball Annies." Those dogged the steps of ballplayers, and no need to urge them into action with the athletes they adored.

Nor did Katie have doubts, the Annies were pursuing her own on-the-loose Husband.

She sought to shut out the consideration, whether he accepted them.

All the while, such road-time away from the park meant she must be strictly on her own, except for the rare times when Elsie and Semanthia would drop in on the off-Marberry scene. Any socializing with her woman-hungry coaches and players, even at mealtimes, could be disastrous to her on-field relations with them.

Then face it, the skipper's dining-out meant no chance that the provocatively bloomered redhead could get lost from the obvious stares of other people nearby. She didn't dare return the obvious male glances passed out in hotel dining rooms or lobbies. It was positively unfair, she told herself, how certainly some men could spot a lonely girl.

Katie could but agonize through those days, counting the hours till she would be back in Marberry with Jimmy and Mom and Dad.

But even that return would be agony-spiked; her once-protective Husband would simultaneously be leaving Marberry with his Lions on another road-trip. Oh, the folly of her big mouth, telling Muggsy she wouldn't see him again until he apologized before her team!

At least there was one well from which she could draw the sweet water of support in those supremely distraught times:

Her team (THE BIZARRE BURGLARS, they had often been referred to) were now a consistently winning ball club.

Finally and actually, first place was within their grasp.

Chapter Thirty Eight

"I have no joy in this contract." - Macbeth

Oppositely for Muggsy and his once-champion (but now thoroughly flattened) Lions, just nothing went right.

Back in Marberry, and after suffering their twelfth straight reversal, they found themselves in fifth place.

Wrote the CLARION sports editor:

Local Baseball fans seem hardly excited these days for the chance to watch their Lions. They are avoiding Lions Park in record numbers. To resurrect a hoary saying from the athletic world, "The stands are so empty, you can shoot deer in there."

Well, what is there to draw fans to owner Cliff Hartwick's once-exciting ballyard? The local team that has grabbed the United League confalon for the past two years is sinking fast, large bubbles now emerging at the surface. Today, fifth place. Tomorrow, the cellar? Look out below!

Reasons for the Lions collapse? Perhaps many of those, certainly spearheaded by the utterly tragic loss of forever dependable third baseman and indefatigable team leader Butch Holcomb. But past that and many other causative influences, something destructive has put an octopus-hold on Lion manager Muggsy Banton. Apparently, a shattered marriage has snuffed out the desire that once made him a flaming leader, who was being thoroughly scouted for a managerial post in the Big Leagues.

To worsen the situation, Muggsy's team has collapsed in tune with him. No hitting, no pitching, stupid base-running, and a fielding collapse by Lions who go through the motions but show no resemblance to Winners.

Observed the Marberry newspaper's Baseball reporter, one George Periwinkle:

True, the Lions haven't done well of late. However, with a top-flight leader such as Muggsy Banton, they are due to quickly pick up ground in the United League standings, likely beginning this afternoon. It's a long worm that has no turning.

Re-reading his own journalistic spiel, George would hope his words of good cheer had at least convinced himself.

In her ground-floor apartment, Elsie read the same reports on Lion doings.

"That horrid Muggsy certainly deserves anything and everything bad that can happen to him. And dumb ol' George doesn't know what he's writing."

In the midst of which haughty put-down, Elsie's doorbell did ring with insistent overtones.

Her visitor was George, the determined Romeo. He had been drinking, to some excess, to salve his wounds of heartache. But the liquor hadn't begun any healing.

"Well, George, you pest! What do you want this time?"

"I'll show you, Elsie darling, what I want and am determined to get," he told her in tones that were both endearing and stormy. He pushed past her, into the apartment.

"Elsie, my love, you and I must come to a meeting of souls right now, no more fooling around. I love you, my precious, I truly do. I mean to take you away with me, just the two of us in the bliss of a faraway hideaway."

George's adored one only laughed scornfully.

"That's what you say, you...you...mere man, you. I reached understanding a long time ago. But you're too dense to catch on."

"Then, my sweetness, I have but one final alternative."

He went into much the same crouch as a wrestler assumes before springing at his opponent.

"You, skinny pipsqueak? You couldn't move me a yard or an inch."

"Then, Elsie, my heart's desire, I'll just have to show you."

The big Blonde stood her ground as George charged her. He grabbed a lovely arm and tried to pull her to the door. She stayed where she was.

He moved behind her, and sought to push her through the open door. Still and absolutely no headway could he gain.

No other alternative left, he advanced from the front, tackled her at her knees, and threw her over his shoulder, caveman-style.

"Stop, George...stop, you idiot! What will the neighbors think?...George, let's talk this over like thinking people who know how to communicate."

They neared the door, and George's plan seemed securely in motion, in spite of her frantic kicking and flailing her arms.

"No stopping...this time," he puffed under his load, feeling a rush of joyous accomplishment he hadn't reached in a long time or ever.

"Got a romantic hideaway...all prepared for us star-crossed lovers."

"George, I'll call the police."

At that instant, something interrupted his forward march. Perhaps Elsie was squirming too vigorously. Or maybe the rug wasn't firmly-enough anchored on the slippery floor to stand such scuffling. Whatever, down plunged George, plentiful Elsie on top of him, a hopeless tangle of bodies, but at least she had a slim cushion in her fall.

She finally disengaged herself, arising to straighten her clothing.

George Periwinkle was out colder than any proverbial mackerel.

Elsie looked down scornfully at her would-be kidnapper. She went to the kitchen and returned with a pitcher of ice-cold water. She threw that into George's face.

Suddenly he sat up, bewildered.

"What happened? Did a house fall on me?"

"No, just your 'dream girl', you idiot, insufferable male. Now get out of here, phony Casanova, and stay out."

No quitter, the dazed reporter still sought to insist he'd take her away with himself.

With little effort, Elsie pulled woozy George off the floor and shoved him through the door. He landed roughly on the front lawn, as she slammed the door behind him.

After yet another Lion defeat the next afternoon, George and Muggsy left the ball park in the reporter's carriage. Muggsy had sold his red gas-mobile; it had belonged to a happy time of his life, no way it should be included in his bedraggled hours of today.

"Muggsy, you sure look down and almost out. I hate to see that."

"Nothin's much fun anymore."

"It's bound to get better. Or, maybe like some Wise Man From The East was supposed to have put it, 'Tomorrow it gets even worse, after that it gets better'."

George's attempt at gentle whimsy was a lost cause.

"I'm not sure about anything anymore," muttered Muggsy morosely. "But hey, what happened to you? Been in a fight or something? That's some ostrich-egg on your forehead."

His friend was rueful as he recounted the day before and his visit to Elsie, ending with his being dumped violently onto the not-soft front yard.

"Man, you picked on an Amazon. Better rassle with someone your own size."

"I'm beginning to think you're right...either that or simply club Elsie into submission like the cavemen did to their women. Trouble there, I love Elsie too much to hurt her."

After a while, they passed a carnival spread out over a vacant lot not many blocks from Lions Park. George pulled to the side of the road.

"What say, Muggsy, we go in there for some laughs?"

"Helluva idea! Between us two down-and-outers, we need at least a dozen solid haw-haws."

They wandered through the noisy grounds, watching animated carnival-goers scurrying by. In the midst of that hubbub, both could briefly forget their blues.

They stopped before the Geek, who amazed the crowd by "biting the head off a live chicken." Though George, forever the inquisitive reporter, had to wonder, whence the endless supply of fowls? After all, the sign above the performer noted that his show was repeated every half hour. George suspected that some sleight of hand (or mouth) was defying their viewing processes.

They came upon the Fat Lady, "all 428 pounds of her." Muggsy said he'd hate to get stuck with her feed bill.

The "absolutely amazing" Sword Swallower seemed to defy indigestion.

"Hey, this is all right," came merrily from Muggsy. "I'd forgotten how much fun these shows can be."

Literally buried in the farthest corner of the showgrounds, and next to the exit they finally headed for, they spotted a baseball-throwing game. The concessionaire was a wearied little old fellow whose customers were currently at a minimum, and for a simple reason: most of them were out of money by the time they reached his booth.

The old-timer leaned on them, last-chance, as likely marks.

He called out in what was left of his pitch-tones, "Throw some balls, gents, win some fabulous prizes to take home to the little Ladies."

Muggsy felt sorry for the elderly gent, and threw a dollar on the counter.

"I'll try six balls, and..."

Then he took a closer look at the stand's proprietor.

"Well, I'll be a monkey's uncle...George, have you met Sam Streck? I know you've read a ton about him in Baseball books."

Sam Streck...now there was a name to be etched in a player's (or fan's) brain. Muggsy remembered hearing about Sam from the time he'd first heard of The Big Leagues.

For the records Sam had compiled as a sparkling second baseman and cleanup hitter, that one still formed a copious core in the game's earliest and most dynamic chapters.

And again, Sam had toured with Cliff Hartwick on springtime jaunts.

Eagerly did Muggsy reach forward to shake the wrinkled hand.

"How are you, Mr. Streck?"

"Near-to-middlin', Muggsy, and I'll thank ye to do away with 'Mister'. From yourself, plain ol' 'Sam' will do just grandly."

"Haven't seen you at our games for quite a while now."

In an aside to George, Muggsy explained that Sam lived directly behind the left field fence at Lions Park, "Oh...about the 375-foot mark..."

"No, cain't get around so good on these pins no more."

Both visitors to the booth had to remember the Baseball bromide: On old ballplayers, it's the legs that go first.

"But I do see a lot of your team from my roof, first-rate view that is, 'specially with my binoculars."

"Sure, I shoulda remembered that. So how's your Wife?"

"Cain't say for sure," was the suddenly glum reply. "Since she joined them dadratted Bloomer Girls, my Daisybelle's moved out on me, after 52 years we'd been hitched. Now she's sent me notice, she wants a dee-vorce. Said she wanted to be 'all-the-way ee-mancipated', if you can believe that. Though damned how I can figure she'd make a living...she's not even a real good cook, though I put up with her efforts all these years 'cause I'm fonda her."

"Sam, I've got somewhat the same sick situation."

"So I've heard, Muggsy, sorry about that...But hey, I went 'cross town to watch your Wife's team play, just t'other day. Could only stay a few innings, though. The way them women down front was yellin' like banshees, coulda busted my eardrums if I hadn't high-tailed it for home early in the afternoon.

"Still, I gotta tell ya, Muggsy, you must've taught her our game mighty fine, the way she's changed-over that miserable bunch of mostly has-beens and never-was's into one sharp ball club. Though I hate to see any decent lady prancing in public in her skivvies like your Wife does..yeah, and like my 75-year-old Daisybelle does too...at least your lady still has the figger to pull it off some impressive. Mine's so doggone skinny now (though she used to have a gorgeous figger, I tell you!), them ridiculous bloomers make her look like a stalk of celery sticking out of an over-plowed field. Wish I had a picture of her to show her how silly she looks, then maybe she might quit that show she's tryin' to put on."

Manager Muggsy did hold much empathy for the Baseball immortal standing before himself.

"It's awful," he told Sam, "what's happened to good women."

"Oh Sam, I'm sorry...I forgot to introduce you to George Periwinkle, a damn good Baseball reporter."

"Mighty pleased to make your acquaintance, young fella. Have to say you know a dang site more about ball games than the other so-called Baseball writers I've come on."

"Thank you, Mr. Streck. Coming from you, that's truly appreciated."

Out of reportorial curiosity, George motioned to the concession stand before them:

"Mr. Streck, how come you're running this ball-throwing stand?"

"Ol man's gotta keep on making money, if'n an old man's gonna keep eatin'...Besides, I feel at home 'round baseballs; they can still remind me of my best days."

From Muggsy: "Pardon me, Sam, but it looks like you aren't doing such hot-shot business here."

"Nah, but maybe if you two guys threw some, and folks saw you at them balls 'n pins, my trade would jack up in a hurry. Wouldja mind, be my shills? I won't even charge you for your fun."

Muggsy thrust forward a dollar bill.

Sam sought to hand the dollar bill back to Muggsy, but that one almost fiercely refused it.

"Glad to throw, Sam, but we'll pay our way, or no deal."

"Suit yerselves, thank ye again."

With just two tosses, Muggsy finished off the pins. Sam handed him a bright feather for his cap, 'midst spectator buzzing.

"Your turn, Reporter. Win a feather to match the manager's."

"Haven't handled a ball in a while."

"Aw, give it a whirl," was Muggsy's encouragement.

George picked a worn horsehide from the pile. His long fingers wrapped around it in familiar, almost loving style, or so it seemed to Muggsy.

The arm unwound in a rhythmic motion, the ball sped true to the mark, and every pin went flying.

Flabbergasted, Sam Streck and Muggsy stared at the scatter-pile of wood.

The onwatchers yelled their approval.

"Holy cow!" uttered an amazed Muggsy. "George, where in blue blazes didja get that natural motion and all that swift? For sure, not from pounding a typewriter."

Sam whistled, unbelieving, as he picked up what was left of a pin. The impact of George's throw had broken it in half.

"Jumpin jee-hosephat, whatta throw...young fella, you sure you're not Christy Mathewson in disguise?"

The crowd begged George Periwinkle to throw some more. But the tall scribe was embarrassed by the commotion.

"Naw...I was just lucky on that one. Oh sure, I played a little ball a long time ago...but..."

He collected his feather, then added a dollar in Sam's money-basket.

"Gee, thanks, guys. Will ya just look at all the folks behind you two right now, waiting for a chance to throw? Looks like my best day-and-night ever."

"Nothing, Sam," said the manager. "And, whenever you want good seats for any Lion games (on the house, of course!), they're yours. We'd sure be honored, too, for your throwing out the first ball at one of our games, anyoldtime. Would mean a lot for our fans to see one of the game's all-time greats."

"You're so kind, Muggsy, and I'll sleep happy for your invite. But I make it to my roof easiest of all."

Sam watched them walk away, his eyes locked on the confident stride of George and on that strong arm too. He gazed again at the shattered pin in his hand.

"'Played a little ball a long time ago'....oh sure."

Chapter Thirty Nine

GAMBLING WISDOM FOR TODAY: "A betting parlor is where a person can be saved from losing any money by not seeking any further money in the first place." ...Wisdom said to be uttered by one of the "Chicago Black Sox" after some of their number were suspended from Baseball for allegedly (never proven) throwing the 1919 World Series.

Came the following morning, and Muggsy went out to his lawn for his copy of the MARBERRY CLARION. The blazing headlines grabbed him:

CENTRAL LEAGUE BASEBALL "FIX" SCANDAL REVEALED.

"Hey, Muggsy, looks like they finally trapped those crooks," a neighbor called out.

"Sure looks like it, and hip-hooray for whoever broke the case," the Lion skipper called back, as he read on: Two players involved in the dirty gambling case, when finally confronted with overwhelming facts against themselves, had quickly pleaded guilty to taking bribes for throwing games. They had fingered the leader of the conspiracy as a doctor-gambler, one Phillip Sutton.

Following which, some ambitious journalist at THE CLARION had combed the paper's morgue to learn that Dr. Sutton had once been engaged to marry Miss Elsie Peabody, now the head of the local Women's Emancipation chapter, which owned the Marberry Burglars Baseball team. So Elsie's-and-Phillip's announcement photo (that taken by a reporter/photog named George Periwinkle at Lions Park) was used with the story.

"Sonofa....?" muttered Muggsy. "I just knew there was something sleazy 'bout that bozo Sutton. From the first minute I laid eyes on him, I didn't like that piece o' betting trash."

The CLARION story proceeded onward to reveal that the two guilty players had completely cleared the third, who'd been under suspicion for some months.

That one was Hubert Jorgenson, a highly promising first baseman who had disappeared three years earlier at the onset of the gambling investigation.

The guilty ones admitted that Jorgenson had been set up as the "fall guy" for the whole scheme. And that the reason for his disappearance was his fear of being framed by Dr. Sutton, now firmly in custody.

What really rocked Muggsy: The solution of the case had dragged the city of Marberry, Pennsylvania into the spotlight. In the CLARION editorial offices, when picture of those involved were brought forth, staffers had immediately noted the amazing likeness of Hubert Jorgenson to one of their own number, reporter George Periwinkle. There was, to be sure, the present absence of a moustache. Also a changed hair style. But otherwise, the features seemed identical.

When questioned then, reporter Periwinkle had soon confessed that he was indeed the long-missing Hubert Jorgenson. He also verified the words of the other players involved, those now occupants of a nearby state penitentiary.

"Well, I'll be a mother monkey's uncle," muttered Muggsy, as he read on:

When interviewed, Jorgenson had described himself as a happy man on this day of revelation and complete vindication. His plans were to stay in Marberry at his present reportorial job, at least for the remainder of the current Baseball season.

No, he did not anticipate trouble in getting back to shape for playing ball. He had stayed in good condition through regular workouts in a nearby town, considerable hours of batting practice included.

Hubert was quoted as hoping that Baseball...some team, somewhere...would still find a place for his services.

"Big news, eh Muggsy?" called out the neighbor, as the Lion manager remained glued to the bombastic story.

"Yeah, big news."

In another part of town, Sam Streck read the story.

"Oh yeah...played a little ball...hopes somebody wants him...oh sure. That young man talks a caution, dang near like he tosses that horsehide at my pins. Say, I'd better put in a quick call to Mr. John McGraw, at them Polo Grounds in New York City. He asked me to some day come up with a honest-to-gosh STAR for his Giants."

Chapter Forty

Speaking of slumps: I heard a quote attributed to a Chicago Cub infielder notorious for the never-cease manner in which he wagered on race horses.

Said he, "I've been in losing streaks so bad that I gave up listening to the results of races. All I hoped for was that my nag was included in the late scratches."

A week after the gambling bombshell did hit the wires, these stories topped the CLARION'S sports section.

BUSTIN' BURGLARS BREAK BARRIER, ACTUALLY MOVE INTO FIRST PLACE
and
LISTLESS LIONS LOSE, COMING CLOSE TO CELLAR. Near-empty home park sees 15-1 crushing by Bears.

About that second item, the sports editor did write:

Manager Muggsy Banton of the Lions, for so long an idol in Marberry, heard distressingly unfamiliar sounds through yesterday's demolishing loss. Those were boos from home fans. What set off the worst of the outcry was a seemingly inexcusable mental lapse by Banton.

In the bottom of the sixth inning of what was still a scoreless pitchers' duel, Banton reached first base via a base on balls. He was sacrificed to second, where, with one out, he represented the go-ahead run...the Lions' first chance in a while to grab a lead. But then, for some inexplicable reason, Muggsy wandered several feet off second and went sleepy-eye.

A snap throw from Bear catcher Tex Hardesty nailed him easily. And Muggsy's thoroughly unnerved team never offered another threat through the remainder of the long, dreary afternoon. During which local fans

wouldn't let their manager forget his sleep-walking act. Results: The more they stayed on the once-fiery Lion leader, the worse his team fell apart.

Any day now, we still expect "the new Banton" to reclaim his fire, charging umpire "Blind Tom," screaming at close calls against his team, as in glorious days of yore. Still and again, Muggsy's spirit is apparently shattered by the breakup of his "ideal marriage" to Kathleen Crowley, daughter of James T. Crowley, a prominent Marberry banking executive. While she is currently riding high, wide, and beautiful as manager of the first-place Burglars, for so long Marberry's ho-hum "other team."

Reporter Hubert Jorgenson, continuing at least temporarily as a CLARION scribe, sought valiantly to refute the above thoughts. But in that his typewriter dismally failed him. Limply, he could but hope for better days.

Two days later, the Lions rode bumpity-bum-bump into the United League basement.

Muggsy cornered Cliff Hartwick in that team-owner's office at Lion Park.

When his catcher/manager, disconsolate, shuffled in, Cliff needed but one glance at his down demeanor. And posted the storm-warning.

"Well, hello there, Muggsy. Say, how's Jimmy these days?"

"I haven't seen him. J.T. and Clara asked me to come out for dinner. But whatthehell, that would be sickening for all of us."

Nervously, Muggsy worked his battered and dirty cap from hand to hand.

"Cliff, I hear you're thinking of changing managers."

Cliff couldn't escape the listless expression, the three-day beard, the soiled and unpressed clothes. Still the Lions owner forced a grin.

"Damn foolish scuttlebutt. You know how reporters start rumors when they've nothing useful to write. Say, why don't you and Katie and my bride Blanche and I have dinner together tonight??"

No derailing for Muggsy.

"The paper says you might even hire a girl to run the team, to offset the big crowds at Burglar games, and put some black back in your ledger."

"Aw, Muggs...well, yeah, some stockholders suggested a change. But I told 'em I'm sticking with my guy. If they don't like it, I'll buy 'em out."

"I appreciate the loyalty more than I can tell you. But, Cliff, I want my release from the Lions...I want it right now...today."

"Look, Muggsy, I know you're down, and I hurt for you, honest I do. But we all go through rough times, and we just gotta bounce back...Surely you and Katie will mend things, then..."

"She's found a new life...doesn't need me anymore."

Nervously, Cliff toyed with his letter-opener, stalling for a miracle, "praying for rain," as a battered pitcher, about to be removed, would be described.

"Hey, Muggs, we got too many old guys on this team. You stay with me; next season we'll load up on young, fast kids. Hellfire, who gives a hoot or holler about one bad season, after a lot of good ones?"

"No, I'm not making guys I've played with the patsies 'cause I don't have it no more."

"Damn!" the owner did explode. And was about to cave in, accept his manager's resignation.

But then, tapped on the shoulder by some guardian angel, he grasped lightning from the clouds, or so it seemed. Not his own idea, true, but one implanted in his psyche by his Bride, Blanche du Bois Hartwick.

Repeated of late, as Blanche and Cliff had spent the nights in each others' arms, she had protested against what was happening to their young friends: It was a tragedy to see her favorite lovers torn apart, and so needlessly. She could think of no way to start the repair, until she came on one way through her adored Husband.

"Oui, Amour, you must do it, and tres-quicklike, to mix my native tongue with yours."

As Muggsy, thoroughly downhearted, faced his owner in that one's office, he had to see the almost-startled expression on Cliff's face, as that one prepared to forward the solution of his Blanche.

"You all right, Cliff?"

"Yeah, never felt as all-fire great as at this moment...Muggsy, you get your release...but on one condition: You've got to stay with my ball club, honor your contract with me....through this Saturday evening."

Suspicious, his catcher faced him squarely, waiting for what would come.

"Oh?"

"Yeah. I've scheduled a game with the Burglars for this Saturday, in this park. It's an open date for both teams, just before we hit the road again. All proceeds from the game to the local Boys Club."

Muggsy was a crashing cloud of catastrophe.

"Sorry, Cliff, but I'm refusing you, first time ever. And I'm surprised, really surprised, you'd play dirty pool on Katie and me, putting us against each other in public."

"Have it your way, skipper," was the owner's forcedly casual answer, as he turned back to his desk and the paperwork there. "So I'll have no way-to-go but to hold you to your contract, which, you just might remember, runs through next season."

Muggsy grabbed at any straw in the tempest: "The Marberry chief of police won't allow this game. He knows there'll be a riot coming out of it, especially with the hullabaloo those stupid bloomer dames would make over the show."

"Old chief Kevin Kelly, bless his recently departed soul, would never have permitted it, that's safely granted. But Johnny O'Brien, our new young chief, is far more adventurous. He has told me personally that this town needs such a spark to build civic pride. Besides, he has a bigger force than Kelly did...I know that for sure; Johnny told me it was one of the absolutely strict conditions under which he took the job."

Thus did Cliff Hartwick continue to bluff, with hardly an ace in his hand. He hadn't approached the new chief or Katie with any plans for the game.

Cliff just wished he could take a breather right then, and seek counsel from his Blanche: "Look, lover, you got me into this mess. So whadda I do now, with my best friend hating me from across my desk?"

"Bluff some more, all the way to 'Le Triomphe'," he could clearly hear her urging. "Amour conquers the universe."

"So how about it, Muggsy?" he blazed forward...."Aw come on....another six days with the lousy Lions. Remember how excited you were when you first joined us? You said it was your dream-come-true."

He watched his manager out of one eye as he went back to the papers on his desk, shuffling them and trying not to give away his concern.

Muggsy was still slumped, a hopelessly-beaten baseballer and husband, in the chair opposite Cliff. Only his eyes seemed alive; they sought to bore through the Indian-head design on the rug.

Finally: "You win, Cliff. But consider our friendship dead and buried."

"Aw...." Cliff looked like he wanted to cry big tears, which of course he did. But the gamble was on the table. No room for his own feelings.

Some dam within himself finally broken loose, Muggsy let his feelings go awash.

"Yeah, I'll play in your lousy game against the stinkin' Burglars. After that, I hope I never see another ball game for the rest of my days. I'll be off to somewhere that's a long way from this crumby game."

Through the agony of that preachment, Cliff nevertheless had the strange notion that, somehow, the crisis had turned its first corner. Before him, he had finally seen a flash of the old Muggsy. How he loved that!

Lantern-jaw almost touching his dirty shirt, Muggsy shuffled from the office. While Cliff wiped his brow in desperation.

"Man alive. And may the beseeching saints in Heaven forgive me for such fibs, saying the game was already set. Now those stinkin' Burglars gotta agree to the game...holey smoley, am I ever starting to sound just like Muggsy?"

He signaled for his secretary, and she appeared in the doorway.

"Miss Murphy, please find the address of that Elsie Peabody, the district leader of the Emancipators who own the Burglars. I must send her a wire immediately. And I want a copy of the same wire sent to the Sports Editor, THE MARBERRY CLARION.

"Pardon me, Mr. Hartwick, but I know Elsie's address. I was at her place for a meeting of Emancipation officials. I just...well, I didn't quite dare wear the bloomers here to work."

"I'll be damned...et tu, Miss Brutus?"

"Et me, Mr. Hartwick."

Suddenly Cliff was laughing.

"Hey, looks like we're surrounded. Be my guest, Miss Murphy, and feel free to wear your bloomers before my august clients and myself."

"Thank you, Mr. Hartwick. I keep a pair in my desk drawer here, just in case the bars might sometimes fall. I'll change into them right now."

The wire was sent:

Miss Elsie Peabody, please know we are challenging Burglars to charity game, benefit of Marberry Boys Club, Lions Park, this coming Saturday, August 16. Anticipate you will not favor participation in game for no-chance Burglars have of winning. Still, we await your reply.
(signed) Cliff Hartwick
- for Marberry Lions

Shortly after, the reply did arrive:

Fearlessly, the Marberry Burglars, owned and guided by the glorious Women's Emancipate Crusade, accept Lion challenge. Just as we anticipate resounding success in our every venture, so we have no fears VS

the next hurdle to be conquered, your **Marberry Lions.**
(signed) Elsie Peabody
- for Marberry Burglars

Close behind that one was a wire from Katie:

Cliff, wish you hadn't done this. You are terribly embarrassing two of your best friends. Still, I affirm Elsie's acceptance of challenge to meet/beat Lions. Will arrive home tomorrow morning to complete arrangements.
(signed) Kathleen Crowley Banton

Suddenly it struck Cliff, he hadn't yet received the O.K. for the game from Johnny O'Brien, Marberry's chief of police, no matter how he had bluffed to Muggsy that such was a sure thing.

But Cliff had guessed well. The chief quickly let him know, he couldn't be more pleased with the prospect. He would make all needed arrangements for added forces in the field from his department. And would Cliff please put aside 4 grand seats for him, such as directly behind home plate?

The Lion owner was so happy to accede to that last.

"You seem terribly excited, Mr. Hartwick," noted the bloomered Miss Murphy, re-entering his office.

"I am indeed. I may have lost two close friends by my over-boldness, but at least it'll bring them eyeball to eyeball with each other. Then who knows just what might happen...And may I congratulate you on your bloomers, Miss Murphy...you do look enchanting in them...Watch out, you'll be making some over-the-hill guys feel sprightly again."

Charmingly, she curtsied for him.

"Thank you, sir. You'll be having me feel almost guilty in cheering our Burglars to victory over your Lions."

Cliff chuckled. "I'll tell you, Miss Murphy, how sure I am, that won't happen. I will take the Lions and bet you another pair of bloomers against a box of cigars. Now, how's that for a jim-dandy challenge?"

"A daisy!" assented the secretary.

In that office, same as all around Marberry, tensions were mounting.

Chapter Forty One

WHAT PRICE EXCITEMENT? A son took his Father, visiting New York City from northern Maine, to Yankee Stadium. It would be Dad's first taste of big league Baseball.
 "Dad, for two dollars, you'll see more excitement than you ever dreamed possible."
 "Wa'lll now, I'm not so sure of that," slowly the Dad did drawl. "Seems t' me, two dollars was all I paid fer your Ma's and my wedding license."

Headlines would proclaim the fever-pitch of Marberry fans, blaring type that had abandoned the CLARION's sports section for page one-section one:
EXCITEMENT REIGNS SUPREME FOR CITY CHAMPIONSHIP GAME.

POLICE SLATE MORE-MORE RESERVES AS TENSION GROWS, LIONS VS BURGLARS.

EMANCIPATORS FROM NEW YORK CITY AND WASHINGTON D.C. TAKE LAST OF OUR HOTEL SPACE, VOW THAT "BLOOMERISM" WILL PREVAIL.

Muggsy was first miserable over the impending battle. But gradually, and since he couldn't escape the "trying ordeal", he zeroed in on plans for winning.
 "If we can't stomp them stinkin', stupid Burglars," he finally, and then repeatedly, crowed to anyone who would listen, "then we'd better quit Baseball and take up croquet or crochetin'."

When Cliff again saw his skipper, he had to joyously note Muggsy's again-shaven face, along with his freshened clothing.
 And breathed to himself:
 "Hartwick, you should oughta be objurgated, even flogged with wet noodles for your faintness-of-heart. Just keep on keeping-on listening to your gorgeous and knowledgeable Wife. Come to think of it, maybe those Emancipators are

right...maybe it is the girls' time to rule the world."

On her return home for a day, Katie informed the local press, she was confident her red-hot team would trample the slumping Lions.

However, to herself, she still hoped the defeat of her Husband's team would not be topheavy. Dearly she wanted him to save face so he'd ask her to come home...or so a dilemma-bound Burglar manager analyzed the murky mess that she and her spouse had torn from an otherwise blissful existence.

Meanwhile, across town, diamond disaster poured for the shattered and lifeless Lions still another draught of doom:

Their only available first baseman was struck on the ankle by a line drive, a shattered bone resulting from that.

"Oh no!" moaned Katie. "Now we'll beat them even worse, and Muggsy will never come home to Jimmy and me."

When Hubert reached his boarding house that night, Mrs. Haggleby, his generally bad-dispositioned landlady, awaited him at the front stoop.

"Mr. Periwinkle (or Mr. Jorgenson, or whatever your name is...I swan, I just can't decipher you young folks of today!)...there's a woman waiting in your room. She's wearing those shameful bloomers that had to be made in Sodom or Gomorrah...I declare to goodness, no decent woman would wear underpants outside her other clothes....

"I told her she couldn't go up there to your room. But she'd somehow found out which is your room, and she went up anyway, real flip-like, she did."

Hubert showed fascination for the news.

"Oh? Could this lady be tall and a blonde?"

"Hhmph! In my world, she ain't no lady. And you like tall blondes, now do you?" sniffed the landlady, who was stockily built and had streaky black hair. "Can't for any reason on earth see why. No, this one's sorta small, and a redhead. Never did trust redheads nohow, I sure didn't."

Hubert started up the stairs in long and decisive strides.

"Get her out of my decent house," were Mrs. Haggleby's shrill grace-notes flung after him.

Hubert knocked on his door, though he wasn't sure why.

"Come on," acknowledged a pleasant voice.

"Katie!"

"I had to see you, Hubert. I want you to (please) offer your first-base services to the Lions for the game on Saturday. They need you so badly."

Hubert pulled a chair next to her window seat.

"Please try that one again."

"I said I want you to please offer to play first base for the Lions in their game against us this Saturday."

"Me?"

"You."

"Why? Are you some...what's the word, seneschal?...hovering over this game to make sure everything comes out just right for everybody?"

That stung the bloomered female before him, probably even more than he had meant it to. But, as of that moment, the reporter's feelings were running to the raw side. Still, she bounced back quickly, as she had to in this time of decision.

"I want you to join the Lions, Hubert, because, with you in their lineup, we won't beat Muggsy's team quite so badly, then he won't feel as put out as if we'd beaten them by a big score. And maybe some day he'll come after me again.

"After all, Hubert, you did say in the paper, didn't you, that you'd kept in shape and would soon be ready to play...and...well, didn't you?"

After all of that, Katie fairly ran out of breath.

As they caught a sound at the door. Feet softly moving on the other side?

Hubert quickly moved to the door handle, unlocked it, and jerked the door open.

Mrs. Haggleby, with an eye pressed against the keyhole, fell into the room, landing in mortification at Hubert's feet.

"I hope you're satisfied," he spoke in a harsh tone. "Or are you disappointed that we still have our clothes on?"

He next turned to Katie, "And I apologize to Mrs. Haggleby for your coming up here and starting all this. Women of today are just getting too damn forward, at least a lot of them are."

"I'm sorry too. I should have phoned you first," offered an abashed Katie.

Wails of misery from the old crone: "And I'm sorry too, Mr. Hubert. I just didn't want the neighbors to think..."

Hubert almost smiled at the round-robin of apologies. Instead, he turned his fire back to Mrs. Haggleby.

"Please leave this room," he demanded. "Then we won't be here but a moment."

She departed quickly, eager to be freed from the situation.

"Let's go for a walk," suggested Katie.

"Good idea. This place is starting to feel too stuffy and closed-in."

Their walk began in bewildered silence, neither knowing what to say, each waiting for the other to begin whatever further conversation would be.

Their problem was solved by a man riding by and yelling out, "Hey, Jorgenson, you gonna sell out as a Burglar spy?"

Their laughter at that would lighten their mood.

"That's my CLARION editor. He knows his business like few people I've ever met. Which makes me reluctant to quit my present job. Though I know that now it's time to move on, hopefully back to Baseball, where I belong.

"Yeah, Katie, like you were saying, I am in good shape. Before long I'll be back at my peak form, however high that peak might just be in the battle-cry of Baseball, as I've sometimes heard it described. It'll be tough, though, to find a peak as early as this Saturday."

"I know that, but you'll surely do a lot better than anyone else the Lions can find in a hurry. Maybe you can even grab the Lion job for keeps, or at least until the Big Leagues come after you."

"I love the way you dream for me," he told her appreciatively. "But sure, I'll join the Lions, if they'll have me...and if Scranton, which owns my contract, will give me an O.K. to play here for a while."

"Hubert, I hope you don't mind, but this 'pushy broad' already took the liberty of checking with the Scranton club's owner, to make sure it was all right to talk to you. He most kindly gave me that permission."

"No problem, Mrs. Banton. I'm glad you did that. Makes me feel more sure of the ground I'm standing on."

"And don't worry a mite about the Lions wanting you, Hubert. I also checked with Cliff Hartwick. He was delighted at the thought of you bolstering his team for the game this Saturday, possibly too for the future....Aw, Hubert, I do hope you're not mad at me for taking so much upon myself.

"This sad-souled girl just has to pull any and every string that might bring her guy back to her."

"I pray each night for the both of you...and Katie, you amaze me, I must say; you cover more bases than Detroit's Ty Cobb. Honestly, I never thought of you as such a thorough Baseball executive. Muggsy must have taught you well."

"That he did. In fact, sometimes he taught me so incessantly, he wore me out. I can even wonder, strange as it sounds, if he had this premonition of what was to come, so he just had to do a thorough job. For now, Hubert, I hope he comes after you, whether he does it on his own or because Cliff 'sorta suggested' it.

"Whole lot of conspiring going on."

"Whole lotta; you can stick that in your pipe 'n puff on it, to quote Muggsy."

They turned back toward Hubert's boarding house.

"Hubert, you were so right. I shouldn't have gone up to your room. The 'old Katie' never would have done it."

"I don't think so either. But, like so many girls of today, you seem lost in the new ideas."

"Those ideas, are they really so destructive?"

"Probably not when taken with moderation. But surely they are when they get out of hand, and they separate people who should be together.

"Past the absolute tragedy of the Holcombs, I mean, the sadness of it is when they keep loving people torn apart....like you Bantons, and Sam Streck and his Daisybelle...oh, like so many other couples, certainly including Elsie and me. I mean, Katie, that hurts bad; Elsie's the girl I've dreamed of."

Katie stopped to face the tall young man beside her, and thoughtfully took his hands in her, caring not a whit if the gesture be seen.

"Hubert, I just know that Elsie likes you a whole lot, or she wouldn't spend so much time trying to convince herself she doesn't care...and I can swear to you that she does spend so much time at that. Girls are like that, or didn't you know?

"That awful Dr. Sutton (that crook!) truly hurt and disillusioned Elsie, so she was ripe for the port-in-the-storm that was the Emancipation thing.

"She just must be reassured by a good man, which is you, Hubert, oh it must be you. When it finally happens, Hubert, step on her every time she gets too rambunctious. Don't hurt her. Just step on her some. Believe her Best Friend, Hubert, that's what Elsie wants, and needs... Come to think of it, if Muggsy had stepped on me a few times, maybe I wouldn't be living by myself today...well, not by myself, 'cause I have Jimmy, but certainly without a man through all these awful nights..."

Back at his boarding house, a still-apologetic Mrs. Haggleby met Hubert at the front door.

"There's another visitor in your room...this time a man. And honest, I am sorry for the way I acted."

"Forget it, Mrs. Haggleby. It certainly wasn't all your fault."

In Hubert's room was Muggsy, far more upbeat than the last time the reporter had been with him.

"Hey, Hubert, wanna play ball again?"

"Sure do; you just hired a first sacker."

"I phoned Scranton, to make sure there'd be no hint of tampering with another club's player. They said O.K. for your joining us for now...Funny thing, too, they also said this is the second time today they'd given that O.K...second time?"

Determined to keep the whole scenario out-front, Hubert told his friend all that had happened, all that had been said in the past hour.

"Well, I'll be hornswaggled! So she doesn't want to beat us too bad. What a knee-slapper that is."

"So, first sacker, report to me tomorrow morning, ten o'clock, at our park.

"Better yet, just so I'm sure you'll be there, I'll pick you up here at 9:30 AM. Then we'll high-tail it to the old ballyard in my shiny red gas-mobile which I just bought back, and which my good friend Luther Lincoln is cleaning and polishing for me at a park a couple blocks from here...sort of on the Q.T., get what I mean?"

After which Hubert waxed cogitative.

"Say, Muggsy, do you think if a guy's chased a girl too long and got nowhere for his efforts, should he maybe oughta stop chasing her?"

"It just might work. Yeah, like some hitters want a pitch down the pipe, but others want it high-and-out, where they can unbend for swiping at it. Gotta search for what works best for you.

"Since you say Katie told you Elsie has some warms for you, maybe the stay-away pattern will work best. Anyway, luck to you."

Elsie Peabody might then have been feeling a chill wind.

All she knew for sure that her phone had suddenly stopped ringing with calls from reporter-suddenly returned to Baseball player Hubert Jorgenson.

Slide, Katie, Slide!

Chapter Forty Two

What makes a winning manager? American League prexy Dr. Bobby Brown, the York Yankee third baseman and pinch-hitter supreme during those all winning years when Casey Stengel was the Yanks' skipper, remembered it this way: "Casey could walk up and down the dugout and spot a base hit in a man's eyes."

On the Thursday morning before Marberry's city championship game, a banner headline in the CLARION announced Hubert's joining the Lions. Baseball hysteria rocketed even higher.

There were pictures of Hubert on the front page. Interviews too, with Lions Jorgenson and Banton, the story of Hubert's life, and a re-hash of the attempted fix by Dr. Sutton and cohorts.

"Muggsy's all out to win this one," enthused a Lion fan. "And, certainly more than most managers, he knows how to bring about winning."

From another: "That was a smart move he made, getting Jorgenson to play for the Lions."

"Yeah," a third joined in. "Whoever said he'd forgotten how to fight?"

"Maybe all that's true," interjected a Burglar supporter. "But we still have the number one team in this town."

"The hell you have!"

"The hell we haven't!"

Katie had rejoined her high-flying Burglars on the road.

Still no meeting between her and Muggsy, though Cliff had asked for a promotional shot of them together. She refused, rather anticipating that her Husband would feel the same way.

Muggsy likewise had refused, though only half-sure that such was the best course of action.

Again, like Katie, Muggsy hated the thought of Saturday. But still was impatient for it to arrive.

On Friday night, there was a joint pre-game rally in Marberry's Town Hall. Again, the photogs wanted bloomered Katie and Muggsy together. This time, no escaping the request.

As his pretty, red-haired Wife stood there before him, Muggsy fumbled nervously with his cap. It was the first time he'd' seen her since that stormy session in the Burglar dressing room, which now seemed lonely light years ago.

He had to admit, she'd never looked lovelier. The blue bloomers were at least distracting, as compactly they rested on her well-formed thighs, then leading down to the length of white stockings, which finally found her blue ankle-white shoes. His adam's apple darted here-to-there, like a mouse trying to escape from under a rug.

He hoped his bulging groin wasn't evident to people standing nearby.

The stubborn Bantons waited, each desperately hoping the other would make a move, if not conciliatory then at least genial. But neither one did.

Reporters, local and from far away, were there to grab them for statements:

"Whaddya think, Katie?"

"We'll win, of course we'll win!"

"Muggsy?"

"We'll murder the bums."

They returned to their seats on the stage, followed by simultaneous shouts and shrieks from the audience. The high-pitched voices were, of course, owned by the horde of Emancipators from Marberry and many other places. The shouts, swelling to a cacophonic roar, came from Lion fans.

"Notice the way Muggsy's jaw is sticking out again?" asked a man in the audience. "That's the guy we'll follow to-hell-and-back."

"You tell 'em! He tobogganed downhill a long ways, but he's headed back up in a hurry. Tonight, he's the dude he used to be, all the way to his red bow tie."

Seated next to Katie, Elsie came on strangely quiet, a perturbed miss who seemed to have shed any invincibility either previously held or so imagined. She hadn't yet learned to handle the fragile situation of being not only alone but also unwanted by the man who had previously, and so ardently, desired her.

Repeatedly on that night, she smiled at Hubert, likewise on stage, he with his Lion teammates. For his part, he was too-busily exchanging glances with a stunning brunette down front in row three.

Cliff Hartwick, likewise up there with his Lions, could but keep his fingers crossed. While remembering the final words from his Blanche as he had earlier parted from her, at her cafe, "Mi Amour, always remember, in dreams and love, there are no impossibilities, but only, as we learn at Lourdes', attainables."

Time for the rally to end.

Off to one side of the hall, Hubert waited for Muggsy, being besieged by well-wishing fans.

Muggsy was about to join his new first baseman, "to round third and head for home," when a lilac-perfumed note was pressed into his hand by fingers that just as suddenly had vanished.

Quickly, he read the note, and anyone watching him from close-up could note a rapid flush taking over Muggsy's face.

He hurried to Hubert's side, and muttered, "Uh...here's the key to our house. See you there after...uh, a little while."

And was gone from the scene with a quick move that amazed even Hubert.

Along his hurried line of March, Muggsy would nonetheless pause to read, then re-read the note in his shaking hand:

> **I really want to see you at**
> **my apartment tonight. No. 3,**
> **218 Affectionate Street.**
> **Love, Barbara Mooney**

Slide, Katie, Slide!

Chapter Forty Three

**The seductive Miss Mooney had heard, "Men are
nature's sole mistake." She couldn't presently remember the
author of that one. But could later conclude, that person
must have been a wise authoress indeed.**

Barbara had rather expertly judged the man in her sights, and how, from his
present situation, he would immediately react to her invitation of obvious passion.

In the first moments after Muggsy had read her note, he had been gripped by
an appetite unmatched for himself in a long while. At the Town Hall exit nearest
the stage, he had abruptly excused himself from a horde of kranks, then had taken
a back-alley escape, headed for the silky figure of "that hunka Barbara."

Hurrying over the seven-block route, cutting in and out to avoid much-used
streets, he let his desires fly unhindered through the breezes: Once again, he felt like
a youngster on the prowl. It was actually happening! He'd soon be alone with
voluptuous Barbara, that one doubtless awaiting him in a peek-a-boo negligee and
very little else...But, he reflected, he must pause very early to admire that bedroom
gown, which had probably cost her many days' pay.

When the appreciating was accomplished, he would "strip her down for
action," as the guys put it. He'd place her gently but so firmly on her bed. He'd
sizzle over those heavenly boobs. He'd love every bit of her as only he-man
Muggsy Banton could.

He reached Affectionate Street. He found 218, then saw No. 3 on the ground-
floor apartment up front.

As he approached, Barbara peeked nervously but longingly from behind her
drapes. She hoped he would like her alluring gown. It had cost her many days' pay
but she was not begrudging a penny of that, as she took a final mirror-peek and saw
what it accomplished for her.

Miss Mooney further complimented herself for having a girlfriend deliver the
note to Muggsy, "Soon as the Town Hall thing was ended." Otherwise, she could
never have made it back to her apartment in time to be completely ready for him.

Her dream moment was at hand. Oh, please hurry, knock on my door!

Muggsy was raising his gnarled knuckles to signal his arrival.

When, brutally betraying his attempt to turn back the clock, Katie and then their Jimmy would flash before him.

As if his blood had suddenly drained away, Muggsy came-to. Whatinhell was he doing, chasing this teen-aged piece, making like he was back in his twenty-three-skidoo days? Why...just supposing it was all a setup and he'd been shadowed by a detective? Maybe Barbara wanted money. Maybe Katie was checking on him.

Whatever, it took no time at all for the subdued lover, now drenched in the stark cold sweat of shock, to turn and hurry away by the same path which had brought him.

Back to the apartment on Affectionate Street, so recently scheduled by Barbara as a trysting spot:

The equally appalled Miss Mooney first uttered an oath not in keeping with her usual demeanor.

And stripped the costly gown from herself.

And stuffed it into the nearest wastebasket.

And finally stomped it with a pink-slippered foot.

Naught left but the Niagara of tears to fall over her ripe body as she flung herself on her bed of aloneness.

Forever considering herself a "nice girl", she had given herself to no man, waiting instead for such a night of perfect taking.

Now rejection was her only taking.

From somewhere or many somewheres, she remembered girlfriends spouting: "Men! No way to live with 'em ... or without 'em."

Chapter Forty Four

**Another offering from our resident Wise Man Out
of the East: "Never feel sorry for a gambler. None of them
deserve sympathy, and the good ones don't want it."**

As Hubert, delayed at Town Hall by endless well-wishers, was finally able to approach the Banton home, he heard hurried footsteps behind himself. Of course, it was Muggsy. And, in the following minutes, the tall one heard the full account of his post-rally sally.

Hubert had trouble believing it.

"You mean you had a shot at 'Knockers Mooney' (Well, that's what the guys at THE CLARION call her, in addition to 'The Untouchable'), and you passed it up? Man, Muggsy, you are one toughie for sure."

Muggsy paused in some amazement: "You mean, honest-to-gosh, I would have been the first one?"

"That's how the Book on Barbara still reads."

"Omigosh! But maybe it was for the best, or I'll tell myself."

"Yeah, I don't know how you managed the walking-away, but I imagine that right now, you must be one pooped-out-pappy, like your soul has been drained...Hey, Muggsy, I'm still glad you did what you did. Your Katie is sure as hell worth the effort."

"Yeah," echoed his thoroughly discomposed friend...I think."

Further from Hubert, as they entered the Banton's front door, while Katie and Jimmy spent the night with her parents: "I'm sure glad I moved in here with you, instead of staying at Mrs. Haggleby's. Whatta mixed-up joint that is!"

"Yeah, good for a man to be where women can't get in his way, boss him, try to push him around, all that crud...Hey, didja hear the one about why women live a lot longer than men? It's 'cause women ain't got wives.

"Now, you and me, we're free as can be."

"Yeah!"

"Now, if we could just make ourselves believe that hogwash..."

"Yeah, or even a particle of it."

From a dark corner of the porch, Sam Streck was waiting for them.

Warmly did they greet the legendary ballplayer.

"How are you, Sam? ... How's it going, Old Timer?"

"About O.K., as they measure it. 'Course, I'm like you two in that I ain't got no woman these days, or so the gossip mill says about you two, too. And I'm short as hell on spondulicks. But then I imagine plenty o' guys have gone down those roads and died to tell about it.

"For now, though, I got something power-packed to tell you fellas."

A twin "oh?" came from his listeners.

"No news to you guys, I want your Lions to bust out the rest of my windows with home run shots against the Burglars, the kinda long balls your guys used to poke before they hit the pits."

"Sounds real fine, Sam," Muggsy told him eagerly. "So what's your master plan for making all that happen again?"

"What I'm about to tell you guys: A while back, sorta guessing this game had to come up before long, men and women and our horsehide game being what they are, I went to a couple o' Burglar games. The screechin' dames like to drive me bug-eyed. But stealing the Burglar signs was no problem, none at all, no sirree, it twarn't."

"Like I've heard," volunteered Hubert, "they used to call you 'Bandit Sam' for the way your sign-stealing shook up the Big Leagues."

Sam swelled some that he was still so remembered. And then went forward:

"Yeah, at the Burglar home games, swiping their signs was even easier, because they was the same as yours, Muggsy.

"But then, when this coming game was set, I figured your woman would switch, bright and eager as she is. So I've been on the road for a few days, brushing up on her new signs. Now, no insult to your family, Muggsy, but her new moves ain't worth a hunk of Limburger in a pretzel factory.

"Anyway, whatsomeever them lousy Burglars have planned in the way o' useless moves, I want you fellas to know that ol' Sam has 'em down cold on their signs."

Right there on the porch, Muggsy and Hubert did an Indian war dance, or at least their version of same from what they'd seen in a recent nickelodeon thriller (admission five cents per person.) Their whoops brought neighbors pouring from their homes to see what was happening...After which the verdict thereabouts was slightly unanimous: Ballplayers, however to rise to the general level of social sensibility, were having difficulties in that climb.

The tribal festivities concluded, Muggsy told Sam Streck, "If you were pretty, I'd kiss you."

"So I'm unearthly glad that I was born pug-ugly and have forever stayed that way.

"But look, guys, when you play them fakers, I'll be up on the roof and..."

"Aw, Sam, don't you wanna sit in the dugout with us?" Muggsy put forth. "Our guys would be so glad to have you down there."

"Naw. By now I'm more at home on my own roof. Besides, I can get a better look-see at them Burglar signs from high-up.

"I'll have a set o' flags with me, all colors of God's rainbow they'll be. The one I wave'll tell you what's about to happen, what pitch is comin', what play they got on, like hit-'n-run, or straight steal, an out-'n-out beanball."

"Do you actually mean," asked Hubert in simulated naivete, "that sweet little Katie would have her guys throw at a human being hitter's head, with the ultimate possibility of wounding him?"

"Are you guys feeding me phoney baloney?" the old man snorted. "That little lady has learned the bible of Baseball through and through, also up and down, insides out: Which is, give a batter a fat pitch to hit, and it's taking dinner off the table o' the pitcher and his family. Oh yeah, then yeah and verily, like our preacher used to beller at camp meetings...be sure in your minds that pretty little innocent-looking Katie Banton has it in her to be just as devil-mean as any ballplayer of the opposite sex."

"Naw!" joshed the other two.

"Yeah! I mean, a high haystack meaner than most of us put-down males know how.

"But then, to put some leveling on this matter, I guess it's all just a section of the games people play at each other."

Muggsy wanted to know, "Sam, won't you be too busy up there on your roof, watching and signaling at the same time?"

"Yessirree, that's a most practical factor I'm gettin' around to: Might one of ye know someone alert-like who'd sit up there with me and do my flag-wavin' as I instruct him?"

"I know just the right person," exulted Muggsy. "And be sure that I'll get him lined up for you in a hurry so the two of you can have a rehearsal session. For now, let's go in the house and break open the beer, while we study those signs. Gotta make sure we kick the bejeebers outta them stinkin' Burglars!"

At that moment, Katie might have felt the same icy wind on the nape of her neck that had struck at her best girlfriend.

Would her sleepless night to follow be tinged with the premonition that she was facing odds too tough to tackle?

Chapter Forty Five

Certainly one of the most UN-believable Baseball games I ever saw was on a June Sunday somewhere in the mid-1930's. Such was part of this Phoenix-Arizona's very first trip to New York City, with my Mother and my Big Brother Jimmy.

"El Senor" Lefty Gomez would pitch for the Yankees that day at Yankee Stadium, before a jam-packed crowd of 68,000. Talk about boyhood dreams come true for Jimmy and me! Our sports photo collection back home was loaded with Lefty and his teammates.

The game began sadly for Lefty and his visiting Arizona fan club. He walked the first four Chicago White Sox to face him. Then (I do believe it was) Sox second sacker Jackie Hayes cleared the bases with a line drive that somehow escaped the Yanks' rookie center-fielder, one Joseph Paul DiMaggio, later to be tagged "The Yankee Clipper." The elusive horsehide rolled to the deepest part of center field in "The House That Babe Ruth Built."

4-0 for the White Sox, Hayes on third base, and still no one out. A solemn-faced Yankee manager Joe McCarthy headed toward the mound after Lefty. We were as dejectedly disappointed and quiet as the rest of Yankee Stadium's mob.

But McCarthy didn't travel far. Lefty Gomez again showed his aptness for the unusual, the reason why he was also tagged "Goofy": He simply waved off his imperious skipper, and that didn't happen often against "Marse Joe"....Manager McCarthy, taking heed from the confident gesture of his star left-hander, turned abruptly and returned to his dugout.

Whereupon Goofy/El Senor stayed on the mound and would not allow Jackie Hayes to advance past third base, and

kept the Sox scoreless for the rest of the ball game. In the meantime, there were Yankee home-run shots from DiMaggio, Lou Gehrig, Bill Dickey, George Selkirk and "Poosh 'Em Up" Tony Lazzeri. Yanks won it going away.

Then, for the Arizona fan club seated down front to comprehend the FIVE O'CLOCK LIGHTNING laid on those Bronx bombers by New York sportswriter Dan Daniel was more understandably easy.

Then there was (another among many) simply UN-believable bit of Baseball played, this some thirty years previous in a considerably smaller Pennsylvania community named Marberry.

And in the fierce Marberry winters since then, with old-time fans gathered 'round pot-bellied stoves, no way to forget the long-ago Titanic between their Lions and their Burglars, those teams managed by Husband-and-Wife Bantons.

At Lions Park that day, every seat and every inch of standing room were grabbed hours before game-time.

When Lions manager Muggsy Banton first emerged from his dugout during his club's batting drill, the noise was at least cataclysmic. Repeatedly did the lantern-jawed one doff his cap in response to the storm from the stands.

He looked across the diamond to see his Wife, Burglar manager Katie Banton, bloomered in blue and standing on the edge of the visiting team's dugout. At which Muggsy spat furiously on the green grass before him: "You'd think she'd at least have the good manners not to parade in her under-drawers in our ball park."

A slightly confused duo of Jim Crowley and Cliff Hartwick sat in the first row behind the Lion dugout. They were non-plussed because the two seats between them, meant for their wives, were unoccupied, with game-time on tap. It was then that Jim looked back to breakfast that morning, when Clara had told him, "Don't wait for me at the office; I'll see you at the ball park."

So he had given her one of his two tickets for the game, and had gone on his way.

Now an excited Luther Lincoln was standing by Clara's Husband, handing him a note scented in lavender familiar to himself:

Jim, I won't be sitting with you today, and here's the ticket I would have used. I'm sure you can find one of your buddies who'll be glad to sit with you. But I feel so strongly

Jim did as bade. He saw his red-haired Wife standing and gesturing to him, also blowing him a kiss, from the completely bloomered Emancipators' section behind the Burglar dugout. Clara came to him startlingly enchanting.

Seated next to Clara was Birdie, the Crowley's cook and maid. Large and well-rounded as she was, she had to win the prize (if such there was) for the largest pair of bloomers on hand. But she came on faithful to the cause.

"My Mama's sure dressed funny, ain't she?" giggled Luther.

"Now Luther," chided Jim Crowley, "don't ever make fun of people for what they believe in, and especially when it's someone as grand as your Mama. I think she looks just great."

"Yes, Sir. And Mama sure do look excited 'n happy, don't she?"

Not many seats removed from those two ladies was a confused Elsie Peabody. Her eyes seldom strayed from the newest Lion, first baseman Hubert Jorgenson, confidently holding infield practice with the other black-and-red-uniformed Lions. But Hubert declined to return Elsie's avid glances.

Next to Elsie was the recently rejected Barbara Mooney. Leaping from her seat on her well-formed legs covered by white stockings, Barbara was one of the most vocal Emancipators, doubtless reliving cheering efforts from her high school days.

At brief intervals, the lusty Miss Mooney would shout to the other femmes, "WHICH TEAM IS FOR YOU?"

At which the other Emancipators would leap to respond: "THE ONE IN BURGLAR BLUE."

Through all such tremor, Cliff had to wonder, where was his Blanche?

Just returning to him was a breakfast-nook admonition similar to the one Clara Crowley had given her Jim. And Luther was likewise handing him a note:

are not a tiny mite so fortunate as your own Blanche du Bois. Now please glance across the field, and I will then blow a "forever kiss" to you. Amour toujour!....Blanche

Caught by amazement, Cliff did as requested. He saw his Wife, voluptuous in Emancipator attire, waving to him. At the soulful sight of which, Barbara again leaped from her chair to challenge her compatriots:

"WHICH TEAM IS FOR YOU?"

For but a smidgin' of an instant, the two Husbands had very first considered fretfulness at such goings-on. But now they were clapping each other's shoulders and laughing merrily.

"Oh, what the hell's the difference?" philosophized Jim.

"As long as The Girls are supporting what they believe in, that and having a ton of fun too, let's be happy for 'em...whatthehell. And then may our Lions win."

"I feel just the same way. Surely, it's not life-and-death that we win the ball game. Just have a grand day, as Abner Doubleday intended."

So both of them stood and blew kisses toward their Wives.

Luther Lincoln, now afraid he had caused a commotion with his note-bringing, quickly announced, "I'm gonna sit with Mr. Streck."

He left the scene after depositing the tickets sent by the ladies into the hands of their gentlemen.

Whereupon Cliff likewise departed, if momentarily, to give the available ducats to police chief Johnny O'Brien and to officer Pete Gilhooley, currently supervising the crush out in front of Lions Park. Those tardy fans would be lucky to find standing room, as the roped-off section before the outfield fences already held a mass of wild-eyed humans pushing from four-deep.

"Come sit with us 'soon as you can," was Cliff's message to Johnny and Pete.

And Pete thanked him heartily for the other four tickets, for his family.

In the Burglar dugout just before game-time, manager Katie Banton told her players, "Just play the same good ball we've been putting out. But stay loosey-goosey, have fun. We'll win."

In the Lions' dressing room, manager Muggsy Banton told his team, "I'm sorry for letting you guys down in the past weeks. When a man goes to seed, he makes a mess of all that he does. But today, LET'S BEAT THESE TRAMPS."

He looked over his pitchers. Every one of them wanted the mound versus the despised cross-town rivals.

But Muggsy knew he'd have to go with Bugle Nose Stankorsky, who was well-rested, also thoroughly on fire to pitch this grudge-game.

"Thanks, skipper. I'd have busted if you hadn't tossed me the ball. Before I'm through with 'em, them bloomer bitches (oh, I'm sorry for that, skipper, I know how you still feel about your Wife)..."

"No apologies needed. Knock down whoever you need to, stick it into a Burglar's ear. Hellfire, just toss one into the middle of the bloomer section if they yell too loud. Well...maybe not THAT, but what a temptation!"

The other Lions applauded his thought.

"Gotcha, skip. Guarantee you, I'll give 'em such a bad time as they'll never live to forget."

Only Jumbo Malone protested, if lightly, "Hey, skipper, what about me? Them lousy dames ruined my best suit!"

"You're first in the bullpen, big guy."

"Thanks much."

"'CAUSE WE GOTTA WIN."

Chapter Forty Six

"Time for the battle, Mother." - some sportswriter somewhere.

Muggsy, Katie, and Blind Tom met at home plate.

"No funny business from either of yez," sternly warned hizzoner the ump. "And that means all day long."

Katie smiled sweetly at him.

"But my team wouldn't dream of doing 'funny business' unless of course the Lions start the rough stuff."

"If your cream puffs can't take it, send 'em home now," snarled her Husband.

Blind Tom shrugged his shoulders and walked away. Telling the Lions and Burglars to take it easy on each other was rather like telling Niagara to kindly cease falling.

"PLAY BALL," was Tom's roar through his megaphone. "Lions choose to bat first."

On his roof, past the right field fence, Sam Streck waited, beseeching help from the heavens. Beside him, multiple flags at the ready, was a wild-eyed Luther Lincoln.

"Beat 'em, Lions!" he yelled without letup.

Nor were all the Marberry fans inside the ball park. Open windows of the apartment buildings across from both the right and left field fences were framed with the faces of fired fans, all of them hoping for a home-run ball hit into their cubicle.

Multiple others watched from the roofs and fire-escapes of those buildings.

By those, squeezing into the last inches of available watching-space, buckets of cold beer were hauled up on long ropes for themselves and the people in the buildings. The buckets and the ropes and the beer, plus pretzels too, were sent courtesy of neighborhood bartenders and their bosses.

But then a delay: Manager Katie moved toward Blind Tom.

"I've got a problem," she told him.

"I've heard about that. But I hope you and Muggsy get back..."

"No, not _that_ one. Today, I'm minus a first base coach. Slewfoot has come down with stomach cramps something awful."

"That jerkhead!" snorted Tom. "I saw him downtown last night, finishing off scads o' beer and pigs knuckles and sauerkraut the fans had pushed onto him along with their best wishes...Awright, so whatcha gonna do? Sure you got other guys on your bench who can fill in on first for today, like maybe a pitcher who don't figure to work?"

Katie looked at him beseechingly, all her womanly wiles out front.

"Uh...yes, but I'd like to do something...uh, different.

"Just for today, I'd like to bring Semanthia Smythe down from the stands to coach on first base. It would mean so much to her to be on the field again."

"Wait a minute," Tom instructed her. "Oh, sure, she knows as much, maybe more Baseball than almost anyone in this park. No doubt of that, 'cause I used to watch her play, out in Nebraska and Kansas. Sharp, she is!

"But she's not on your roster. So how can you use her?"

"Wellll...this is just an exhibition game. It would be all right if you said it was."

"How about Muggsy? Gotta get his permission before we bypass the rules."

"So ask him."

Blind Tom signaled to the Lion manager, and that one again trotted to home plate. "Now what the hell? Let's get this game started. My team and I got a train to catch this evening."

The ump explained what the Burglar manager wanted.

Muggsy was ready to immediately blast back, "Naw, no way she can coach on this field, especially dressed in her drawers."

But then thoughts from the past swarmed over him. Those were memories of when he too had worn bloomers on a ball field, playing for one of the supreme Baseball-wise skippers he'd ever known, including to-this-very-day.

Suddenly, the lantern-jaw relaxed, and Muggsy was caught in loud laughter.

"Hey, why not? Sounds like a great idea. Let's give these fans a chance to see the old gal in action. It'll gimme another look too. Sure, bring her out here!"

Katie was already running to the stands, quickly speaking to Semanthia. When she headed back for the field, the aged and bloomered Emancipation leader followed her, signaling wonder from the fans and shrill screams from the ladies behind the Burglar dugout.

Lastly, and before confidently taking her post by first base, Semanthia threw a glance of soulful gratitude toward Katie.

In her secret soul, Katie hoped that Slewfoot would never (at least for today) give away the secret, how his "stomach cramps" had come on, for her plan to once more put Semanthia Smythe out on a Baseball diamond, which had forever held her affections.

But then, before the first Burglar batter stepped to the plate, Semanthia approached Tom with the most of quiet dignity.

"Sure it's all right with you, Thomas?"

"Absolutely sure, Miss Smythe. I got no worries about you above-all knowing the rules, also the ground rules of this here park. And, if needs be, feel free to tell me off like the others do."

A smile caught her face, and she told him, "I don't expect to do that, Thomas, unless of course you give me cause to."

"PLAY BAWWLLL," Tom then boomed again, as the Burglars hustled from their dugout to their positions in the field. After which concussion-like pronouncement, the fans really got on Blind Tom, as if enough confusion hadn't already encountered him.

"Hey, Stupid, so what's the batteries for this game?"

"Tom, you're not only stone-blind, you're a dumbhead too!"

As the catcalls continued, Tom quickly recovered his composure, recovering the megaphone from the Lion dugout.

"The batteries for today's game: For the Burglars, Priddy and Simmons. For the Lions, Stankorsky and Banton...uh, yeah, that's <u>Mister</u> <u>Muggsy</u> Banton."

When the cacophony brought on by that last had subsided at least somewhat, Tom yelled, "Nowfergawdsakes, LET'S PLAY THIS HERE BALL GAME WHILE THERE'S STILL DAYLIGHT."

Mike Priddy took his final warmup toss. Buck Jackson, the first Lion batter, swung three bats as he walked to the plate.

"Get rid of all of 'em, Bucker," Pete Brancato jawed at him from second. "They ain't gonna do you no good today."

At least Pete was utterly correct on the first pitch, as Priddy threw at Jackson's head. The Lions started from their dugout, but Buck waved them back. "I can handle this."

With which he walked halfway to the mound and yelled at pitcher Sam Priddy,

"Awright, Sammy lad, you've had your jollies for this game. But if you or any other brainless thrower on that crumby club of yours repeats it, there'll be blood spoutin' from your brainless heads."

Priddy yelled back something that sounded suspiciously like, "Up your'n too." But his next pitch was closer to the plate, and Buck popped out to Hubert.

The precise signals from Sam Streck's roof began to tell as Bobo Gentry and Herky Jackson hit safely. Runners on first and third, one out, as Hubert approached the plate.

It had indeed been a gamble by Muggsy, moving the newly acquired, and recently untested, first baseman to that vital cleanup spot in the Lion batting order. Still, Muggsy had liked Hubert's easy, natural swings since he had joined the team in red-and-black. And manager Banton had long ago learned to follow his hunches.

Hubert took a quick glance at Sam's roof, where Luther and the old timer were working in tandem. A red flag was flying, the signal for a pitch high and inside, the first cousin to a brush-back or "purpose" pitch.

"Slam it, Hubert!" pleaded Muggsy.

As Priddy threw the duster, Hubert was ready. He took a step back, to be in perfect position, then simply reached up to "tomahawk" the ball, which was soon but a white blur as it took off for far-distant regions. Across the street from the left field fence, a frantic ex-ballplayer saw it coming, knew its possibilities. Just for an instant, he thought it might even clear his house.

"Keep coming, ball, dad blast ye!"

Beside him, Luther was pleading, "Be a homer, oh please be a homer."

There followed the crash of horsehide against the very top of the iron grating covering the window, the same that Luther had installed that morning. He'd told Sam, "I just know our Lions gonna pop some out here today, I just know it.

"'Course," he added confidently, "no bad Burglar can hit it this far."

At home plate, a delirious Muggsy and his Lions climbed over the grinning Hubert Jorgenson.

The next two Lion batters popped up to Priddy. Because Katie, seeing what was happening on Sam's roof, had quickly changed her signals. Still, the Lions did lead 3-0. If Bugle Nose was completely right and ready, that could be too big an early lead to climb over.

The Burglars came in for their turn at bat, and Bugle Nose couldn't find the plate. The first two Burglars drew walks, and those on eight straight badly aimed pitches. Blind Tom called time, as Muggsy conferred with his pitcher.

"What's wrong?" he wanted to know, though the answer had to be obvious to him.

"My hands are slippery as hell. Stinkin' Burglars must've sneaked in here last night and soaped up this mound...at least for the dirt I'm usin'."

Fighting to hold back laughter, Katie followed Blind Tom to the mound.

"Hey, what's going on?" she asked in mock severity. "I thought the Lions were all worked up about finishing this thing early so they could catch Esmeralda on time."

"Those tramps've worked soap into the dirt out here," Muggsy told Tom, "and in our own park."

Katie took on an expression of terrible offendedness.

"Ridiculous! My team wouldn't be so dastardly. We wouldn't even hire an old man to steal signs from his roof."

"Tom, make her tell us where the soap is, or we walk off the field."

"Awwww, poor offended baby. Finally got some of your own sneaky medicine? You've told me you're the world's greatest soaper, how you know every single one of the angles on that dirty stuff. So you find it yourself."

After which, if looks could have killed, little Jimmy Banton would immediately have been a motherless child.

Trying as hard as Katie not to laugh, Blind Tom picked up a handful of dirt from where Bugle Nose had been working.

"See!" snorted Muggsy, "I toldja she was cheatin'."

"Soap, all right. So, Mrs. Katie Banton, show me where there's no soap in the dirt, or I'll immediately forfeit the game to the Lions."

Immediately, Semanthia was confronting the umpire:

"Now, now, Thomas. You know perfectly well that Baseball's rule 417-J-1 clearly stipulates that..."

Tom immediately recited the rest of the lesson:

"Yes, Ma'am...it stipulates that you can eject the manager of the offending team, or each succeeding person-in-charge of that team. But it says nothing about forfeiting the game."

"Very good, Thomas," pronounced Semanthia, who then turned and walked back to her coach's box at first base.

Katie was so impressed by all that, she told Tom, "Oh, all right...it's...there's no soap over...THERE.

"But tell Payne to lay off my third baseman. I won't have his legs cut to ribbons by sharp rocks, like I've seen Payne do to other third sackers."

Tom put his hands on his big hips and squarely faced her in disbelief.

"Just who, if I may ask, is Payne?"

She pointed to Muggsy, "Why he is, of course."

"Haw haw! He's a pain, all right."

Hizzonner took full command of the tyradical situation. He backed off two steps, straightening to his full height, and considerable that was. Next, he bent over and drew a line in the dirt with a huge index finger, that line clearly a battlefield delineation between himself and the Lion manager.

"Muggsy, that line says I'm waiting. Cross it, or kick dirt over it, and you're a gone goslin out of this game in a big fat hurry."

Muggsy took one step forward. "You wouldn't dare toss me. My kranks'd tar 'n feather ya."

"Big talk, Muggsy, but I'm waiting. One more step in my direction does it."

Snarling, Muggsy headed back to the dugout, while Katie laughed resoundingly.

"You shut up, too, Katie, or you're gone just as quick."

Beaten down just as thoroughly as her Husband, she headed back to her own dugout. By then, the bloomered ladies before her didn't know whether to cheer her on or be similarly silent. So Barbara Mooney filled the gap, leading her favorite battle-chant: "WHICH TEAM IS...."

"Pullllayyyy Bawwwlllll," Blind Tom shouted all over again.

His hands then working with dry dirt, Bugle Nose Stankorsky settled down and retired the Burglars in order. End of first inning: still 3-0, Marberry Lions.

"While the game played on," tra la la. Yes, perhaps a slight discoloration of the much-loved old tune Strawberry Blonde. But then it was, and indeed, a melodious moment for Marberry.

In the third inning, still 3-0, the Lions' lead much thanks to Sam Streck's sign-stealing and subsequently Hubert's homer.

But the Burglars were furiously determined to get back into the game.

Their third baseman was a recently-acquired youngster named Harvey Houdini. He was determined not only to live up to the magical sound of his last name, of which he was proud, since it did bring on Harry Houdini, the master magician of that era; past that, he was also determined to make local fans forget that the late Butch Holcomb had been the mightiest third sacker ever to grace the diamonds of that city; yes, even of that entire minor league Baseball area.

Along which lines, in that third frame, Harvey Houdini made a can't-believe-I-saw-it diving stop of a smash by Hubert that seemed headed for the left-field wall. After which, from a sitting posture, the third-basing magician threw out the long-striding Jorgenson by a step at first.

The Burglar fans went wild, except for some of the Bloomer Girls among them. For those distracted ones, a new and multi-flowered hat going down the aisleway behind them was far more intriguing.

One of those ladies, then noting the buzz caused by the dazzling play at third base, asked Elsie Peabody what had happened on the field.

"Our handsome young baseman did a lovely play," the blonde told her in knowing fashion.

"Does that mean we've already won the game?"

"Of course not, silly. We still have to score some more goals."

Clara Crowley, long since become a rapt student of Baseball, listened to that exchange in silence, doubtless remembering times when she had "talked the game" in similar fashion.

"I do declare to goodness," Clara told herself, "there's a whole lot of teaching to be done among us girls. But at least a lot more of us have discovered there is such a game as Baseball."

At the end of that scoreless half-inning, Burglar first-base coach Semanthia Smythe intercepted the perpetrator of that dazzling play at third, as young Houdini was crossing the diamond, headed back to the dugout.

"I must tell you, young man, in my Baseball times I've seen a lot of great fielding plays, but hardly any of them touched what you just did."

She then took her seat in a deserted corner of the dugout.

Harvey, who had heard from older teammates the diamond legend that was Semanthia, was overwhelmed by the gesture. He stood embarrassedly frozen.

Bob Little, coaching at third base for the Burglars on this mighty occasion, noted the scene. On his own path to the dugout, he moved to Harvey's side and asked, "Mind telling me what the lady told you?"

When informed, Bob said, "Son, you can remember that compliment for all your days. Miss Smythe has seen more of this game than the rest of us will ever get close to."

"Brought back to the land of the living," Harvey moved to where Semanthia was seated.

"Thank you so much, Miss Smythe, for the kind words. Would you mind if I sat with you for a while? Mr. Little seems to think I can learn a lot from you, and I certainly believe him."

Her features did glow.

"Please do, son. I'm likewise sure I have a lot to learn from such a superb young player such as you."

Out on Sam Streck's roof, the old man and his assistant had, at least temporarily, put away their flags...now that Katie had changed signs. Sam, adept as he was at the "stealing" trade, found trouble with the lady manager's maneuvering. In fact, he was wishing he'd taken Muggsy's invitation to sit in the Lion dugout, for a close-up view that his eyes could better decipher.

He told himself, "I knew she was sharp, but I never guessed how much.

"Then, too, maybe ol' Sam's head is running outta gas, like in tempus figits."

Fifth inning, still 3-0, Lions and again Burglar twirly Priddy set down the home team in order.

In the bottom of the fifth, Slugger Ennis lifted a towering pop fly that sailed high over third base, headed for "home run heaven," as players could call it. The Lion left-fielder fairly flew in that direction for a last-ditch try at the flying horsehide, as the ball was about to enter the seating section just inside the foul pole, which was fair territory.

The Lion left-fielder dove into the stands. (Miraculously!), he snared the ball out of the hands of a bulky and shouting man with BEAT THE BROADS lettered blazingly across his jacket.

While Lions supporters caught their guy before he could crash into the seats.

The Lions and their own kranks whooped it up, as Tom signaled "OUT."

Katie, though admittedly hazy on the rule concerning this play, decided to make a stand for her team.

She charged the umpire: "That was an illegal catch! The outfielder has to have one foot on the playing field to make the catch count."

For a noisy instant, as the Burglar adherents backed their manager, Blind Tom almost wavered on his call.

But Muggsy settled the rhubarb. Followed by his coaches, he stomped to home plate, waving a rules book in the ump's face. And, pointing to a section in small type in that 'SPALDING'S GUIDE FOR BASEBALL', he roared, "Don't you dare reverse that call! Long as my guy caught the ball, doesn't matter if he was standing on his head on a knockwurst grill."

Knowledgeable Muggsy was right, though many years from then Katie could have won the point via changed rules. For the moment, Tom again signaled "OUT."

Not content with being right, Muggsy further turned his scorn on the opposing manager, who just happened to be his ever-loving Wife, however temporarily disengaged from him she was.

"Whatsamatter, smart-britches? You usta say you loved exciting books. You better try this one all the way to its chilling finish, then see your stupid team LOSE."

Her psyche wounded, Katie still tried, if hopelessly, to bluff the point home. She again charged Tom, shouting that the catch had been "illegally aided" by the Lion kranks who had caught their left-fielder on the fly.

"Naw, the catch is legal, batter is out," Tom insisted, his confidence regained.

"Blind man, you got no guts at all," she shouted at him. "And you're scared to death of Muggsy!"

"Watch yer tongue, Miz Banton, or you're off to the showers."

"You wouldn't dare run me. If you tried it, my kranks up there in the stands would run you outta town on a rail."

For the second time that day, the towering umpire drew a line in the dirt and dared an angry manager to cross it. While he faced Katie and shouted into her face, "Ain't but two people in this world that's infallible.

"Which is the Pope on religion and me on Baseball."

Katie's anger somehow disappeared. After all other combatants had left the scene of verbal warfare, she reapproached Tom and told him quietly but joyfully, "Congratulations. Hey, you finally said it, and you said it just fine. I'm so proud of you, and I know Muggsy is too."

"Outta here!" he roared for the ears of the world. But softly to the lady before him he breathed, "I thank you, Ma'am, I surely do."

For the ears of the world, Katie threw one more blast at him as she turned to walk away, "You're so blind, you oughta be out on a street corner selling pencils!"

Katie retreated to her dugout, play-acting hard to retain an angry face.

Pete Brancato approached her:

"Helluva show, skipper. I honestly didn't think a little ol' gal like you could scrap like that."

"Frankly, Pete," she told him in little more than a whisper, "I wasn't at all sure I could get away with it. That big guy had me scared so bad, I liked to wet my bloomers. But I just had to show you guys how much I'm behind you."

"We got the message, oh yes we did."

Pete was further tempted to ask about that final (softened, as he had closely observed it) exchange at home plate between his manager and the ump. But some things, he reckoned, just better stay private.

Chapter Forty Seven

"RUN, RUN ..... O RUN!" - King Lear

And indeed time did run, swiftly so, in that Marberry City Championship game.

The eighth inning still found the Lions with a 3-0 lead. Bugle Nose was vengefully pouring in his fast ball, and Katie was beginning to worry some.

But then the long-sought Burglar breakthrough: Brancato started it by coaxing a base-on-balls from Stankorsky. He scored when Slugger Ennis drove one to the center field wall. 3-1.

The next Lion was lucky to keep his head in place, as Bugle Nose planted a blazing pitch just inches from where his jaw had been before he fell backwards, out of the path of disaster.

That same Lion, not to be discouraged, slammed the following pitch against the boards in deep center. Two runs scored, and it was a tie game, 3-3.

Just as a calling card, although with no need to slide, Slugger did that at home plate. And gave Muggsy a hard shot to the shin. Muggsy, though smaller by some 60 pounds, immediately backhanded the big guy across the mouth, drawing blood.

Blind Tom had a war on his hands, as both squads rushed to the scene, both the players from the dugouts and their relief pitchers being readied for action.

In an instant, fights had broken out all over the field.

Up in the stands, kranks of the two teams charged each other.

Katie, lost in the feeling of it all, likewise started from her dugout.

But Slewfoot restrained her.

"Please stay here, Mrs. Banton. This isn't for you."

She acquiesced, watching such a brawl as even the battle-wise Lion Park had never seen. Above all, she watched her Husband.

Muggsy roamed the battlefield, mixing with one Burglar after another, deliriously venting frustrations he'd bottled for too long, far too long as it now seemed to him.

Once he was knocked down, and the oversized Del White fell heavily on his long-weakened knee. Katie saw her man writing in awful pain, but briefly. Back to the war he did limp, swinging at every blue shirt in sight.

Del White was enjoying himself to an equal extent. Which is to say he simply couldn't find enough Lions to swing at.

Then Hubert stood in back of him.

"Look out!" yelled the ex-reporter, trying a trick he had once read of in a nickel novel.

Del responded by turning around just in time to catch Hubert's hard right to the jaw. And went down, cold to the world around him.

Over-buoyed by success, Hubert tried the same trick on Slugger Ennis. For his trouble, he was likewise blasted into dreamland.

This brought Elsie onto the field.

"You...you...BULLY, YOU!" she screamed at Slugger.

The target of her revile turned to cast a joyous eye on the big blonde.

"Wanna wrestle, Babe? Hey, let's go at it, no-holds-barred."

She thought it wiser to turn her attention to Hubert, still unconscious in the dirt.

"Poor Hubert, poor dear Hubert," she wept, lifting his head and brushing dirt from his face.

Hubert had been about to return to daylight. Still, so completely enjoying Elsie's long-delayed affections, he maintained his dead-to-the-world posture for additional minutes.

FINALLY, Hizzonner Blind Tom, the ump, aided by some of chief Johnny O'Brien's finest who charged into the rhubarb with batons at the ready, got matters under control. He first considered ordering a lot of players out of the game. But then, considering the violent feelings throughout the ball park, he merely threw up his hands in despair. And shouted "PLAY BALL" still another time.

Muggsy was limping badly. Del's landing on his knee had brought back the anguish of times past.

Katie saw him fighting back the pain, as he again tried to crouch behind the plate. She wanted terribly to run to him, but knew she mustn't.

"Muggsy doesn't want sympathy," Cliff had told her.

Silently she wept for her Husband.

3-3 into the bottom of the eighth.

By way of a walk, a stolen base, and a sacrifice fly deep to right field, Katie's team worked a runner around to third base, with one out.

Bugle Nose was weary-wild. Muggsy went out to check on him.

"I'm all right, skipper, honest I am. I gotta finish it, beat these creeps."

"If you can stay in this game, hurtin' as you are, dammit, I'm stayin' too!"

But Bugle Nose walked the next two Burglars on just ten pitches, to load the bases.

He then struck out the next two batters.

Muggsy, same as his Wife across the field, scarcely dared look to see what would happen next. He knew Jumbo was ready to come in and save Bugle Nose, but Bugle Nose had been so determined to stay that he could only delay the change.

What did happen next was decidedly UN-believable:

Pete Brancato slammed a vicious shot over Hubert's head. It was rising in its flight, up-up in a line for the right field wall, surely to clear the bases, maybe even a grand-slam home run.

But, as it went by him, somehow Hubert's intense leap put the tip of his glove on it. He secured it as he was falling. Somehow then, scrambling to one knee, he gunned the horsehide at Muggsy, as Slugger thundered down the line toward home plate. Muggsy grabbed the ball, diving forward to block the hugeness of Slugger coming in like the Five P.M. Freight.

Ignoring his pain, terrible as it was, Muggsy put everything in his being into blocking the plate, slapping the ball in Ennis' teeth.

"Yer out!" boomed Blind Tom.

The crowd noise was past description.

Top of the ninth, and the score was still locked, 3-3.

Muggsy limped pitifully into the dugout to rally his troops.

Elsie stood and waved to Hubert as he passed by her. But he gave her only the briefest glance of recognition as he went in to sit by his manager.

Nothing for the Lions in their top of the ninth.

Even Sam Streck had given up on cracking "only-a-girl" Katie's changed signs.

Blind Tom made an announcement, as 'SPALDING'S RULES OF BASEBALL' said he must:

"It is now five-fifty o'clock. The Blue Laws of this great State of Pennsylvania clearly state that no game may continue after six o'clock P.M."

The first Burglar batter in the bottom of the ninth struck out on three of the hardest consecutive moves left in Bugle Nose's arm. But then the Lion pitcher most definitely had had it. Quickly, the Burglars put three runs across the plate. Muggsy rushed in vengeful Jumbo Malone.

The rampaging Burglars answered that too-little-and-too-late move by scoring four more times, still only one out.

10-3 seemed insurmountable, especially with the Burglars' Priddy still throwing so easily.

Katie checked her watch: Five-fifty-seven.

She checked her runners on first and second, Brancato the lead man and then White. No speed there, and, besides, with a 10-3 lead, almost no chance they'd steal. All they'd want was to end the game, celebrate some, then go to dinner.

Her two feeblest hitters were due up. The game should quickly end.

But Muggsy, she feared, would never be able to accept the shellacking from the team managed by his own Wife. In final despair, he would, she just knew, quit Baseball, in despair, go far from Marberry, never again to come home to herself and Jimmy.

From all such, Katie had a sad, faraway look. But her Dad and Muggsy had built a solid foundation of never-quit into her Baseball being.

Her only savior now was her knowledge of the rules of the game, patiently drummed into her by Muggsy.

She ran from the dugout, notifying Hizzonner, "I'm now taking over for my runner on first base."

Hizzonner was both hesitant and dumbfounded. He reached to his hip pocket for the answer from 'SPALDING'. He found no reference to the sex of people allowed to play the game.

Katie further leaned on his hesitation: "If Muggsy can be a player-manager, so can I."

"So play your little games, Ma'am," was Tom's only answer.

He signalled the change to the scorekeeper, then watched Katie tap Pete Brancato. Pete headed for the dugout, last-second turning back with a grinning/understanding, "Happy landings, skipper. You know all us guys are for you a thousand percent."

Over his shoulder, Tom saw Muggsy approaching him. He waited for an argument on Katie's move. Muggsy listened quietly to Tom's narration of that.

Muggsy had been ready with strong protest. But something made him back away from argument. To Tom's amazement, the Lion manager nodded quietly in assent, a strangely quizzical smile tugging at his lips. Quickly then, Muggsy returned to his dugout, to watch further proceedings alone, from a far corner.

Over at first base, Semanthia Smythe moved from her coaching box to Katie's side.

"I see what you're doing, Katie. It's horribly bad Baseball, but then this is only a game...and you are playing for keeps. Let me wish you the most of success."

Hubert, taking practice throws in his own agile style, told her brightly, "Always pleasant to have you with us, Katie Banton."

Katie felt sure then that Hubert too understood her move.

But at second base a storm of anger was raging. Del White, the Burglar runner there, was throwing his palms upward in a frantic beseeching of the heavens. Such as, "WHATTHEHELL WAS THAT CRAZY BROAD UP TO NOW?"

Del's fury had to remind Katie of the evening when he had attacked her in the dressing room.

She ignored Del, but soon he got his answer.

She watched Jumbo Malone, out there on the mound, shaken by her entry into the game.

Jumbo held the ball, hesitant before going into his motion.

Whereupon the blue-bloomered Katie broke for second base, sliding in safely. Hysteria mounted in the still-packed stands.

From Semanthia Smythe, "Slide, Katie, Slide!"

Del had remained frozen at second, unable to believe what was happening. Finally, though, with no choice, he broke for third. But far too late. A snap throw from Jumbo nailed him before he could get within three feet of the bag.

Two out. Hoots of derision rained on Katie...especially from a certain gamblers' section of the stands, where heavy money had been bet on the Burglars. And where those punters were now beginning to faintly sense that they'd been had.

Katie seemed to have other problems. In sliding, she had ripped the seat out of her blue bloomers...although, later on, the Lion second baseman would swear he had seen her tearing frantically at them as she launched her slide.

Katie seemed so embarrassed that, with a peek at her watch (now showing five-fifty-nine) she melted into a torrent of tears.

Blind Tom advanced toward her, seeking some "decent way" (he was later quoted) out of the thoroughly embarrassing situation.

Still sitting on second base, to hide her nakedness, Katie let her torrent become a flood. She continued that until...after another peek at her watch showing six-o'clock-and-one-minute-thereafter...distraught Hizzoner returned to home plate for a final announcement. (He did this because Mr. Spalding said that he must.):

"By the Blue Laws of the Great State of Pennsylvania, this game is called. Since the ninth inning was not completed, the score reverts to the end of the eighth inning, which is a final 3-3 tie."

Slewfoot rushed an oversized warmup jacket out to Katie.

She wrapped herself in it; then, in thorough acquiescence, she left the playing field. Oh yes, she did sneak one quick look at that corner of the Lion dugout where her Husband was still watching the mad scene in thorough quietude...oh, with perhaps the trace of a knowing grin on his face.

Chapter Forty Seven

**"HE WHO TURNS AND RUNS AWAY,
LIVES TO FIGHT ANOTHER DAY."
- a thoroughly shattered military leader
    from sometime/somewhere**

Such words could well have returned to Lion manager Muggsy Banton, at least in one form or another, as, hands on hips, he continued to view the pandemonium all about himself. He refused to join the deafening jubilation of his team and his kranks for escaping certain and decisive defeat at the hands of the despised "crosstown tramps".

J.T. Crowley and Cliff Hartwick patiently held their seats for a while, amazedly taking in the noise mixture that was drowning Lions Park.

Still, when Cliff saw a certain loved one approaching where they sat, he quickly departed, looking for his Blanche du Bois.

Of course, the new arrival at J.T.'s side was his Clara.

Lovingly, she pressed a hand to his and told him, "Jim dearest, I do hope you understand why I did what I did today. Now please, let's go home, provided of course that you too wish to."

A huge grin grabbed her Husband.

"I'll be so pleased if we will. Further, if you'll excuse my reverting to bawdy, it's been a while since I've lowered the bloomers from the delightful likes of you."

Clara turned scarlet: "Jim!"

But then, after an added thirty seconds to savor the proposal, she let it swarm all over herself, delightfully so.

"Oh my, yes, it has been a long while. And yours, Jim, is one daisy of an idea. So whyever are we wasting precious time? Afterwards, let's burn the bloomers to a pile of ashes."

On the Streck's rooftop, Luther Lincoln was utterly dejected.

"We didn't beat the bad Burglars!" he repeatedly uttered.

"But Luther, neither did them bums beat us," Sam would then tell him.

"But I wanted us to win."

"Son, if you ever grow as Baseball-wise as Mrs. Banton was out there today, I'll be glad to take lessons from you, provided I be still on this sod."

Trying to brighten, Luther left the rooftop just as a tiny and withered old lady in blue bloomers reached that scene.

Sam held out his arms to her.

"Well, hello there, Daisybelle My Pretty."

But she stopped a few feet from her Husband.

"Samuel, I'd like to come home for a while, give our marriage another trial, after the first fifty-two years."

"Yippee!" was Sam's exultation.

"Still, I'm not almighty sure, Samuel. Your Wife has heared a heap o' modern thoughts whilst she was away, and I don't want to be the same ol' slavey that your Daisybelle used to be. Of course, too, I'll still wear my bloomers and attend "Emancy" meetin's when I get the notion to."

"Yes, of course, Daisybelle My Pretty. I hereby promise to take out the garbage in time...And may I say you look powerful enticing in those bloomers!"

"Thank you, Samuel, and glad to be here. Frankly speaking, you always was my knight in shinin' armour, as perhaps I recently forgot to tell you."

Midst the melee still swarming over the playing field at Lions Park, Barbara Mooney was in sprightly chatter with young Harvey Houdini. And a closely observing watcher on that scene could have noted that they were excitedly repeating "YES" to each other.

As the fans finally began to dazedly depart, Blanche du Bois Hartwick was in earnest conversation with Semanthia Smythe. As Cliff waited discreetly in the background.

"My dear friend, it has been such a day of joie de vivre, and how marvelous that I was able to meet you by arriving before contesting time in this seating for your madames and mademoiselles. Though I 'declare to goodness', as I have learned from the language of my new nation, I just don't feel very comfortable in these outside bloomers."

"Blanche, between you and me, I don't either," Semanthia confided. "Still, our mighty movement must push on with such a symbol."

"I'm pleased to respect that. And now I must tell you something else, because at the moment it is weighty on my mind, as Americans state it:

"You see, in my la belle France, I used to put in what seemed to me to be endless hours of practice on my beloved ballet, even if with no results that could be called le grande. Again, and often, I DID have a chance in the halls of Paree to watch those of true expertise make oh-so-graceful pirouettes, attitudes, and all other movements characteristique of the ballerina...which ungraceful I could never complete, even though I prayed at Lourdes for assistance in that. I could not miss one such gloried chance for looking.

"Now, I see these tres marvelous Baseball people performing. Oh, how they return the performances of le grande ballet, with their impossible moves of grace made time after time. Once again, I am in the fascination of my days of being young and overjoyed."

"I never thought of Baseball in that way. But I surely see what you mean. Those men capable of making it to the Big Leagues, or near to that, must have, as you say, 'tres marvelous' coordination of mind and body.

"My dear friend, Blanche, you and I must attend more Baseball games together...ballet performances too whenever possible. At which you certainly may feel comfortable in any clothing of your desire. Though today I have appreciated your support more than I can tell you."

Leaving the field, Katie was approached by a citified and over-serious Baseball writer from New York.

That one demanded to know, "My dear Mrs. Banton, if you will entertain this query from a fourth estater whose career has long been one of watching the cream of Baseball talent play in our metropolis of New York City: But why in heaven's name did you so foolishly try to steal second base when there was already a runner present there, leading to a loss of certain triumph?"

"Yes, wasn't that just too silly? But a sophisticated gentleman such as yourself has certainly observed how impulsive we silly girls can become, how absolutely flighty! Which may just be why we're not allowed into your glorious national pastime. Still, and through all my pubescent years, my overwhelming passion was to recklessly steal a second base. Do you think that's just possibly because of faulty toilet-training? Anyway, on this day, I just did it! Can you and your knowledgeable Baseball readers ever forgive my impetuosity?"

The haughty metropolite, for once naked of a closing put-down, stood open-mouthed as Katie tripped away in seemingly utter abandon.

As Hubert left the Lions' dressing room, acceding to a throng of autograph seekers along his line of march, a lady tall and blonde moved to his side, seeking to take his hand. But he did not immediately acquiesce.

Of course, the new arrival was Elsie Peabody.

"Please, Hubert, forgive me for the awful things I've said and done."

"Nothing to forgive, Elsie. We all must fight for what we believe in."

His overwhelming inner fire wanted to take that luscious woman to himself. Still, now warmly holding her hand, he resisted the desire.

"Elsie, so much has happened in a hurry. Right now, I'm not sure of anything, most of all myself. But I do want us to be special friends, even though I'll likely be leaving Marberry before long. See, I have a telegram from Frank Chance, the manager of the Chicago Cubs. He's bought my contract, and wants me to join his team next week. Oh, my goodness, girl, I'm headed for the Big Leagues! Such a little while back, I couldn't have dare dreamed of that."

Elsie stalled some hopes. "Hubert, I couldn't be happier for you...But may I at least come to the depot with you when you and the Lions leave tonight on your road-trip?"

"Yes, I'd like that a lot, to have you say goodbye to us and Esmeralda. May I come to your apartment by eight o'clock?"

As Muggsy limped from the dressing room in awful pain, his reinjured knee weightily bandaged, his Wife moved to him.

She brought a crutch sent by Bob Little, but Muggsy would have none of such assistance. His support came from the sight of Katie, in the lacy white blouse and pink skirt that had so long been his favorite.

Katie grabbed an intervening instant to cut off the swarm of autograph collectors descending on Muggsy, beseeching them to please await another day.

Mr. and Mrs. Banton moved forward in a searching of souls. But then the same terrible dread captured both. Would rejection follow? After all the bitterness inside of each, how much could have changed in a hurry?

Such hesitation having lasted a "lengthy" thirty seconds at most, she was in his crushing arms. She wouldn't move away for a precious while.

"Please, Muggsy, let's go home to Jimmy. He and I both miss you so badly, need you so terribly. Now...well...we've been hoping you might feel the same way."

He continued to press Katie to himself, as it had been in all his dreams. Even if those of recent vintage had ended in nightmares of futility.

"I've notified Elsie that I've resigned my manager's job."

"I'm so glad."

"And Slewfoot is the new skipper of the Burglars."

"Ol' Slew's a great choice, one helluva Baseball guy."

"Oh please, let's hurry home for the little time before you meet Esmeralda."

"Relax, girl. My coaches will take the Lions on the road for the next week or two. So we can be a family again. After that, if you want, you and I can join the team 'out there'."

"Oh yes," she breathed, somehow not being able to stand close enough to her lover, little matter how warmly they were touching. Perhaps frivolously breaking into the moments of love-rediscovered, it had to remind her of an ancient vaudeville routine where the Romeo beseeched his Juliet, "Closer, my sweet, oh closer!" And she would tell him, "Hey, ya big bum, if I get any closer to ya, I'll be on the other side of ya."

So it happened, Mr. and Mrs. Muggsy Banton (to be forever enshrined in horsehide lore as 'The Merrily Married Managers'), finally rounded third and headed for home.

JOE E. PALMER

Author/Sportswriter

11997 Foxboro Drive - Brentwood

Los Angeles, California 90049-4110

(310) 4778568

FAX (310) 8208760

ABOUT THE AUTHOR: Joe E. (He prefers to ditch the rest of his second name) Palmer was born in Phoenix, Arizona. His Father was one of the founders of the American College of Surgeons, also of the American Cancer Society.

Joe E. graduated from Bellarmine Prep, San Jose-California, an adjunct to Santa Clara U. Also from the University of Notre Dame, 1942, BS in Pre-Med. He has noted, he did not complete medical school (Georgetown) as had two of his Brothers. However, he did fulfill some of his medical karma by serving as Pharmacist Mate 1/C, USNR, in the Normandy invasion area, also the north-central Pacific combat area, as designated "senior medical officer" on LST 1103, also being in charge of all alcohol on the ship, which would carry beer, Marines, and toilet paper. He will tell you that, for weird adventures afloat, the cruise of the 1103 made the USS Caine, of literary mutiny fame, come off as child's play, somehow traveling alone through enemy waters with only light weaponry at hand.

Back in civvies, Joe E. formed Palmer Addresing & Mailing Company, Beverly Hills-California which has press-release served the L.A. Dodgers ever since their arrival from Brooklyn on 11/15/57. Also worked with the Angels, Rams, Lakers, and the Raiders.

He has covered Sports for THE SAN FERNANDO SUN, PACOIMA POST, EL MONTE HERALD, BACKSTRETCH and TURF DIGEST magazines. Most extensively, over 35 years, he served the fiercely independent CALIFORNIA (thoroughbred) HORSEMAN and THE MALIBU TIMES.